The Hummus Series

T.K. RICHARDS

First printing, 2021

LNK Publishing

ISBN-13: 978-1-737043867

www.tkrichards.com

Author's Note

Sign up for my newsletter here:
https://tkrichardsnewsletter.ck.page

www.tkrichards.com

Follow me on social media here:

Love is composed of a single soul inhabiting two bodies.

— ARISTOTLE

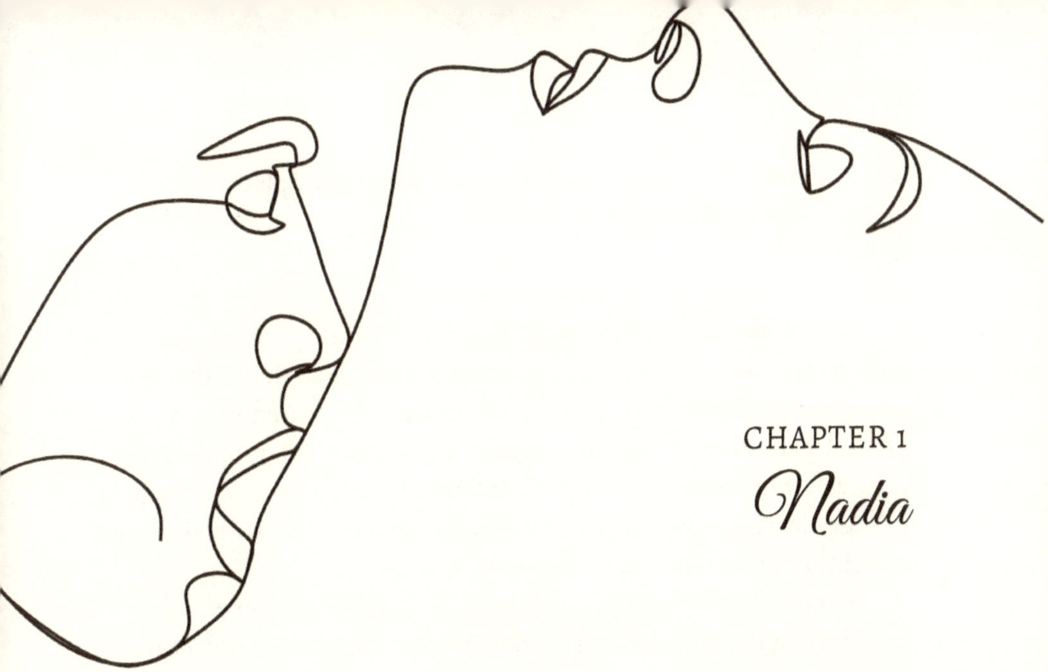

CHAPTER 1

Nadia

This is humbling. Sitting in a room full of strangers because I can't get over a man. What a bunch of losers. Wait a minute, I'm here so I guess I'm a loser, too. Why would I take advice from Carmen 'Can't Keep a Man' Woods? I would die if any of my friends saw me in here. Note to self— Give Carmen a tongue-lashing tomorrow— better yet, never mention I was here.

I can barely hear myself think with Lady Chatterley sitting next to me. For the love of God, someone please shut this woman's mouth. I have been smiling and nodding the entire time she has been yapping her purple lips, but I haven't heard a word she's said.

Well what do we have here? This one seems pretty full of herself. I can tell from looking at her designer shoes whatever problem she's facing, it is most likely her fault. I shouldn't say such things. I don't know this woman, yet still I want to call her Ms. Look at Me. She can't stop looking in the mirror long enough to see what is actually happening in the world—like how I am intensely watching and judging her. Shame on me. A giant panther could have entered the room and she wouldn't know it. Look up sweetie you're not cute enough to be clueless.

My God! Who let King Kong out of her cage? Note to self, 'don't let her kick me in the ass.' She has to be the tallest, most statuesque white woman I have ever seen. Please don't sit by me, please don't sit by me. Whew! That was a close one. I might slip and say something slick and she would wipe the floor with me. Next mental note— Nadia, stop talking about these people.

Now what do we have here? Possible lesbians, perhaps? Jeez, I hope not. I can't bear to hear what issues they are having. I thought once you gave up on men, you should be happy by process of elimination. Right? How could any woman on woman relationship have problems when a man isn't involved? Guess I'll find out soon enough. If they do turn out to be a couple, I'll treat myself with donuts tonight. I beg someone, anyone, gas me now.

Is the therapist here already? Is she one of these women I have talked about horribly, waiting for the right time to speak? I don't want to be the guinea pig, nor do I want to sit here and waste my time looking at strangers all night. I have talked about them to myself which I really need to work on. Note to self— Work on your bullshit, and stop talking about people.'

The metal door creaks as it flies open from the hands of a petite, well-dressed woman, rushing in with folders pressed against her chest. Her maroon- colored lipstick, and black cat-eye frames announced she was fashionable, and perhaps well paid, which was a good sign.

As her heels clanked across the wooden floor, I had a change of heart. This didn't seem like a place I belonged. As she continued to get settled in, I stood and grabbed my sweater from the back of my seat. Avoiding eye contact with everyone, I fixed my mouth to say, 'I'm so sorry, but I can't stay,' but was intercepted by the therapist.

Coherently and unapologetically she spoke. "Forgive me for running late, I couldn't get my husband off of me."

'*Wait, what? Did the therapist greet us with personal information? About herself? Maybe I will stay after all.*'

I repositioned my sweater and made myself comfortable, eager to hear what she was going to say next.

"Allow me to start by asking you all this question. Are you open to sharing your deepest, darkest, most liberating sexual encounters with the people you see in this room?"

The room fell silent. We all looked around at each other with skepticism. Crickets chirping outside the windows, music from cars passing by, and chatter from the hallways filled the room as our whispers remained on pause.

"I urge you to answer my question honestly, as it is important for you to be successful in this class. My name is Dr. Bartley, and I'm here to help you— help yourself."

She looked around the room, assessing us from what I could gather. No one had found their voice to answer her question, and as the silence continued, she began writing in her notebook, looking up at us from the rim of her glasses.

"I'm going to assume those who have remained seated are responding yes. Yes? Okay then. Let's get started. You with the mirror." She pointed to the girl I nicknamed Ms. Look at Me.

"Me?" she asked, tapping her designer shoes.

Her heavy lined eyes looked confused, and her caramel face had a bit of fear written on it suddenly.

"Yes, you. You are primping in the middle of the day. Why?" Dr. Bartley questioned.

"Don't you want to know my name first?"

"We'll get to names a little later. Right now, I'm interested in knowing why you are staring at yourself in the middle of the day? In a class for people who are sexually frustrated no less."

"Um, because you never know who you're going to meet," replied mirror girl.

"Did you plan on meeting someone to impress in here?" Dr. Bartley asked.

"Maybe."

"And how about you?" Dr. Bartley pointed her pen towards me.

"What about me?" I asked looking her in the eye, past the glass on her ebony frames.

"I saw you getting ready to leave as I walked in. Tell me why?"

"I had second thoughts about staying," I firmly replied, refusing to allow her to bully me into submission like the first two women.

"May I ask why?"

"I don't think I belong in here." I sassed.

"So why did you sit back down?"

"Honestly, when you blurted out you couldn't get your husband off of you, I was intrigued. That was one hell of a way to enter a room," I said, causing a stir.

"Your response tells me you are interested in other people's lives. Am I right?"

"I, I, I wouldn't use those exact words. I just found what you said to be very honest. You know. I have never met a person bold enough, or unafraid to enter a room as their true self. Nowadays, everyone is either faking it, or trying to be something they're not." I explained with surprising support from the room.

The girl I labeled as Lady Chatterley sat opposite of me, humming in agreeance, catching the attention of Dr. Bartley.

"You appear to have something to add." The good doctor looked down her nose. "What brings you here?"

"A former attendee recommended I sit in one of your sessions." She stammered.

"Do you often take advice from unlicensed professionals?"

"I beg your pardon." Lady Chatterley scoffed.

"What I am asking you is, where is your own mind? Your own train of thought? Where is your courage to do what you think you should be doing? Don't worry. We'll work on those factors in the weeks to come."

I read the room. Of seven attendees, three sat in their seats with expressions of enthusiasm on their faces. The possible couple were having a conversation with their eyes, and Lady Chatterley appeared to be uneasy as she raised her hand to speak like we were in school.

"Can you start with someone else? Please? I don't want to go first."

Dr. Bartley answered with an impish grin across her lips. "Of course. Class let me inform you. I am all about expressing how one truly feels. I encourage my class to speak freely and honestly. I will push you to stop hiding and reveal the person you are when no one else is around. Your true self. You will have to get personal, and dirty, and detailed in here, so again I ask, is everyone in here comfortable with my methods? And this time I would like a verbal yes or no."

"Yes." Everyone answered except me.

"I was right earlier. I don't belong here. Good luck to you all," I said, avoiding direct eye contact with the room.

The immediate silence was uncomfortable. Quickly, I crossed my tote with my sweater and jetted to the exit. Lately, I have been second guessing myself about everything. I know to follow my gut, yet I disobeyed it, and sat back down. *'Big mistake.'*

Trust is one of the areas I needed extreme help with, and trusting a room full of strangers with my most personal, intimate details is not where I wanted to begin that journey. Such a conversation could be had with my closest friends, whom I'd be spending the day with tomorrow. *'I won't tell them about the class. Only about dumping Evan. They already call me Naïve Nadia. No need to make it worse.'*

Despite the overcast and heavy weekend traffic, I wiggled my way through the backroads of Charlotte to Taylor's shower. Five minutes late, but on time before the bride threw a hissy fit, I arrived with the cheese and fruit tray, bottles of chardonnay, and tequila. The shower was a hit, filling the country club with the bride and groom's side of the family, an overflowing table of gifts, and libations flowing amongst the room.

The party was near its end when Levi, the groom, arrived to pick up the gifts, and his bride to be. He tried to break up the party and tear Taylor away from us, until it became clear we weren't ending our night early.

Outnumbered and aware of the company before him, he loaded his car with the presents, and waved his scrawny arms at us as he left.

We snacked on the remaining food trays, to balance the number of bottles we were most likely to empty. Our group never needed to go to a party. We were the party.

Shannon, the outspoken wild one, was in rare form. Always forward and unapologetically direct. Tonight, was no different. After over indulging on tequila, she overstepped with invasive questions for the bride. "Are you ever going to tell us what he is like in bed?"

The room chuckled as Isla passed the near empty bottle of tequila around the table.

Taylor smirked. "You never share such information about the one."

Shannon's face stiffened. Her golden eyes locked on Taylor, and her lips barely hid the cracked smile she forced. "He's that good huh."

All of us squealed in high pitches followed by laughter, while Taylor blushed, revealing the unspoken details, simply by smiling so hard. Her rosy flushed cheeks could no longer hold her resting bitch face.

"Good for you Taylor," I said. "You are right. It's none of our business."

"What's going on with you and Evan?" Taylor questioned as her caramel hands reached for the last drop of tequila.

"Not a damn thing. I know you guys think he is a keeper, and he does look great on paper, but **I** am just not into him." I emphasized.

"Why not? I wish a man like Evan would sweep me off of my feet." Isla scowled in my direction.

"Look, I already feel bad about stringing him along. Trust me on this one. If you knew why I have to break up with him, you might sympathize with me."

With great hope, I wanted them to take me at my word. Such a wish might have been possible if they were of sober mind. "Then tell us why," they said in unison, like a rehearsed choir.

I finished off the remaining tequila in my glass, and chased it with a squeeze of lime between my teeth. Gasping from the burning pains in my chest, I bought myself a few moments before sharing my quandary. "He is incapable of giving me an orgasm." I hid my face with shame, peeping at my friends through the cracks of my fingers.

Taylor and Isla looked at each with smirks between them, Khai took a sip from her cup with raised eyebrows, and Shannon couldn't help but be Shannon.

"Come again? No pun intended." Shannon chuckled.

I knew her too well to know her pun was indeed intended. Once the banter and laughter faded, I pled my case.

"I've never had an orgasm with him. Sex with him is so horrible, I can't describe it," I blurted, hiding my face.

My friends looked at each other in silence, which is strange because they always have something to say. I could tell from looking at each one of them, they were calculating their responses, and waiting each other out to speak first.

"You are going to let a good man go, because of bad sex. You're crazy, Nadia. Do you know the percentage of women who have to fake it in the sack, but have a good man to come home to? Do you think a lot of women are sexually satisfied? Let me break it down for you. Studies show only twenty percent of people, married or single, actually experience the best sex of their lives. Get you a vibrator, handle your business, and keep your man." Shannon lectured looking down at me from her ginger colored nose.

"You seem to have it all figured out don't you, Sha? Pass the wine please?" I asked Khai in desperate need of a swig to survive Shannon's sermon.

"You know I'm the one in this circle who knows the most about sex." Shannon bragged.

"Just because your yellow ass talks about it the most, doesn't mean you know the most." Isla added.

"And you do? As I was saying, you better not throw a perfectly good man to the woods when the rest of us are meeting pathological liars, cheaters, sword fighters, video game freaks, and what not." Shannon definitively rested her case.

After taking a bow, she tooted her own horn further, telling me her advice was free of charge *this time*. I balled up a paper napkin from the table and threw it at her.

Khai then decided to chime in. "Have you told him he was bad in bed?"

I admitted I didn't want to hurt his feelings. And with that statement, I proved to be a walking nincompoop.

Men rarely make decisions with the consideration of a woman's feelings. They live their lives selfish and entitled with the world handed to them, while women have historically made the dumbest decisions in their life based on a man. Girls choose a college based on a boy. The television show Felicity was surely about a million girls worldwide. Women have agreed to public marriage proposals, to save the integrity of a man she has no intention of being with long term.

Always the nurturer, women everywhere are sparing a man's feelings. Ignoring their own needs and wants and desires, to be pleasing to or for a man. I know this firsthand.

The love of my life, Dylan, or who I thought was the love of my life, wasted my early twenties. I could have moved to New York and become a dancer, or experienced the rough streets of NYC and become a groomed writer at a major publication.

Instead, I met a big shouldered sexual God with a head full of course hair, and a smile that could charm the panties off of a nun. It is because of him, I stayed in North Carolina after college. Afraid if I left he would find someone better, or we would grow apart, or he wouldn't want me anymore, and cheat on me because of the distance.

It is also because of him, I have yet to trust a man with my heart, and overanalyze everything in my relationships. His ghost lives in my head and my bedroom, even though he did turn out to be a serial cheater, with me living in the same city as him, a compulsive liar, and extraordinary gas lighter.

Evan is better than Dylan in every way, except between the sheets. His kindness is appreciated, he calls often, is a considerate human being, and his resume is desirable. But that's it.

My friends couldn't understand the torture I feel when we're intimate. He's too good of a person to tell the brutal truth. My only solution was to end the relationship, and leave the hurtful comments to his next partner.

"Nadia, Evan is crazy about you. Shannon is right. Fake it and stroke his ego, then get yours with a toy when you need it." Khai encouraged, raising her sketched eyebrows as she took another sip.

'I don't think she bought what she said either.'

The mention of a bedroom toy, served as a segue for Shannon to become livelier. Describing what brand she recommends. Exaggerating with tales of how she became addicted to one in particular.

Unfortunately, Shannon's wild stories didn't remove the attention from me completely. "Do you love him? Like at least a little bit?" Taylor asked.

"I have love for him, but no, I can't say I love him, love him."

"You guys, this is about Dylan again." Taylor teased me. "Look at her. She is still hung up on the douchebag with the bomb-diggety dick."

"This is not about him." I lied.

"Yes, it is! You are still hung up on your old flame who cheated on you, and made you feel insecure about yourself. All because the sex was *immaculate* as you put it?"

"This is not about him for the last time."

I convinced no one, but I refused to let on. Beneath the digs and jabs, I knew my friends were concerned about my well-being. When I love, I love hard. And getting over Dylan was beyond rough in the beginning.

I suffered extreme dark days during that time, and I knew my circle never wanted to see me in such a state again.

"We want you to be happy," said Isla. "Forget about that lame prick, and move on with your life. It's been what three years?"

"Five," I mumbled.

Taylor could tell from the sour look I gave her, I was pissed she brought Dylan up. She sat quietly, while everyone else piled on with their thoughts about what I should do.

Casually she interrupted. "I think breaking up with Evan was the right thing to do. If a guy isn't satisfying you in the bedroom, you will not take him seriously. I know I wouldn't. And look at you. Stunning and miserable. If he doesn't make you happy after doing all the things you ask of him, then he isn't the one. You want magic. And fire. And passion. I get it."

"Well you just answered my questions about your sex life." Shannon clinked her glass with Khai.

Taylor scolded Shannon for prying yet again, while I fought the urge to remain upset with the one person now showing me support. I was missing everything she mentioned. I was bored and unhappy with Evan. I wanted what I had with Dylan, before his true colors were revealed, and what she had with Levi.

Dylan's whip appeal kept me thinking about him all of the time. My phone was glued to my hand, making sure I didn't miss his call. I yearned for his touch in the middle of the day. Snuck home during lunch for quickies. Everything Taylor said was true. When a man isn't doing his job in the bedroom, he doesn't cross your mind, or give you the shivers when you least expect it. I never looked for Evan's call, or yearned for his touch. I tolerated him because he was nice, and I suffered from the responsibility to be polite. To be a kind woman.

Sex shouldn't be a deal breaker, but it was a deal breaker. After nearly six months, I had given my best to a dreamy guy, waiting for something to kick in.

Shannon joked. "Dylan really dicmatized you."

She was correct. I have been comparing every man I date to him. At some point, I joined the club of women who had a hard time getting over a man not worth my tears, time, and energy. The worst men always handled their business in the sack, and are the hardest to move on from.

Old women speak truth when they say, you have to lie under a new one to get over an old one, but that statement needs some amending. You have to lie under a better one in my opinion.

"Let us set you up with someone," Khai suggested.

"I'm not donating my reserve dick," said Shannon.

"Wait, what?" I asked. "I don't want any of your hand me downs. I can find a man on my own thank you."

"It's not about finding a man. It's about getting you laid with some good *D* so you can move on with your life. I knew a guy so hung he gave me a bladder infection. You might be able to handle him. I sure couldn't." Khai snickered.

"Thanks, but no thanks to the Emergency Room dick. I'll pass."

We burst with laughter. Isla stood at the table and made a toast to finding me a thoroughbred in the sack. They all raised their glasses. "To finding Nadia a thoroughbred in the sack!"

Glasses clinked amongst them, as I held my head low in humiliation. Taylor diverted the attention back to her with news about our upcoming seven-day wedding getaway. She discussed the details and itinerary of our trip to London in a week.

Khai lit up at the mention of the word's getaway and week, expressing she was overdue for a break, and in desperate need of some girl time.

Taylor made the trip sound surreal, constantly repeating, "We are going to live like The Royals, or at least close to it. Levi has rented buses, and a private chauffeur during our stay, along with scoring us access to clubs, and passes for a major festival happening on the weekend."

Taylor made it sound as if we were going to party like rock stars, which was up her alley. She devoted the past year to plan her extravagant affair: scheduled family activities to occupy us during the week, designated days for rest— which we were going to need after wine tasting, game day, and a two-hour train ride to Paris.

I had been eyeing flights to Ibiza, Spain from London, and asked if any time would be permitted to do something of our own choosing. "I want to see the big magnetic rock, Es Vedra. It's supposed to have healing powers."

Taylor shut down the notion of us not obeying her every command, for her wedding, and quickly dismissed my query. "We have a jam-packed week. Maybe next time." She continued with her speech, killing the mood, and our buzz with the nonstop details.

Finally, Shannon saved us with her usual antics. She interrupted Taylor and asked, "Are we going shopping, and what kind of men do they have to offer over there?"

Isla was now tipsy slurring in her words, and added. "I heard a rumor the men in London are the world's worst lovers."

"I guess we'll find out won't we Isla." Shannon gave Isla a high-five.

Their shenanigans returned the liveliness back into the room, and we sipped a few more rounds, listening to Isla and Shannon match each other wit for wit. An oldie but goodie came on the radio, and we sang along and grooved in the open area by the table, dancing our drunken heads to the tunes, until Levi returned to shuttle us home.

CHAPTER 2

London

Visiting a different continent, and country, could now be checked off my bucket list. The anticipated destination wedding weekend was upon us, and thanks to Khai upgrading my seats to first class, the long flight went smoothly.

By early evening, all of the bridal party assembled in Taylor's suite, to check in and receive our orders. Wired with excitement, even though we were on a tightly run ship, we tended to the list of duties given to us.

While welcoming the guests at the reception in the hotel lounge, the girls and I scoped the premise for possible prospects. Levi's family provided certifiable eye candy, as well as a few of the hotel staff.

The start to our getaway seemed promising. After exchanging pleasantries with both families, Isla took it upon herself to ask the concierge of the Friday night happenings.

According to the itinerary, we were scheduled to go clubbing Sunday night, but we were too excited to spend our first night in Europe stuck at the hotel. Secretly huddled in the lobby, Isla whipped out a list of events to check out nearby. It was settled. We were going out on the town. Now, we had to break it to Taylor.

She wasn't thrilled with our plan, especially since she was unable to join us. Veering from her itinerary, wasn't how she imagined the start of the weekend, but she graciously gave us access to the limousine for the night.

After a quick change into skimpy outfits, the fab five minus 1 made its first stop. A few blocks away from the hotel, a nearby pub stood on the corner. The girls and I looked at each other confused. Surely, the concierge didn't think we would have a good time, at a place playing music we didn't know how to label. The place was practically empty, and the scene was trite.

Without mumbling a sound between us, we backtracked back into the limo, fearing the night was going to be a bust.

Isla asked the driver, Tony, if he was familiar with any of the places on the concierge's list. He scoffed multiple times as his eyes read from top to bottom. He then asked if she wanted to hear the truth. Isla nodded yes.

With confidence he said, "You ladies won't enjoy any of the places on this list. These are the safe tourist attractions. A group of young ladies like yourself would enjoy the clubs the locals go to."

We pretended to have a private sidebar conversation about what we should do, but Tony could hear us.

"I say we stick to the list. I'm not trying to be a human trafficking victim," said Khai.

"Who would buy and sell you Khai." Isla snickered.

Khai nudged her then added. "We are not home. We can't trust anyone. Not even Tony here, no offense." She motioned her head towards him.

"Taylor said he is bonded and will be with us all week, so I'm guessing we can trust him." Shannon raised a brow.

Khai asked Tony a serious round of questions, typed out his full name and license number in an email to her sister, and made him swear he would do as we commanded.

"I will take good care of your party. Would it be of interest to you, if I drove by the hot spots not mentioned on the list?" Tony asked.

The four of us agreed with a simple nod.

"And Tony sir, I am live streaming this outing, so our whereabouts will be public," Khai announced.

"Sounds good Madame."

The line in the car rang loudly enough for us to hear in the rear. Tony called a friend by the name of Prano, who had connections with nighttime entertainment. He explained our dilemma to the high-pitched voice on the line. We struggled to understand what was being said between them, due to their heavy accents and broken British lingo, which sounded alike yet different somehow.

The background of his whereabouts sounded like the place we needed to be. We gave him the okay and arrived at Tower Nightclub, placed in the middle of a block, with a heavy line of people waiting behind a velvet rope.

Tony drove us directly in front of the entrance, and thanks to his contact, we bypassed the line to go inside. "No woman left behind." Khai reminded us as we entered.

The place was leveled with people of all colors, and the music was blasting techno rave tunes. The music scene was different than in the States. The hot songs were blends, mixed over a faster house music sound, which was popular in the U.K, thumping with heavy bass lines and noisy effects.

We settled at our table sharing appetizers and cocktails, when the music transitioned to classic reggae dancehall, my favorite genre. Off I went to the middle of the dancefloor to show off my moves.

I had to create my own space on the floor. Once I let loose, the crowd surrounded me as I threw my cilantro colored fringe dress and hair around.

Heavy into the moment, and feeling alive for the first time in a while, I danced as if I knew a crowd was watching. A spotlight appeared above me, singling me out in front of everyone.

The crowd surrounding me clapped and cheered me on, fueling my ego to carry on the way I did at frat parties back in college. I fed into the way they were receiving me— until another dancer came from the darkness, and made his way into my light.

He circled me before engaging, and when the beat dropped he began thrusting and winding on me from the rear. I felt his bulge against my back, so I turned to get a good look at him. He wasn't the most attractive man, nor was he my type, but I couldn't deny he had rhythm.

I paused and watched him with my hands placed up on my hips, doing moves I couldn't dream of in an acrobatic fashion. He taunted me to battle him, and instead of gracefully giving him his respect, I waited for his moment to end, then joined him once the bass kicked. I circled him, throwing my flimsy strands everywhere, and challenged him as if he were an old companion.

He responded to my invitation as if we knew one another, and went back and forth creating a frenzy in the crowd. I let him get the best of me until it was quitting time, then I surprised him with a slowly risen high kick, and held it in place for a few seconds.

While holding my balance, I tossed my hair and pretended to file my nails, causing the crowd to go wild. My consort bowed down to me, and I in return curtsied him. Together we bowed to the crowd as they applauded us, then shook hands followed by a friendly hug, whispering compliments to one another.

I strutted back to my table for some much-needed rest, but before I could sit, I was asked to join Isla in the ladies' room. We snaked our way through the crowd when I noticed a short, latte colored guy appeared to be following us. I freshened up in the mirror while Isla used the loo, debating if I wanted to worry her about the suspicious man.

Upon our exit, the guy in question stood with his back against the wall near the men's pisser. I grew nervous.

He stepped forward. "Pardon me, I'm friends with Tony, the chauffeur who brought you here. Hayden's my name but people call me Prano."

Immediately I recognized the high-pitched tone. "Nice to meet you Prano. I'm Nadia, and this is Isla."

I imagined him as a tall, slim, fair-skinned figure from his voice on the phone. He didn't match the person I created in my head at all, but he was still cute enough. His eyes bounced between Isla and I, and he smiled on the side of his mouth. He was just as nervous to meet us as we were him.

"Thanks for letting us come in tonight," said Isla.

"It was no problem at all. Really. Lovely meeting you both. I planned on coming over to your table and introducing myself, and a few of my associates here tonight. But before I could do so, the Deejay wanted me to find you." Prano pointed at me. "He wants to thank you personally for putting on a show out there. You have some really nice moves."

I blushed like an idiot. My cheeks were so full, they nearly burst. It was as if I had never received a compliment before. "Thank you. If he really sent you out of your way, I guess we can go say hi." I looked to Isla for confirmation it was okay with her.

"If you wouldn't mind following me, I'll take you to the stage." Prano led with a step.

"I guess it's okay." Isla shrugged her shoulders. "If he is fine, I call dibs."

'Dibs on a man.'

"Isla, please. I'm not going there with you tonight. Besides, he asked to meet me."

The side of the stage was guarded by a hefty security team, sectioned off by a velvet rope. Limited seating was available, so we stood and waited, too long for Isla's taste.

Song after song blasted from the nearby speakers, still no sign of this deejay who wanted to show his gratitude. Isla grew impatient and asked Prano to escort us back to our table, without asking if I was ready to bail.

"You go ahead. I'll be right behind you," I said.

Her face grimaced. "We travel in pairs. Always."

I convinced her to give the guy a few more minutes, as a line dance song came on. Prano assured us his friend would join us in a few minutes, claiming to know the playlist.

Rudely, Isla suggested. "Can you light a fire under him."

Prano climbed the stairs to the dimly lit booth, signaling thumbs up from above. Moments later, the music changed and Prano returned with an average height, slightly tanned white boy behind him. He was medium-build, with curly brown hair cut low on the sides and nape of his neck, thick eyebrows, hooded light brown eyes, and a square jaw outlined from a five o'clock shadow. A crisp white fitted t-shirt hugged his chest, and tailored white jeans hung correctly around his waist. It was hard to not stare at him.

"Ladies this is Mash. Mash this is Nadia, the lady you asked to meet, and her friend Isla," said Prano, smiling at Isla.

"Nice to meet you ladies, especially you, the dancing queen." He kissed the back of my hand.

I blushed. Unable to speak as the gorgeous specimen eyed me from head to toe. When the cat finally let go of my tongue, I flirtatiously said to him, "Dancing Queen. Stop. I was just enjoying the music."

"Ah, an American. You surprise me yet again."

"I know we don't sound sophisticated like you Brits. You're easy to understand by the way. I was having trouble earlier with your friend."

"I love your accent." He gazed into my eyes without blinking.

I blushed again, looking at his full lips, then his eyes, then his lips once more. *'They look tasty,'* I thought to myself, searching for the right words to say next.

My accent was all over the place at times. I had my home voice, which was country twang, my work voice, which was considered proper, and my Geechee tongue, which I spoke with my grandmother. Sometimes I spoke all three without realizing it.

Finally, I complimented him in return. "I love yours as well."

"Tonight, must be my lucky night. A great beauty gave me the boost I needed to get through this set. You see I just arrived back in town for a big event tomorrow, and I'm fatigued to say the least," he confessed.

"When Prano said your name, I thought I recognized it. We're here for a destination wedding, and there is a big outdoor party we're going to tomorrow. I remember reading your name on the flyer."

"Yeah, a few hours away in Glastonbury. I won't rest until my set is over. As soon as I'm done here I'll load up again, and hit the road. When is the wedding?" he asked, looking at his watch.

I felt I had bored him quickly, and didn't want to humiliate myself further. "Next Sunday. Well, good luck tomorrow. It was nice meeting you," I said, salvaging my pride before being dismissed.

"My apologies. I checked my watch to see how long I have before this song ends." He explained.

"I understand. I don't want to keep you from working. We need to get going anyway, since we have an early morning."

"So, you're here for a week?" He grinned.

I nodded yes.

"I hope this isn't too forward, but if I give you my information, will you reach out to me. I'd really like to talk with you some more, maybe you could stop by my tent tomorrow. Check out my set? If it's cool with you?"

"I'd love to."

"Here's my card. All of my social media is listed, and this is my mobile on the back. I really hope I hear from you Nadia."

I studied the card, thinking of the perfect response before walking away. *'Talk to you soon. See you later. I'll be sure to call.'*

"You will," I replied, lifting my head from studying his information.

Our lips met surprisingly. *'Mmm. An accidental kiss. Or was it. He didn't pull away so easy.'*

We shared a smile from our faux pas moment, and for a few seconds locked eyes, until he recognized the song was about to end.

"I was aiming for your forehead but you— I should apologize, but I'm not sorry." He admitted.

"It's fine. Don't miss your cue. I'll be in touch." I sauntered away slowly.

He winked his left eye at me, then ran up the stairs to the booth, while Prano led Isla and I through the crowd.

I'm not sure if I walked, glided, or floated to our table, but I was in heaven, as well as in shock. This was the first time I found a Caucasian man attractive, and felt chemistry so powerful with a stranger at first sight.

Men of different persuasions made passes at me before, but I never flirted back. Never gave them a chance, or a second look. But this time I engaged. A smoldering, brown-eyed babe, with skin the color of buttermilk had my stomach doing pirouettes. And I liked it.

Before taking a seat, I slipped my cell number to Prano, and asked him to give it to Mash. As my head was in the clouds, I could hear Isla telling the girls about our thirty-minute disappearance.

I was in a zone, off somewhere with my thoughts, fascinating about my encounter. The kiss. The feel of his lips. The way his eyes shone. The way I wanted to ditch my friends, force my way back into VIP, and taste him once more.

Moments later Shannon shoved me, waking me from my trance. They were all staring at me, waiting for me to chime in and validate Isla's rambling. I had a lot to say, yet speechless at the same time. I sat there smiling at them like those masks you see at Mardi Gras, dodging their questions, and staring past them at the tinted glass on the booth.

I wondered if he was heavy into his job, or looking at me, too. "Earth to Nadia. Tony is waiting for us at the door." Shannon nudged me to rise as I took one last look at the stage.

I was hounded on the way back to the hotel. The girls begged me for details, but I wasn't ready to discuss it. What was there to discuss? A gorgeous man asked to meet me, accidentally kissed me, and gave me his number. I was still processing it all myself— My intrigue and arousal of the man.

Honestly, I didn't know how to communicate what I was feeling or thinking, and lucky for me Khai was too tired to badger me once we made it to our room. Before falling asleep she playfully said, "Don't think you are off the hook. I want answers in the morning." Then dozed off within seconds.

Lying across my bed, I giggled and smiled to myself like a simpleton. I needed to shower the club scent off of my skin, but couldn't pull myself out of my daydream to do so. Sleep was calling me, but my thoughts were on repeat of the accidental kiss that moved me, and then my phone buzzed.

Prano delivered and gave Mash my number. He texted.

> M: *I'd like to see you before I get on the road.*
> *Can I stop by?*

I didn't want to say yes and seem desperate. I also didn't want to say no. I wanted to see him as well. I was nervous to talk to him in a quiet setting with just the two of us at such a late hour, so I hesitated for a long time not knowing how to respond. The next message popped up.

M: *I hope I didn't wake you.*

I held the phone close to my chest, while my mind raced on how to reply. I was in London, on a destination wedding vacation with love in the air, and a new experience on my heels.

Filled with uncertainty and giddiness, I decided I would take full advantage of whatever came my way, live outside of my comfort zone and replied.

N: *The Mandarin in Hyde Park.*

I took the shortest shower of my life, and threw on a pair of jeans and a fitted tee, washed off my make-up, brushed my teeth, and moisturized my face so he could see me in my natural state. I applied some lip balm in case our lips touched again, and pulled my hair back into a ponytail as the next message came through.

M: *I'm in the lobby.*

As the elevator doors closed I became uneasy. '*I should have made him wait to see me,*' I thought, but it was too late. I was already on the ground floor, and there he was, standing near the front desk waiting for me.

I walked over to his leering face, exuded with confidence, and plopped in front of him. Twisting and turning about flirtatiously, as the bass in his voice nearly made my knees buckle.

"My crew is out front giving me hell for coming over here." He grinned with his head down. "I couldn't stop talking about you. Even if it's only for a few minutes, I had to see your face."

"I'm flattered." My cheeks flushed.

A short silence occurred while we stared at each other, smiling in between eye contact, waiting for the other to speak.

"I must admit you make me nervous. Do I make you, nervous?" he asked, in a deep tone.

"A little."

"That must mean something. I hope we find out what." He seduced me with a tempting look in his eyes.

"Yeah, I hope so, too."

"Forgive me for staring. I'm normally cool. It's something about you...I can't take my eyes off of you."

"You know you didn't have to come all the way over here. I could have sent you a picture."

"It wouldn't have been the same."

"Why not?" I tilted my head.

"Because I can't kiss a picture," he said, then stole my lips.

He pecked them delicately, once with his eyes open looking into mine. I returned the gesture and closed my eyes, tasting a trace of liquor that mixed well with the sweetness of his tongue as we locked lips.

We lingered, long enough to hold hands, and make our first official kiss perfect. And it was, perfection from two strangers.

"That was exactly how I imagined it." His eyes held mine.

I unlocked my hands from around his. Our index fingers remained intertwined.

"I'm glad you came to see me." I felt my heart skip a beat.

"So am I. I know what I'll be dreaming about on the bus. I'll tell you about it tomorrow," he said, letting go of my fingers as he backed away to the sound of the horn blowing for him outside.

"I look forward to it. Good night." I walked backwards towards the elevator.

He waved, high-stepping to the exit. "I've changed my mind. Send me a picture!" He shouted across the empty lobby, captivating me with his perfectly lined teeth until the steel doors closed between us.

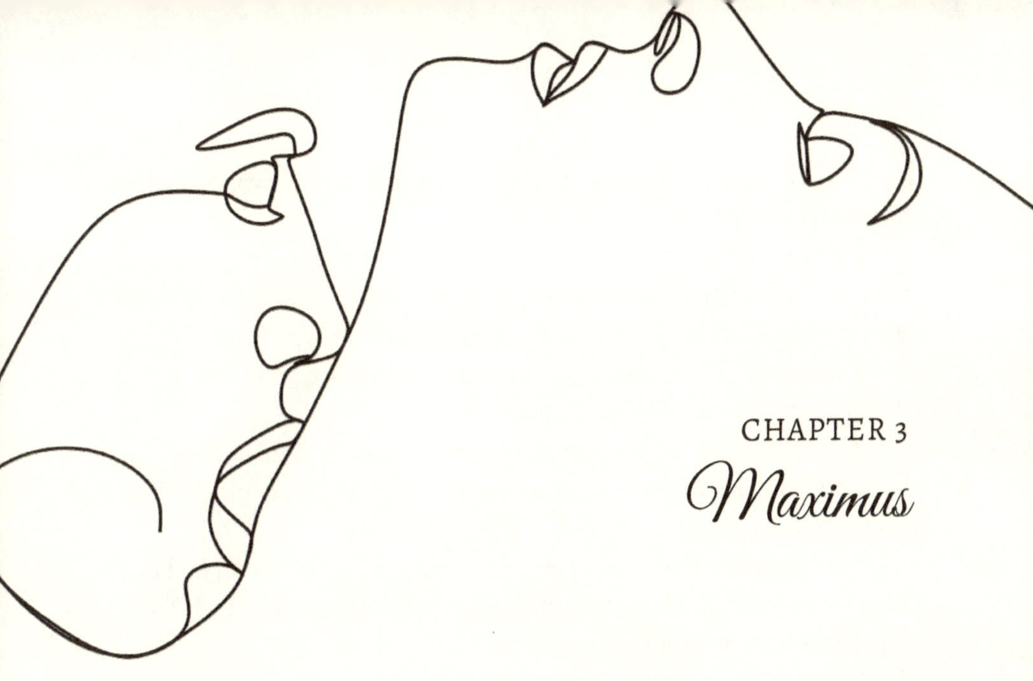

CHAPTER 3

Maximus

En route to the festival, every corner of the bus had something different going. Some slept, read, or sat quietly to themselves, while others made the drive entertaining. Telling jokes, playing card games, passing bottles of hooch, and making bets of sporting events back home.

The sweetest of dreams filled my head as I napped, and when I woke I admired the country roadside of the terrain.

At times, I caught a glimpse of myself in the reflection of the window, grinning about my late-night visit, and planning what to say when I saw him. Three hours later, we arrived in Glastonbury. The butterflies returned to my stomach, fluttering in circles, and my chested tightened in knots. The feeling was familiar, yet scary. I hadn't felt those flutters in years, and to feel them so quickly about a man I knew nothing about, threw me for a loop.

The field was packed with free-spirited party goers, resembling the crowd at Coachella. The entrance line was so long, I assumed we would make it inside when the shows were over for the day.

To distract myself from the impatience growing inside, I checked my emails until we were admitted, then called Mash to let him know I was there. My call went straight to voicemail, and I was torn if I should call again, fearing I was interrupting, or worse, being blown off.

The day was quickly slipping away, from the long line to enter the parking lot, the hours waiting in line to get inside, then the half hour walk to the main stage. A few of us didn't care to watch the concert from far away, or on the mega screens. Instead we split into pairs, doing as we pleased until ten o'clock.

Khai partnered with me to explore the grounds, but not because of shared interest. She was eager to meet the mystery man who had me smiling all morning.

We watched a few artists perform we had never heard of, had our horoscopes read for fun, and undoubtedly had a contact high from the marijuana swarming the gardens.

Hours later, I grew anxious to be in Mash's company. Khai and I footed the fields, until we found the tent Mash was scheduled to perform in. My palms grew sweaty as I texted him.

N: *I'm outside.*

He responded seconds later.

M: *Come to the back of the tent by the loading truck.*

We entered through the slim drapery next to a generator. Eyes from every direction were upon us, as we stood in front of two huge security guards. "Nadia!" shouted a voice to our right. "They are with us!" Prano yelled to the guards letting us pass.

The backstage crowd stared at us as we walked over to the seating area, as if they could tell we were foreigners without hearing us speak. A bad habit I had since childhood reappeared while working through the crowd. I began mocking a horrible impression of a British accent, saying "Pardon me," as I swept through the onlookers.

He kissed my cheek and my chest pounded fast and hard. My eyes twitched from nervousness, and as his hand wrapped around my waist, I nearly melted from his touch. The way he looked at me, made me feel desirable. I feared I could lose control with him. Be wild and carefree without remorse. *'So unlike me.'*

To break his spell, I ruined the moment by blurting out, "What is your real name?"

"Maximus Sharper," he answered, leading me to a sofa behind a curtain.

'Mmm, a strong name.'

My left leg crossed his right leg when we squeezed tightly in the corner of the couch, leaving plenty of space for Khai and Prano.

"And your surname is?" he asked.

"Melton."

"Melton? I don't think I know any Melton's." He clutched onto my hand placed on my thigh, running circles on my leg with his other.

Khai glanced from the corner of her eyes, then raised her eyebrows at me allowing him to fondle my skin. I smirked, letting her know I saw her reaction, then carried on with my conversation.

"So, did you dream about me?"

"I dreamt about our kiss. Is it too soon for another one?" He leaned in and smiled.

"No sir."

He pulled me in close by my shirt, and lightly swept his fingers around the back of my neck. Planting his luscious lips against mine, I gulped in his air as he took in mine, unapologetic for our public display of affection. Like a schoolgirl, I began counting the seconds not knowing when to pull back.

This kiss was hotter and longer than the one from the morning. Heat sparked between us, as neither he nor I showed signs of letting up. My knees were now in his lap, and both of my arms wrapped around him.

Khai interrupted us by clearing her throat a few times. "I'm Khai by the way."

I wiped my lipstick from his lips, and giggled. We turned towards my good friend, and I formally introduced her to the man of the hour.

"I haven't seen you smile like this in a long time," said Khai. "All is forgiven. Nice to meet you. Prano and I are going to give you two some privacy, but not too much." She joked.

"I promise I will behave." Mash held up his hands.

When Prano and Khai disappeared behind the curtain, Mash and I shared a laughable lip embrace, then cooled things down.

We conversed with the twenty minutes of free time he had remaining before his show. Our words connected like a game of scrabble. Our energy flowed in sync. The chemistry between us was explosive, and magic felt present when I was near him.

Time flew by so fast, it seemed like we had been talking for only a few minutes instead of twenty. The show coordinator called for him, and our lips touched once more.

"Have dinner with me tomorrow night?" His hands stroked my cheek.

Looking into his eyes, I envisioned being pressed beneath him with expressions of joy on my face. I could look into his eyes for days, nights even, and listen to him talk for hours.

His accent drove me wild, and the five o'clock shadow filling in on his face, reeled me further into his abyss. The longer I looked at him, the wilder my thoughts ran. "What time should I be ready?" I answered.

"Pick you up at seven."

For a moment, I contemplated hanging back until his set was complete, but we travel in packs for safety. I couldn't abandon Khai, nor did I want to look like a stage five clinger.

I argued with myself. *'He didn't ask you to hang back. Let him take you on a date and get wined and dined.'*

He walked me to the side of the stage, where I joined Khai and Prano. We watched him work for a while, then trekked back to the meeting point. Bypassing concerts in session, parties, tents and kiosks throughout the fairgrounds, we spent just as much time walking as we did watching shows.

Large crowds accosted us, carrying us away in their flock. We held hands to prevent being separated, as painted faces screaming and circling about, frightened us while trapped. The increasing size and weirdness of the crowd grew every second. Slightly worried, I drew in closer to Khai, and fought our way out of the drunken horde, safely returning to the meeting point.

The rest of our party regrouped, and Tony drove us back to the city. After a long flight, a night out, a catnap, a long drive, and the long day at the festival, I was exhausted. I slept on the bus, and throughout Sunday morning. Even after skipping breakfast and brunch, and spending the afternoon in bed, I was still physically tired, but found energy to get ready for my date with Mr. Sharper.

I didn't trust myself around him. I was participating in public displays of affection, and kissing him like I had known him longer than three days. The more I realized how reckless I was behaving, I was glad Khai and I chose to share room expenses. If I had a room to myself, I felt certain both of my feet would have been off of the floor before our date.

Preparing for this date became a strategic exercise. The dress I originally planned on wearing was overly, sexually enticing. Without a clue of where I was being taken, I opted to wear a blue one-piece jumpsuit instead. It had an open neckline which accentuated my healthy bosoms, then loosened as it left my curves down to the hem.

Since this was a special occasion, I accessorized with my custom Billie Hilliard bracelet cuffs, but only wore three-inch strappy heels for comfort. I placed my flat shoes in my oversized purse, and when Khai wasn't looking, added my toothbrush, a pair of panties, some leggings, and my make-up bag.

Maximus knocked on the door, and my heart fluttered. I felt like a teenage girl going on her first date, and lost all of my cool knowing he was on the other side of the door.

Before answering, I made a mental note to be as quiet as possible, and not say anything stupid.

I opened the door. "Damn," I mumbled.

"I'm sorry." He grinned.

His light brown eyes glistened as he greeted me with a single red rose and kiss on the cheek. I recovered my verbal fumble with, "Huh, oh nothing. I was talking to myself."

'I'm already muttering like an idiot.'

My mind betrayed me and let my tongue speak what I was thinking. I couldn't help myself. The man was fine as hell, and handsome as ever.

We hugged, long enough for me to sniff the orange notes of his cologne which blended well with his natural scent of take me now.

"Shall we?" He took me by the arm.

I clung to his manliness, admiring the sharp way he was dressed. His garments looked tailored. Fitted black slacks and a black pullover, with a light blue and black oxford shirt peeking at the collar.

I held on to him so tight, I knew he could tell I didn't want to let go when the elevator arrived. I was already smitten, picturing myself stroking his freshly trimmed beard, while looking up at him on the bed fucking me slow. Thank God Khai was there to block me from spreading wide eagle.

She liked Mash from the short time she spent with him, but still didn't trust the fact we were not on home soil. She made me promise to ping her my location every hour. Being married to a cop, she felt forced to share the safety tips Brian, her husband, taught her. But I wasn't worried. Foolish, maybe. Lustful, indeed. But not worried.

Mr. Sharper demonstrated what I never experienced in a grown man. He escorted me around his city in a vintage town car, made eye contact with me when speaking, placed his hand in the small of my back frequently, and held a full conversation while explaining the significance of well-known tourist attractions.

At dinner, he pulled out my chair, stood when I left the table, and didn't laugh as I wanted to try fish and chips at the upscale establishment. He ordered it as an appetizer after insisting I try his favorite dish, and I admired how he took charge, just as he did our first kiss.

Afraid I was going to humiliate myself, or say something stupid again, I kept quiet at dinner, creating an awkward vibe. He began to grow uncomfortable, and I couldn't pretend any longer, so I admitted what I was doing in an effort to lighten the mood.

He laughed at my honesty and confessed, he thought he had done something to offend me which caused me to withdraw.

The tension left the table and our vibe returned to normal, as I began talking his head off. Telling him about my failed career attempts, my childhood dream of becoming a famous dancer, and how I now hoped to become a successful writer.

He listened to me ramble while stuffing my face in between, then I revealed what was really on my mind. I told him he was the first white guy I ever kissed, and went on a date with.

He sat pensively after my revelation, and I grew worried I had blown it by being too direct. I suffered as he sat in silence, looking at his near empty plate, fumbling his fingers against the white tablecloth.

I looked away as there was no eye contact between us, then he spoke. "I wanted to carefully craft what I am about to say. I'm flattered to be the first white guy you have spent time with. If I may ask, what took you so long?"

"I. I..." I stammered, choking on my words.

"I'm just joking. But in all seriousness, I would like to know why you gave me a chance?"

"It seems strange saying this, but there is something about you I can't explain. I wish I could articulate what I want to say better, but for some reason I can't. It's like there are no words to describe it, but it exists. I probably sound crazy right now."

"Actually, you don't. I know exactly what you are trying to say." He smiled at me with his eyes.

I swirled the wine in front of my lips, sniffed and sipped slowly. I returned his stare and confessed. "I've received offers outside of my race before, but I never felt compelled to accept. Until now. You are the first I've ever been attracted to."

"Are you comfortable being out with me?" he asked.

"Are you comfortable being seen with me?"

"Why wouldn't I be? You're beautiful. And since we are talking about this, you may as well know, I have gone out with women of all persuasions, but you are the first to have this effect on me."

'Same.'

I was in trouble, falling fast and hard, and worried about the future instead of enjoying the present. Terrified my heart was going to get broken. In the back of my mind, I thought the only thing that could save me, was if the rumor about British men being horrible lovers turned out to be true. He had no idea, but I knew I was going to find out the answer to that question tonight.

The amount of food we ordered was gluttonous. Maximus

suggested we take an after-dinner stroll to walk some of it off, and led me down a few lesser crowded streets.

The sound of traffic surrounded us as we walked a few blocks, and ended up in a courtyard across from Buckingham Palace. The gold and white lights lit the site so bright, I could see it clearly from where we stood.

He placed his jacket around my sweater, as the night air turned on its chill, staring at me marvel at the historic palace. The glimmer in my eyes lured him in, and we found ourselves kissing in the moonlight, wanting more of one another, and not wanting the night to end.

"Are you ready to go back to the hotel?" he asked.

"No. But if you need to get some rest I understand."

"Rest is the last thing on my mind." He traced my hand with his fingers, and gazed into my eyes.

"So where to then?"

"I'd love to show you my place?"

"I'd love to see it."

We drove a little under an hour from the city into the suburbs. Curvy roads, dark streets, and many hillsides later, Mash entered a code into a gated community, with at least three acres between each home in a dimly lit neighborhood. The houses were huge, and I grew anxious to see where we were going to end up.

He pulled into this beautiful mini castle like home, with mild lighting outside its exterior, and greenery for days. I thought to myself, *'He must be one hell of a deejay to afford something of this nature.'*

It was intimidating. My small three-bedroom starter home could fit inside this colossal house. I felt out of my league and became quiet again, shifting back into awkwardness.

My silence was broken when Mash asked me what I thought about his house. I thought it was a lot of house for one person, but I didn't dare say it aloud. "I love it. It's beautiful." I smiled.

"Thank you. I was thinking of downsizing next year, but I like the area."

"I admire your taste. Did you do the interior design?" I inquired.

"I hired professionals. I couldn't pull all of this off."

"Well they did an excellent job. It's clean and modern, but most importantly it reflects a man lives here. It's sexy."

"Come on, let me show you around."

He began the tour with his man cave/studio, where he housed all of his collectible toys, a bar for hosting, and a Styrofoam room where he recorded his music. We then walked into each of the five bedrooms and workout area near the living room.

Along the walls were mounted abstract paintings and nothing personal. Floating shelves, but no pictures of a mother, child, or himself. Only paintings and random wall decorum, of what I perceived as an expensive Indian collection.

Next, we entered the living room where a massive, curved screen television rose from the floor. I acted impressed but I wasn't. All men seem to be fascinated with oversized TVs, and the latest electronic gadget.

Below it was an electric fireplace I desperately wished he turned on. The house was beautiful but nippy, and I was hoping this would be the room we lounged in, so I could get warm in front of the fire.

I pulled my sweater closer together and hoped he noticed. I thought he did when he took one of the decorative fur throws from the sofa, and wrapped it around me. I was wrong. He covered me so we could climb five steps from the left side of the living room, where he led me through a double glass door to an outside pool area.

I couldn't see the landscape, but I imagined it was beautiful. We cuddled under the fur blanket, admiring the stars in the sky as the moon's reflection hit the waves in the pool.

We conversed about music, movies, our likes and dislikes, and cultural differences without checking the time, which moved on significantly.

"I have an important question to ask you." His tone of voice turned serious. "What is your favorite song of all time?"

"Ugh, that's a hard one. I love so many different genres."

"But there has to be one song you love more than any other piece of music. When I asked the question, what song popped into your head?"

"Sting, *When We Dance*," I professed.

"Voila, your favorite song of all time."

"I do love it. It's definitely in my top five. What's your favorite song?"

"Bob Marley, *Waiting in Vain*."

"Ooh, another good one."

"It is, isn't it?

A breeze of cold air infiltrated the blanket. I shivered and drew closer to him, pressing my head against his chest for warmth. He squeezed my shoulders, and I relaxed— nestled next to him.

"I'm assuming you like reggae music from the other night." He grinned to himself.

"Very much so."

"What's your favorite Bob song?"

"*Chances Are.*"

"You surprise me." He scoffed.

"Why?"

"I thought you were going to name a more commercial, more well-known one by The Great Late."

I had run out of words, and silence found its way back in as we stared at each other, wondering what the other was thinking. He took me by the face and kissed me so tender I felt a tingle in my chest.

"You're freezing." He rubbed the coldness of my cheeks. "Let's go inside."

He led me to the stone colored rug in front of the fireplace. With the flip of a switch, the black glass revealed a red and brown fire behind the panel. We canoodled in front of it until the blanket was no longer needed, continuing the tender kiss he planted on me outside. My sweater was tossed, then his sweater disappeared, as the heat from the fire, and from us, sweltered the room.

He let me unbutton half of his oxford shirt, while fighting the urge to explore me with his hands. I found his restraint admirable, but I knew he wanted to ravish me, so I played his game and stopped undressing him. "You didn't finish giving me the tour," I said, punishing him.

He rose to his feet and helped me off of the rug, holding my hand as he escorted me to the kitchen. I noticed him looking at me, then looking away when I caught him.

I laughed to myself, wishing I could read his mind. Imagining the conversation he was having in his head, since I pulled the brakes in the living room. *'I just couldn't be a cliché giving it up on his living room floor.'*

He paused in the hallway and pressed me against the wall. Stealing a few soft kisses, and running his fingers up and down my arm. I wanted to shout, *Take me!* Instead, I held it together as the intensity continued to build.

"Why don't you have any pictures on your walls?" I distracted him.

He backed away, still holding my hands and replied, "I thought photographs belonged in photo albums, not walls."

"Okay," I said, feeling I had overstepped.

"Whose picture should be hanging around?" he asked.

"Um your parents, or one of you mixing, or one of your favorite moments maybe." I responded and questioned at the same time.

"Maybe I will. I hadn't put much thought into it. I'd be happy to share my photo albums with you if you want."

I didn't answer. I motioned my head to the room up ahead, then led him towards it. "What a kitchen!"

"I have used the stove maybe twice, and I've never used the oven." He snarked.

"Seriously? I could get fat in a kitchen like this. You have everything. I mean literally everything."

"Yeah, but it's no fun cooking for one." His eyes followed me.

"So true. I cook and invite my crew over to eat all the time."

"So, you cook a lot?"

"Cook and bake."

"I hope I get invited to one of those dinners. I'd like to see you in action."

"Trust, I can burn."

"You can what?" He scowled.

"Burn. Where I'm from it means I cook really well. Slang or Ebonics is what some would call it. I might whip up something for you while I'm here. Ugh, do I spy another pool table in your dining room?"

"And that brings us to the last room in the house."

Adjacent to the kitchen was an obvious dining room, where a second pool table sat in place of a dining table. I felt I had already pried, when I asked about the pictures, so I waited for him to volunteer, why he designed his fine china room so poorly.

Circling the table while eyeing him with suspicion, I waited for an explanation. He played my game as I ran from him, making him chase me, then he caved.

"Yes, there is a table downstairs, but what can I say. I love the game. It is my favorite pastime, and my stress reliever. Sometimes I don't want to walk all the way downstairs, so I put another table in this empty space," he said proudly.

"You don't owe me any explanations about your house, but the fact you did has earned you some bonus points. I think it's cute. Plus, it is still a table, right?"

"Right. I knew you were smart. You get it. But uh, I didn't know I needed bonus points." He closed in on me. "You're the first person to ever walk through my entire house."

"Yeah right." I tapped his shoulder. "I'm not calling you a liar, but that just seems a bit far-fetched. I mean come on. A house this beautiful? It's hard to believe no one in your life has ever walked down these halls."

"It's true. I've been here a month or two, over a year and you are the first."

I couldn't look him in the eye. It was hard to believe he hadn't had a woman stay over, and roam his house for a night or a weekend. Looking away, I used his same words from dinner.

"Why me?"

"I wish I knew why I chose you to be the first. I know I'm definitely vibing with you," he answered.

"I'm feeling you as well."

"Ah! She said she's feeling me," he said aloud. "So it's mutual then?"

"It seems so."

This would have been the perfect time to be a mind reader. How could I really know Mr. Sharper wasn't playing with my emotions? I was really enjoying his company, and getting to know him and the world he lived in.

He was smooth, and I couldn't tell if he was being pretentious with me. Those sweet, tantalizing kisses we shared had me wanting to explore him below the surface, and I was too far gone to know, if he masterfully played me like a game of chess. "When will I get to see your house?" he asked.

And there it was. The second reference of coming to visit me. *'God, I hope he is for real.'*

"My house? It's nothing like this. It's cozy, and clean and decorated to my taste, but it's nothing compared to yours. Would you really come to the States to see me?" I leaned back to look him straight in the eyes.

"I'm already planning it in my head."

"You're serious, aren't you?"

"I say what I mean, and I mean what I say. I told you at dinner, I felt a connection with you the moment I saw you. I couldn't take my eyes off of you. Watching you move, was the only reason I let the song you were dancing to, play all the way through. I didn't want you to stop dancing, or for it to be the last time I saw you. No one has ever had that effect on me before. Ever."

"I haven't felt close to anyone for a few years now," I confessed.

"What about right now?"

"Right now, I'm feeling like a teenager. Do you remember the tingling feeling you'd get when your crush would walk by you in the hallway, or look your way?"

"I do. My crush is standing before me, and I'm feeling a tingling sensation looking at her."

"You've been feeling a sensation of some sort for most of the night." I teased him.

"I've traveled many places Nadia. I've seen many world beauties, but none have measured up to you."

"What if it's just lust?"

"I'm definitely lusting you, but I'm also falling in love with you.

I'm a firm believer when you know you know," he said, towering over me.

I failed searching for the truth in his eyes. I stared in them and became blinded by a combination of lust, desire, and naivety. I clung to every word he uttered, believing his words were honest and pure.

"Will you let me love you?" he said, now molding my chin with his fingers, and nibbling my lips.

"Love me or fuck me?" I sighed, desperately wanting his kisses to continue, and they did up and down my neck.

He slipped his fingers between my breasts, slowly unzipping my suit. "Both."

And there was the smoothness again. *'This is too soon for this to be love. Right? It would be insane to let this man fuck me after three days. Right?'*

We knew a little about each other— but I still couldn't resist the physical desire exploding inside of me. I wanted him. Bad. Badly. Properly. Now. Nervously, I shuttered as he removed the straps from my shoulders, still seducing me with his gaze. His hands began to stroke the top lining of my bra, and my senses heightened from his gentle touch— almost giving me the healing of reiki, but not yet quite there.

I took his hand and placed it over my racing heart, so he could feel his effect on me. He grinned, then delicately whispered in my ear, "May I touch you?" in the deepest, most virile tone.

I became heavily lubricated— there was no need for foreplay. I melted into his grasp as I felt the hook of my bra become unfastened. He stood back, and waited for it to fall onto the floor giving me a once over, then smirked on the side of his mouth.

He had me on display, studying every inch of my topless body. "I'm going to remove those now." He pointed to my tangas.

"Okay." I sighed, as he stepped back towards me, fell to his knees, and slid his fingers between my hips, pulling my panties to my feet.

As before, he examined me, but this time I was fully naked, and could feel his hungry breath upon my navel. I trembled as he read me, giving him my power, and closed my eyes awaiting his next move.

One ankle lifted, then the other, as I quivered from the anticipation of what was to come. Suddenly, I felt the presence of his fingers upon me. They were warm, feeling the curves of my buttocks and exterior of my walls.

Quickly, he jerked his hands and pulled me closer to his face, where he landed the softest kiss on my lips down below. My eyes opened, and I looked down to see the bottom half of his face, missing in between my legs. "Aye Papi," I muttered.

Not only was this man causing my pussy to pulsate, he now had me speaking in random Spanish.

I ran my fingers across his head while he held me in position, then balanced me on one leg, placing the other across his shoulder, never skipping a beat on his tongue service.

I occasionally enjoyed a good licking down below, but it was never an act I required. Thanks to Mr. Sharper, my position was rapidly changing about foreplay as I, for the first time, quavered and released from oral stimulation.

This new lover of mine, was undeniably experienced in tongue play, and had to have sensed I was about to come. As soon as my body began to trill, he stuck his finger on my clitoris, and applied pressure, while generously open mouthed kissed me from my navel to my breasts.

He lingered there for at least a minute, sucking on my nipples until he finally released his finger from my trigger spot. "So, you speak Spanish?" he asked, rising to stand on his feet, then wiped his mouth with his shirt.

Not an inch of fat was on his abs. The black and brown stubble on his chest begged me to kiss them. I did so softly before answering with what little voice I could find.

"Not really. I don't know where that came from."

He flashed his whites at me. "I think you're ready for me."

I nodded yes as he steered me towards the wall where he lifted my thighs with his wrists, and placed his wood against my crevice. I heard plastic crumbling, and smelled the latex as he drew back, and rolled the condom down until it smacked. '*Thank goodness we didn't have to have that talk,*' I thought to myself as I sighed at the pressure, neglecting to look at his package.

I'd never seen an ivory cock in person before, but I was about to feel one. My shoulders tensed and my back locked at his first attempt to enter. "Breathe," he commanded. I didn't realize I was holding my breath, but Mash was paying close attention to me, and could feel me tense up upon his entry. I obeyed and exhaled. "There you go. You can take it. Good girl." He sultrily coached me as I gripped him inside my walls. "Hold on to me." He warned before feeding me to the wall, leaving my imprint in the indigo cracks.

Back and forth, up and down, fast then slow, he stroked without any struggle to lift my body midair. He moaned and complimented how good I felt to him, as I held on for dear life, just as he instructed.

Tightly gripping my arms around his neck and atop his shoulders, I was panting with delight and moaning in his ear. "Maximus, Maximus."

The sound of my voice made him thrust deeper and deeper. I was in mind-blowing ecstasy and taking the full beating, pinned between him and the wall with no way out. Mash was heavily endowed and possibly ruining me, but I was loving it. No one could top this performance and he knew it. He was owning me. Staking his claim. Planting his flag in my life box.

My shyness faded the more I pulsated in his clutch, and I pulled his head back so I could finally make eye contact with him. He liked I was finally engaging, and not letting him be the only aggressor, grunting slightly louder, showing me his sexy grin, and kissing me fervidly, but slower than the motion he was grinding.

His attentiveness to hit every corner made me spasm, and our eyes connected as I arrived at orgasm number two.

As I rained on him, he switched his movement to subtle, long strokes. Applying the pressure I needed to get it all out. "You okay?" He removed himself.

"I am more than okay." I whined. "Did you?"

"I held it back. I'm not done with you yet." He delivered a swift kiss to my lips, then took me by the hand.

He led me over to the pool table in the dining room. I could barely lift my feet to follow him, but somehow managed to in my weak state. Without any more chatter, he turned my back to him and positioned me up against the table, placing one of my feet in the ball socket while the other remained on the floor.

He kissed the back of my neck with an open mouth, then lower, and lower, surprising me with a sudden insertion to my warmth.

I screeched and grabbed onto the green velvet, accepting his entrance while listening to him enjoy me. "Nadia, you feel so damn good." He groaned.

Mash was relishing in my body, my juice, my lines— and I was pleased to please him, enduring all he had to give. The pain and the pleasure were a lot to handle, but the sensation of his hands massaging my back, and the tugging of my hips, enthralled me with levels of pleasure I never imagined.

From this angle, he waxed my ass like he was the karate kid, until he segmentally arched my back from pulling my hair, lifting my head off of the green velvet and let loose.

It felt like thunder, though thunder can only be heard. His exhalation was boisterous, assuring me his reveling inside my love, would classify tonight as one he would never forget.

I lied motionless with him still inside of me, waiting for release. My shoulders slumped from pure relaxation, and a good sleep working its way in. Maximus pardoned my body, and I turned around to look at him, and to look at it.

I was mesmerized. It was tawny and wider than I had ever witnessed, longer than average, and absolutely perfect. I looked up at his face, then back at it once more, unable to look away.

"You made quite a mess."

"I had some help."

He stepped away into the kitchen and discarded the rubber. He returned with two bottles of water, as I stood not knowing what to do with myself. He sat me on the edge of the table, positioned between my legs.

Caressing my back as I sipped, I wilted in his arms. "Come on, let's take a shower and go to bed." He carried me to the master bedroom, and sat me in the middle of the black marbled double vanity.

Once the steam rose from the running water, I cleansed his scent off of me, while he gathered my clothing scattered all over the house. When I was done he wrapped me in a towel, and escorted me to his bed where he had a t-shirt laid out for me. He pulled the sheets back and I climbed in, waiting for him to join me, sleepy and unable to get comfortable in the unfamiliar setting.

When he was finally next to me, he sat up fumbling through his phone. Mine buzzed nonstop in my bag, and for some reason I asked permission to answer.

We looked at each other, both confused by the question. I answered Khai on Facetime, ready for my lashing.

"It's good to know you are okay," she said.

"I know I forgot to ping you." I stretched my bottom lip then smiled.

"Why the hell are you smiling so big? And are you lying down? And where is your make-up?" She grilled me.

"I only answered the phone so you could see I am okay. I'll talk to you later."

"And you are glowing! Where is Mr. Maximus?!"

"He's right here."

"Hi Khai," Mash said in the background.

"You are alright with me Maximus!" Khai cackled.

"Good night." I urged.

"I guess this means you aren't going with us to Paris in the morning?"

"No, I'll have to miss Paris. Bring me a chocolate croissant please."

"I most definitely will. Talk with you tomorrow."

"Good night Khai." Mash added.

"Good night fornicators." Khai laughed.

We laughed at being called fornicators for a good minute. "Are you okay with missing Paris to hang out with me?" He kissed the back of my hand.

"Yeah it's cool. I really wanted to go to Ibiza anyway."

"Ibiza? Why?"

"I'm fascinated with the big mythical rock Es Vedra."

"I've had a few shows out there and never paid any attention to it. I've definitely heard about it, but my visits were mostly work related."

"People say they can feel an energy from it. I was just curious to see it, and feel it for myself."

"Well I'll make tomorrow worth your while since I'm interrupting your plans." He squeezed my hand.

"You're a good interruption. I have no complaints."

He leaned over and told me to check my phone. A copy of his schedule for the week, highlighting the days and time he would be free during my visit, sat in my inbox.

He then invited me to join him in Paris for a show on Friday. I reminded him I had obligations, and would have to miss his show because of the rehearsal dinner.

"I keep forgetting you are here for a wedding. Sooooo, I guess I'll see you at, or after the wedding? If I'm invited?"

"You can be my plus one, and you better not stand me up." I gave him a stern eye.

"Ha! She's bossing me now."

"What I meant to say was, I'd love for you to be my plus one."

"I thought you'd never ask."

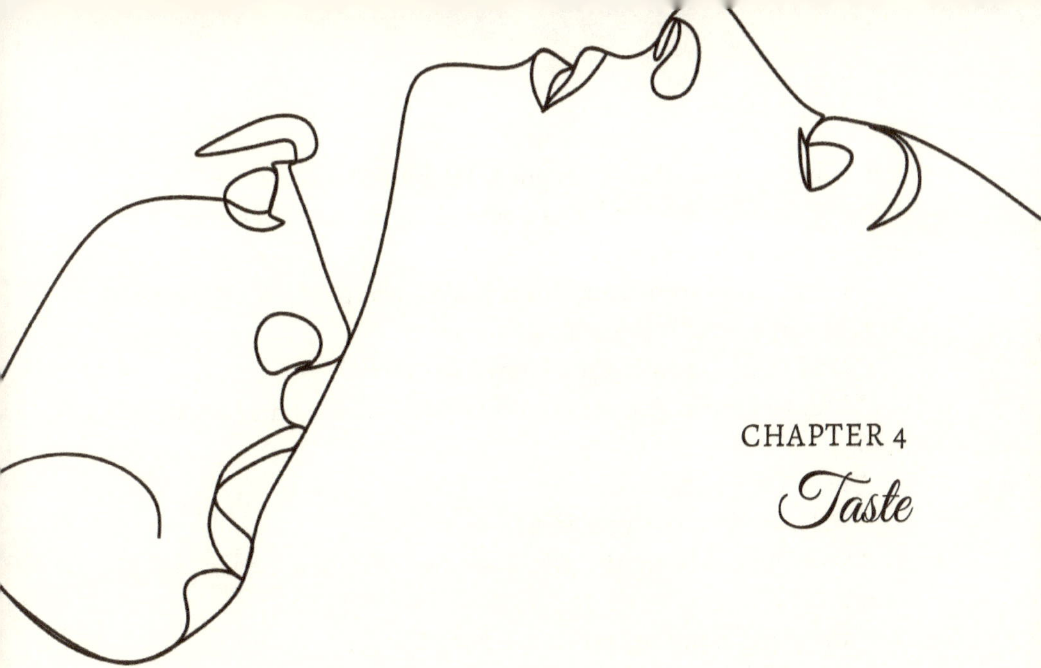

CHAPTER 4

Taste

The clock read 4 a.m. and I was wide awake. Under normal circumstances, I would be fast asleep at this hour. Alone or wishing I was alone. My thoughts were running rampant, and my body was growing impatient for those thoughts to come to fruition.

Lying still on my back in the middle of the bed, I was trapped under one arm and afraid to move. My eyes wandered from left to right, searching for clues and details he hadn't shared, or may have wanted to keep hidden.

His room was neat and well organized. Everything was in place from what I could see. The pillows on the lounge correctly tucked down the middle.

The marble abstract piece, properly placed in the center of the nightstand next to a book and a lamp. And all dust free. I could only assume he hired a maid service for the upkeep, or he had a girlfriend he neglected to mention. *'Don't go down that road,'* I thought, but it was too late. The can of worms had been opened, and I wasn't going to be able to get it out of my head, unless I went back to sleep.

I closed my eyes and listened to Mash sleeping peacefully next to me. Instead of joining him, my mind continued to race— reminiscing how good I felt up against the wall in the kitchen, to imagining him with other women, then I coughed. He twisted a few times, finally releasing me from his hold, and I turned on my side away from him and pretended to be asleep.

He slid closer to me, and from behind whispered in my ear in a deep, groggy voice. "Is something wrong?"

"No," I lied. "How did you know I was awake?"

"I felt you move. Are you comfortable?" He kissed the back of my head.

"Yeah, I'm good."

"Tell me. What's on your mind?"

"Everything. Mainly the past three days, and how I ended up in your bed."

"You being in my bed isn't a bad thing I hope?"

"It certainly doesn't feel like a bad thing."

I was back in his embrace. His arm wrapped around my waist, and he stretched the t-shirt he gave me, to kiss the back of my shoulder.

"Then what's wrong?" he asked.

"There lies the problem. Nothing is wrong. I'm over here already thinking about Sunday— when I have to get on the plane to go home."

"Kotch. Don't think about Sunday."

"What does kotch mean?" I snickered.

"Relax."

"I'd like to, but something else is bothering me. I was also wondering who is going to be in this spot when I leave. Please, don't judge me for being jealous, when I have no right to be. I just got a little curious as to why you are single. I mean come on, there has to be someone keeping you company."

"If you are asking if I have a girlfriend, the answer is no. I have no reason to lie to you. I have a few friends I can call if I don't want to be alone, but nothing serious. And none of them have been in this bed."

"No offense, but I'm calling bullshit."

"I told you, I feel something for you I haven't with anyone else. I have other bedrooms, and yes, I have entertained in them, but never in here. This is my personal space. Why are we talking about this again?" He huffed.

"Because this is what I do. I overthink things, open my mouth, and everything goes to shit."

"I think you feel what I feel and you're scared. Admit it."

"I am a little scared."

"I have no intentions of hurting you. Do you believe me?"

I hesitated.

"Say you believe me." He pushed.

"I believe you."

"Now say you trust me."

"Nope."

He pressed firmly against my back, cocked and loaded, ready to strike. I had been lying awake, waiting for a second round. "Say it," he demanded, searching for my tickle spot.

"I said I believe you have no intentions of hurting me."

"Now say you trust me."

"Un uh." I screeched with laughter, until he silenced my giggles by sucking on my neck, mixed with tongue traces and gentle bites grazing my skin. "I trust you," I gasped.

He took a pause and smiled at me. Kissing me from my cheek, to below my chin, and then my shoulders he softly whispered, "You don't have to worry about anyone else."

I didn't believe him, though he was convincing, smiling at me in between kisses. His rod grew larger against my thighs, causing my papaya to *kegel*. Ready to wrinkle the sheets, my legs opened wide for him, ready for the taking, and grinded upwards hoping he would slide in.

Our eyes locked as he grabbed my bum, squeezing it like a stress ball. I removed the t-shirt he gave me, then begged him to put it inside. He touched me and grinned at the drip greeting him, then pressed his weaponry against my wetness.

"I want to feel the real you. May I?" he asked.

"Are you clean?" I sassed.

"Yes. I always use condoms, but I want to feel you skin on skin. You said you trust me."

"Don't make me regret this." I poked his chest.

"I promise I won't."

"Ah!" I sighed from the penetration.

"Breathe my love," he said, watching me welcome him. I exhaled as he held me tight around my waist, accelerating forward and fully inside, groaning at the sensation of pure flesh.

With my arms cuddled beneath him, the slow grind of push and pull ignited an awakening in me I couldn't fight. Him grunting against my chest, somehow made me feel even closer to him.

Tighter and tighter, I cradled his head against me, rocking back and forth in unison. He came up for air and I grazed my teeth against his shoulder, catching what he threw at me. His head lifted and our lips met for soft pecks, and quick compliments to one another.

"I love how I feel inside you," he whispered.

"I love how you feel inside me," I moaned.

"You're driving me insane woman."

He dove deeper and applied his lips to my forehead, swept my hair off of my face, then tugged it from the nape. Watching me turn into putty as he pummeled and massaged my head simultaneously, I drizzled on him, causing him to shriek. "Messy girl," he taunted, then enhanced his strokes, intensifying my orgasm.

I screamed out, "Do whatever you want to me!"

And he did, taking it up a notch to next level shit, digging into me like crates. Wearing out his welcome with one of the toys he fancied in my box, he skillfully lifted my right leg, and flipped me over while still inside. I yelled, "Oh shit," as he went directly back into thrashing me from behind.

Lying flat on my stomach, I could feel every inch of him against the back of my canal. I had given him total control, and he proved I was now in his world. And I liked it here. I loved it here.

I clenched onto the pillows as he held me down by my shoulders, and worked me over, moving in circles, then pausing, then circles again. "Baby I'm close!" he shouted, "You are too much for me from the back!" And he climaxed animalistic this time, howling in delight, and panting as if he just completed a mile run.

Falling beside me he panted, smacking my ass, unable to speak. Seconds later he mumbled, "I have to meet this couple and thank them for bringing you to me."

I nestled close to him and slipped my feet beneath his, and finally lost the battle to a deep sleep.

~

Unaware of the hour, I felt a presence above me and opened my eyes. Mash was fully dressed standing over me, telling me to sleep in while he ran an errand. "Leave clean sheets," I muttered before drifting back into the darkness.

He hadn't returned by the time I fully woke. I rose from the soiled sheets, looked around his drawers to appease my curiosity, then jumped in the shower a second time.

I returned to the bed wrapped in a towel, changed the linens, and took advantage of thumbing through the photo albums, he left at the foot of the bed for my amusement.

The first book painted a colorful story of his teenage years. Pictures of him in a private school uniform, team sports, posing with album covers, and shadowing deejays, completed the first half section. The final portion displayed more moments of him carrying records, and what I assumed were girlfriends.

The next book was filled with old pictures of what had to be his family. Black and white portraits of beautiful people, which explained his striking looks. It dawned on me, we hadn't discussed our family history of where our ancestors hailed from. I made a mental note to bring it up in our conversation, if we experienced a dry moment.

Flipping through the second book led me to the conclusion he had an interesting story to tell. It became obvious he was more than a Brit, and I couldn't wait to hear what he revealed.

While reaching for the third book, I realized I was completely air dried. I dressed in the leggings and tee hidden away in my bag, then plopped back down on the bed to finish snooping.

This book was the most questionable, and impressive by far. A plethora of photographs with actors, athletes, singers, and models I recognized from runway shows and commercials.

Turning the pages, I was hit with multiple, beautiful women smiling back at me, which played my insecurities like a fiddle. I began to imagine some of them lying on the bed staring at me, smirking at my existence, teasing I didn't belong. I slammed the book shut, envious of the women who made it into his memorabilia. *'Everyone has a past,'* I said to myself, then snapped out of it.

The garage door hurled and roared, and I rushed to the vanity to pull my hair back and fix my face. Mash walked in holding a small white paper bag in one hand, and shopping bags in the other. His face curled as he glanced up and down at my attire, then chuckled as he teased me. "You had plans of spending the night I see."

"I bet you're happy I did." I sassed.

"Fucking ecstatic."

His ego increased tenfold, without any signs of returning back to normal after discovering my secret. "I got you a few things, but it looks like you won't need all of them," he said, placing the shopping bags on a bench at the foot of the bed. He then handed me a pastry box from the small white one. "I'm sorry you missed Paris with your friends."

I opened the box. A freshly baked chocolate croissant with two strawberries, soothed my morning hunger as I pulled the flaky pastry apart. With a mouth full I chortled, "As you can see I was starving. And thank you. This is heavenly."

"Only the best for you."

"Where are my manners? Do you want some?"

"No thanks. I'm enjoying watching you have a go at it."

"Good. Because I really didn't want to share it."

I closed my eyes and bit into the last piece, savoring the flavors, while wishing he had brought two of them home. Licking the chocolate from my fingers, then chasing it with a strawberry, I pranced in my stance and nodded to Mash, motioning you did good.

He turned the shopping bags upside down, covering the bed with new tags, a box of flats, and an array of panties and matching bras. For reference, he took my clothes to a boutique, and brought back a few outfits for me to wear.

"Did you pick these out?" I asked.

"No. A friend did."

"Your friend has taste. So, was this the errand you had to run this morning?"

"Sort of. Get dressed. We're going to be late. I'll wait for you downstairs."

His assertiveness was attractive, but I began to wonder if I had given him too much control. I also wondered why I liked it so much. I was aware I could be naïve, but never had I been submissive, and did whatever I was told. *'Maybe he just wants to show me a good time while I'm here,'* I thought, as I popped the tags on a bohemian print skirt, solid magenta tee, and denim jacket.

I spruced up my make-up, threw on the flats, and off we went. A short twenty-minute ride further into the country, led us into an open-air field. *'Oh, Dear God! Please don't let him think he is about to fly me around in that thing. I'm already impressed! I'm already impressed!'*

Fright was written on my face, when a short elderly man appeared from the rear of a personal Beechcraft plane. "Park over there for me," he shouted, then tipped his hat.

I dragged getting out of the car, regretting I hadn't spoken my mind. As Mash opened my door, the gentleman walked over and shook hands with him, then extended them to me.

"Nice to meet you." He helped me out of the car.

"Nadia." I gave him my hand.

"Nadia, meet Mr. Hunt, a longtime friend of the family."

"And a pilot I hope." My brows raised.

"For thirty years now," Mr. Hunt asserted.

"Suddenly, I'm not so nervous anymore."

Mr. Hunt laughed, then escorted me over to the plane, while Mash gathered bags he had stashed in the trunk. The steps lowered and we boarded, receiving a full tutorial on safety and emergency information, and what if scenarios.

I gripped the edge of my seat at takeoff, counting the minutes until we were settled in the air. Searching for a distraction, I pestered Mash to tell me where we were going, but he remained tight lipped.

He dug into the bags and pulled out a Sudoku book, pencils, a mystery novel he hadn't finished, and a bag of chips— offering me each of the items, refusing to answer my question.

The plane leveled in the sky moments later, and I released the arm rests from my clutch. Mash gave me a cocky once over, then tapped my hand. "We'll be there in a few hours. Sit tight and enjoy the scenery."

I stared at him without blinking for a few seconds, attempting to read his mind. His poker face was stern as he circled words in the book, and so I gave up and did as he suggested. I sat back, pulled my earpiece from my purse, and listened to my calm playlist. *'I bet he's taking me to Paris to meet my friends.'*

An hour into the flight I grew bored and anxious. I leaned over and helped solve a few puzzles, read some of his book, then asked him to give me a list of the songs he produced.

We shared our playlists from our phones, and he complimented my arrangements and selections, "You have open ears. I've never seen a playlist like this before. You went from Kings of Leon to Nina Simone, Coldplay, OutKast, Prince, Edie Brickell, Fiona and Jay-Z in your shuffle file."

"You'll love my Texas rap on there, too," I added.

"Why is it called Texas rap, and not just rap?"

"Because of how it sounds, and how it flows. They call it chopped and screwed. Stick with me kid, you'll learn something new." I clicked my tongue.

I played him a few songs from Houston artists. His reaction was priceless, having never heard a record chopped and screwed before. I looked on as he took it all in, and assumed he was contemplating new ideas from the way his lips mouthed words to himself.

When he removed his headset, I pried into his business. "Do you care to discuss the photo albums?"

He turned his head and scoffed. "I was wondering when you'd bring that up."

"So, private school?"

"Yes. My mother is Italian and my father is full Brit. My dad raised me after they divorced. He came from wealth and believed my mother couldn't make me become a man, plus he had control of the money, so you know how that goes. He wanted me to be the next big thing. Forcing me to try my hand in everything he liked. Soccer, Lacrosse, Tennis, Rugby, Polo, Boxing.

'That explains the body.'

"Did you like any of those sports?" I asked.

"I was into boxing— up until I was knocked out. I continued training, but stopped sparring. Anyway, my interests didn't matter to my father. I was always attracted to music, but he didn't approve. I had to sneak around in clubs, and learn how to work turntables, speakers and mixing boards. When I went off to university, I made a name for myself on campus."

"And look at you now. He must be proud."

"He wasn't around long enough to see me get to this level. He passed away."

Maximus turned his away and stared out of the window. I met eyes with Mr. Hunt watching us in her rearview mirror.

"Sorry to hear that. My dad passed away three years ago. It's an experience you'll never get over."

"Losing someone you love, when the relationship was full of turmoil, is even worse. But you can't change a person, so it is what it is."

"There it is!" Mr. Hunt yelled.

I wobbled to the closest window, prepared to see the Eiffel Tower from the best view possible. During our quiet time, I put two and two together. The croissant was a clue I assumed, so I braced myself for the big reveal. "What the!" I screeched, looking at miles and miles of turquoise water leading the way to the magical rock, Es Vedra in the distance.

"You brought me to see the rock! I'm in Ibiza! The Baleares Islands of Spain! I can't fucking believe it! Excuse my language. Holy shit! I didn't think I was going to see this place!" I exclaimed.

"You were so close, and the way your face lit up talking about it, I figured I owed it to you, since you know. You missed Paris."

"I thought you were taking me to Paris to meet my friends, hence the breakfast croissant, but this is so much better! I can't believe you did this for me."

A black line dripped from the corner of my eye. I fought to hold my tears, but one resisted flowing back into my glands and exposed itself.

"Come here," Mash said, reaching for me.

I returned to my seat.

"Buckle up sweetheart, we are about to land," said Mr. Hunt.

Carried away with emotion, I became putty sitting next to Mash. We kissed, necked, caressed and rubbed, becoming aroused at an inopportune time.

The decline disturbed our moment. "I can never repay you." The glee I felt inside spread across my face.

"Your excitement was repayment enough," he said.

My feet touched the soil of Spain. My skin felt the breath of the calm water surrounding Es Vedra. My eyes magnified a landscape of beauty. My nose inhaled the scent of the crisp trees spritzed in the air, and without making it to the beach, I was already in love with the place.

Four hours were spared to tour, and explore the historical city. For starters, we shopped at the many outposts, where I found an array of organic oils and beauty products. Some of the brands were familiar, and the others I came to know.

After buying more than enough goodies, we taxied to the white sandy beach of Cala d'Hort, and dined at Restaurante Es Boldado. The mysterious rock Es Vedra sat beautifully in the view, making me anxious to take a stroll near the water before high tide.

As the sand on the beach invaded my sandals, I soaked in the energy of the magnetic rock I had been dreaming to visit. Mash stood at my side, watching me take it all in.

Meditating with my eyes closed. Listening to the waves crash and burn. Its presence was majestic and commanding, and everything I hoped it would be. Calming yet thought provoking of its existence, mystifying and legendary, wondrous and extraordinary.

We wandered until we reached the famous tower, Torre des Savinar. It was rumored to be the best place to witness the sunset, and from what we experienced I could concur. The skyline melded from sapphire to bloodshot, as the sun slowly declined into the water, capti-vating us both.

A peacefulness flowed within me, as Mash was draped his arms around me from behind, gripping my waist, stealing kisses on my neck. The burning ball in the navy sky began its journey to the other side of the world, and a familiar feeling cloaked my chest. I was over-come with emotion, overwhelmed from the perfect past couple of days, and overjoyed to be in the company of a man who made me feel wanted. "Do you feel that?" I asked.

"I do." He pecked my cheek.

"I can't explain it. It's so beautiful, and so, I, I..."

"Sometimes there are no words."

But there were words. I just couldn't say it. I wanted to, but I was being cautious, and mildly childish not wanting to be the first to say I love you— as if it mattered.

'Why would it matter who said it first? If it's real, it's real.'

Maximus chose action over words and planted his saccharine lips on mine as a breeze of cool wind trapped us, sending chills over my body and up my skirt.

"It's time to go home," he said.

I smiled into his glimmering brown eyes. "I like the way that sounds."

"What do you like about it?" He grinned.

"The home part," I said, kissing him one last time under the heav-enly sky.

'Ugh why couldn't I say it?'

Mr. Hunt delivered us safely to the London countryside. The hours crept by slowly, making my urge to physically thank Mash unbearable. Once we landed, I waited for him in the car as he settled business with his longtime friend, yearning to show my gratitude. Watching his lips move as he talked, I grew profoundly aroused, slipping my panties off, and placing them in my jacket pocket before he made it to the car.

As he drove us back to his place, I brushed my hand in his hair, and stared at him handling the curves of the road. When the path straightened, I took my panties out of my pocket, and dropped them in his lap.

"When did you...?" he asked.

"Pull over," I said, unzipping his pants.

The car jerked to the side of a dirt path, near bushes leading to the woods. His wood stood at attention, as I slid his trousers down a few inches, and marveled at it, rubbing it in the dim moonlight escaping through the clouds. It was the color of roasted red pepper hummus, longer than average, and wide like a mushroom at the top.

'No wonder I'm swooning.'

In excitement, he neglected to put the gear in park, and the car rolled a few feet. After shifting it correctly, he turned off the engine, then I grabbed him by the face and kissed him, short but forcefully.

Pulling away I purred. "Un uh. Allow me," I offered, while shoving him back against the seat before I dove.

He huffed at the touch of my jaws, wet and slippery, cupping him whole inside of my mouth. He moaned and called out, "Nadia," as I teased him at the tip with my tongue, then held him at the roof of my mouth, swirling my tongue in circles.

His moans deepened from the oral massage as I sped up the pace, up and down nonstop until he jolted. He locked onto my hair as I lowered completely down around him, controlling my reflex, then slowly releasing him from my clutch.

With tamed strokes, I rubbed him while taking a quick breather, then returned for one more taste while both hands pleasured him, as if I was grinding pepper. "I love you," he whispered indolently. I amplified my kisses for a few seconds more, then reduced to slow soft licks, triggering his body to slump over in elation.

I rose to face him, lifted my skirt, and sprung on top of him, screaming from painful delight. "Ih-Ih." I sighed, gripping onto the headrest.

He thrusted his dick upward, "You look so fucking beautiful tonight," he said, holding me in place just below my back.

I regained my composure and matched his rhythm, slow deep strokes kneading my walls side to side. He reached for my face and I cradled his hand against my shoulder, while he ran his other hand down my back.

Escaping my hold, he placed both hands behind my shoulders and we locked eyes as he gripped them tightly. He stared at me with pure passion in his eyes and I grew weak. "I love you, too."

"Say it again," he begged.

"I love you."

"I loved you first."

His deep voice in its sultry state affected me uncontrollably. Harder and faster my hips grinded, while his hands spread my cheeks east and west. Sweat soaked between us, and our heat fogged the windows on the driver side of the car. "Ah!" Mash bellowed, holding me in place as I rested my head on his shoulder, savoring the moment.

Disheveled and gratified, I returned to my seat and the engine revved. Mash exhaled deeply. "Let's try this again. I need a smoke," he confessed, then drove us to the house.

We didn't speak for the twenty-minute ride, and I grew worried my forwardness was too much, too soon. I attempted to end the silent streak. "I'm going to hop in the shower."

"You know where the towels are," he said, and headed outside.

I watched him hit a joint sitting pensively by the pool, then left him there as I couldn't watch anymore.

I had showered, put on another one of his t-shirts, looked at my friend's pictures online, and nearly nodded off waiting for him to come to bed. An hour later he showered, and sat up scrolling through his phone, far away on his side.

As I waited for him to speak, I drove myself insane with worry. *'Say anything. Kill this silence please. What did I do to mess this up? He said he loved **me** for Christ's sake. Today was too perfect to end like this.'*

The past taught me not to react and be patient, so I did. I was confused and wanted to cry, but I refrained out of pride. My back remained facing him, but I could feel his eyes upon me.

"Nadia."

"Yes."

"About today..."

"It's okay. You don't have to..."

"I don't know what I'm going to do when you leave on Sunday," he said.

Shocked to hear him say such words, I turned around to face him, greeted by his solemn, handsome face. "What?"

"I've been thinking. Sunday is fast approaching and I don't want you to leave."

"You do realize you haven't said a word to me in over an hour, and I have been over here trying to figure out what I did to ruin this perfect day we shared."

"I didn't mean to make you feel uncomfortable. It wasn't my intent. I was just trying to come up with ways this could work for us."

"And."

"I just told you. I don't want you to leave. Today was one of the best days I've had in a long, long time."

"Me, too. How about we do as you said. Let's not think about Sunday." I slid next to him.

A simple slip of the tongue and expression of rage over an hour of silence could have ruined everything. His confession stunned me, more than his profession of love. He said it. I said it. But did we mean it? We were somewhere on the borderline of love and lust, and having been addicted to someone physically before, raised the question of did I truly know how I was feeling.

I fell fast, but I fell nonetheless. The past seventy-two hours felt surreal. Love was here, looking me in the face, showing me what it was like to have it in my grasp, and I didn't know what to do with it.

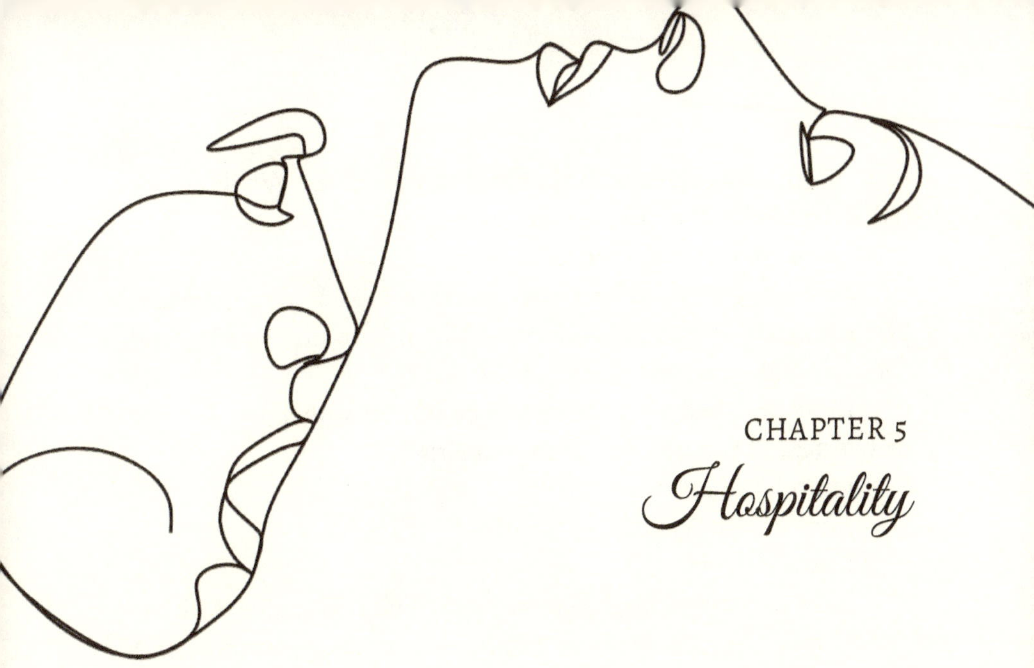

CHAPTER 5

Hospitality

Travel began to wear on my body, and enigmatic pleasure added to my fatigue. Knowing he was concerned about a future with me eased my mind, and allowed me to relax in his home, and in his care.

I slept past midday, and probably would have slept longer if I had placed my phone on silent. Multiple phone calls back to back disturbed my rest. I had found a comfortable spot in the middle of the bed, and once you lose such a place there's no getting it back. I rolled over and checked my log, curious about the urgency of calls ringing nonstop. All of them belonging to Taylor.

I lied there with the phone in my hand, preparing myself for a conversation, I knew was going to be one-sided. I took a deep breath and returned her call, regretting it the moment I pressed connect.

"Hello Stranger," she answered.

I could hear rustling in the background, confirming she wasn't alone, and had placed me speaker. I took another deep breath, preparing myself for one of her performances. "Stranger?" I frowned.

"I haven't seen you since Saturday. We were supposed to be enjoying this trip together, and you have run off with some random white boy with your nose wide open. What's going on with you?"

"Whoa," I said, not happy with her word choice or tone. "Let's back this train up. I'm not with a boy, I'm with a man. You didn't see me before I left on Sunday, because we were all taking it easy."

"Nadia, you missed going to Paris."

"So what? I told you I preferred going to Ibiza over Paris remember? And going to Paris was optional. Why are you making a big deal about this? Do you need me for something?"

"I just can't believe you chose to be laid up with a guy you just met, instead of going to Paris with your girls."

"I wasn't laid up yesterday."

"Then do tell. What did you do?"

"I went to Spain."

Taylor scoffed and laughed in her wicked way, mumbling with the phone muffled by her hand. A commotion of noise ensued when I heard her faintly say in the background, "This bitch just said she went to Spain yesterday."

The voices of Khai, Shannon, and Isla became clear when Khai took over the conversation. "Nadia, everything is cool. What Taylor is failing to communicate, is she feels you have forgotten why we are here. But don't worry, I think it's just a bridal moment."

Taylor shouted from a distance, "I'm not having a bridal moment! She is supposed to be here!"

"Excuse me ladies," Mash interjected. "Taylor, I told Nadia I wanted to meet the bride and groom, so would you and your mate have dinner with us tonight at my house?"

"You should go," Khai whispered.

The line grew silent. I rolled my eyes at Mash, waiting for Taylor's theatrical performance.

"Sir, thank you for the very nice offer. Mash, is it?" she asked, knowing the answer to her question.

"Just say yes already. You know you want to." I interposed.

She huffed. "Well I guess my answer is yes then."

"I'll text you the address. See you at seven." The words swiftly left my mouth before I ended the call.

~

A pool table sat where a dinner table belonged. A highly critical and emotional guest was coming over, and dinner was to be served by my hands. With limited hours to prepare, the market run extended to multiple store runs, in search of foldout tables and chairs, a tablecloth, candles, vases, kitchenware and fresh flowers.

A pear and apple salad with a honey-lime vinaigrette chilled in the fridge, while my famous diced tomato short ribs, creamed potatoes, and sautéed spinach travelled through the house. For an added bonus, I baked Levi's favorite yellow cake topped with chocolate almond icing for dessert, and set it next to the floral centerpiece I arranged.

Taylor and Levi arrived on schedule. Mash welcomed them inside, and Taylor's eyes could not stop sizing him up. She became fixated with his hand around my waist, and hardly parted her lips, while Levi participated alone in the conversation. "Why are we still standing here?" I asked. "Let's get some drinks in those hands."

As we walked to the living room, Mash thanked them for bringing me to London. Levi was his normal modest self, cool and collected, and dismissed the notion they had anything to do with fate.

Taylor, on the other hand, replied, "You're welcome." I knew then we were in for a long night.

The men set off to smoke cigars in Mash's studio, while Taylor and I took a quick view of his house. Subtle sounds murmured behind me as she looked around each room, never offering a compliment.

When we made it to the kitchen, she stared at me as I carefully proportioned the dinner plates, smirking and shaking her head. "You seem right at home. Playing Suzy Homemaker," she chided.

"I made the apple and pear salad you like." I deflected.

"He seems to really like you." She continued.

"Taylor. I've never fell for someone this fast before."

"Fell? As in?"

"You know." I puckered my lips.

"You can't be serious." Taylor laughed. "You two are so— different."

"Have you seen how fine he is?"

"He's okay, but still. He's... and you're..."

"Yeah we are. And it doesn't matter. We click. I don't care about color. Only him as a person, and how he makes me feel. And he makes me feel damn good. I'm in love."

"Girl stop playing." She fanned me off.

"Judge me. Tease me. Do or say whatever you want. I've been bitten and I'm smitten."

"Okay calm down Foxy Brown. It's been what four days?" She rolled her eyes.

"I know it sounds crazy, but it's true."

"Do you love him like you loved Dylan?"

"Dylan who?"

Taylor stood with her mouth slightly parted, and a look of disbelief on her face. Mash and Levi's voices grew closer entering the temporary dining room, snapping Taylor out of her zone.

She surprised me and carried the salad to the table, and I trailed her with the dinner plates, enjoying the sounds of the men getting on so well.

I considered Levi one of my male best friends. He was always a delight, a great role model for the youth, patient, and respectable. Being the great conversationalist he is, he kept the table talk interesting with discussions of business, sports, books, politics of the west, and entertainment knowing it was Mash's field.

"If you don't mind me asking, how much does all of that equipment run you?" Levi asked.

"Quite a pretty penny. It's taken me years to get everything I needed for a fully functioning lab, but it was worth it. Studio time costs an arm and a leg. Now I can work from home and save my coins."

"You seem to be doing well for yourself— for a deejay," Taylor added.

"Babe, that's inappropriate." Levi scolded her.

"It's okay. I do more than deejay at clubs and spin records. I do sound engineering, sound mixing, radio guest spots, and produce music. My next project is producing the score for a movie coming out this winter."

"By score you mean add the music to the scenes, right?" Levi asked.

"Yes. It will be a major accomplishment for me."

"Have we heard any of the music you produced in the U.S?" Taylor asked.

"Probably not on the radio, but satellite radio spins them. Techno is bigger over here than it is in the States."

"It amazes me how different things are here. I can't get past the driving on the wrong side of the road," I said.

Levi, Mash and I laughed at my comment, while Taylor stewed at how great we were getting along.

Mash shared a look with Levi. "You'll get used to it."

Levi chuckled. "Nadia, you did good with this one."

I nodded and rubbed the back of his neck, avoiding eye contact with the opposition across the table. Taylor rejoined the conversation, and changed the subject to her wedding.

Mash didn't know Taylor well enough to know she was baiting him. Unaware of her trap, he thought it would be good to say something about the wedding to appease her. "Is it okay if I come to the wedding as Nadia's plus one?" he asked.

"Weddings are for people you are close with. You know family and friends, and we don't know you like that." She bitched.

"Don't listen to her man, of course you are welcome. Baby, the man has invited us into his home. Don't be rude." Levi reached for her hand.

"That's the second time you've chastised me tonight."

Levi and I put our forks down knowing where the night was headed. We had years of experience with Taylor's flip side. Her ugly head had arrived, looking for a fight, and wouldn't stop until she got one.

"Am I the only person here who realizes how crazy you two are being? Nadia, can you honestly say this isn't moving too fast?"

"I told you it was moving fast, and I'm on board. I'm happy."

"And you?" Taylor pointed her fork towards Mash. "Is this your first interracial relationship, Mash? What is your real name?"

"Wow. And no, it's not. My legal name is Maximus Sharper. Get is Ma, Sh, Mash for short."

She scoffed. "You live half a day apart— by plane at that, how serious can you be with my friend?"

I tapped Mash on the leg, and shook my head *no* to not answer her. Levi and I shared a look, then I faced Taylor. "Don't speak to him like that. He invited you here, and you're being beyond rude. What's up with you?"

Taylor was blown away I confronted her behavior. She huffed. "This is all insane to me. You two are acting like you're so in love. You know nothing about each other."

"I know enough, and I do love her," said Mash.

I lifted my head and shared a smile with him. He leaned over and kissed me gently, then looked to Taylor.

"And we don't owe anyone an explanation of what is happening between us."

She looked to Levi to speak on her behalf. "I'm not chastising you Tay, but baby he's right."

Taylor threw her hands up. "Apparently, it's 3 to 1, so I'll go back to minding my business. I've said what needed to be said."

I took a deep breath. "Let's agree to disagree here. Everything is cool. When you bit my head off earlier, I assumed you were feeling like I was stealing your thunder. I promise you that is not my intent. I'm here for you. We just want to spend as much time together as we can before I leave."

"Baby, apologize to them," said Levi.

"No need. I know she's stressed out about the wedding. We're cool." I patted her hand across the table.

"Well I'm glad we got that cleared up, because I think I found my first bromance," said Levi, pounding fists with Mash. "Now can we cut this cake?"

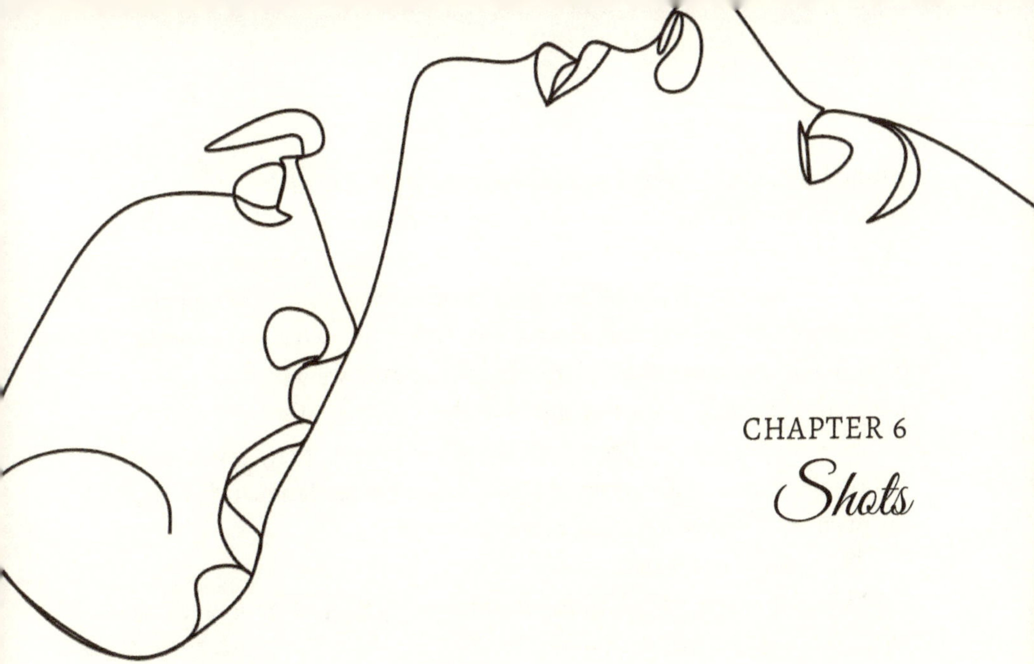

CHAPTER 6

Shots

Naked I lie in his arms, my eyes closed enjoying his caress against my back. My hands pressed against his firm chest, my head next to his. "Morning," he said.

My eyes greet him and I smile. "Five more minutes. Please." I begged.

"Then five more minutes it is."

The morning was opposite of the night prior. With friends we laughed, danced and drank ourselves into slumber, but woke to the realization our secluded days had come to an end. This day was inescapable. He walked me inside and we said our goodbyes at the elevator. I did a quick change into my purple Team Bride t-shirt, and I was back on duty, fulfilling Taylor's every wish and command.

London weather was fickle. Sunny with wicked winds, making it chilly and warm depending on the hour. The overcast and breezes didn't serve well for some of the planned family activities. During the downtime, we stood around and gossiped, half-assing around when it came time to pick up where we left off. The constant stop and go killed the competition, and purple versus green ended earlier than planned.

With lunch an hour away, improvisations were made as the family selected someone to sing a solo, forced the younger children to entertain, and fought one another for the microphone to speak about the wedding— the ones who weren't asked to be a part of the ceremony.

The caterers arrived and like good worker bees, the wedding party saw that everyone was seated and fed, before ourselves. The bridal party table was then allowed to clock out, and we gathered at our assigned table lastly, a few feet shy from the elderly section.

The memo hadn't been received to everyone, that Taylor was feeling a certain way about my absence, as her cousin Janine pried into my business. "Where have you been?" she asked.

"Around," I answered.

"I haven't seen you. I thought you were jetlagged or something when you didn't come with us to Paris."

"No, I wasn't jetlagged."

"She was in Spain," Isla blurted.

"I didn't know we had the option to choose where we wanted to go," said Janine.

"We didn't," said Isla. "Did you and Taylor work everything out?"

"Yeah. I think she had a good time last night."

"Oh, so there was drama." Janine inquired.

"No, there wasn't any drama, but since everything is cool now, I have to know. What is it like being with a white man?" Shannon asked.

"So, it was you they were all whispering about." Janine told.

"They were whispering about me?"

"It wasn't like that. When we went to Paris, Taylor was upset when she found out why you weren't there is all. They may have overheard a thing or two, but it's nothing to fret about," Khai added.

"Now that that's squared away. Give us the *deets*," said Shannon.

"My lips are sealed. And don't ask me anything about the past couple of days."

"Then tell us about the nights." Shannon joked. "Come on Nadia. You've been gone for like three days. If it was whack, you wouldn't have stayed over there so long. Now quit playing and give me something. You got down with the swirl, now tell your girl." Shannon squeezed my shoulders.

"Why do you think I fucked him?"

"Didn't you? Can you verify if London men are the worst lovers?"

"No comment." I turned up my nose.

"I know you did it. From now on Nadia, I'm calling you GK. Grandma Klump. *"That's the only white man make me moist!"* Shannon quoted in the voice of the famous character.

The entire table burst into laughter. Tears formed in my eyes as I cried laughing at her antics. An uncanny rendition of the scene from *The Nutty Professor* movie.

"Do not call me that!" I begged, wiping my eyes.

"He is a hottie. I know that much?" said Shannon.

"How do you know?"

"I looked him up online. Hell, everyone's met him except me."

"Pull up his picture. I want to see him, too," said Janine.

"Shannon did more than look up his picture," said Khai.

"He is a celebrity. They always put their personal information out there. What people make per movie, net worth etc... You're in good hands." Shannon signaled the ok symbol with her fingers, then showed his picture to Janine.

"Oh yeah. I'd ride up to his house butt naked on a horse covered in honey." Janine joked.

Her comment led to more tears and crying laughter amongst us. A few of us gasped for air. The others searched for napkins to wipe their lids, and the elders at the table nearby all smiled at us. Isla remained indifferent.

"What is your problem?" Shannon asked Isla.

"Why do you think I have a problem?"

"Because that was funny, and you are over there all stoned face."

"It wasn't that funny." Isla frowned.

"Don't worry about her Shannon, her beef is with me. She called dibs on my guy, which is ridiculous."

"Is that why you've been starting shit? I've been peeping how you've been getting in Taylor's ear. Not cool," said Khai.

"Isla, how do you call dibs on a man? Please do tell," Shannon inquired.

Snickers filled the table as all eyes were upon Isla. "If you will excuse me." She removed herself.

Shannon began her line of questioning once more, asking for details of my sexual conquest, and the appearance of my lover's lumber. I refused to share the details, but she wouldn't take no for an answer. She began explaining why her curiosity was getting the best of her.

"I just want to know if white men look like black men down there. You know, like you can be with a light skinned dude, but his thing will be brown, or you can be with a dark-skinned dude, and his thing will be reddish brown, or..."

"We get the picture Shannon," said Khai, giggling with the rest of the table.

"Seriously, what color is it? Inquiring minds want to know."

"I would say hummus," said Janine.

"Hummus? Hummus tastes just like it sounds— Hum-Ass," said Shannon.

The table paused in silence for a moment. A mixture of chuckles from Shannon's pun, and images of Janine's description pictured in our heads. We all looked at each other, guilty and tickled. Several hmm's and huh's were expressed, and collectively we burst into loud cackles, creating a stir and landing the attention of Taylor.

She waltzed over with Isla at her side. "Y'all better not be over here laughing at me."

"Don't worry. We're not." Khai assured her.

"What's so funny?"

"Shannon," we all said.

"I promise I'm behaving," Shannon replied in defense.

The laughter wasn't as boisterous as before, but it continued, and Taylor begged to be in on the joke. Janine took it upon herself to speak up.

"I was being my delightful self, telling your friends a few stories and what not. You came over just in time. Tell us, who could be the vanilla in your sundae?"

"You do realize our grandmother is sitting right there." Taylor pointed.

"Your grandmother might have a story she wants to share." Shannon teased.

"If she doesn't, I do!" shouted the grandmother's sister.

Shannon and Taylor's great-aunt snapped their fingers at one another, then shared a head nod of solidarity.

"She knows what's up," said Shannon. "Now let's see if it runs in the family. Who is on your list?"

"Nick Jonas," Taylor whispered.

"Is he legal?" asked Isla.

"If he isn't he will be when I'm done with him."

"Yeah let's hurry up and get you married," said Khai.

"I'd do Brad Pitt," said Shannon.

"Did you see him in Snatch?" Janine asked.

"Hell yeah. The scene when they burned his mama's van is why he is on my list. Come to think of it. He was smoking in Mr. & Mrs. Smith, too. Since you've already dipped your toes in the clear ocean, would you do it again?" Shannon asked Janine.

"Most definitely. Seth motherfucking Rogen."

"I can see that." Shannon concurred.

"He's like a total package for me. Funny, cute, high as hell, cool, and a head full of curly hair. Hell to the yeah."

"I have always thought Thor looked like he packed a punch," said Khai.

"He was wearing a piece in Vacation. It was not real," said Shannon.

"How do you know?"

"I researched it."

"Well he's still my pick." Khai shoved Shannon.

"And a damn good one." We assented.

"Don't leave out Captain America either," Janine chimed in.

"Yeah, he's very seasoned," said Taylor. "What about you Isla?"

"I support black love. I've never given it much thought." She turned up her lips.

"You told me you would fuck Jon Snow!" Taylor blabbed.

"I told you that in confidence!"

"Like you would ever meet him." Taylor teased.

"Jon Snow and Daario Naharis." I cosigned.

"Which Daario?" Isla asked.

"The first one."

"Yes *Lawd*. That Daenerys is a lucky bitch."

"Who the hell are y'all talking about?" Shannon asked.

"It's a Game of Thrones thing." Our voices synchronized.

"Why are we talking about this again?" Taylor asked.

"You know why." Isla snarled.

Levi pulled Taylor away for what looked to be a serious chat. Hand gestures, pouting, and pleading appeared to be the theme of their conversation. She returned to the table, gave me a dirty look, then accused Mash of being a troublemaker. "Your little friend has invited Levi, and his groomsmen on a party bus with strippers."

"What's wrong with a night out of fun and bar crawling?" I asked.

"Call him and tell him to rescind his offer," she demanded.

Under severe scrutiny, I dialed him. *'Don't answer,'* I sang to myself. Heavy music blasted through the line. No greeting, just vibrating bass and chatter in the background.

"Sorry about that love. I wasn't at a stopping point. Is everything okay?" he asked.

I sighed. "I don't think so. Taylor would like to have a word with you."

Before I finished my thought, Taylor swiped my phone from my hands demanding answers.

"How many people can this bus hold? How well do you know these strippers? Who are these people coming with you?"

"It's a party bus. Quite a bit I imagine. And I'm bringing the artist I'm working with at the moment. Whom I need to get back to."

"Expect all of us tonight. We're crashing the party."

"Taylor, I didn't mean to cause any trouble. It's my way of helping him celebrate before the wedding."

"What time do we leave?" She insisted.

"7."

"We'll be ready. See you then."

She handed me my phone as I gave her a death stare. I apologized to Mash for interrupting his work, then ended the call. Shannon could no longer contain herself.

"So we're going out tonight?" She bounced in her seat.

"It looks that way," I answered, pacifying my anger internally. *'Stay calm. It's her wedding. Let her have this one.'*

Across the room I locked eyes with Levi, who was shaking his head in disappointment. I mouthed, *"Sorry,"* as a defeated look crossed his face. In unison we shrugged our shoulders, continuing to play along with the bridal tantrums and ridiculousness.

To avoid further conflict, I skipped hanging out with the others at the sauna. I hadn't had a moment to myself for days, so while Khai was busy taking advantage of the hotel amenities, I hung back in the room for some me time. I showered, threw on my pajamas, pulled out my tablet, and fell asleep before tapping a key.

Shortly before gathering in the lobby, Mash texted.

M: *Come upstairs to room 414.*

He greeted me wearing a towel around his waist, wet in some parts, seducing me with his smile. "You know we don't have time for this." I grinned, stripping him bare and running around the room from him. He begged for a quickie, but pleasure had to wait with everyone waiting on us downstairs.

The bus rolled into the lot, and a cloud of smoke floated from the doors as they bolted open. The recording artists sat in the rear, the strippers posed on the pole, and the party had already begun without us.

Acquaintances were made once the wheels were in motion. The men crowded the rear, and the women housed the front. Bottles of liquor, cigars and weed loosened up the stiff bunch I was with, with the help of the strippers forcing us to dance with them.

They showed us some of their moves, and we shared some of ours, then the music mix blended into our favorite song. All of the brides-maids jumped up, bounced and shouted, "I get it how I live it!" Sending the bus into a frenzy and vibrating the floor.

Harv Legend, the artist from Mash's session earlier in the day, groped my legs as if he were entitled to them. I brushed his hands away, and made my way towards Mash blowing smoke with Levi sitting across from him.

Harv's eyes followed me, forcing Mash to signal *She's with me* with a hand gesture.

"Is this wifey you were speaking of?" Harv asked.

Mash nodded yes.

"Man's not foul." Harv held up his hands.

Playing it safe, I toned down the dancing. Partially because of the grope, but also the contact high I had from the ganja flowing freely. Between the weed, and the sexy smoldering way Mash looked when he lowered his bottom lip to the side to exhale, I was turned on.

I sat in his lap and kissed him zealously in front of everyone. "Don't do me like that after you denied me in the room," he said in my ear.

"You miss me huh."

"You look sexy tonight. I love seeing you so carefree like this. Reminds me of the night we met."

"You look handsome as always. Who taught you how to dress?" I flirted.

"I put my garms together."

"Your friend keeps looking at us." I side-eyed toward Harv Legend.

"He's fam. He's harmless. Forget about him. I'm more concerned with getting you out of these jeans you have painted on. I can't wait to get you home tonight."

"You mean the room?"

"Wherever you and I are together is home for me."

"Hmm," I said, squirming on him. "I just got a little wet."

"Naughty Nadia. I might have to bend you over in an alley some-where. All of this teasing, I should warn you. There will be no love making tonight. *Capisce*? Do you think you can handle it?"

"I know I can handle it."

'I hope I can handle it.'

Bar one interrupted our provocative moment. The crew went inside, enjoyed a few rounds at the bar, and took over the mucky, minuscule dance floor, while Mash and I made out under a dart board in the corner. The way he felt pressed against me ignited a fire in my jeans. It reminded me of my high school days, when I allowed my first boyfriend to hunch on me for five minutes against the wall in the den. The only five minutes of alone time I ever had with him in my house, before he found a girlfriend who actually put out.

I forgot how hot this made me. The urges bursting like flames, and throbbing uncontrollably. *'I wish I could have him right here, right now.'*

"Posse out!" Levi shouted, and the crew scattered back to the bus.

"I hope this bar crawl goes by quickly," Mash whispered, pulling me from the brick wall.

I stepped on the bus and the girls pulled me away. Grilling me about how openly affectionate I had become. Harv sat next to Mash, and the bass in their voices carried along with the music. With my back to them, I overheard Harv ask, "How in the hell did you pull her?"

"I got lucky," Mash answered modestly.

"The bird is bad. She could have easily been mine if I saw her first."

"Maybe, but I saw her first and here we are."

"Don't switch. Man's not on the defense. Easy."

"We safe."

Their lingo was hard to follow as their slang was unlike ours. It was choppy, and proper, and confusing at times— primarily because of enunciation. Not understanding completely what was said, I politely gave Harv a tight-lipped smile when I sat in Mash's lap, in hopes he would be cool, and take an interest in someone else.

He got the memo and returned to his friends at the back of the bus. A short ride later we arrived at Bar 2.

Half of the bus went inside, while the other half continued to dance in the aisles, and on the poles. We stayed behind this time, contemplating the safety of a quickie in the alley behind the bar. The absurdity of it made us laugh, and so for the remainder of the night we agreed to distance ourselves.

Bars 3 and 4 were neighbors on the same block, far away in an area that resembled uptown back home. Bar 3 was cleaner than stop one. My boots didn't stick to the floor, and the wood on the bar shined.

A fuzzy navel on the rocks served me well, alongside lemon pepper wings and fries. The guys crowded Levi at the opposite end loudly chanting, "Cheers!" and other male repartee and obscenities while throwing back shots.

"Next!" yelled a groomsman.

One by one we trickled in the bar down the block. This being the final stop, the entire party huddled at the bar, and did shots on the count of three.

"It's a celebration!" Shannon shouted.

We surrounded the bride and groom with hugs and cheers, then took to the small dance floor, filling the place to capacity. The girls and I got wild on the dance floor, dancing dirty and singing loudly.

Mash's eyes were glued to me frolicking about, but I pretended not to notice, loving every minute of his attention. "Posse Out!" shouted one of the groomsmen, and for the last time, we reloaded the bus to end the night.

By the time we arrived at the Mandarin, smoke veiled the bus, and everyone was sloshed. Without any regard for other passengers in the elevator, Mash and I acted like sex crazed maniacs. Buttons were broken, jackets stripped. My hands up his shirt, and his down my blouse.

The ride was steamy and the heat didn't stop once we stumbled inside our suite. What remained of my top was torn as we made our way to the bed. My jeans were the only thing in our way from touching familiar skin. I was hard-pressed against the linens when Mash unzipped my boots, aggressively slid my jeans down my legs, and stared at me with a beguiled face.

Heavily, I breathed with anticipation when he reached down, and put my boots back on. He pulled me off of the bed and said in a masterful tone, "Dance for me." I took my time getting into a slow rhythm up against him, swaying in the silence, then untying his boots.

My finger pressed against his chest, and guided him to the chair next to the bar where I poured him a swig. I glided across the room and retrieved my phone from my jacket, selected the mood playlist and Paula Cole's '*Feeling Love*' set the tone.

Rubbing my hands across every sensuous zone of my body, I teased him with slow movements, body rolls, and flexes. Giving him what he wanted. His own private show of me in red lace lingerie.

Playful taps to my cheeks and high kicks pointing my heels to the sky, I reeled him over to the bed, where I posed with my back arched and tossed my hair.

He grabbed a patch of it, lowered his face to mine, and kissed me roughly tasting of pure vodka. "Remember what I said earlier. There will be no love making tonight," he whispered in my ear, then flipped me over and spread my legs far and wide.

He sucked my vulva hard with my lace thongs still on, then suddenly destroyed them as they frayed in half. There was nothing gentle or soft about his kisses to my pussy. These were fast, wet licks with vigorous suction and cupping. I pulled his shirt off in the midst of him making a meal out of me, and placed it in my mouth to keep down my screams. He held my hands down at my side until he was ready to enter, and this time he wasn't gentle like our previous encounters.

"Uh," I gasped at his insertion as he moved forward toward me, tonguing me hard and restricting my hands above my head. He kept his word from before. This was a strict fucking and exploration of my walls. There was no remorse in his strokes. No regret in his poaching. No shame in the sounds he made.

My boots were now touching my hands above my head as he continuously pounded me into the bed. He removed his shirt from my mouth and kissed me a little softer this time, then whispered, "I want to hear you taking this dick."

He found pleasure in my moans and restraint. Suppressed beneath my inhibitor pummeling pure joy from my juice, I had no room to wriggle as I was locked in his clutch. Pinned together as one, I couldn't stop him if I tried, and I didn't want to. I was tipsy, tired, and taking it— most of all loving the thrashing he promised to deliver.

I screamed to the heavens, "Papi, Papi, Papi!"

He shuddered and opened fire. "I'm about to shoot to the moon!"

Neighing atop me, his hands clasped my neck with a mild squeeze, then he fell next to me. Winded. Breathless. Complete.

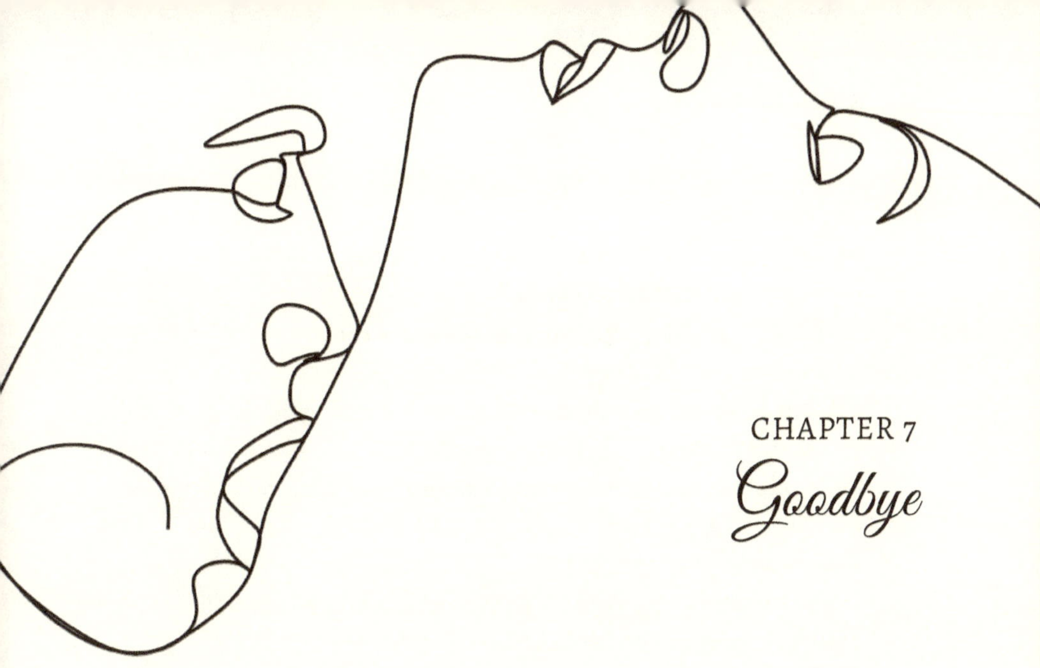

CHAPTER 7

Goodbye

Underneath the loading zone we parted ways once more. Paris this time. He watched me walk through the revolving door, reveling in the damage he'd done hours before. He texted.

M:*I won't be like that always.*

N:*A good manhandling is alright every now and then.*

A full day of bride responsibilities began with a trip to the Shoreditch district for shopping, followed with wedding prep at the hotel spa. I was in no mood for hours of walking, and trying on clothes after the smashing I'd received, but to keep the peace I didn't stray from the schedule.

We returned to the hotel and gathered in the salon/spa for manicures, pedicures, and hair trials. Full service massages weren't a part of the package Taylor selected, but I was in need. My legs, feet, and back enjoyed a deep tissue massage, as I waited for my turn with the manicurist— charged to room 414.

With the entire bridal party present, the spa offered selections of Rosé, Pinot, and Champagne. We sipped while being pampered, then gave a toast to the bride for hosting a memorable getaway.

"If it weren't for you cousin, I would have never come to this place. But I'm glad I did. Being a bridesmaid is not my forte, but when you said it was a week-long event of fun out of the country, I said why not," Janine confessed.

"And thank God we don't have hideous dresses," said Shannon.

"I wouldn't do that to you guys."

"And last night! I haven't had that much fun in years." Janine celebrated.

"We did have a good time. Didn't we? Aren't you all glad we crashed the men's party?" Taylor took credit.

"Here, here. I was so messed up I hooked up with one of Levi's cousins," Shannon confessed.

"Which one?" Taylor asked.

"I can't remember his name. I'll point him out at rehearsal."

"That's a damn shame," said Khai.

"She's not the only one. Right Janine?" Miri, Janine's younger sister revealed.

"Stop telling my business."

"Which reminds me, does anyone here want to trade roommates, because mine brings home random men in the middle of the night," Miri chided.

"Who did you hook up with Janine?" Taylor asked.

"The rapper guy." Janine lowered her head.

"He was trying to get at everybody. Why did you let him hit?" asked Shannon.

"I was messed up. His team was doing a party pack in the back of the bus. I took a molly or ex and got serviced."

"They sounded like animals in the bathroom. I had to put a pillow over my head. No one wants to hear their sister having sex." Miri complained.

"Okay from here on out. No one is to hook up with anyone else. Got it?" Taylor ordered, and we all snickered.

"General Tay, you can only babysit one punani. Yours," said Shannon, causing everyone including the service team to cry with laughter.

Nightfall quickly approached, and I made a second attempt to get some writing done. Avoiding the blank page, I read emails, sorted every item I purchased, and organized my luggage to make everything fit. *'2 days until I see him again, then back to reality.'*

Finally, I sat against the headboard, reflecting on the past few days. There was so much to journal, I didn't know where to begin, so I typed whatever came to me in flashes. The club, dancing, kiss, concert, kiss, romantic stroll, sex, the plane, the rock, the sunset, sex, sex, the dinner, the crawl, the make out session in the bar, and sex again.

I chuckled when I proofed my outline and saw how many times I wrote sex. Then I thought about it, about him, about how he made me feel, and how I missed him already.

Thirty minutes later, my journal had turned into a first chapter draft of the past week. *'There's no way I could go into detail about us,'* I thought and closed my computer.

I still felt him from last night. My hands crept in between my legs pressed together, holding myself in an attempt to savor the feeling. In a fetal position, I dozed off. Completely tapped and missed my paramour's call.

The ringing of the hotel phone woke me the day before the wedding. *This your wake-up call. Enjoy your day*, said the recorded voice.

One last hurdle before the main event, the rehearsal dinner. My assignment— oversee the decor.

The morning was spent catering to Taylor. Collectively, we had to see that she remained calm, verify the hotel staff arranged the decorations according to her wishes, iron her clothes if need be, and make her feel like royalty which was why she chose England for her destination wedding.

Levi's grooms relaxed while the bridesmaids ran around like chickens with their heads cut off. Happy hour began early for them, showing up glossy and red-eyed, giggly and frisky.

The vibe was stressful yet energetic, and I learned weddings were an emotional time, watching Taylor cry on and off until it became contagious. When we lined up she cried. When Isla and Drew, the best man, walked in the bride and groom's place, she cried, making Levi cry. Then Isla cried, creating a wave of tears in the party and family members.

Time ran over in the rehearsal as emotions ran high. The banquet manager saved the night, interrupting our last run to remind us of our dinner reservation.

The hour was late, but that didn't stop the drinks from flowing. Family and friends sang praises of the happy couple, taking turns as they saw fit, to stand and share special moments from their past, and wishing them well in their future. A toast was made to the bride and groom, then dinner was served.

Continuing from earlier, the drunken groom party became bold and flirtatious, working the room with hopes to get lucky. I excused myself while the others mingled to answer a call, and returned promptly to complete my list of duties for the night.

Unaware I was within listening distance, Isla had my name on her tongue, ridiculing my behavior to Janine and Taylor, who stood by and allowed the bashing. Anger was my first reaction, but it quickly faded as I reminded myself Isla was jealous and had every right to be. I waited a while before gracing them with my presence, and carried on as if I heard nothing, being a good friend and not ruining Taylor's moment.

With the wedding only a few hours away in the afternoon, I turned in early. I didn't disturb Mash since he was working, and out of boredom I wasted money, ordering a movie that ended up watching me, exhausted from the harrowing day.

Braids draped in the front of our hair, with loose wavy curls falling from the ends, the bridal party circled Taylor in her room, perfecting her strands and her straps, securing her fears from the unknown, and praying for a perfect day. The tears returned and her hands shook with nerves, delaying her glam team to have her ready on time.

Running fifteen minutes late, Levi stood outside of her room, and shared a moment with her. The last push she needed to get the show on the road.

One by one, we preceded her down the aisle in our mint colored gowns and fuchsia florals in hand. The ceremony began with a solo from a member of Levi's family, then a poem read by Taylor's aunt.

The minister performed a lengthy service with a scripture reading, followed by a short story about the roles of a husband and the duties of a wife.

I searched the room for Mash, hoping to catch a glimpse of him since we barely spoke after he left. *'Where is he?'* I wondered, after scanning the crowd with no luck.

Taylor's waterworks returned during the lighting of the unity candle, and Levi wiped away her tears. The room including myself cried along with her, though mine were a mixture of happy and sad tears. I was moved by the love in the room, but sad the time with my love was ending.

Man and wife were pronounced, then cocktail hour entertained the guests as we posed for a million photographs on the hotel property. Watching the newlyweds love on each other made me grow antsy to get to the reception hall.

The celebration began, the wedding party introduced, and still no sign of Mash. The first couple dance ended. Taylor danced with her father, Levi with his mother and then mother-in-law, and the dance floor opened to everyone. It was then I realized. *'He's not coming.'*

It wasn't the way I would have said goodbye, but I understood the gift he was giving me. Our time would forever be cherished, I just wished I could feel his arms around me once more. If I had known our last kiss, would be our final kiss, I would have held it a while longer.

Listening to speeches and toasts and watching friends and family dance, I lost my composure. I needed to get to my phone, which was forbidden during the ceremony.

I slipped out of the reception and went up to our room, searching for something with his scent on it, but he had packed all of his belongings when he left for France. The only thing remaining in the room with his aroma was the pillow he slept on. I held it in my arms, imprinting the fragrance on my brain.

My phone had zero missed calls and one unopened text, not from him. I paced the room in disbelief. *'You did this to yourself.'* And I did. I let this happen. I lost control. I ignored my brain and listened to my heart. I was to blame.

A knock on the door disturbed me from my insanity. I ran to it with hopes I had worked myself up for nothing. Still no Mash. It was Khai. She had been watching me play pretend all day, and came to console my aching heart.

"Is everything okay?" she held my hand.

"I'm such a fool." I cried.

"You're far from a fool. What's going on?"

"The fairytale is over. He's not coming."

"What did he say?"

"Absolutely nothing. No call, no text, no show. And I get it. Why prolong the inevitable when he was already free from me ya know? Why leave Paris and come back here. He's not tied to me. He doesn't owe me anything."

"Sweetie, you're getting yourself all worked up. And for nothing I'm sure. He wouldn't just ditch you like that." She assured me.

"How do you know?"

"I saw you two together with my own eyes. He's crazy about you. Not to worry you, but maybe something happened. Like he missed his plane, or someone stole his phone so he couldn't call you. I'm sure he doesn't know your number by heart. No one knows anyone's number by heart. Calm down. Okay. If you haven't heard from him tonight, then worry. But right now, you need to come downstairs and enjoy yourself. Let's get you cleaned up."

She wiped my dripping mascara, and touched up the red areas on my face, concealing the emotional rollercoaster I was experiencing. We returned to the party, where I masked my true feelings by dancing with a persistent groomsman.

Once he became hard to shake, I faked a cramp and sat alone in the spectator chairs. Straight-faced and forlorn, occasionally faking a smile.

Simpering face Isla spotted me sitting alone. It was the moment she'd been waiting for all week. Tension ran down my spine just looking at her, but I had to be strong, and not let her belittle me, or get me riled up. *'Keep your cool. Don't let her see you like this. Don't give her the satisfaction.'* I preached to myself.

"Where is Mister 1s and 2s? I haven't seen him around for a few days. Trouble in paradise already?" Isla probed.

"Humph. Mister 1's and 2's. That's cute. How long did it take for you to come up with that one?"

"I'm just teasing. But for real though, where is he? I thought Taylor said he was your plus one?"

"You and Taylor have been doing a lot of talking about me and my plus one. Why is that?"

"What do you mean?" She stuttered, horribly hiding her guilt.

"I heard you last night. And I quote, "This weekend was supposed to be about you, and Nadia's been running around town with her nose wide open over a fling. She's in la la land." End quote. Sound familiar?"

"Did you seriously think it was something more? You're smarter than that."

"Isla, humor me. If he chose you that night, what would you have done?"

"Don't deflect. I was simply saying it was embarrassing how you were carrying on. But seeing as though he isn't here, I'm sure you've snapped back into reality. Sorry it didn't work out the way you wanted." She smirked.

"Now look who's deflecting. You didn't answer my question."

"You didn't answer mine. Do you know what your problem is Nadia?"

"Her problem is she isn't dancing with me," Mash interrupted.

Reaching for my hand in a tailored tan suit accentuating his broad shoulders, and a powder blue oxford shirt, he rescued me from Satan's daughter. I rose to my feet, coyly smiling with my head down, elated he was in front of me.

He escorted me to the dance floor and I gleefully followed his lead. "Do you know what you're doing captain. This is a fast song." I teased.

"Let's pretend it's a slow one," he said, holding me close. "You look amazing by the way."

"You clean up well yourself. Very dapper look you got going on here."

"Have you been crying?" he asked, kissing my neck.

"I had a slight meltdown, but I'm okay now."

"Why? What happened?"

"I didn't think I was going to see you again."

He held me from the nape of my neck, and placed his head against my mine, "I'm sorry I'm so late. I would never do something like that to you. I had a few errands to run before leaving Paris. One was finding these guys a wedding gift. Then of course, I had to get you something. I had to fight traffic, rush home to get dressed, get back in traffic, and now I'm here."

"Like I said before, I overanalyze everything. I thought you were making a clean break from me without all the drama."

"Look at me," he demanded, holding my chin up. "I told you I love you the other night. I mean what I say, and I say what I mean. Never forget that."

"I love you, too."

"I would have called, but you told me you wouldn't have your phone at the wedding. I got here as fast as I could. You have no idea how gutted I've been these past two days. I've done nothing but dread tomorrow. I want you to stay."

The thought had crossed my mind, but it was wishful thinking. I didn't dare tell him that. Instead I replied, "I wish I could."

"Tell me why you can't."

"You know why. My life is across the ocean."

"You can write from anywhere. I want you here with me. Let me show you the world. I've thought this through and I know it can work." He pulled me in closer.

"You're serious, aren't you?" My brows furrowed.

"Promise me you'll think about it." He sighed in my ear.

"I promise."

I inhaled his scent as we continued to dance, wrapped in one another's arms, slow dragging to the fast song playing, and the slow one after that. The dance floor was cleared to witness the bride and groom cut the cake. Levi and Mash shared a congratulatory embrace, and got on as they did earlier in the week. He placed an envelope in Levi's hand. "This is from the both of us."

We joined everyone at the banquet room doors, throwing lavender and dried flowers at the wedded couple, glowing upon their exit. To speed up the bridal party duties, both the maids and grooms delivered the gifts to Taylor's parent's suite.

Mash and I disappeared to our room filled with a range of emotions. We lied in bed laughing at the tele, snuggled close with sporadic moments of passionate lip exchanges. He wiped my tears when they fell, gazed at me in silence, and avoided eye contact with me when I added items to my luggage.

He stared at the floor from the edge of the bed in the middle of the night. I crept behind him, contemplating his request to abandon my life across the ocean. While kissing and squeezing his shoulders, I listened to him sigh, studying the brooding brows above his distant eyes in the mirror wanting to shout, "Of course I'll stay with you," but I was afraid. Afraid to be alone in London without my friends and family nearby as a safety net. Afraid he was who I had been searching for and I would mess it up. Afraid to take a chance.

"This is going to sound weird, but may I have the t-shirt you wore tonight?" I asked.

He removed my arms from around him, folded it neatly, and placed it in my bag. He sat in the chair near the mini bar, and poured himself a shot. "Leave me something of yours as well."

"Like what?"

"Whatever you want me to have." He avoided eye contact with me.

"Can we at least discuss how and when we are going to see each other again?" I huffed.

"I'll send you my schedule. You pick which city you want to come to, and I'll fly you in."

"What about you coming to see me?"

"I'll come when you tell me to."

"Are we okay?"

"Yeah. I just hate this day has finally come."

He threw his head back and gulped the harsh brown. I minced to the bar and stood in front of him, stroking his hair while pressing his head against my stomach. He looked up at me and told me he missed me already, kissing the back of my hand while rubbing on the back of my thighs. I hadn't felt his touch in two days, and my legs withered at his fingertips. It was time. He knew it. I knew it. We had become addicted to one another. Sexually. Wholeheartedly.

He grazed my nipples with his teeth. Toying with them, forcing the nerves in my drip to pulse. My bosom saluted him, pointing at the tip with each nip. I stood in front of him, holding on to his shoulders with a confounded mind, wondering what was this hold he had on me, but also how was I going to get along back home with him.

Seductive kisses began to melt against my skin. His approach was tender this time. Delicate strokes brushed up and down my back. Elongated kisses upon my neck. Now standing, he danced with me in circles around the small space beside the bar, then carried me to the bed.

His fingers drew lines from my feet, all the way up my legs as if he were making a mental image of them to keep. Then he kissed the exterior of my orifice with a closed mouth. Not once. Not twice. Several slow and gentle pecks, observing the shocks in between.

'*Was this our last time together,*' I wondered.

I squirmed as I wanted him inside of me, but he made me wait for him. His tongue licked me everywhere it could reach, Frenching my lower lips as if it had a tongue of its own. I groused with my hands running through his hair. Sighing for him to ease the pain of my departure. And then he hovered over me. Waiting to give me what I craved.

Lingered atop of my desperate begging body, he looked into my eyes and rubbed his thumbs across my cheeks, then traced the outline of my bitten lips with his index finger.

I grew weak from the impeding attention being given to me. "Put it in," I begged. He refused. He wasn't done studying me. I pled again. "Mash, please let me feel you inside me." He wouldn't budge. He was in control, showing me what I would miss if I left.

And so, I lie there patiently beneath him, gazing into his eyes and brushing his face against mine, going mad from depravation, bracing for his vast entrance. "Unh," I whimpered from gratification the torture was over.

He grinned as if he was looking forward to hearing the sound leave my mouth. Back and forth we moved in unison, looking away deep into each other's eyes. "Stay," he said. I looked away. "Stay," he repeated, resting his head on my shoulder.

I gasped in between jabs, never responding to his request, losing the battle of holding back my tears.

My grind from below excited him. He wrapped my legs around his waist, moaning insatiably from the build-up. My ass encompassed his pressing palms, bringing me up further as he drilled for my black gold.

"Let me hear you say my name one last time," he ordered.

"Maximus," I moaned.

"Again."

"It's not the last time."

"Again."

"Maximus," I cried.

"I love you."

The climax was bittersweet. I hadn't felt so good and so bad at the same time ever in life. I was riddled with guilt, and without explanation, but mainly perplexed at his word choice. *One Last Time.*

Distance doesn't work well for most relationships, and I took his words to mean he was giving up before we started. I listened to him drift off, then slithered from underneath his arm. So much was on my mind I couldn't sleep. I texted Khai.

N:*You up?*

K:*I am now.*

N:*Can I come down? Please?*

K:*Sure thing.*

Khai placed the bolt lock outside of the door to keep it open for me, and sat propped up on the bed looking at me with her-*this better be good*-face. I sat at the foot of the bed and spilled my guts. "You know how you've always been there for me?"

"Yeah." Her voice dragged.

"I don't know what I would do if I didn't have you in my life."

"If this is about Taylor and Isla being shady to you, don't sweat it.

We're friends, but sometimes friends get jealous of one another. It'll blow over."

"Maybe. But you know how the two of them have their thing, and you and I have our thing, and all four of us have Shannon?"

"Yeah, that's true."

"He asked me to stay Khai. I won't have you to run to if I do."

"Stay as in move here?" Her voice heightened.

"I guess. I haven't asked him to go into detail about it. He just keeps repeating stay, stay, stay."

"Do you want to?" Khai sneered.

"I have no fucking clue what I want! I wanted a good man. I found him. A gotdamn diamond in the rough to be exact. I've wanted someone to love me. And not just say it. But show it. And he does that. But why does he have to live on the other side of the world? If I stay, I'm giving up my world— for a man...That's sounds so bizarre don't you think?"

"It is a hard one. Especially this day and age when we are all talking about women's rights, and the fight for equality."

"And here I am considering doing something as bonkers as staying in another country for a man."

"But he's a good man." Khai's brows raised.

"Is he? We've known him for seven days. No, no, no I can't stay. My mother would kill me. I'd lose my best friend. I'd be over here all alone. Just forget I even came down here and bothered you."

I stood to leave, then sat back down in confusion. Silence sat between us as Khai stared at me half smiling, and half laughing at the back of her throat.

"Nadia, did you come down here so I could tell you what to do?"

"Maybe. No. I don't know. Probably."

"Well I can't make this decision for you. But I will say, you should clarify what he means by stay. Maybe he wants you to stay for a few extra days. That wouldn't be so bad. Ask him."

"A few days wouldn't be a problem."

"Exactly, but you have to have the conversation."

"And what if he means a few weeks?"

"Then you need to decide if he's worth you giving him that kind of time and attention. What are you afraid of?"

"That this will end like it did with Dylan. Being used and betrayed and thrown away like a piece of trash. That if I stay, he'll get bored with me and ship me home when he's ready, and I will have lost all of my respect." I wiped away my tears before they fell.

"This one is nothing like Dylan. I've seen how Vanilla Ice looks at you. And you him." She joked.

My mouth fell open, and my tears fell as a hard laugh echoed from my stomach. Trying to catch my breath I uttered, "Don't make me laugh." But we both fell over guffawing.

Moments later we simmered down, and Khai alerted me. "Everyone saw how he looks at you. I bet you didn't know all eyes were on you two when you were dancing. And I saw his face when he showed up tonight."

"He said he loves me."

"And I believe he does."

"I said it, too."

"I knew it!" She jumped up from the bed and clapped her hands.

"You think I'm crazy, don't you?"

"I think you're scared more than anything. Look, if you stay, you won't lose me girl. Hell, your man is rich he can fly me back and forth. By the way. Before you go I need to remind you, you owe me something."

"What?"

"The 411. Is it good girl?"

"Do all donkeys have a cross on their back?" I sashayed away and grinned at Khai's hands muffling her open mouth.

Mash was in the same spot I left him in. I crawled next to him and kissed his arm, his face, his shoulder and his neck while watching him sleep. I put my foot under his shin and stared at the clock, waiting for the alarm to sound. Eventually, the night got the best of me and I woke to a ringing telephone, and a fully dressed Mr. Sharper.

The room was silent, filled with tension and sadness. The housekeeping carts squeaked as they were pushed from room to room near our door, and became the topic at hand. "They begin early, don't they," I said. He glanced in my direction with half an impish grin.

I threw on the sweat suit I arrived in, and zipped up my final bag. Mash gathered the load with me close behind, and the click on the door triggered him. He stopped before making it to the elevator, held my hand, then offered to drive me to the airport. "That won't be necessary, but thank you," I declined.

Our fingers entangled on the ride down until we reached the lobby floor. Mash settled the bill while I stood with the other passengers waiting to board the shuttle. I encouraged the others to go ahead of me, waiting for my girls and Mash with my bags.

My hands began shaking as I stood on the curb, then I felt his hands cover mine from behind. He wrapped me in his arms one final time and felt my body quivering.

"You okay?" he asked.

I nodded yes, lying as best I could.

"Stay with me," he said, as the girls handed their luggage to the attendant.

"It was nice meeting you Mash," said Khai.

"Nice meeting you, too. All of you. Hopefully we'll get to hang out again soon."

I trembled. *This is the moment I dreaded.'*

"And thank you for taking us on the bar crawl. When you come to the States we'll treat you right." Shannon shook his hand.

"I'm going to hold you to that." Mash forced a smile.

Khai looked me up and down, and then in the eyes. She placed her arms around me, and I dropped a tear, visibly shaking in front of everyone. She squeezed my shoulders, then said to Mash, "You take care of our girl now." Shannon turned around and questioned me with her eyes.

"Take care of our girl?" she mouthed.

I widened my eyes and handed my keys to Khai. "I'll call you if I need you. Love you and be safe."

Shannon's mouth dropped. She put her arms around Khai and I, and we hugged like teens going off to college. The driver split us up, calling for the last round of passengers. I watch them board the shuttle, shaking in my boots, second guessing my decision as the bus pulled out of the lot.

Mash swung me around and plastered his lips on mine with an audience watching. "Are you ready to take me home?" I asked.

He gloated. "You have no idea."

Tapping on the coated glass and making heart symbols with their hands, my friends shouted *love you* nonstop, as the shuttle engine throttled. We watched them fade in the distance, then loaded my bags in the car. "To the outskirts we go," I said.

My heart pounded, and my arms turned slightly damp of nervousness. I felt brave about my choice, and excited to be adventurous for the first time. I was living on a prayer, and taking a chance with my heart. Knowing the risk was high, and stepping out of my own way, certain I had found something profound.

I opened up a part of myself that was closed off, eager to explore a new chapter.

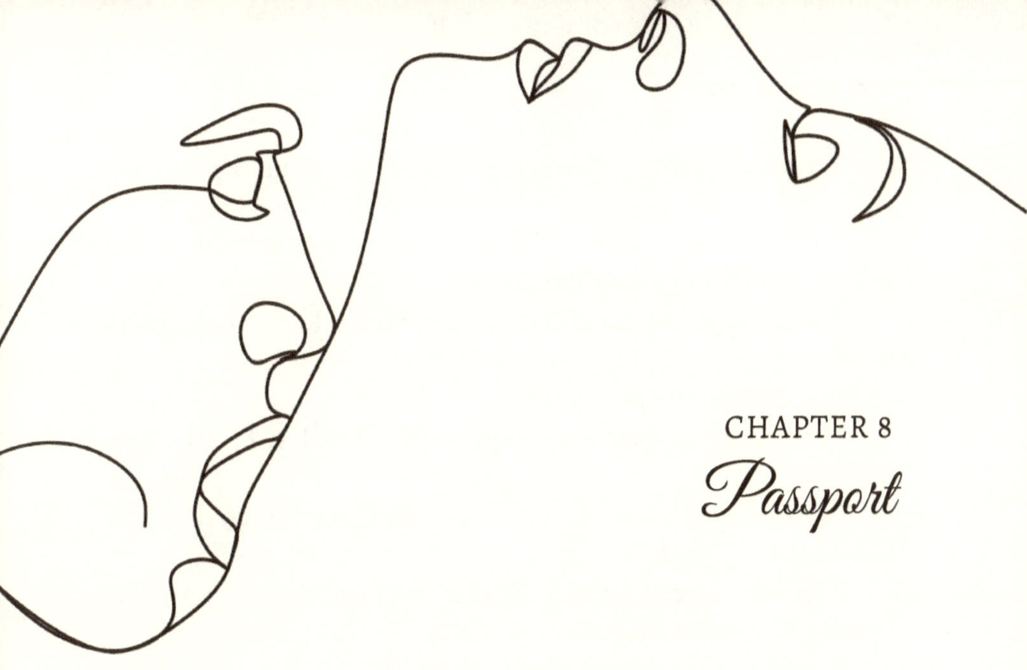

CHAPTER 8

Passport

Stay. The one syllable word needed clarification. A few extra days to enjoy each other's company seemed ideal, but I avoided initiating the conversation, in fear it would ruin the vibe between us.

Our chemistry was unmatched. We weren't finishing each other's sentences or anything like that, but we were in sync. He made me feel welcome in his house, persisting I call it home.

Whenever he saw me working, he gave me space and room to breathe, or when he'd be gone all day to work on one of his various projects, he made sure I had access to money and one of his vehicles. And that was just the first week.

His level of consideration wooed me so, I dreaded the uncomfortable exchange we needed to have. Creating a genial atmosphere, I set up the folding table and chairs in the middle of the kitchen floor, and cooked one of my best meals, setting the mood for the discussion. As always, he greets me with a kiss the moment he arrives home. His hand finds the same spot between my waist and my back, and no matter what kind of day he's had, he lets me know he is happy to see me.

I tell him dinner is ready and to meet in the kitchen. We sit and chat for a bit, then casually I mentioned, "I looked up flights today, and I need to book something weeks in advance for a good rate."

"The rate doesn't matter. I'll cover it. What date are you looking to fly?" he asked, adjusting his frames.

"I was hoping we could discuss that. When do you want me to leave?"

'God I love him in those glasses.'

"Why would I want that?" His voice lowered as he stared me down.

"What did you mean when you asked me to stay? A few days? I've been here over a week."

"Honestly, when I asked, I didn't have an end date in mind." He hypnotized me with his gaze.

"I don't want to outstay my welcome is all."

"You still don't get it, do you?" His lips parted.

"I think I'm starting to."

'That's a come-hither look.'

We lunged across the flimsy table and burned from the passionate fire between us. The cheap table surprisingly held up against our quick stint of fucking in the middle of the meal.

This had become my new normal. A simple look, or accidental graze against my skin ended with my legs in the air, or me bent over the couch.

I had no idea when I was going home, and the time had come for me to face my mother with an answer to that very question. By the end of week two I was in Paris, following my lover around in the city of lights, narrow streets, delectable pastries, and historic museums.

I took photographs of old dated buildings, and attempted to converse with the staff of the hotel in their language— desperately I tried to remember what I learned back in high school. The fashions of the women walking the streets were all awe-inspiring, but the highlight for me were the indulgent chocolate croissants.

Mash served as a tour guide showing me the normal attractions, and hidden gems people like himself only knew about. His access to places was notable, and during this trip I learned how important he was. I was blinded by his kindness and attention in the beginning, overlooking how the world viewed him and his work. Quickly, I became acclimated to the world of fame.

Sitting out on sound check, I laid back in the penthouse suite his promoters provided, and overlooked the city. The Eiffel Tower glittered over its admirers, and the streets were buzzing. The owner of a café across the street, swept the sidewalk just before turning her signage to *fermee*.

Moments later she locked its doors, and set off holding the hand of whom I assumed was her daughter. I watched them until they turned the corner, exhaled a few times, and dialed my mother.

"Your grandmother and I had a nice chat about you little girl," she answered.

"Good things I hope. How is she? How are you?"

"I'm my usual self, but your grandmother is not. She said you haven't called her in weeks. You normally call her every day."

"She's right. I haven't been myself lately."

"Oh, we know." My mother scoffed.

"Is she mad? Are you?"

"Truthfully, as long as you are safe, we are fine with whatever it is you are doing. What exactly are you doing? Besides laying up with a strange man. And spare me the details."

"I'm writing. And traveling. I'm in Paris right now. It's beautiful Ma. We should have done things like this. You know?"

"Traveling wasn't our thing. I'm glad you're doing it though. Is your friend with you?"

"Not at the moment."

"Well tell him as long as he doesn't hurt you, he won't have anything to worry about. Your friends have given me his address, so I know how to find him."

"I'm in good hands Ma."

"Seems so."

"I just wanted to tell you that, and tell you I miss you, and I'll see you soon. I love you."

"I love you, too, baby."

Weight lifted from my shoulders. I mistakenly thought that was going to be the hardest phone call of my life. I expected to be chewed out for my reckless behavior and rash decisions, and was grateful I received understanding and support instead. Then I remembered, I had to call my favorite person in the world, Grams, who was sure to cut me with her sharp tongue.

The car returned to chauffeur me to the concert. On my way out of the lobby, I stopped at the postal stand and wrote Grams a few lines. *'This should buy me some time before my lashing,'* I thought, before leaving it with the concierge.

Nightlife in the city reminded me of the years I spent in college. Seeing the crowds of women laugh amongst themselves, and having a good time, made me wish my friends were sharing this experience with me. *'I missed that opportunity, but it was so worth it.'*

For a brief moment, I became sad. I understood how it looked when I bailed on them to go to Spain. It came across as selfish, but I was sure they would have done the same thing if they were in my shoes.

As I passed several groups of women, I began to miss them, and wondered what they were doing back home. Then I remembered it was bowling night, and I wasn't missing anything except shit talking in a smoke-filled alley wearing borrowed shoes— having a good time nonetheless.

Backstage was reminiscent of Taylor's wedding day. Stressful, fast paced, lively, and crowded. A stage hand escorted me to the dressing room tucked away in a dark corner. It could have used a major facelift, cleaning, painting, or demolishing, but as I sat and looked around, I understood why it looked like a pit stop. It was. Acts from all over signed the walls, dressers, and chairs. It was the image of filthy history, and for entertainers a rite of passage.

The clamoring of the crowd amplified the artists as each went on. I stood stage right with the other VIP pass owners, watching Mash and the artists perform.

Unlike his gig at the tent, this crowd was massive and electrifying, and by the end of the show had made their way backstage somehow to meet the acts. It was unsettling to watch woman after woman throw themselves at the artists. I stood far away in a dimly lit shadow of a boulder taking it all in.

Fuming in jealousy with flashbacks of deceit. Mash was humble and acknowledged all those who approached him, which was a great look for him. I, on the other hand, had been given a front row seat to a world I was sure my insecurities couldn't handle.

The stage hand found me in the corner, and escorted me to the car down a hallway to a tunnel, where the artists come and go. I sat there for nearly thirty minutes waiting for Mash to come out, and when he finally did he looked beat.

"All done," I asked.

"That was insane at the end. Where were you?"

"I got lost in the crowd, so I stepped back to give the fans their space."

"Did you enjoy the show?"

"I was blown away. I must admit. I didn't know you were this big of a deal. Seeing it firsthand is different from reading tabloids."

"Stop." He covered his face and blushed.

I could have and should have let it end there, but doing what I normally do, I continued to reach. "How do you handle all of the fans coming at you like that?"

"What are you getting at?" he answered my question with a question. "I feel like there's more to that question."

"Humph. I'm not too keen on seeing women put their hands all over you." I regretfully admitted.

"Imagine being the person who doesn't enjoy people putting their hands all over you. It sucks, but it comes with the territory of what I do."

"I didn't think of it that way." I bit my lip.

"Well, you're about to see more of it. I just got an updated schedule, and we'll be hitting the road pretty heavy over the next few weeks, so get ready."

'We? Next few weeks?'

As Mash prepared for his crammed schedule, he spent hours away from the house rehearsing with the acts for the upcoming shows. I made an effort to keep myself busy by enrolling in exercise and dance classes, and people watching at cafes for writing inspiration.

The house was peaceful with Mash gone most of the day, and the quiet time allowed me to mentally decompress and write diligently. Submissions about travel, western news from an eastern perspective, and romance excerpts kept me occupied the many hours I was alone.

When boredom struck, I revisited the non-fiction story I began writing at the Mandarin, adding bits and pieces to it, giving myself a few shameful giggles.

Shy of a month, the hectic schedule began with the first stop in Cannes for a film festival. Mash had been hired to work a few parties, and as requested gifted me with passes to screenwriting workshops and seminars. It felt good to do something of my own interest, and not exist as the travel companion following him around all day.

I was on my own in the streets, sight-seeing and taste-tasting when the seminars ended. Basking in the sun on the beach, taking full advantage of my me time.

As Mash's schedule opened up, we won and lost money in one of the casinos, before sailing on a private yacht with one of his industry associates.

Snooty and elite minded people lounged on the vessel. Models in bathing suits, champagne every few feet, and A-list actors and actresses acting holier than thou.

My insecurity went into overdrive every time a famous woman tugged on Mash's arm, or tapped him on the shoulder, overly smiling in his face. I didn't think I would ever get used to feeling inferior to powerful women. *'How do I measure up,'* constantly crossed my mind in the presence of these people. They were desired beings making their own money, compared to me the penniless shadow.

The boat docked near our resort, so we strolled through the villas taking in the night air. Mash asked about the seminars I attended as an icebreaker, then questioned my behavior on the boat. "Talk to me."

"About what?"

"Earlier tonight? I noticed you shut down. What caused that?" He paused his steps.

"Just wasn't my crowd." I pulled him along.

"Is that all?"

"Yep."

He knew I was lying. He could feel something was wrong, but he didn't pressure me to say. He took me by the hand and respected my moment of withdrawal, though my silence rattled him. *'Lack of confidence is a turnoff,'* I said to myself, wrapping my fingers around his. "I'm fine." I assured him, knowing eventually I would be.

The next morning, we flew to Amsterdam. Two days in the city didn't give us time to explore the way I had hoped. Amid the rumors of it being well known for its red-light district, I wasn't interested in seeing sex-trafficked women work. I preferred to visit the museums, and taste the world-famous crepes as research for a travel submission, but time didn't allow it. Neither did the congestion of the city. I bust my ass riding a bike as the streets were overly crowded, and spent my short time taking it easy in the room.

Before leaving the Netherlands, I mailed post cards to my mom and Grams, filling them in on my travels, then it was wheels up. Four days until the next show I had no interest in attending.

After taking a day to recuperate from Cannes and Amsterdam, I began looking at flights again. I was homesick. I was tired. And I was losing myself in someone else's world. His world was exciting nonetheless, but my receiving rejection letter after rejection letter murdered my sense of self. My mind constantly wondered, *'What am I doing with my life.'* I needed to regroup.

Without discussing it with Mash, I booked a flight on the night he was due in Barcelona. I had three days to tell him, but couldn't muster the courage. Nor was there ever a good time to do so, being that he was exhausted when he made it home.

Every night he greeted me with a kiss, showered, ate, and laid under me while I keyed my soul away, still attempting to prove I was worthy of my craft. With nothing to lose, I submitted a synopsis of my Mandarin piece, to a production company in search of material to produce, then woke Mash to tell him I was leaving.

A light stroke to his shoulder led him to twist. Delicately, I massaged his shoulders to wake him. He grunted and mumbled for a few seconds, eventually opening his eyes. "Something's up," he muttered.

"I have to tell you something."

"It must be bad news."

"I'm homesick." I confessed.

"This again."

"I booked a flight."

His eyes widened as he lifted and leaned back against the head-board. He looked straight ahead, avoiding eye contact with me. "I kind of felt you were getting sick of me with the late nights and the shows, but I didn't think it was this bad."

"I'm not sick of you. I just need to go home. For a little while. I was thinking maybe you could come see me when your schedule opens up."

"What will you do when you get there?"

"For starters, check on my mother. Check on my house. Maybe drive down to visit my Grams."

"And then what?"

"What is with your tone?"

"I'm not understanding what is going so wrong here, that you are rushing to go back home."

"My life dammit! I just told you I was homesick. I never said anything was going wrong here. I just need to be around my people. Be around my things. Not feel like a kept woman or a shadow puppet. Hell, I'm practically a citizen."

He turned towards me but said nothing. He was looking through me and I couldn't take it. I couldn't take him or the silence. I left the bed and continued to rant. "Do you know I haven't had one article published since I've been here? I feel like I'm losing myself."

"I didn't know you were feeling that way. You never said."

"You never asked. You just keep putting off the discussion of when we would go to the States together."

"Nadia, if you had left after the wedding, I would have visited you by now."

"I'm not so sure you would," I said, pacing the room.

"I would have. But you stayed, and I thought if I played my cards right, you would never want to leave. It never occurred to me you would get homesick."

"You have done everything right. I love being here with you. I'm just..."

As I paused, he followed me to the window. I looked into the darkness, searching for the words to end my sentence. He placed his chin atop my shoulder and wrapped his hands around my waist. "Do I make you happy?"

"Very much so," I said, leaning my head against his.

"Then what can I do to remove this scowl from your pretty face?" he asked, stroking my cheek.

"Maybe take some time off and come home with me."

"I give you my word, we'll set a date. I'll have some things moved around tomorrow, then we'll go from there. Cool?"

"Un huh."

"I planned something special for us this weekend. Say you're still coming with me."

"Have I ever let you down?"

"Not once." He turned my face towards him and kissed my lips. "So this is what it's like to argue with you huh?"

I blushed and placed my arms around him. "That was not an argument. More like a disagreement."

"I don't know— you got a little feisty a second ago."

"You call that feisty?"

He grinned. "It kind of turned me on. Do you need help getting the rest of it out of you?"

"Oh no. I have work to do."

"So do I." He picked me up and carried me to the bed.

'Why can't I say no to this man?'

In the morning, I cancelled my flight home and packed for Barcelona. I was curious about these special plans he spoke of. Once again, my feet touched the soil of Spain.

Its colored beauty could not be ignored from the sky, but to see the murals and buildings up close were breathtaking. My host knew the ins and outs and kept me on guard for pickpockets, while we roamed the city exploring the streets and museums.

The next day was an early one, as Mash wanted to show me more of the city before reporting to sound check. We took a brief stroll in the Gothic Quarter. Narrow lanes and eerie architecture eventually led us into a shopping market, with novelty and keepsake items targeted for tourists.

My eyes locked in on a kiosk selling handmade rings, made from wire and beads. The intertwining of a black and blue band spoke to me, and with permission the attendant allowed me to slip it on my finger.

My face expressed I liked the piece before I could verbally say so, and without asking, Mash purchased it. He then asked the artist to take his measurements, and make him one to match mine.

With an hour to kill before picking up the order, we ate street food, sat and listened to a band, followed a map of the well-known historic churches, then returned to the market.

The craftsman earned a healthy tip, by crafting matching bracelets with the identical pattern of the rings. I couldn't stop admiring my matching set. It reminded me of the hand-crafted jewelry sold down-town on the market in Charleston.

I stuck my hand out and dangled my wrist side to side at least a dozen times, fascinated at how the colors moved and shined in the sunlight.

"You love it that much?" Mash teased.

"I do. I respect the work of creative people, and I love to support artists. I know it's only wire and beads, but working with beads requires talent."

"You can have my bracelet. One for each arm."

"Thank you. I'll take it."

"One more thing. Marry me tomorrow."

"Don't play." I smirked at him.

"I'm serious. It's the only reason I wanted the ring."

"I thought you just wanted to match mine."

"Yes. As husband and wife."

"My feisty side didn't scare you away?"

"I've had this on my mind for a while now. I had this whole thing planned out for when we went home, but I don't want to wait. Let's do it here."

The look on his face exposed his truth, as he gazed at me with love in his eyes. "Tell me the worst thing about you," I said.

"I'm jealous." He confessed.

"So am I."

"I've seen enough to know I will weather any storm with you. Say you'll be my wife. Say you'll marry me."

The concierge in our hotel located a priest to perform the ceremony on the beach. I bought an inexpensive white sundress in the village, and tied white flowers around the thread in the hotel sewing kit. Pinning it into my hair, I walked barefoot on the beach, admiring my soulmate in his white t-shirt and slacks.

The wind and the mist blew my straight hair curly, while the sun blessed its light for those spectating to see. Hand in hand, we eloped. No big show. No drama. Just he and I, vowing to love each other forever.

CHAPTER 9

Mrs

I smiled to myself for most of the flight home. Thinking about the way my husband couldn't have picked a better moment, a better place to ask me to be his wife.

My face was flushed, looking down at the stillness of the ocean beneath me. Giggling to myself as I reminisced about our consummation. The flickering candles. The calla lilies thrown all over the floor. The tenderness he displayed the moment I undressed when we returned to the room. The wind against my breast, the second time we made love on the balcony. The beast he became outside slaying me against the glass door.

We were rabbits before, so I didn't know what to call us now. Jack rabbits maybe? Whatever the species, we were animalistic with each other. I couldn't get enough of him. And now, his home was truly my home. Our home. The way that sounded put a bandage on my being homesick for a while.

Instead of searching for flights to America, I was scheduling when and where we would honeymoon, researching dual citizenship, and contemplating how to break the news to my mother. To my friends.

The response from the embassy took days, and the information we needed turned out to be complicated. I had to prove I was living with Mr. Sharper for over a week, then we could apply for a license in

21 days to make our union legal. I would also have to apply for a visa. The only visa I was ever interested in was the kind that swipes.

My first time travelling out of the States, led me to see parts of the world I never imagined I would visit, and changed my life. I no longer felt I was losing myself. I finally understood I was gaining a partner. The person I had been looking for.

Mash's tight schedule allowed us four days to honeymoon. Giving me total control, I chose Italy. It was the only place I could get the perfect wedding gift— The best pizza in the world, and meet my mother-in-law.

Valeria was stunning. Frail and tanned with strong cheekbones and wavy chestnut brown hair. Mash looked a lot like her. She cried at the sight of him standing in her doorway, speaking her language with what I assumed ended with many emphases after each word. "Vita! Vita!" she shouted.

Thumping noises came from the top of the house. A cute middle-aged woman peeped around the wall and shouted more words in Italian. I stood patiently by the door, watching the two women pinch Mash's cheeks and chin and hug him. It was the first time I saw him cry. Which led to me shedding a few tears.

Shortly, they settled down and he reached for my hand. I joined him at his side as he introduced me as his wife. Valeria held her face then held mine. "Bambino," she said.

My eyes widened and I responded, "No bambino, no bambino." I shook my head side to side.

'Hell no I'm not ready for that. Should I be offended?'

Vita then stood next to her and eyed me from head to toe. My heart pounded literally being in Valeria's hands. The two spoke Italian to each other briefly, and I looked over to Mash for help.

He placed his arm around me and joined their conversation, then Valeria sweetly said, *"Figlia."* She and Vita hugged me, gave me an extra once over, then pulled me by my arms to the sofa. I didn't under-stand a word the three of them were saying, but I picked up on *tele-fono* when Vita started making phone calls.

Within the hour, the house was packed with cousins and uncles from all over Vomero. The news Maximus was home travelled quickly, and the news he married a cocoa colored American surprisingly went better than I expected. His family showed me love and made me feel welcome, speaking in very little English and forcing me to eat. Our union received the warmest reception as his family blasted music and cooked food way into the night.

The former Mrs. Sharper wouldn't allow us to stay in the hotel we reserved. She forced us to stay with her in Mash's old room, with the thin walls, full size bed and loose headboard. We laughed most of the night, trying to sneak in a quick one, eventually giving up and dozing off.

By morning the house was already filled with family. Some who spent the night because it was a special occasion, and others who wanted to get a jump on the festivities. It was a repeat of the previous day. Family all around. Music blasting. People dancing. Matriarchs cooking. Children running. Everyone singing.

Before the sun set in the evening, my new cousins drove us around the never-ending hills to a spot overlooking the city, and Mount Vesuvius in the distance. The buildings looked like they were stacked on top of one another, but the sight was one to behold.

Cousin Primo convinced us to check out a sports bar where he bragged to any and every one, his cousin was famous. I put on a brave face as I watched everyone, except me go berserk when a team scored a point in the soccer match on the television. The place rocked with stomping and cheering, celebrations and beer splashing, from the tall glasses being thrown around.

The family kept the same energy when we returned to the house with more food, music still blasting, and more blankets laid out for the night. Seeing Mash around his family was an image I would always remember. He came from beautiful, loving people who instilled their values in him somehow from a distance. It was a side of him I needed to see, to cancel any doubt he was the one for me.

In the middle of the night he woke me, nibbling on my face. "You picked the best place for our honeymoon. What made you decide to come here?"

"Ibiza would have been ideal, but I know we're going back there this summer. And I wanted to meet your mom. Plus, I didn't want to go anywhere tropical."

"Why not?"

"Because I've been too embarrassed to tell you, I fall into the stereotype when it comes to water," I mumbled beneath my pillow.

"We do have a coast and seas you know."

"I know, but you don't think of boats, and oceans when you think of Pompeii. You think of the volcano and landmarks."

"True, but what stereotype?"

"I can't swim. I've tried to learn, but I can't hold my breath long under water, and when I try to move in the water, I go nowhere. It's quite comical."

"I can teach you."

"I will frustrate you."

"No, you won't. It'll be the first thing I teach you. The second will be how to make a proper mix."

"My mixes are fine."

"Remember I've seen your playlists." He joked and tapped my nose.

I squeezed his in return. We wrestled and giggled then he pressured me into taking a lesson from him. "I'll give it one lesson. But I'm telling you I'm pretty bad." I warned him.

"I love a challenge. I'll have you swimming like a fish by the end of the summer."

"God, you're confident. Go back to sleep."

"I had something else on my mind." He placed my hand on his wood.

"The walls are too thin," I whispered. "You know someone will hear us."

I rubbed his cock regardless of my excuse, breaking him free from his boxers. He tasted my lips. "I don't care. I want you now."

"I hate saying no to you." I sighed.

"Then don't."

I slipped under the covers and kissed him softly on the tip of his head, then slicked him with strong pulls from my throat to my lips. My plan was to suck him off quietly, so the family wouldn't hear the headboard knock against the wall, or squeaks from the bed as I was being pillaged. But my performance was stellar, and Mash's delight was far from quiet.

I rose from below and looked at him with a smile and shrugged my shoulders, then placed my finger over his lips. He flipped me over to the edge of the bed, then pulled me to my feet. I dropped to my knees for a second taste of him, gliding my hands against his abs, and looking him directly in his eyes. The taste of salt tinged my tongue. I froze and grinned at him.

He lifted me from the floor and bent me over facing the wall, boisterous in his delight, unconcerned with the listening ears. I restrained vocally, whimpering as low as possible, until the painful pleasure overpowered me. A gleeful sigh escaped when our skin slapped in rhythm as my husband placed one hand around my neck, bringing me closer to his body with a light choke to hold me in place. He grunted uncontrollably into my back, surely waking the house.

The next morning, I went into the kitchen, greeted with snickers from the aunts and my mother-in-law. It was obvious they heard us.

"What a beautiful glow you have this morning," said one of them in English, and the rest chuckled at my expense.

"It must be the water here," I replied.

"Mm hmm," said Valeria.

Italian words circled the room with giggles between them, *bambino* and *presto* frequently in their exchange. I smiled to let them know, I knew they were going in on me, then Mash and I left for a day out to ourselves.

Traffic was heavy on the short drive to Pompeii, but the scenic route made it worthwhile during the stall. The buildings along the route were picturesque, and the mosaics the first I had ever seen.

The closer we were to the city, we withdrew from our original plans of visiting the ruins, and roamed the streets instead. The highlight of the day was finally tasting what I heard was the best pizza in the world. I wasn't lied to. It was *magnifico*. I moaned with every bite, and didn't speak until I met the owner. After explaining how far I travelled to taste his heavenly pie, and commending him on its supreme flavor, he whispered his secret in my ear. *L'acqua naturale.*

Before returning to a house full of family, we strolled down the cobblestoned streets in the neighborhood, enjoying the starry night sky, searching for zodiac signs and visible planets. We picked up cartons of gelato for the little ones, and spent our final night with family trading stories— Mash translating for me, and eating until our bellies nearly burst.

The night ended with a surprise from Valeria. In front of the entire family, she placed a ring in Mash's hand. He translated her wish was for him to place her mother's ring on my finger, and made me promise to continue the tradition. I repeated, *"Lo prometto,"* and the family cheered as Mash slid it in place.

The house remained filled with Pasini's for a final night, but it didn't stop us from repeating last night's activities— most likely being cheered on from every room in the house.

The next morning, we returned to business as usual, departing for Copenhagen. A one night stop, for a show I was not looking forward to attending. The name Harv Legend spilled from his lips as the headliner, and I laid low the moment we checked into the hotel.

Travel had gotten the best of me, so lounging in the room while Mash went to work wasn't a bad idea. Missing out on the famous crepe station, museums, and favorite spots Mash raved about, had to wait for a future visit. I was spent, leaving my bag packed due to our early departure merely hours away.

Mash arrived some time over in the night, lying next to me fully clothed. The alarm sounded and the in and out trip ended just as it began. The fact I didn't hear him when he arrived was telling of my exhaustion level.

To perk us up for the trip home, he stood in line at the bistro, fetching us coffee and scones, while I settled the bill at the desk. I reached for the receipt from the clerk and a hand snatched it away from my grasp.

"So, we meet again. I thought you were long gone back to America." Harv Legend grinned on the side of his mouth, continuing to be persistently annoying.

"Hello again. I hear you had an amazing show last night. Congrats. Now if you'll excuse me." I turned back to the clerk.

"How do you know we had a good show?"

"My husband told me."

"Husband? You and Mash?"

"Yes. Now if you'll excuse me."

"Queens belong with Kings." He grabbed my hand.

"Don't do that." I jerked away.

Folding the receipt in half, he toyed with me. Presenting and taking it away. I huffed in frustration, then he finally handed it to me. "Mash is cool, but he doesn't know what to do with a Queen like you."

I reached for the paper, and he held it tightly in his grip before letting it go. "And here I thought I got lucky running into you. Remember what I said." He rubbed my shoulder.

I maneuvered backwards, not knowing what to say or do as Mash appeared behind him. He reached forward and slapped his hand from my shoulder. "Harv, I thought we already went through this."

Harv's eyes grew big from the shock of Mash's actions. Stunned, he stared at Mash with a dumb look on his face, then attempted to deflect his wrongdoing. "I hear congratulations are in order. Seems like you would have mentioned that last night. But then again." He scoffed. "You two be easy."

'What does that mean?'

"Don't disrespect my wife again."

"Calm down big *mon. You no wan it wit a real bad mon,*" Harv jargoned.

"Let's just go," I said.

"Grimey fuck!" Mash groaned, and stood in front of me, protecting me by using his arm as a barrier.

"Oh you're a tough guy now?"

"I think you want to see if I'm a tough guy." Mash balled his fists.

"People are staring at us. Let's go. Please," I pled, pulling him away.

The matter wasn't discussed right away. Through checkpoint, the skywalk, and boarding, we avoided conversing with one another. I couldn't find the right words to say, and he wasn't in the right headspace to hear me. We were miles in the air before our eyes locked, and the silence was broken.

"Thank you for standing up for me." I leaned into him.

"I did what I was supposed to do." He kissed my forehead.

"I'm sorry that happened. I tried to handle it."

"Don't apologize for him. He was being a total wanker."

"You know you said were jealous, but you also have a bit of a temper. Promise me, you won't get into any trouble." I held onto his forearm.

"Don't worry. Everything will be fine."

But I was worried. Not because I was naïve, or believed life was a fairytale, though mine had been lately. I was worried if I had gotten out of my way, and gotten into his.

Upon exiting the airport, a massive number of alerts buzzed his phone. His demeanor worsened minute by minute, so I kept quiet as he fumed. We sat in the lot for at least half an hour as he rigorously texted, and stared off into space. '*How could I not be worried?*'

Eventually, he cranked the car and sat with a grimaced face. I was afraid to ask if everything was indeed fine. I sat quietly and uncomfortable on the ride home, waiting for him to offer some sort of an explanation. He didn't.

As the day grew sour by the hour, rest and relaxation seemed ideal once we made it home. Thanks to the constant turn of events, it was hard to wind down, and I found myself doing what I always did whenever anxiety found its way into my space— I cooked like a madman and cleaned like a janitorial service.

I turned the rotting bananas into a banana nut loaf, and opened cans of tomatoes and added herbs and spices until the delightful smell of chili filled the house.

I unpacked, did a few loads of laundry, food prepped for the week, shampooed my hair and dusted around the house with the conditioner dripping, and changed the linens.

Mash had been on his phone since we returned, blowing on smoke out by the pool. He suddenly called for me. "Put on your bathing suit!"

I ignored him.

Moments later he shouted, "Let's go!" His calls went unanswered. He came inside and cornered me with red eyes, and a goofy smirk—high as a kite, feeling good no doubt. "Outside now."

He wouldn't take no for an answer, so I gave him my word I would be out in five minutes. I dressed in my suit, and grabbed towels for the both of us. Standing near the sliding door, I overheard him on a call with a gentleman constantly repeating, "We've got to fix this. We've got to fix this!"

"She's my wife. Cancel all future shows with him." I heard him say.

My worst fear had come true. My being in his life was creating chaos. I gripped the door handle, frozen in time, listening to the conversation while my mind got the best of me.

"I'm sure if he knew she was your wife he would have never disrespected you," said the male voice from the speaker.

"He was out of line. On the contrary, he knew she was with me."

"And what are you doing getting married? It goes against the image we've worked so hard to give you."

"What are you saying?"

"Your brand is at risk if word gets out you have a wife. Girls see you as the hot deejay they want to spend a night with, and the shows sell based on that fantasy. Women are 70% of your audience and fan base."

"Wow, Davie. And here I was thinking it was my mixes and musical talent drawing in the crowds."

"You and I both know this business is about more than talent. And you are talented kid, but this is the world we live in. You've got to work with me here. Do me a favor and keep the news of your nuptials quiet for now. I'll be in touch in a few days with word on how we are going to spin this."

The door jolted and I was busted standing there. There was no need to pretend I wasn't eavesdropping, so I confessed, "I heard every word. I'm sorry you're going through all of this because of me. I haven't told anyone we eloped yet, so the secret is safe with me."

The goofy look had disappeared from his face. It was now blank, and I didn't know how to read him.

"You're not a secret," he said.

'That's good to know.'

"Let's do this another day. I'm not in the mood to learn tonight."

"No. We're doing it now."

"Has anyone ever told you, you were bossy?" I playfully asked.

He lifted me in his arms and threw me in the shallow side. I stood up in the water and he jumped in beside me, "You're the first to tell me that. Now do as I say." I looked at him like he was crazy and we laughed. "In all seriousness, show me what you can do," he said in a sweeter tone.

Embarrassing myself, I went under and did the moves as I always had, then returned to the surface. It was laughable, but he didn't make fun of me. Instead he put his arms around me and said, "You're going to do just fine. Lesson one, go under again and open your eyes this time."

"No. It stings. I need goggles."

"Get comfortable not having them. Take your time. We've got all night."

I went under countless times, but never opened my eyes. I waited for him to grow impatient with me, but he didn't, which I found frustrating. Again and again I buried my head, insisting we give up, but he wouldn't allow it.

My frustration soon turned into anger, then finally I did it. We stared at each other for a brief moment beneath the surface, then he smiled at me. I rose to the top, wiped my eyes and pushed my hair back. My patient instructor swam to me and gave me a kiss, proud of my effort, not giving a damn about the chaos going on outside of our house.

The following afternoon we were back at it. I was told to get comfortable with my opening my eyes in the water, before learning how to properly hold my breath below. Up and down he moved my head with a three count, relentless with his method. *'God he will not let up.'*

One hour— every day— I had a lesson. Kicks, strokes, and breathing techniques. By the end of the week I was floating on my back and swimming a small distance. It was a small victory for him, but a huge one for myself.

I was instructed to stay out of the pool, while he fulfilled his contractual obligations over the weekend with Harv Legend. The ink was barely dry of making our marriage legal, and we were already in the midst of our first hurdle— because of me.

His career and brand was facing ruin, he was now at odds with a longtime colleague, disputing with his management, and having to lie about his personal life. I couldn't help but feel responsible. My compromise to abandon my home seemed trivial, compared to what he was facing, and I was the common denominator of these newfound problems.

To ease my sorrows, I opened a bottle of wine to keep me company for the evening, ending in a drunken stupor. Mash called after sound check, sharing the details of his meeting with his PR team and Davie, his manager, "I'm not on board with the way they want to spin. They want me to deny I'm married in interviews, and stage photos eluding I'm dating around." He seethed.

He sounded terribly flustered, and I wasn't in the right frame of mind to pacify his frustration. Primarily because I blamed myself.

"I was thinking, maybe I should leave. Not because I want to, but because it's the right thing to do. Let's face it, you wouldn't be in this mess if it weren't for me."

"Rubbish. How much have you had?" He laughed.

"I'm almost done with this bottle, but I'm speaking facts. Your life can go back to normal if I wasn't here." I rambled.

"I told you not to worry. I'm taking care of it." He exhaled deeply. "You should have been here with me. I'd be all over you right now. Show me something to hold me over."

I flashed my breast and screamed of embarrassment. Mash blushed and grinned, promising he'd be home as soon as the final show closed, while I promised to sleep off the tipsiness.

It pained me to be the root cause of his drama. My feelings were being spared, but the truth was the truth. The last thing I wanted was to be his downfall, and when the alcohol wore off in the morning, I opened my notebook and wrote a pro and con list of our relationship.

I was halfway down the page when I received a notification on my phone. I took a pause and learned I had a new follower on social media, a few direct messages, and one missed call from Khai. I sent her a message that I would call her later, then checked my social account.

"Son of a bitch!" I shouted. My new follower turned out to be Harv Legend, and the direct messages were from him, along with a photo of a woman and Mash in what perceived to be a deep conversation.

My chest felt as though it could cave in. My head felt a sharp pain from the back that pierced like a yo-yo, and I threw my phone to the opposite side of the bed.

Wanting to look at the pictures again, but knowing I shouldn't. I jumped up and painted the floor with my slippers, dragging my feet while coming up with an explanation of what I saw to soothe my soul. I looked out of the window, then caught a glimpse of myself in the glass. It was as if outside mimicked how I felt inside, as the rain depicted tears on my face before they fell. *'This can't be happening.'*

The first tear fell and I dialed Mash. No answer. I tried a second time. No answer. I needed to hear him say nothing happened last night, or the picture was taken before we met, or the photo was staged, and he had no choice but to go along with his manager's ridiculous plan this one time. Anything. I needed to hear his voice give me a reasonable explanation to make my rage go away.

After he didn't answer the third time, a million worse case scenarios plagued my thoughts. I went back to the photograph and examined it. The malicious Harv Legend uprooted my world with this image. I enlarged it looking for the wedding band, the hotel name in the background, or a logo of some sort. Finally, I caved and read the message attached:

> *From what I saw tonight you are fair game.*
> *I told you Queens belong with Kings*
> *@ me.*

Immediately I thought of what he said that morning he and Mash squared up. "Seems like you would have mentioned that last night. But then again..."

'*What did he mean then, and what did he mean now?*'

The longer I didn't hear from Mash, the more enraged I became. My thoughts got the best of me as I waited for my phone to ring. Harv ran a brilliant number on me. Since I had time to think, I realized I was caught in a trap.

If I mentioned the photo to Mash and who sent it to me, he would most likely lose his temper, and only God knows what would happen— but I would be at fault for telling him. If I waited to show him the messages when he got home, I would be blamed for not telling him right away. It was the typical conundrum for a woman— always holding the blame no matter what.

Within seconds, I skipped being mad, jumped over angry, bypassed rage, and embraced crazy. The drama, questionable deceit, and humiliation was too much for me to handle, on top of already feeling like the catalyst of a potential downfall. And the fact that I failed to reach my husband after three attempts. Multiple scenarios ran through my mind:

'*Is he with her right now?*
Is that why he didn't answer my call?
Why the fuck would he play me like this?
Is this a staged photo his PR put together?
How can a person make you feel so loved,
and betray you at the same time?
It doesn't make sense.
What are my friends going to think?
God I look stupid. Again! I know he loves me.
He treats me like any woman
would dream of being treated.
Will I ever know the truth? I trusted him.
What the fuck is going on!'

Then it hit me. I had seen the girl in the photo before. I ran to the bedroom and flipped through his albums until I searched the right one. It was the memory book with the pretty models and famous people. There she was. Smiling in at least ten or more pictures with him.

I threw the album across the room, breathing heavily like a monster. Unable to calm down, I went into the kitchen and threw myself into some serious cooking and baking. My go to when I'm stressed.

I baked and prepared casserole dishes, two flavors of cookie dough, eating the chocolate chip dough raw. I baked a sourdough loaf and sautéed peppers and onions to dress up a sandwich. I stood against the island and took a bite, bursting into tears, spitting the perfectly dressed hoagie on the floor to catch my breath.

I wasn't this woman. I didn't want to be this woman. I didn't like this woman, as I had already been her years before. The fairytale was over, and I was tired and defeated. I dumped on myself for abandoning my okay life, for what I thought was a better one, and could no longer fight the inevitable.

I packed what I could in two suitcases, and framed a picture of us in Italy, I had stuck in the crevice of the mirror on the dresser. I placed it in the center of the pool table in the dining room, and said good-bye to the house I thought was going to be my home. The taxi called for entry through the gate, and I lugged my bags outside and set the alarm. As the driver drove me away, a song I used to know so well came on the radio, and I sang along to it in my head. *'Good morning heartache, what's new.'*

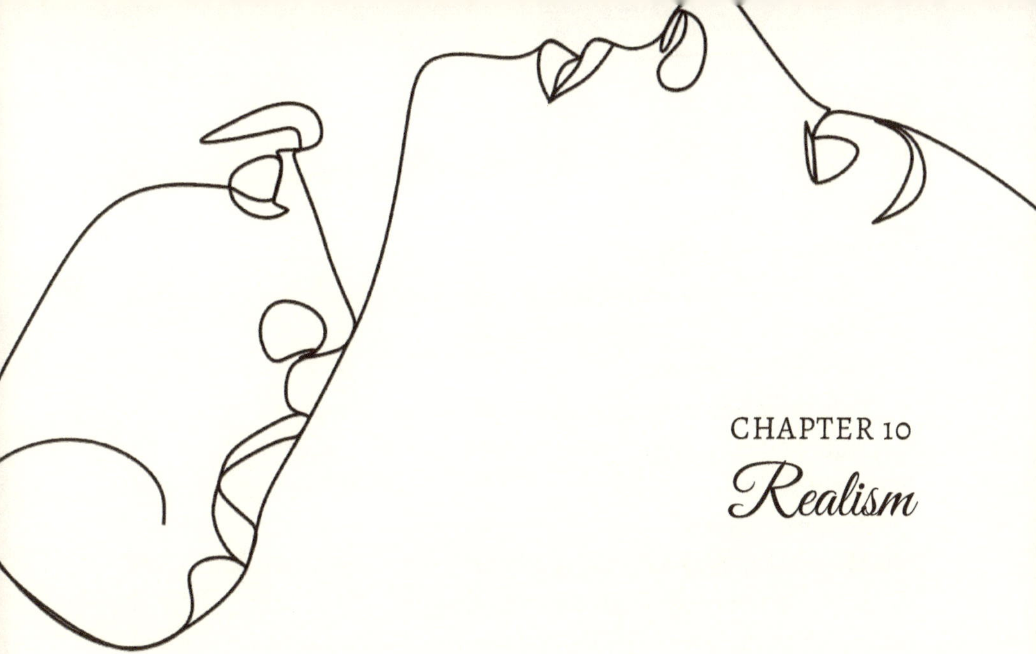

CHAPTER 10

Realism

The credit from my cancelled flight months ago came in handy. I caught the next flight into the States, Denver, then waited two hours for a layover to GSP. I silenced my phone for a "peace" of mind and roamed the airport, searching for the apocalyptic art people raved about. Creepy as fuck. Fires, coffins, and weird looking children of the corn figures.

I love art but the one mural I found was made of nightmares. I went back to my gate, beyond happy to get the hell out of Satan's airport.

The real home of home. Mama's house. My voice of reason. I don't think she's ever hugged me so tight, or so long. To be in her embrace soothed my bleeding soul, and just like that I felt like a little girl again. Her house wasn't the house I grew up in, but the scent of it was the same. A blend of roasted coffee and baked goods lived inside the walls, with a hint of bleach and ammonia in the air.

We sat in the kitchen playing catch up, waiting for the timer to ding, to take her sweet bread out of the oven. I turned my phone on to show her pictures of my travels with continuous interruptions of texts, calls, and voice messages.

"Something seems important. You ought to get that," she said.

"It can wait. I wanted to show you one picture in particular."

"Oh my. Weren't you a smashing bride." Ma held her chest. "When was this?"

"About a month ago."

"When do I get to meet my new son? Is this what you came home to tell me?"

"Sort of?" I fidgeted.

"Well you don't need my approval because it's already done. And you know I was going to tell you, you looked beautiful as ever. So, what is it?"

"I think it's over."

My mother laughed deep from her belly. The timer dinged and she removed the bread from the oven and placed it on top of a towel, on top of the toaster. Sighing and making comical noises she asked, "Over. Why?"

"It's a long story."

"It always is." She scoffed.

"And before you say it, I know marriage takes work but...We've hit a huge bump in the road."

"Is it that bad? Because honey to be honest, you look happy to me."

"I was happy, but I don't think I'm going back."

"What do you mean was? I know the look of love when I see it. Especially on my baby."

The phone rang again. "Is that him?" Ma asked.

I nodded yes, unable to survive her stare.

"Talk to him," she said.

"I need more time."

"Okay Ms. Need More Time. Some other woman is going to take your time."

"One already has. I think."

"Start from the beginning."

Mom listened to my dilemma, and shared a story with me about perspective and perception. She went on to tell me that sometimes things aren't what they seem, and without me hearing what Mash had to say, I was making a mistake. "A picture is worth a thousand words," she said. "People don't always have good intentions. Are you going to allow the person who sent you that photo, to control your happiness?"

After making her point, she finished schooling me by saying as long as I knew the truth about the fake pictures, other people's insight shouldn't matter. "People are going to think whatever they want to think anyway, and in a marriage, communication can make it or break it," she said, handing me a slice of the warm bread.

I sat on the stool nearly healed from the taste of my mother's cooking, ready to hear my husband's explanation. I returned his call and he answered on the first ring, looking at me through the glass with seething eyes in utter silence. "Hey," I mumbled.

He took a few seconds to respond. "What the fuck babe, I've been calling you all day."

I was shocked by his callous tone and word choice. "I turned off my ringer. I needed to figure some things out."

We sat in silence, waiting for the other to speak. "Why did you leave?" he asked, in a softer tone than before. "Where are you and when are you coming home?"

"At my mother's house, and I don't know the answer to that question."

"You have no idea how I'm feeling right now. I rushed home to be with you, and find you've left me. And for what?"

"For starters, I don't want you to resent me. I don't want to be the reason you lose everything you've worked for."

"I would never resent you. I told you to let me worry about work. Come home."

My heart rate increased and my palms began to sweat. There wasn't an easy way to ask him about the picture. I blurted out, "Did anything happen this weekend? Something I should hear from you and no one else."

"I have no idea what you're talking about."

"Check your phone. I sent you something."

We stared at each other through our screens, waiting for the message to transmit. "Bloody hell. Where did you get this?" he asked.

"Harv sent it to me."

"Bollocks! That barmy maggot! Is this why you left?"

"Who is she?" I demanded.

"No one. Nadia, I don't know what else to do to show you I love you."

"I know you love me."

"Then why are you giving up on us so easily? I promise you. It's nothing. I will explain everything to you. But I want to do it in person. I need you to know I would never do anything to hurt you."

Having to wait for him to explain the image infuriated me. I didn't need an answer in person. I just needed clarity. My hesitation to answer his question bothered him, so he asked it again.

"You know I would never hurt you, right?"

I huffed and scowled at him. "That's what makes this so hard. I believe you. It's a lot to take in, but I believe you. What confuses me is the picture, and the things Harv says. In Copenhagen, he made that remark about you, and now he's saying from what he saw I'm now fair game? All of this code language makes me wonder what is he not saying."

"He's being a dick. I'll take care of him. You, take some time. You did say you were homesick, so do whatever it is you need to do, and I'll tell you everything when you get back. You still love me?"

"I wouldn't be hurt if I didn't love you."

The pain in my chest didn't leave after we spoke. It felt like a wrecking ball knocked the wind out of me, and left a huge dent in between my breasts. I was more confused than when I left, and tossed all night with a cloudy mind. I beat the sun and my mother up, and suggested we drive to Goose Creek to pay my Grams a visit.

Mom skimmed through my phone, admiring the photos of my travels while I sped down the highway, arriving at the retirement village in record time.

After two and a half hours of listening to the oldies at the crack of dawn, we signed our names in the record book, and I powerwalked to my grandmother's room. Seeing her never failed to brighten my day, and I was long overdue for one of her hugs.

I peeped my head into her room. She sat in her rocking chair, dressed comfortably in a blush sweat suit with her long, silver silky hair pulled behind her ears, and braided to the side. I was jealous my hair never grew as long as hers, but I did inherit her texture and wave pattern, which made up for what I lacked. "There is my pretty lady?" I said, entering her room.

She turned to her side and looked at me, fanning her hand and turning up her top lip. "Well, gal why didn't you tell me you were coming? It's been a long time." She kissed my cheeks. "You still got a little sugar in there."

"You know I love surprising you," I said, kissing her forehead.

I held onto her tightly, smelling her perfume from the 1950's mixed with mink oil, and dove soap. She patted me on the shoulder. "Yes, you sure do. You look good gal. Skin so plump and smooth."

"I am the chocolate version of you."

"Which is even better. Less wrinkles when you get old."

Ma finally arrived in the room. "Leave some hugs for me." Grams turned towards her and gave mom her cheek.

"Oh, I got both of you today. Is the good-looking boy with you, too?"

"Momma behave."

"You know I will do no such thing."

I told her I came alone and she asked to see another picture of Mash. I pulled up some of our travel photos, and showed her how to swipe left and right. "This sure is from the future." She scoffed, then arrived to the one of us in Barcelona. "Nadia, you are every bit of me I tell you what. I would've married him too if it was safe back in my day. My baby girl snagged her a husband. Such a handsome boy. Grams can dig it."

"Momma." My mother ridiculed.

"What *chile*? You are always cramping my style. You know that's why I won't come live with her. I'd never get to see my boyfriends if I moved in her jailhouse."

"Did you say boyfriends with an s?" I asked.

"You heard me right. I have one on every hall in here."

"How is that possible?" my mother asked.

"Easy. One is a night hawk, one is in a wheelchair, and the other one can't half see."

"I've missed you so so much Grams?" I curled over in laughter.

"If they have men my age over there who look like him, I'll move in with you baby girl. Book my ticket tonight."

"Momma please. You aren't moving anywhere."

"You hear the sheriff talkin' right?" Grams joked.

"Okay I'm ringing the bell. You two always go at it. How have you been doing?"

"Really good today, but I have my days, arthritis and all."

"You feel like getting out of here today?" I asked.

"Hell yeah, if you're not too tired. I want to see the water. I can smell it for God's sake, so I'd like to see it."

"Let's go."

On our way to the beach, I noticed The Creek had been updated since my last visit. I remembered it as nine busy streets surrounded by green landscape and moss trees. Now mom and pop businesses and shopping plazas stood in lots that were once flat grassed terrain. The amount of street lights doubled if not tripled, and the population and diversity was significantly diverse.

In less than an hour, Grams removed her shoes and walked bare feet in the sand until she reached the water. She looked like a young woman as she played footsie with the waves and dusting off seashells. I could tell from her smile she was reminiscing of old times, and mom and I watched her become one with the sand as the grains sifted between her toes.

I joined her in the water, while Mom stood in line at the booth for chair rentals. Grams and I were in sync, and she hurried in one of our special talks for the few moments we had alone.

"My gal went and got married on me," she said.

"Are you mad finding out this way?"

"Not at all. All I care about is you being happy. Are you happy?"

"That's a complicated answer Grams. I love him."

"Hell, I would love him, too. But happiness is what I want for you."

"I'm happy, we just have a few wrinkles that need ironing."

"I'm sure you'll tell me all about it when you're ready. Just remember. You ain't nobody's fool. If you can't get the wrinkles out, get a new shirt. Uh oh, here comes the warden."

Listening to the waves roar a few feet away, we stretched beneath three rented beach chairs and umbrellas. Basking in the breeze with worthy conversation between three generations for hours, I forgot about my dilemma for a short while. My mind needed that break, and my soul needed what my grandmother had always given me—strength.

Once the sun set, we grabbed a quick bite to eat, and said goodbye to Grams. We headed back upstate where I spent a few more days with my mother, then I returned to Charlotte, to the abandoned place I called my own.

Khai had done a great job taking care of my plants. I did a thorough walkthrough, dusting what needed to be dusted, changed the linens to fresh washed sheets, tossed the spoiled milk from the fridge, sorted my mail, and settled in. I pulled out my laptop and stared at a blank page, not knowing where to begin, and realizing I had nothing to come back to.

Before the five o'clock traffic began, I surprised Khai at work. Popping my head in her office I teased. "They said the weed man is in here."

"Oh my God! What are you doing here?! Is this why you didn't call me back?!" She hugged me.

'Oops I forgot to return her missed call the day the chaos erupted.'

"This trip was a spur of the moment thing," I said.

"Is Mash with you?"

"No, he had to work." I sort of lied.

"So we can get some girl time in?"

"Yes. I'm in desperate need."

We met the girls at one of the better, and upscale clubs in the city for happy hour. While we waited, Khai ordered appetizers and the first round of drinks, filling me in on what her phone call was about.

Taylor and Levi were having marital problems, but no one knew the reason why, and her father-in-law moved in with her family, so she's been using my house as an escape. Before she finished telling me about the strain it has put on her marriage, Shannon arrived.

"What's up Grandma Klump? You remembered us little people!"

I stood to hug her as Isla waved her hand and spoke in a fake

British accent, "Lady Nadia has decided to grace us with her presence. To what do we owe the pleasure?"

"It's good to see you too, Isla." I scowled.

We air kissed cheek to cheek as Taylor surprised me from behind. "You finally came home," she said, squeezing my shoulders.

"It took me a minute, but I finally made it. Now give me all the tea."

Shannon lit up like a light bulb, describing her latest boy toy while Isla kept the details of her mystery man secret.

"How are you and Levi doing?" I asked Taylor.

She moaned something jumbly under her breath and deflected. "How is London?"

"I don't know. It was great at first, but now...I have a lot of decisions to make."

"Would these decisions have to do with you getting married and not telling us." Taylor snitched.

"How did you know?"

"We all know. Mash told Levi, and Levi swore me to secrecy, but you know I had to tell the girls."

"I wanted to tell y'all in person, and show you the ring his mother passed down to me. You want to see pictures?"

They passed my phone around and swiped while I gave them the details of Barcelona and how Mash proposed, how beautiful Italy was, and how I made my head wrap for our ceremony.

"Look at you with those flowers in your hair. Levi and I should have done this. Simple, intimate and romantic," said Taylor.

"Your wedding was beautiful Tay." Everyone at the table synchronized to pacify her.

"Humph." She scoffed.

Khai gave me the side eye. She spoke of marital problems between Taylor and Levi, and it was clear something was going on there.

Taking the negative light off of Taylor, I mentioned Mash's management wants us to keep the marriage a secret— curious to see how they would respond, and who would agree with me.

"I say go along with the lie," said Taylor. "His image is his livelihood, and from what I saw, it's worth it to lie."

"Sorry, but I would want everyone to know I'm the wife," said Isla.

"What does Mash have to say about all of this?" Khai asked.

"He says I'm not a secret and not to worry. But I feel like I'm in his way."

"Did he say that?" Shannon frowned at me.

"No."

"Then stop doing the Nadia thing and jumping to conclusions." Shannon offered.

"The Nadia thing?"

"You know what you do," they said in unison.

I clutched my fake pearls at their synchronized depiction of me. Once again, I was the butt of the joke, but it was fine. We laughed as if nothing had changed over the months I was away, but something had. Me.

I couldn't bring myself to show them the picture, or tell them the full story of my dealings across the ocean. The old me would have blabbed every detail, but the new me chose to be happy in the moment, and to keep some things to herself.

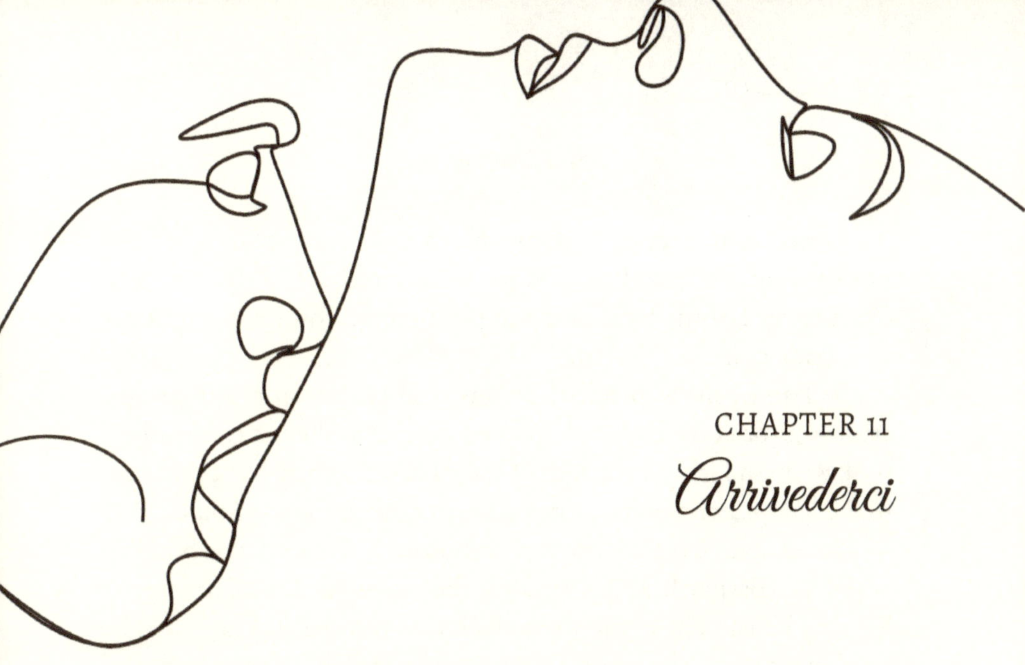

CHAPTER 11

Arrivederci

Now what? I was no longer homesick. Mom was doing fine without me, my friends were carrying on, and our reunion was just like old times.

A night of embarrassing photos and laughs, relieved me from my racing thoughts. But now it was morning, and with it came a hangover from hell, loneliness, and the constant question burdening my brain. *'What should I do?'*

I was lying on my favorite high thread count sheets with one eye open, and the other closed like Uncle Fester, when the doorbell rang. I robed and opened the door, greeted to orchids at my feet. I shouted to the delivery man, "Wait! I'll get you a tip!"

He replied, "No need! It's already been taken care of! Thanks!"

The card read:

Counting the days ~ Love Mash

I grabbed a juice and a stale bagel from the fridge, toasted it, took a bite, and threw it in the garbage. Above the trash can was my calendar with a red circle on today's date, which meant there was a group meeting tonight. I searched for something else to snack on, but only found crackers, took them with me upstairs, and texted Mash.

N: *I love you, too.*

I reacquainted myself with my sheets, and slept until hunger woke me a few hours later. I dressed for what remained of the day, then drove to my favorite mom and pop pizza shop across town to give my taste buds a pinch of heaven.

Bell and banana peppers, onions, and cheese on a soft doughy crust— just as I remembered. I closed my eyes as the taste soothed my soul, when suddenly, I thought of Italy. I couldn't help but compare it to the best pizza I ever had, forcing me to smile at the good times.

Bored and avoiding my lonely house, I drove to the building where Dr. Bartley held her sessions, then kept on driving arriving at Taylor's house. The tension was thick between she and Levi, a knife wouldn't suffice. She begged me to stay longer than I intended, and when I finally broke free I thought of a saying Grams used to teach me. *'If God took all the problems and threw them in the air, everyone would grab their own.'*

She was absolutely right. Feeling their vibe propelled me to reach out to London. I was ready to hear his explanation and make a decision. But just like the day I left, no answer.

The next morning, I shopped for grocery and prepared my homemade salsa and guac for bowling night. Another fun night out with my friends, was better than sitting alone in the house thinking about my problems, and why I hadn't heard from my husband.

The crowd at the alley was mixed with newcomers and old faces. Some I recognized from the wedding, and others I couldn't place. The groomsman I danced with at the reception served as a buffer and made a joke at my expense.

"Hey Mrs. Copperfield," he said. "One minute I saw you in London, then the next minute you vanished."

"Sounds like me. Drew, right? Levi's college buddy?"

"Yeah. I asked about you a few times, but Levi said I moved too slow. He said you stayed over there and got married?"

"I did."

"Was it the guy you were dancing with?"

"You saw us?"

"Everyone did."

I smiled, remembering Khai said the exact same thing to me.

"Time to whoop ass!" Brian, Khai's husband yelled.

"Congratulations, and good luck tonight." Drew winked his eye at me as he walked off.

"Your team is the one who needs it." I snapped my fingers.

We separated into teams and began the competition, Mars versus Venus. Alcohol always led to a night of laughs and an occasional altercation. Towards the end of the first round, the women were leading on the scoreboard, and the men were losing gracefully.

It was a drama free night, and after we took round one we huddled for some girl talk, while the losers stormed the bar to buy the second-round drinks.

"Someone told me when you get married, you become more desirable. Is that true Nadia?" Shannon asked.

"I would say yes."

"Me, too," Khai added. "I've had men come out of the woodworks, but the gag is those men wouldn't marry a soul. They just want to fuck you and send you back home."

"Khai you cursed!" We gasped.

"Well it's true."

"Women are no different. They want to sleep with your man just so they can stare you down and throw it in your face," Shannon added.

"You would know." Isla teased.

Shannon invaded Isla's personal space and danced in a raunchy manner. The two playfully tussled, entertaining us until Taylor interrupted. "Why are we talking about this?"

We looked to one another, realizing we were close to getting answers of what was going on in her house. Khai changed the subject. "I heard Isla went hummus shopping."

Isla hid her face and blushed, then looked at me. "I don't know how you do it. We had nothing in common."

"You have to get the right one." I bragged.

"By the way, our friends want us to fix whatever is going on between us. Are we good?" Isla tested me.

"We're good." I held out my hand to shake for a truce.

"Ladies, get your pretty asses up! We are about to redeem ourselves!" Levi announced.

Team Venus went toe to toe with Team Mars throwing strikes, turkeys, trash talking, and celebrating with in-your-face choreographed routines. The men drank so much beer, we thought we had an edge on them until the final frame, where we lost by a gutter ball from our weakest link.

The night was young and the party continued at Khai's house. Brian cranked up the grill, Khai brought games outside near the pool, and Shannon's new beau took charge of the music.

As I watched the couples interact, happily and miserably, I realized I was ready to go home, and not the one a few blocks over. The one on the cusp of daylight, with the man I wanted to be happy and miserable with. *'Guess I have made up my mind.'*

Stepping away from the party, I eased over by the fence for privacy and finally made contact with London. Something was off. I could hear it in his voice. He was vague and sounded on edge, which unnerved me. Our conversation was short, and it felt like I was talking to a stranger. Not one I love you at the end. I wondered if our time apart gave him clarity— I was indeed bringing him down, and with all of the awkward silence between us, I didn't mention I was ready to come home.

After my uninspiring phone call, I returned to the party to tell everyone I was going to call it a night. "Don't go," they all said, convincing me to stay a while longer.

Caving into their request, I hung around and pretended to be fine when I was losing it inside. I circled the yard one final time, making sure I spoke to everyone before I made my exit, then did the unthinkable. I removed my sandals and jumped in the pool.

"Somebody go in there and get her!"

"She doesn't know how to swim!"

I rose to the top.

"Yes I do!" I yelled.

Three seconds under, rise to the top. Three seconds under, rise to the top. I swam from one side to the other as my friends grew louder and louder, muffled under the water. I reached up for the edge and pulled myself to the surface.

Water dripped from my hair and into my eyes as I stood in the shallow, smiling from ear to ear clearing my face.

"So you're a show off now," the deep voice said.

I opened my eyes to a grinning Mash kneeling before me. "Hey you," I said, lifting myself higher to meet his lips as fast as I could. "What are you doing here?"

He pulled me out of the water. "I came to bring you home."

My soaked clothing dampened his as I pressed against him, locking my lips with his as if it were for the first time. Chatter in the background didn't break my concentration. I was in the arms of the one I wanted to be with, and didn't let go of his tongue until our hosts shouted, "Get a room!"

"Who knew he was coming here?" I asked.

"Just me," said Levi. "My wife can't keep a secret."

I gave him a fist motion.

"Levi, you said it was hot down here. You should have said boiling." Mash joked.

He removed his shirt and his shoes, picked me up, and I wrapped my legs around him. I hugged him tightly around his neck, and screamed as he leaped in the pool. My eyes closed when I felt the water on my feet, but I opened them once Mash pinched me, and kissed him underwater.

We rose from the deep end, my arms still around him, spinning and playing in the water, convincing the others to join us.

The night ended with a splash party, Mash and I abandoned before everyone else. I skipped the tour and led Mash to my bedroom. Our bedroom. I was in a rush to feel him inside me, but he took his time to give me what I wanted.

He shampooed my hair in the shower, building up the sensual stamina to come. I was in agony, yearning for our bodies to bond once more. He kissed me after every rinse, teasing me with finger play in between. I shuddered from the cold air blowing above, then warmed with heat when he tasted my quivering lips between my thighs.

I turned my back to him, but he had something else in mind. He lifted me between my legs and carried me to the bed. On my knees, I fell atop the satin spread, and he held me in place grazing my ass cheeks with his teeth.

He spread them apart and wet his fingers, massaging my forbidden with gentle, circular strokes. Screams of passion parted my lips as my face was buried, muffling my cry, until he lied me on my back.

I squirmed even though I hungered for him. "You remember how to take it. Look at me," he said, and submitted his plow. I clutched on to him as tight as I could, moaning and sighing in his ear. "Good girl. Oh, how I've missed your sugar." He dug deeper and faster.

Abruptly he positioned me on my side to the edge of the bed, digging in me sideways, yowling at the touch of a newfound corner as I switched between circular motions, and galloping charges from my throbbing womb. I spread my ass open so he could see his excavation, heightening his intensity. Barely keeping quiet he held onto my shoulders, and released his load while locked inside of me.

My drip held her grip while I waited for him to regain his strength, and release me from his hold. I clutched and vibrated on his wood, happy to have him where he belonged. I thought about when he said wherever we are together is home, and he was right. I belonged at his side, and he was home for me.

Lying next to me, he ran his hands through my hair then all over my body, studying my face while adorning me. "How do you feel?"

I panted. "Like all is right with the world."

"It is now. I missed you. I baked the cookies you left in the fridge, and it made me think of how you only eat the crispy ends and give me the middle, then I was reminded of how you don't eat the crispy end of cake. I can't make sense of it." He mocked.

"I know I'm quirky."

"Yes, you are. But I fell in love with quirky."

"I'm already lying here naked, you don't have to flatter me."

"I also fell in love with that swift tongue of yours."

"It's not the only thing you fell in love with."

He rolled me on top of him, sweeping my face, and reading my eyes. I played with the stubble on his chest searching for words, unaware I was putting him to sleep. He was tired and so was I, but I stayed awake until he drifted off, then laid my head on his shoulder, giving in to the night taking us under its spell.

In the morning, he told me he signed with new management, and we could move on from the nonsense. I spoke my truth and told him I didn't want to be kept a secret, and we agreed to move one from that narrative.

I waited for him to bring up the weekend in Cardiff. It was clear he was avoiding the subject when he mentioned how great my bed felt. It did sleep well, but it wasn't top grade like our bed in London. It cost significantly less, wasn't nearly as soft, and I personally upgraded his sheet thread count when I moved in.

I lifted from his chest and took it upon myself to bring up the matter. "Just tell me nothing happened so I can calm my mind."

"Nadia, nothing happened. Harv knows I despise her. He saw it as a way to get back at me. Reaching at its finest."

"I don't want to ever feel like that again. I drove myself crazy with theories. I needed to hear you say this is nothing. But then you didn't answer your phone, and I lost it. Deep down I know you wouldn't do anything to hurt me, but looking at that picture over and over gave me a little doubt."

He kissed my hands and stroked my hair. "The night of that picture, I told her I would file a restraining order if she came to any more of my shows."

"Who is she?"

"An old friend."

"And she was in Copenhagen, am I right?"

"Yes. But can we not talk about her?"

Normally, I would have badgered him and made him tell me everything I wanted to know, but I trusted my gut and left it alone. "I was thinking, since we're both here we might as well file for a marriage license, so I can change my last name before we go back."

"I love that idea Mrs. Sharper."

∽

The papers were filed and Maximus Sharper was properly introduced to his mother-in-law. Determined to have me wed in a traditional setting, we stood in church with her after Sunday service, and said our vows at the hands of her pastor.

Mash surprised me with a written vow, using the pro and con list of our relationship I wrote the night I was in distress. He said to the congregation, "I won't read everything on this paper, because I've crossed out the things that don't matter. My wife needed several reassurances of my love for her, and being the analytical person she is, she compiled a list I found. I've walked around with it in my wallet for good luck ever since, and I want to let her know that her list is also my list. My wife Nadia— She makes me happy. I have grown as a person because of her, and having her in my life has changed me for the better. And I love her. I love her. I love her. She also wrote I taught her how to swim, but I would like to add, she taught me what happiness is."

My mother's pastor didn't get a chance to say the words – *You may now kiss your bride.* Mash reeled me in and kissed me before the words left his mouth, becoming man and wife in front of family and friends, making it official on two continents.

Fear no longer controlled me. I was no longer afraid of change, and ready to live life abroad with a man who is incomparable, and worthy of me. Excitement filled me for our journey ahead, leaving my old life behind, and beginning a new chapter that felt promising in a foreign land. The place I now call home.

The List

Cons: ~~Interference with career, drama with colleagues, jealousy, financially challenged.~~

Pros: Makes me happy, changed for the better, grown as a person, sleep better next to him, taught me to swim, I love him, I love him, I love him.

Bonus Scene

Second Honeymoon

CHAPTER 12

Puerto Plata

Ｔhe Lyft dropped the newlyweds off in the loading zone of the airport. Maximus wheeled their bags inside to the check-in counter and stopped.

"Where to?" he asked.

Nadia nudged his shoulder. "What do you mean where to? Home, silly."

He kissed her forehead. "We just exchanged our vows, Luv. That calls for a second honeymoon. Pick a destination. Anywhere you want to go in the world."

Nadia backed away and smiled at the seriousness in his eyes. She looked at the board of flights, then back to him and scoffed.

"Puerto Plata," she blurted, calling his bluff.

Maximus questioned her assertiveness with a smile. "Done." He placed her hand in his, then led them to the ticket counter.

Ten minutes later they were seated in first class aboard a plane flying to Miami. They toured the airport, browsing books in a bookstore during a one-hour layover, then two hours later, the heat of Santo Domingo brought sweat beads across their foreheads.

～

The rocky turbulence from the flight was nothing compared to the leather gloved driver whipping and wheeling the shuttle van to the resort in Puerto Plata.

Nadia held onto the seat—and her husband—for dear life as the driver smiled and joked, leaning with every sharp turn with his eyes roaming from the sharp curves of the road. When they arrived at the resort, she dropped to her knees and missed kissing the ground by an eighth of an inch.

"Thank God! We made it!" she shouted.

Mash laughed at her theatrics. "I forgot this is your first time traveling to these parts. Most shuttle drivers handle the roads like that over here." He passed the driver a tip.

"How uppity would I sound if I said I want a car service to take us to the airport when it's time to leave?"

"What about a helicopter service?"

"Seriously?"

Mash chuckled. "We'll be fine."

The staff greeted them with mixed drinks topped with pineapples and cherries floating at the rim.

"Welcome to Lifestyles Holiday Resorts."

Nadia whispered to Mash, "Like the condoms?"

They snickered leaning against one another.

The hostess continued, "Mr. & Mrs. Sharper, our trusted associate Marco will drive you to your villa. Your welcome packet will be on the bar when you first enter your quarters. It has all of the information about our resort. And with your all-inclusive package, I am sure you know if we have it, it is yours." The hostess smiled. "We hope you enjoy your stay."

Marco and another attendant loaded their luggage into the back of an extended sized golf cart.

Mash tapped their chauffeur's shoulder. "Marco."

"Si. Si."

"I'm going to need you to take it easy on the road. Okay?"

A big smile grew on his lips as his head nodded continuously like a fluctuating stock market chart. "Si. Si."

Mash wrapped his arms around Nadia and held her tight along

the short drive. She nestled in his arms as the warm breeze and slow, scenic route brought her at ease.

They reached the villa half of a mile down the path. Mash helped Marco bring their bags inside, tipped him generously, then made his way over to his wife.

"Are you tired?" he asked, lifting her onto the kitchen counter.

"A little."

He lifted her t-shirt and kissed her neck as the cloth momentarily blinded her.

She sighed. "I see you aren't."

He grinned and covered her mouth with his, softly extracting her tongue with fond kisses he patiently waited to land over the course of the evening.

Her back melted in his hands and sunk into him. In between warm pecks on her brown skin he confessed.

"I wanted to fuck you on the plane, in the bathroom in Miami, and on the side of the road once we landed, but the opportunity never knocked."

"Trying to make me a member of the mile high club, I see." She ran her hands down the back of his neck. "I would have let you fuck me in all of those places if you had asked." She teased, spreading her arms wide and arching her back as she lowered the back of her head to the hard, white and grey, granite countertop beneath her.

Worked up from the anticipation of getting Nadia alone, Mash skipped the elongated foreplay and act of making her beg for him. He was desperately in need of her healing waters. Eager to reside in the warmth of her passion.

Moving with urgent desire, he pushed her skirt above her hips, pulled her panties off with a vigorous pull from the damp padded center before Nadia drenched them with the drip he wanted to coat him, and inserted two fingers between her slit.

"Drenched as always," he murmured, sliding her near the edge.

Nadia lifted her calves on his shoulders, smirking at his compliment.

He groaned, withdrawing the two fingers to fill her cup with his blessed appendage. Her favorite part of him aside from his giving lips and captivating brown eyes.

Sinking his teeth into his bottom lip from the sensation of her tender grip saturating his girth from his rigid insertion, he whispered, while gazing at her perfect body. "My wife. If I could bottle this feeling I would."

That quick feeling of her walls clenching around his dick whenever he entered her always made him lose his mind. Lose any sense of reason. For she would always be his reason for anything going forward.

Tugging on her outer thighs, he lowered his torso to kiss her mouth. "Mrs. Sharper," he sighed, tasting her lips once more before stroking deep, strong, and slow. "You never disappoint," he said to her, motioning his hips in circles, tattooing the tip of his widened head into her corners.

Nadia whined. The vibration of her moans drove him to propel deeper. He wound his hips, grinding in her flesh as her slick walls lubed his throbbing dick.

Her waistline thrusted forward, coordinating with his play by play until they both scored in her goal. He grunted alongside her screams of passion. Together succumbing to the height of lust, love, and existential bliss.

Huddled into each other's arms atop the counter, Mash joked. "Now that we've properly christened this place we should have a good time."

"How did you pull this together on a whim?"

"The new management team. Once you told me where you wanted to go, I messaged my new assistant, and she took care of everything during our flight. I'd say she passed the test. Wouldn't you agree?"

Nadia nudged her forehead against his shoulder. "Yes."

He leaned back and looked at her. "I've tired you. Let's go to bed."

He carried her into the bedroom. As his knees bent to lie her on the bed, Nadia hummed against his chest.

"Un uh. Shower first. I want to sleep on clean sheets and spend all day in bed with you tomorrow."

"You're the boss."

The sun shone for hours before Nadia caught a glimpse of the island's radiance. The sleeping beauty slept through the noise of pots clanking, spoons tapping bowls, cabinets opening and closing, and Mash sneaking kisses to her cheek to wake her.

Unable to sleep, he was awake when the personal chef assigned to their villa knocked on the door. He had roamed the marble floors which kept the house cool from the outside temperature, snooping in drawers of the mostly white furniture decorated with accents of pale blue décor, multicolored sea shells, and random jars of white and brown rocks on the dressers in each of the three bedrooms.

They'd overlooked a white paper bag filled with local jellies, jams, and sweets on the table in the foyer at the entrance sitting next to a note welcoming them to the village, and the layout of the resort. Mash tasted the confections just before the chef arrived, happy to show him to the kitchen to fill his growing hunger.

He wet a towel from the sink while the chef unpacked, grinning as he wiped the counter he and Nadia graced the night before.

"Any special requests, Mr. Sharper?"

"We'll have whatever's your specialty, some French toast, fresh sliced fruit, and juice for my wife."

The chef sautéed pepper filled omelettes, steamed potatoes, Mash's request for Nadia, and stood by for further instructions.

Mash bit off the omelette, fixed he and Nadia a plate, complimented the chef, then told him to take everything he cooked home to his family.

Hours later, Nadia rose from the bed and joined her husband

sitting outside on the balcony. Wrapped in the top sheet from the bed, she hugged him from behind.

He placed his hand on top of hers, releasing a cloud of smoke into the wind. "You missed breakfast. And lunch."

"Thanks for letting me sleep in." She rubbed her chin into his back. "Where did you get that?"

"Scored it from the chef," he said, leaning against the balcony.

"The chef had a cigar?"

"And weed." He smiled, looking over his shoulder.

Nadia's hands pressed firmly against his chest. "What else have I missed?"

"Nothing much. Just a beautiful day, but you needed the rest."

"And now I have nothing but energy for you to burn off." Her hands found the waistline of his trousers. She tucked her fingers below the belt, and stroked down his shaft to the base. "I'm wide awake now."

The sun dipped closer to the coastline. They watched it fall behind the blue horizon, leaving traces of its golden silhouette in spouts towards the white sands below them as the warm breeze added a layer of arousal.

Nadia teased. "I bet you won't last long enough to see the top of the sun dip its head into the ocean."

Mash grinned. "Oh yeah, you're well rested." He turned his back to the sphere. "What do I get when I win?"

Nadia gently tugged on his dick, squatted on the back of her heels, and sucked him off with the intensity of a hand squeezing a lemon, then softly like she had the best soft serve in her mouth.

Mash struggled to compose himself, marveling at the sight of her full lips making love to his cock. Her closed eyes and circling tongue boosted his confidence. Her pretty face swallowing his manhood with full desire for him.

"What was that?" She licked her lips, rising to look him in the eyes.

"I love watching you do that to me," he whispered, holding her stray hairs blowing in the wind.

Nadia dropped back to her knees. He caressed the corner of her mouth with the other hand, and Nadia surprised him, adding his finger to the oral play. His dick stiffened harder than the railing he was leaning against, jolting at the risqué move, ready to spring back into action watching her mouth fill until tears streamed from her eyes.

Boisterously he sighed, checking to see if they were being watched. Then, his urges stopped her stellar performance. He removed his parts from between her lips.

She hopped up. "Why'd you stop me?"

"I can't hold it."

He pushed her inside, closed the sliding glass door behind him, then pressed Nadia against it face forward. She braced herself against the glass with her hands, smiling that she was about to win the bet.

Mash licked his fingers, spread her ass cheeks apart, and pivoted inside her throbbing pussy.

"Every Goddamned time," he said, scraping the sides of her pussy in beast mode, reveling at the sound of her breast shrieking against the balcony door like a rag shining a glass table.

The open curtains shook from the vibration. The handle rattled from every jolt. Every stroke. Every thrust.

Nadia trembled from his dominance. Fogging the glass pressed against her face with growing hunger in her belly.

With the sun minutes away from disappearing into the abyss, her narrowed eyes watched it sink. In her euphoric state, it was like watching magic take place within an arm's reach. Delight taking over her body.

Mash pressed harder against the roof of her constricting walls. With each twist of her hips, he compelled her with a strong hold against her flesh. She grunted from the pressure. Breathless. Her sweaty fingers slid down the glass with a weakened back.

"Aye, Papi you win," she mumbled, watching the sun take a permanent dive for the evening.

Mash's lips curved a devilish grin. He stepped back and turned her towards him, then lifted her against the wet glass.

Kissing her fervently, he muffled in her mouth, "I won the night we met."

Nadia smiled, but lost it as Mash ambushed her pussy without warning. She belted a sensuous moan. Her back squeaking on the glass from the condensation as Mash fucked her like she was new pussy, and let loose an implosion between her thighs as darkness owned the sky.

They fell back on the bed.

"I'm starving," Nadia said breathlessly.

"I had the chef prepare you French toast and fresh fruit this morning. But it's still early enough to grab dinner. Get dressed. I'm taking you out."

Dinner and dancing at a restaurant outside of their village delivered the perfect night under a clear, starry sky, blended drinks, and live music. Mash two stepped while Nadia danced circles around him, capturing the attention of the wallflowers admiring them all around the venue.

Marco spotted the couple. He approached them with a tanned woman at his side.

"This is my friend, Duff. I recommend her tour for sightseeing outside the resort."

"Si. Allow me the pleasure to show you how to experience the city like the locals."

The next morning, The Sharpers packed an emergency survival kit inside two backpacks, and embarked on an adventure with two other couples, The Malloys and The Doctors, of Puerto Plata's best kept secrets.

They trekked landscapes in Pino De Teta that led to a hidden waterfall, safe for sliding into a pool of bubbling blue water. Mash and Nadia passed on the exploit, laughing at the other couples' screams of fear on the way down the slide.

Once everyone was united at the bottom of the pond, the wet couples raved about the experience of the fall as they hiked to a mountain top for the final destination just past a narrow bridge they had to cross to overlook the clear blue ocean from a secret high point.

The point connected with a path leading into a village where local vendors sold keepsakes, baked goods, clothing such as sundresses, wraps, and hats, and tents of farmers selling fresh fruit.

Nadia received a lesson in the purity of the grapefruit. Tasting the white flesh of one grown locally by a farmer nearby.

"It's sweeter than the pink ones I normally eat," she said, walking away with a bag of them.

~

Mash bravely tasted a sliced guanabana cut by a woman freely swinging a machete. Nadia held up her grapefruit to the woman, afraid to try the exotic produce. Mash pinned her in his arms and forced his lips on hers to taste it. She squealed and squirmed, powerless to his hold.

He whispered in her ear, "It's sweet. But not as sweet as you."

Nadia stopped fidgeting and welcomed the flavor from his mouth, leaving with a second bag of fruit to haul back on the path over the bridge.

Later that evening, they joined the couples they explored the city with for dinner inside the village. A night of drinks and laughter completed their final night in paradise, sending them back to the cottage, greeted by an un-welcomed guest.

"Mash!" Nadia screamed, from the bathroom.

He hurried to her call, finding her frozen against the wall pointing to the corner of the mirror.

He looked up and choked on swallowed laughter. "Don't panic. I'll get it."

Nadia hummed, locking eyes with a lizard staring back at her until Mash returned with a glass, and a pan from the kitchen.

Carefully, he coached the reptile into the glass and trapped it inside with the pan. Nadia followed him to the balcony, instructing him where to release it.

He glanced at her with a side-eye. "Do you want to do it?"

She fanned at him and they shared a laugh as the creature jumped into the tree branch resting against the house.

Mash studied the look on Nadia's face and teased her. "It wasn't going to hurt you," he said.

Nadia turned towards the moon half hidden behind clouds. "You don't know that," she chuckled. "But you do know I'm ready to go home now. Right?"

"I figured as much." He stood beside her. "We leave tomorrow at noon."

Their hands weaved together.

"It is beautiful here and we did have fun. Wouldn't you say?"

"I always have a good time when I'm with you. It's a shame we haven't walked on the beach though."

"But we did witness another amazing sunset."

Mash kissed the back of her hand. "You witnessed it. My eyes were on something else amazing." He palmed her ass.

She squealed. "But none of them will ever beat Ibiza."

"Never."

In the morning, they welcomed the sunrise outback in a hammock, and walked barefoot in the white sand. They returned to the house, greeted by the staff and chef outside near the pool where a smorgasbord had been prepared for them before their departure at Mash's request.

Mingling with the staff, they indulged on the feast, then finished packing so the staff could transfer their luggage to the van.

"What happened to my helicopter ride?"

Mash squeezed Nadia's hand. "I thought you were joking."

She braced herself for the wild ride to the airport. Their trusty "Buckle up," he teased, and whipped them from the curb.

Mash laughed. "I've got you."

Safely they were delivered back to Santo Domingo. Ten hours later, the newlyweds arrived in London.

When Nadia's feet touched the ground at Gatwick airport, she held onto her husband's arm and sighed with relief, then looked up at him leading the way to the car waiting for them outside.

"Home sweet home."

Book Two

A Taste of the Forbidden

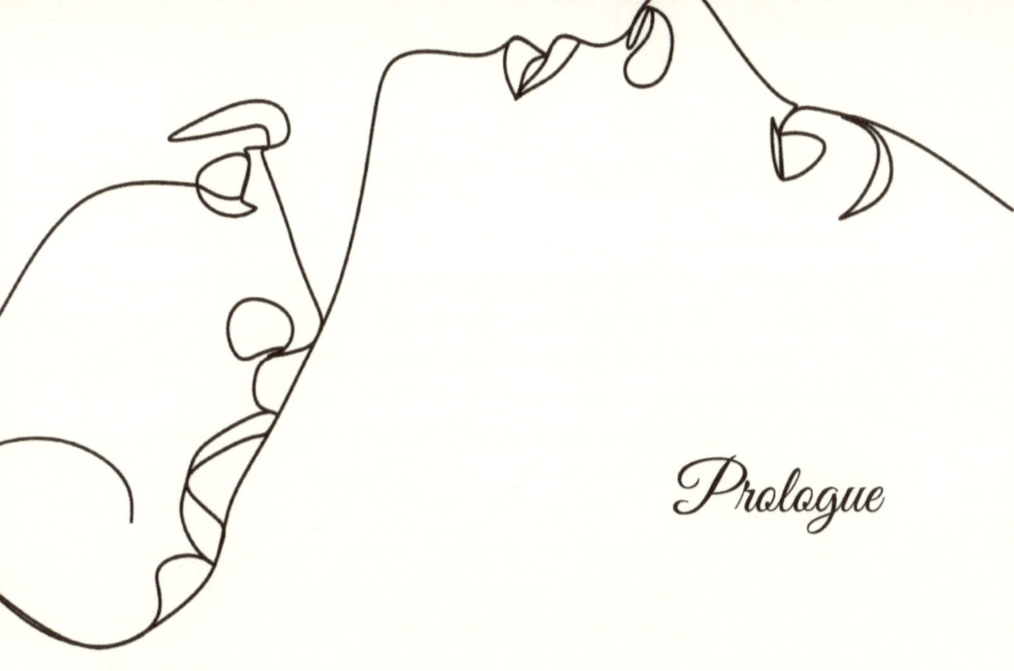

Prologue

He was warned. Before we eloped in Barcelona, I questioned if it was wise for two people who had not had an argument to get married. We dove into this marriage exceedingly fast with blinders on, and neither of us cared. I was all in for whatever the world of Maximus Sharper flung at me. The spell I was under didn't leave room for the voice of reason, and we were convinced we were destined for each other. Now I bear his last name.

My life changed dramatically fast. Two years abroad in the cold and gray land of London, my writing career was still in limbo, but I wanted for nothing as Mash's career continued to flourish under new management.

He was now an in-demand mixologist, creating countless mixes for A-list artists, and attaching his name to the less established beginners in the industry—Transitioning them from starving to breakout stars.

As a couple we were in sync, but alone I suffered. I felt inadequate without success of my own.

In order to fill the void of my lack of accomplishments, I went against my husband's wishes and took an entry level position as a Trainee Negotiator for a real estate firm.

I love beautiful homes, but convincing people to buy them was not my forte.

I learned the business of London's real estate exceptionally fast. It was expensive, the agents were cutthroat and competitive, and I needed to be a shark to swim amongst them.

In doing so, I missed several of Mash's shows, which was the primary reason he opposed my taking the job in the first place.

My work created a slight discourse in our house, but it helped me learn my way around the city, and introduced me to people I couldn't wait to write about.

After nearly a year of employment at the firm, I grew to like working in real estate, which was a mistake. As soon as I got comfortable, my time there ended due to a lack of sales.

I cried for a day or two, but with the support of my husband's hefty wallet, I took what I learned, and opened a private office as a licensed realtor in the Shoreditch district.

Working for myself meant I controlled my schedule, and could once again travel with my beloved.

I'm sure this is why he was so on board with the idea.

But it was exciting to become an entrepreneur, and not feel like dead weight. And as for Shoreditch, I had found my tribe. I belonged with the various diverse creatives, artsy folks, colorful streets, and coffee shops—Even though I was *posing* as a realtor.

'Nadia M. Sharper' was painted in bold white font on the glass of the front door of *my* office. Sure, I made one sale in three months, but I opened my doors every day, waiting for my second sale to walk through the door to free me from failure yet again.

I sat in my plush chair meant for a fortune five hundred CEO that Mash insisted I have, with hours of downtime. The swanky space wound up serving as my writing hub away from home instead of making sales.

Being surrounded by creatives helped the juices flow with a simple glance outside the window. When I needed a break from writing, I turned to Plan C—Buy homes and flip them for a profit.

But as the pressure mounted and my confidence began to flail, I lost interest in all of my ideas, and decided to travel alongside my husband. Just as he wanted.

The weekend he was due in Marseille, I surprised him as he was about to board the plane. It was the first time we'd be traveling together in months, and it felt like it did in the beginning—Sweet adventurous escapes with my personal tour guide showing me parts of the world I never imagined I would see.

Unfortunately, I was introduced to more than landmarks and historic sights with my famous husband in the land of the French.

CHAPTER 13

Brand New Me

I hadn't missed the clouds of cigarette smoke in the clubs, but I did miss seeing Mash come alive onstage, and my guilty pleasure of people watching. After a few peach flavored drinks, I got a little loose and danced provocatively against the railing near the stage. Mash blushed at me grooving solo in my corner, so I simmered down, and fought the urge to move to the beat.

The ambiance of the crowd, the loud sounds of the bass booming from the speaker, and Mash focusing on his work suddenly turned me on.

Oh how I love a working man. Who doesn't?

I fanned myself with a club flyer to cool down and shy away my raised nipples piercing through my top. The peach schnapps and vodka also played a role in my sudden yearning to be pillaged by my husband hard at work.

I turned away from the crowd until my boobs were no longer on high beam, then refaced the stage to continue watching the show.

Mash winked at me. My face flushed from his flirtation.

Oh shit. He knows that I'm heavily aroused.

To keep my nipples from telling the world I am in need for some action and the naughty thoughts flashing in my head at bay, I crowd surfed the faces from the atrium section. The horde was heavily

155

engaged with the music. Shades of partygoers below the color changing LED lights were enjoying themselves. Some more than others. But the vibe I felt from one of the faces in the crowd didn't come across as friendly.

A woman stared me down for far too long. If she could shoot venom at me from that distance, I'd be poisoned.

Her gaze was beyond intense when we locked eyes. So extreme that a chill traveled down my spine, and my skin felt like it froze amidst the heat in the club.

I waited for her to blink, but her menacing face didn't budge because she wanted my attention. And I didn't break my gaze either, letting her know that I didn't scare easily.

She finally folded, and I turned toward the stage, cheering on my husband who decided to play my favorite song. Suddenly, it dawned on me. I recognized the woman. Her silhouette, long face, and dark eyes screamed at me from the back of my mind. She was the mysterious woman in the photograph Mash and I never discussed. The bitch I wondered about from time to time. Mostly when I was pouting over something silly.

How do I play this? I thought. *Should I lock eyes with her again? Then, roll them when she stares back? Or do something clever to make her jealous?*

Jealousy won.

Winding my hips on the side of the stage, I eye-fucked *my husband*. His face turned pink and red, and his interaction with the crowd took a pause as he bit the side of his lip. His smoldering features turned serious as he signaled to some guy behind him, pressed a button on his equipment, then stepped forward in my direction.

His hands wrapped around my waist to still me from winding my hips. "I see Naughty Nadia came here tonight. You wanna quick one backstage?"

I moaned in his ear and smirked at the girl in the crowd studying us from below. She squinted her eyes as I showcased my effect on the man she obviously came to see. But he was with me.

If she didn't know me before, she knew me now, but I still knew nothing about her. Something told me I was about to learn more than

I wanted to, but that lesson would have to wait, as I was beguiled with the man who put a ring on my finger. Naughty Nadia was at the party, and she wanted pleasure, even if it was against the dirty wall of a dressing room.

I placed my bag around the knob before Mash locked the door behind us. Forcefully, I unbuttoned his pants, and yanked down his zipper. He was ready without any participation on my part.

I stroked his penis in my hands as his face pressed against mine, then we fervidly locked in a sloppy kiss. I could feel the speed of his heart increase with my hands wrapped around his gyrating muscle beating like a marching band.

His fingers slipped between my orifice. "I knew you wanted me twenty minutes ago," he said, gliding my drip around the apex of my inner thighs.

Quickly, I dropped low and wet his wanton whistle. He sighed of gratification as I licked him with a circular motion of my tongue, then enclosed his head in my mouth for one quick suck.

"Ha-ah-ih," he respired, running his fingers through my hair.

I rose to face him. "See, there you go. Getting excited trying to mess up my hair. You'll get more of that later tonight."

He pressed my back against the door and lifted my right leg. I exhaled in heat, anxious to feel his girth separate my walls.

A gentle tug on my thong bared my pulsing flesh for his dick to stand up in my pussy with ease. Above my head, he gurgled sounds of pleasure from the tightness of my warm embrace hugging his sturdy stride breaking me open.

He grunted, and I whined, bracing myself for the lashing my pussy was happy to receive.

I clenched my juices to coat him and moaned. He groaned as his strong, long thrusts withdrew screams from my mouth like the people on the opposite side of the door enjoying the show.

"You know how to make me come quick. Don't you girl?" He sighed, then tongued me as he approached his peak.

I timed each push and pull until I was lost in the zone of our souls being weaved together. Then, he came inside of me, breathing heavily against my cheek, holding me tighter than a bear hugging a tree.

Unable to move I asked, "You good?"

"When I'm with you, always." He slid out of me gently. "You?"

"You won't hear me complain." I searched for a napkin in my bag. "You better get back out there." I jittered from a cramp forming in my toe, then lined the tissue around the seat of my thong. "I'll be out shortly."

Mash frowned, securing the zipper on his jeans."I wouldn't dare leave you back here alone."

I rushed to make myself presentable, then we headed back to the stage arm in arm. The audience cheered at his return under the flashing lights, and he reveled in it, holding up his hands with a proud grin on his lips.

I cheered for him, too, but mostly for the private performance I had just received.

For the remainder of his set I behaved. No provocative dancing. No enticing him from the side of the stage. I sat patiently in the seat I was provided, and played the role of a good supportive wife while scouring the crowd for the hateful eyes piercing through me moments ago.

They say seek and you shall find. And that is exactly what I did with the ghost of my husband's past. A rising problem I sensed that returned to haunt me.

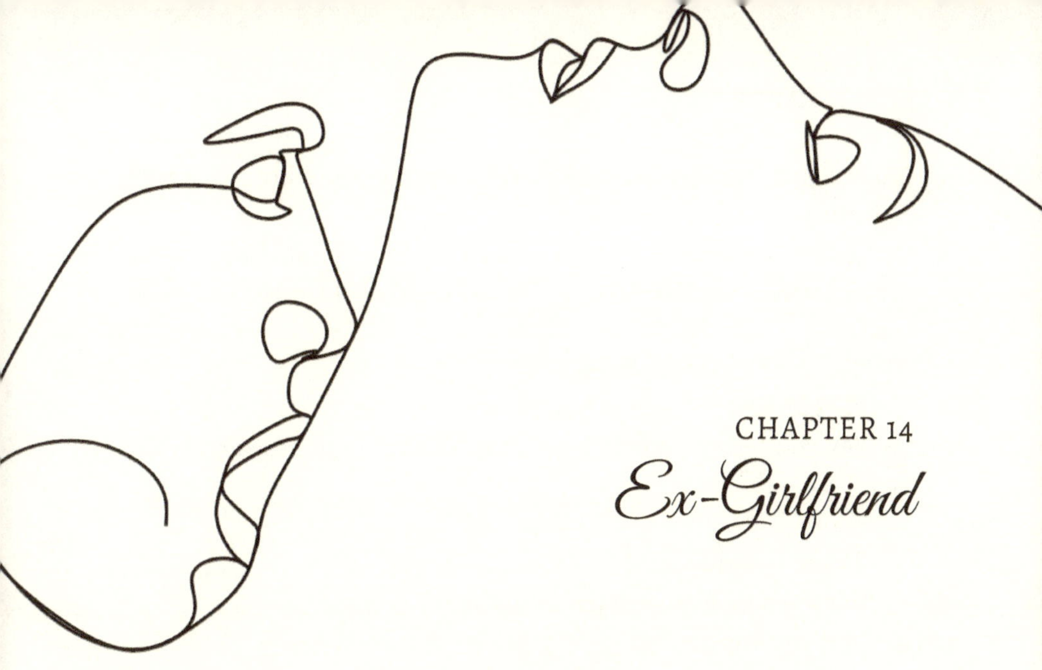

CHAPTER 14

Ex-Girlfriend

What truly happened the night in Cardiff, rose from the back of my mind from time to time. Mostly when I was PMSing and looking for a reason to bitch about something. Also, because there was no closure.

Ignorance is bliss to some. Count me out of that lineup. *If only I could let it go.* I started playing twenty questions in my head. *Why didn't he want to talk about this girl, and why was she making her presence known all of a sudden? — and on our second anniversary nonetheless.*

I kept quiet during the short ride to the hotel, purposely driving Mash insane. *He should have never let me know the silent treatment kills him.* He grew fidgety in the back seat, constantly knocking his knees with a balled fist, tapping his heels vigorously on the car floor. *He knew something was up.*

Either he saw her in the crowd, too, or my silence made him uncomfortable, and I was no holds barred once we reached our room. Calmly I asked, "Are you going to come out with it, or do you want me to belittle myself and ask the obvious?" He opened the balcony doors and lit the unfinished joint hiding in the crease of the window sill. If I could place a sure bet, he was carefully crafting his response.

And judging from the bullets of sweat forming above his eyebrows, I patiently waited for him to answer.

Orchestrated circle clouds of smoke left his lips until he killed the silence between us. "She is the girl in the photo that bastard Harv sent you."

"No shit Sherlock. Who is she?"

"An old acquaintance of nonimportance."

"So, you've said. What's her name?" I asked, not interested in the least.

"Nomi."

"What does she want?"

"How would I know? I haven't spoken to her."

"But you saw her."

"Apparently, we both did."

Mash tapped his gar against the brick and stepped back in the room. A breeze followed him inside as we briefly stared at each other, waiting for the other to blink.

"You know we never fully discussed what happened that night." My eyes pierced his.

"And you want to do that now? At 4 a.m.?" He scoffed.

"Why was she there?"

"Again, I haven't had any communication with her, and Nadia, the last thing I want to do is talk about an ex-girlfriend. We've had a great night, and it's our first time away together in months. Can we please table this for another time?" He begged.

"Fine. We'll finish this in the morning. Just know, I don't plan on asking you about this again. You need to come clean with me about whatever dirty little secret you have with this woman. Am I clear?"

"It's our anniversary and we're here for two more days." He sighed. "Why ruin it over nothing? Forget about her and enjoy everything I have planned for us. Okay?"

Fuming internally, I managed to utter, "Good night."

The presence of this Nomi heaux awakened the bitch in me Mash hadn't met yet. I clock watched during what was left of the night, thinking about the way she looked at me. Looked at him. Looked at us.

I practically lied on the edge of the bed, clinging onto the sheets to keep Mash's arm from covering me as he slept like a baby. Either he had nothing to hide, an innocent conscience, or the late set he worked had him spent. But he slept peaceful and sound, while I stared at him until the sun came up like a mad woman.

As anxious as I was to badger him in the morning, my mind imagined the worst. I needed a distraction and some space, and let him sleep in. My baggy eyes and restless body visited museums, tourist attractions, and a café on my list of sites and places to visit in the city. I declined all calls, then slowly made my way back to the hotel when I knew he'd be gone to his set.

The sleepless night eventually took its toll on me, while anger fueled my restlessness. My fickle mind chose not to stay in and sleep, but slip into a bit of mischief instead.

Posing as a regular patron, I lurked about in the darkness wearing cut off denim shorts, and a skinny black tank with a shirt tied around my waist, skimming the entry line for what's her face in the crowd. Behind chic glasses I bought earlier in the day, I hid my face and styled my hair in a bun, attempting to pass for a college girl.

Once I made it inside, I sat at the bar until the crowd overflowed the floor, then made my way upstairs to a table in the corner with a bird's-eye view of the dance floor. A white bolder hid my frame from the stage as I observed the room—anticipating I'd see Nomi's face in the crowd.

A text lit my phone from Mash.

Mash: "*At least tell me you are alright.*"

I waited to respond as I watched him pick up his phone a few times in between songs looking for my reply.

Nadia: "*I'm fine. See you when you get in.*"

The angst on his face humored me after he read my response. His shoulders raised and he smirked to himself. A thread of guilt swept over me for making him wonder of my whereabouts. *You better sweat,* I thought to myself, laughing internally at the change in his demeanor.

We wouldn't be at odds if I didn't feel he was withholding information. It was also possible I was all worked up over nothing, which wouldn't be the first time. I knew this man loved me. There wasn't any doubt in my mind he did, but whatever he wasn't telling me ate away my soul, and I felt justified in torturing him until he filled me in.

My poor clueless husband was now grooving with the beat, whereas before he looked bored on stage. I laughed out loud in front of a group of strangers standing near my table—Receptive of their stares as they weren't in on the joke. I continued to giggle at the sudden pep in Mash's step. *If only he knew I was watching him like a hawk a few feet away.*

~

My ploy of crowd surfing was a bust. There was no sign of Nomi after nearly two hours of searching through the horde, and Mash's set was coming to an end. I rushed to the exit hiding behind the people standing near the rail, wiggling between them when my gut spoke to me. *Don't leave just yet.*

I listened.

In an obscure spot across the street, I made myself comfortable leaning against an old foreign car whose name I couldn't pronounce. Watching the crowd of people come and go, I examined the faces under the buttery colored light above the club's entrance. Still, no sign of her.

A few feet away a pack of drunk clubbers hopping into the last cab freed an open space on the street. I eased over to the shadow where they stood, and caught a glimpse of the side entrance in the alley. Bingo. There she was with two females in her company, standing where Mash was due to come out.

I didn't smoke but I could have used a cigarette once I spotted her. The temperature of my blood rose to boiling, and my hands grew clammy with sweat. My chest was pounding so forcefully, I could hear it inside my head and swore I saw it thumped my tank top above my heartbeat. I took deep breaths stomping the pavement towards her, questioning if confronting her was the right thing to do. *Is listening to what she has to say going to bring me peace? And how will I know if she's telling me the truth? Fuck this, I'm ending this shit tonight, and letting my presence be known.*

I took my hair down and covered the top half of my body with the shirt tied around my waist, and blended in with the fans. Five minutes later the side door opened, and Mash walked out addressing his admirers, signing posters, and posing for photographs.

As he posed with a couple, one of Nomi's friends intruded, and pointed in her direction. They shared a look before she walked over to him, and my chest dropped into my stomach.

I stepped in closer and zeroed in on their conversation catching the tail end of it. "Leave me the fuck alone." Mash berated her in front of everyone. The crowd grew loud with gasps and chaos, and Nomi stood on her toes in his face.

"Don't be like that baby." Her lustful eyes looked into his as she dragged her whorish nails across his shirt.

I wormed through the horde and eased into their proximity, alerted by the madness growing from the bystanders. They pulled out their phones and began recording the commotion as Mash unleashed on the two of them.

"You and your friends need to stay the fuck away from me!"

I tugged on his shirt, and turned to the couple waiting for their photo op. "Did you need me to retake your photo?" Mash's eyes widened. "Baby, these lovely people are still waiting for their picture with you," I said with raised brows and a soft smile.

He returned my smile and posed with the couple, then took a few more shots with patrons before taking my hand and hurrying me into the limousine. I didn't look at him.

"What were you...?" he asked.

I put my hand up to silence him. "We're almost at the hotel."

His hands trembled during the ride. I reached over and placed mine on top of his. He removed my hand, and placed his arm around my shoulder. The heat from his chest provided me with warmth from the breeze seeping in through the cracked windows. I listened it to race with the beat of my own, hoping our exchange would lead to resolve.

Inside our suite, we stood at opposite ends, waiting for the other to speak. "I'll go first," I said, studying the twitching of his lips as he gazed at me with narrowed eyes.

"Where did you come from?" he interrupted.

"What the hell is going on?"

"You first," he demanded, pacing the floor and running his hands through his hair and down his face mid yawn.

I took a few deep breaths and calmly answered him. "I couldn't sleep so I spent the day roaming the city."

"All day?" His voice heightened as he questioned me.

"Yes, all day."

"Nadia, we have security guards for a reason. You can't just wander off in a strange city you know nothing about alone. And when I call you, answer your phone for fucks sake."

I leered at him. "I made it back in one piece."

Mash stood before me and gripped my shoulders with his fingers. "Listen to me. Don't ever leave without telling me where you're going while we're traveling. Do you understand?"

"Yeah, I hear you."

"It was reckless and selfish. Anything could have happened to you. I could have been hurt. Or needed you..."

"I said okay. I heard you. I'm sorry. Wait. Why am I apologizing?" I removed myself from his clutch.

"Where did you come from tonight? You said you were here."

"And then I was where you apparently needed me."

"I did need you." His blistering tone simmered. "I do need you."

I escaped his hovering, followed by his shadow against the wall on my heels. I stopped short and turned to him. "People were recording you lashing out at those girls. It's probably all over the gossip channels by now."

He grabbed my hand. "Thank you."

"You're welcome."

His lips curved on one side. "So, you were spying on me?"

I scoffed and sat in the lounge chair in the corner. Removing my flats, I looked up at him and shook my head. "I wasn't spying on you. But I did see what I needed to see."

"Which was?"

"How you and your ex would act with one another if I wasn't around. I got my answer. Now, tell me. What does she want? And talk now or I walk."

"Enough of the leaving me bit. Nomi is not a nice person, and I'm being respectful of women with my choice of words."

"She's a bitch. I can see that first hand. But why is she showing up all of sudden? Getting in your face? Looking at you how I look you?" I pursed my lips.

Mash sighed then removed his shirt, baring his chest to entice me. *It was working, but I held my composure.* He lied back on the bed. "I told you I had friends when we met, and Nomi was one of the few I could call to come over and keep me company. We had some wild times, but that was then."

"Was she your girlfriend?"

"A friend. And the night in question something happened, but not what you think before you jump to any conclusions."

"Are you kidding me right now?" I threw my shoe at him.

He caught it with one hand. "I didn't sleep with her. Calm down."

"Sure you didn't!"

"When I made it back to my hotel room, she and the friend she was with tonight were in my room— naked. I told them to leave, some awful things were said, and I lost my temper and threw them out in the hallway. Nomi caused a scene and threatened she would tell the tabloids I assaulted them. I panicked, not knowing what other tricks she had up her sleeve. A hidden camera in my room perhaps. Who knows? So, I packed my bag and checked out. That picture is of me checking out."

"In that picture she was in your face?"

"She was high. Begging to have the room because the hotel was booked. I took care of the charges, but put the room in her name. I went to another hotel."

"You were in Cardiff for days. Three to be exact. How do I know you didn't have any other interactions with her? How do I know you really put two naked women out of your room? Most men dream about banging two women, and you dismiss a threesome like it's nothing?" I rolled my bracelet off and threw it at him.

Mash chuckled. "Been there, done that. Nadia, I'm not new to this scene. Alcohol, cocaine, ex, orgies— it's all history now."

"Cocaine and orgies? Iyiyi."

"That is what they wanted tonight. Access to drugs and a hookup."

Hearing two women approached my husband to fuck and fly didn't sit well with me. I knew his lifestyle could get wild, but seeing it in real time disturbed my soul.

"Can we go to bed now?" he asked.

"Suddenly, I'm not tired." I mumbled.

"Do I hear a challenge?" Mash fled to invade my personal space.

"You wish." I pushed him aside. "And let me be clear. I'm not inviting another woman into our bed."

"Neither am I. I'm not sharing you with anyone." He picked me up and threw me on the bed.

Stealing kisses from my neck while I squirmed beneath him, I interrupted his attempt to kill the conversation with affection.

"How do you think they got in your room?" I asked, placing my hand between his lips and my cheeks.

"Davie is the logical answer. Though he denies the allegation."

"You had plenty of chances to tell me all of this." I lied still under him.

"Babe, nothing happened."

"Proof of your innocence would be great. I mean, I can't blame Nomi for wanting another night with you, but I'm having a hard time shaking the jealousy I feel. I think I want to leave in the morning."

"No." He stated, calm yet stern.

"Excuse me?" I shoved him from on top of me.

"You will accompany me tomorrow night. You will be seated close to the stage, and we will leave together. End of discussion?"

I didn't respond. I felt his demand in my bones, and knew that was the end of our argument. His explanation had given me a headache, and my chest tightened lying next to him during our heated moment.

I exhaled deeply, then headed for the shower. Once again on my heels, Mash followed me. Fully undressed, erect, and aware I wanted no part of him.

Pressed against my back, his cock jutted, begging for my attention. My weakness for his touch normally caused me to cave, giving into the satisfaction of him fucking my brains out, figuratively and literally. The mental elevation and higher vibration we journeyed together when physically connected made it hard for me to say no, but I fought off the urge. I avoided looking into his eyes, kept my back to him, and cleansed my body swiftly, wanting him in the worst way.

Refusing myself pleasure and residing in my anger, led me to revisit the few heated disagreements we had. Discord that led to some of our best raging sex moments. This felt like it could be one of those times, but I was determined not to fold. Determined not to look into his eyes, which I could do for hours, and resist the temptation of the one-eyed monster I craved rigging my oil slick. *Not this time.*

Playing hard to get excited him even more. *Always up for a challenge this one.* He pressed deeper into me, as if I didn't recognize the firmness of his penis moments before. His hands glided across my shoulders, massaging them with kneading thrusts as the soap from his fingers lathered my back.

I allowed him continue to work my body because it felt too good to stop. Allowing his fingers to slowly slide everywhere they pleased until I was covered from head to toe with white bubbles.

I stood still, facing forward towards the shower head, getting lost in the sensation of his manipulation. He then reached for the cloth in my hand, and scrubbed my back in mini circles, touching all of the sensitive spots that required his touch and attention.

Growing weaker by the minute, my eyes rolled back and my posture wilted, in his hands and by his hands. I replayed his story in my head, believing his words to be true, but still wanting some form of proof. I needed it. My pride required it to not feel dumb for taking him at his word.

Now pulsating between my drenched cheeks, he rinsed my body, using his pillowy lips to delicately suck the water beads from the back of my shoulders. I imagined him already inside of me, locked and loaded with a full hard on, as he toyed with my body from behind—rinsing away the lather on my breasts with palms of water, while teasing my neck with his tongue.

I exhaled in heat, like melted putty in his hands. His fingers skid south of my navel with an intended purpose to flick my golden spot. I tensed knowing if I let him touch me there, I was his to devour, so I turned around to face him, and kissed his cheek. "Thank you." I grinned, then exited the shower.

Quickly I dressed for bed in one of his t-shirts and pajama pants, jumped beneath the covers, and pretended to be asleep when he toweled off in the room.

"You left me hanging in there, but don't worry. I took care of it myself. I haven't had to charm the snake in a long time, but I still love you. Good night." He climbed in behind me and laid his arm over my waist.

I cuffed my chest tightly and squeezed my lips, trapping laughter in my throat. Quietly, I swallowed each chuckle, feeling the burn from his eyes down my back.

Mash never liked when we went to bed angry. Over the course of our short marriage, I was the only one with the bad habit of doing so. No matter the fight, disagreement, or misunderstanding, his arms always ended up wrapped around me, and this time was no different.

By morning, he rose as if all had been forgiven. I declined his invitation to see the city, and barely spoke a word to him all day. By nightfall, I did as he ordered and accompanied him to the club, adored him for the cameras during his set, and waited for him in the car while he mingled with his fans.

While Mash was signing autographs and posing for pictures, I spotted Nomi staring at me through the lightly tinted window. A deep sigh parted my lips and a heavy load pressed inside of my chest at the sight of her. I have never cared for confrontation in my life, but her presence disrupted my peace.

I slipped out of the car on the opposite side of Mash, irrational, tense, angry, and annoyed. As I approached the nuisance, my thoughts were unclear and led by anger.

Pointing my finger in her face I warned her. "I will say this once.

Let this be the last time I see you hanging around my husband. If you see his name on a flyer, or hear he is in the same city as you, alter your plans."

"Aren't you cute. Keeping my spot warm while Maxi has a tantrum. Don't get too comfortable." Nomi smirked and shared a laugh with her friend.

I giggled. "He said you were a bitch. He really does know you well. The stunt you pulled in Cardiff has earned you a spot on my hit, I mean shit list, so if I were you, I'd tread lightly."

"Enjoy him while you can. It won't last. I'll never be out of his system." She turned to her friend again, cosigning her every word.

"This ring says you've been out of his system for a while now, and from the way he screams my name, I'd say enjoy those memories you're holding on to. I hope you enjoy the rest of your desperate night, and stop embarrassing yourself. Has been."

With a fake smile laced upon my lips, I waved good-bye to Nomi and her friend, bumping into Mash who I assumed was rushing over to my rescue. His knuckles formed in one hand as the fingers on his other hand tapped the side of my stomach softly. "You okay?"

I nodded.

"What were you doing?" he asked.

"I put an end to this ridiculousness." I gritted through my teeth, and placed my palm on his chest.

"Are we good?" He kissed my forehead.

"In time we will be. Can we agree, I deserve some time and space to process all of this, and sort it out for myself?"

"How much space and how much time?" He slammed the car door shut.

"However long it takes." I squeezed his hand, searching for support in his eyes.

CHAPTER 15

Gin & Coconut Water

The will power I possess to scoot away from the hardness pressed below my cheeks in the middle of the night, and early in the morning should be awarded. After days, sometimes weeks of my doing so, it begins to wear thin for the both of us as its punishment— For him and me.

Though I suffered from the lack of his touch, and placed a border between us with a body pillow that magically ends up on the floor by morning, I held true to will of no intimacy. Using no sex as punishment was not my finest hour, especially when it carried on past a week, and I had grown comfortable in the petty game of tit for tat, forgetting what we were at odds about.

I woke one morning and inched over to his side of the bed. It was cold and empty. I searched for Maximus throughout the house with no luck, realizing I had become the villain, and couldn't quite process how I allowed the tables to be turned on me— Despite my infantile behavior of making breakfast for one, ordering takeout for one, and stocking the cabinets with the foods I liked. If that wasn't enough, the drawn out silent treatment, and never responding to his *I love you* texts, had sent him over the edge. Some days I texted a response, and was certain he saw the moving dots on his phone, but I couldn't bring myself to press the send button. And that morning I felt the repercussions of my silly actions. I had gone too far.

Everybody plays the fool at some point, but when it's your turn it's sucks pure ass, and I was in a terrible, frustrating state to say the least. Ironically, the hurt I felt during that time decided to move on without my permission and tell me we were over it, waking me to an empty bed and an empty house, waiting to receive the '*I love you*' text I ignored so many times before.

~

Work was slow which gave me time to reflect on my anger issues, dedication to vengeance, and inner she-devil I oddly found satisfaction in. I had watched Mash sulk all week, but it was my turn that morning.

The noise of the city served as the perfect distraction, yet my thoughts wouldn't allow me to write. Every word flowing from my pen expressed feelings of sorrow, regret, and the absence of love, and the delete button left me with a blank computer screen staring back at me. Still no text from Mash.

After studying the pixels on the white page for minutes unknown, finally I composed a script regarding a fictional account of my true feelings of the turmoil at home. My insecurities about the beautiful— I hated to admit that— ex-girlfriend lurking about. I tapped into deep, buried anger, jealousy, and personal struggles I'd locked away from previous heartbreaks. One in particular.

Thoughts I never shared with anyone but the page as the words began pouring out of me. My keys tapped nonstop, potentially creating my first masterpiece until my focus was disturbed by the bells chiming above the front entrance, and a velvety male voice asking, "Is anyone here?"

I stuck my head out from my office. "Hello. I'll be right with you." Quickly, I threw my blazer around my shoulders and stepped into the lobby area. "Sorry about that."

"The lights were on so I let myself in." He smiled.

The image went along with the voice, and did not disappoint. I hadn't seen a chocolate man this handsome since I left the states, and I wondered where he had been hiding. I eyed him from head to toe, then laughed internally at my thoughts. *Of course, a handsome stranger would turn up when I'm on the outs with the hubs.*

Hardly servicing any customers, I had to pull myself together. I erased the grin on my lips and cleared my throat. "Pardon me, how can I help you today?"

"I'm looking for Nadia Melton, or Nadia Sharper." My last name lingered on his lips.

"It's Sharper, now. And you are?" I scowled.

"You're Mash's wife?"

"Yes, I am. How do you know my husband?"

"We run in some of the same circles. He's quality on the tune scene. Huge following from what I hear. Mint guy." He grabbed the new growth of chin hair on his beard.

Carefully I crafted my response after watching his fingers smooth the roughness of his beard. "Please forgive me for not following. I am still learning the use of some words over here. I'm not sure what mint guy means."

"Sorry, it means he's cool." The gentleman chuckled.

"Then yes, you do know him. What can I help you with today? Are you interested in purchasing a home?"

"I am, but I'm also here to discuss another matter with you. You submitted a project to my production company, and I wanted to meet with you to see if you were open to a few changes, and possibly working together."

"Seriously? Which title?" The excitement in voice escaped me.

"The short story entitled *'Run'.*"

"Ha! What a way to end my day," I said, placing the closed sign on the door.

"You know I never forget a face. I saw you in Cannes a few years ago. You and Mash were on my yacht."

"I remember being on a fancy boat, but I didn't know anyone there. To be honest all I remember was smiling and shaking hands with people, and mispronouncing names."

"It is a pretty busy event, and select crowd. I understand."

"Forgive me if I seem out of sorts, but I'm in shock to hear about my work. After a while I gave up it was well received."

"I found it fresh. You should be proud of your submission. Let's say we schedule a few meetings to discuss your script, the changes I have in mind and so forth, then later arrange a meeting with my fiancé about seeing what homes are on the market."

"Most definitely. Excuse me while I fetch my planner."

His eyes followed me as I left the lobby, so I contained my shimmy dance until I was fully inside my office. I saved my masterpiece of emotions on my laptop, then returned to the lobby with my calendar cued to schedule the appointment.

"I didn't catch your name." I asked a second time.

"Yohan Stallworth, but my friends call me Yogi." He reached for my hand.

"Nice to formally meet you, Mr. Stallworth." I reached forward to shake his.

"Please, call me Yogi."

A tingling sensation traveled from the back of my hand, up to my shoulders, then into my chest. His handshake was firm and short, but I could feel the strength residing in them. I sighed to collect my wild thoughts and hid the frustration rising from the impossible openings he held in his calendar. My schedule was wide open, landing three meetings within the next two weeks— One day to meet with his soon to be Mrs., and two days to discuss the direction of my script.

An embarrassing rumbling sound from my stomach imposed during our chat.

"I apologize. I haven't eaten anything all day." I hid my face behind my hands.

"I could use a bite to eat myself. I'm free for the next few hours. What do you say we have our first meeting right now, and continue this conversation over a working dinner? My treat."

"I'll grab my purse."

Mr. Stallworth reeked of wealth. His cologne smelled as if it were made specially for him, and his skin shined like chocolate silk. I assumed he spent time at spas getting facials, exfoliated, and groomed by staffers tending to his every need.

The suit he wore was custom made and tailored to fit his physique precisely. The more I glanced over him I felt intimidated, and I didn't understand why. Mash introduced me to a life of money, but Yogi's presence felt like a different kind of money— like longer money, and I was positive he had more of it.

I cheesed like an idiot during the walk to his car. I couldn't shake off my level of excitement, knowing one of my works had finally caught the eye of someone who could help me reach the level I aspired to achieve. Two years ago, I was aboard this man's yacht, and now a guest in his luxury Mercedes, being chauffeured to a working lunch. *What were the odds?*

The driver parked curbside, directly in front of a Jamaican restaurant a few blocks away from my office. It had been a while since I incurred the spicy flavor of jerk chicken cooked correctly with rice and peas, and the moment we walked inside, I nearly *foodgasmed*.

I ogled at the edible meals on customer's plates as we were seated, immediately ordering an appetizer. "Plantains and coco bread please." My voice dragged as I pled. The waitress smirked and giggled to herself while placing a fork and knife rolled into green paper in front of me.

"*Ya* familiar wit' Jamaican cuisine." Mr. Stallworth surprised me, speaking with an island accent.

"I know my way around a Caribbean menu." I nodded. "I didn't pick up on an accent earlier."

"It comes out when I get around my people. When I'm conducting business, I code switch so I'm easily understood."

"I see." My eyes stretched, noticing his eyes were more hazel than whiskey brown.

"You look uncomfortable. Did I say something wrong?"

"Not at all. It's just when I first came here I wasn't treated so well by a Yardie. It wasn't anything serious, but he caused me a great deal of headaches."

"Wha ya know 'bout a Yardie? Was he a romantic interest?"

"He wanted to be, but didn't handle rejection well. He had a horrible ego, and was really disrespectful to me."

"All man not the same. Don't judge us as one. I can't speak on his behalf, but he should have known better. Jah teaches us to respect thy woman."

"Thank you." A curve rose from the corner of my mouth.

"Look. You're smiling again. All is right with the world."

While waiting for the apps to arrive and place our order, Yohan showcased a mixture of professional Mr. Stallworth, and Yardie Yogi. We touched on my story, topics pertaining to black culture in the states, the U.K., and in his native homeland of Jamaica. I took notes of our conversation for a documentary idea I had in mind about the history of our people I hadn't executed as of yet.

The waitress returned with the coco bread and I stuffed my face while ordering jerk chicken, rice and peas, mac and cheese, with a side of curry chicken for later. Yohan copied my order, except he chose a side of yams and curry goat with a gin and coconut water.

He explained the changes he wanted to make to my piece, and the direction he pictured the short film could expand. Time got the best of us as we ate our dinner, talking for nearly two hours, as refills of water settled the spicy tongue I missed dearly.

"It's getting late Mrs. Sharper. I must be on my way to another appointment."

I checked my messages. "Yes, I need to be on my way as well. I enjoyed our meeting, and I look forward to working with you."

"Welcome aboard." We shook hands once more.

The chauffeur parked next to my car. Yogi, in gentlemanlike fashion, opened and closed my door. The driver waited for me to leave the lot, then pulled out behind me as I merged onto the highway. *Still no text from Mash.*

Having not heard from my better half, I dialed Khai, and shrieked lightly into her ear. She put me on pause, then connected us on a conference call.

I screamed louder. "Guess who has a short film in the works!" I gasped for air.

"It's about time someone gave you a shot!" Khai exclaimed.

"Who are you going to be working with? And is this a paid opportunity?" Shannon asked.

"I don't know the money details yet. I have to find an agent, a manager, a publicist. Just look up Yohan Stallworth."

"I'm pulling him up right now. Let's-see-what-we-are- working-with." Shannon sang. "Damn!"

"Damn is right." Taylor cosigned.

"He is a seasoned brother, but never mind him. How are you and Mash going to celebrate tonight?" Khai asked.

I scoffed, debating if it was time to discuss the drama with the dreaded ex. Again.

"I'm a little salty with him at the moment, but this would serve as reason enough to make peace."

"Why are you being mean to my friend?" Khai sassed.

"Remember the infamous picture?"

"Yeah." They answered simultaneously, then the line fell silent.

"Turns out some shit did go down that weekend."

"Oh hell nah!" Shannon exploded. "Did he cheat on you?"

"You two always go to the extremes and come up with the worst possible scenarios." Khai fussed.

"He says he didn't, but you know how my mind works." I sighed.

"And why don't you believe him?" Khai chastised me.

"Because the story is cockamamie. His former manager came up with some hair brain scheme, which led to some sort of disturbance, forcing him to check into another hotel, and it all sounds a bit too much. I told y'all how I felt about the ridiculous staged photo business mess. That girl has been a huge thorn in my side. She has threatened and stalked him. I had to step to her."

"You did what?!" Shannon bellowed.

"It's a long story. Since I put her in her place, we haven't seen her since. But still, her presence lurks and it bothers the hell outta me."

"Don't allow that heifer to drive a wedge between you two. If **your husband** says nothing happened, you should believe him. You don't want him to think you don't trust him." Khai advised.

"Well I... um... do trust him. But it feels foolish not to question the matter since he shares a past with this girl. Ya know?"

"Nadia, go home. Tell your husband your good news, and apologize, to him." Khai instructed.

"Why am I apologizing?"

"Because I know you've been giving that poor man the silent treatment?" Khai added.

The phone call went silent until the giggles from Shannon and Taylor created an uproar.

"You and your grudges." Shannon cackled.

"Whatever. It's times like this I wish you all were close by. Y'all should come see me for a few days. What if I buy the tickets?"

"I would love to getaway, but I've been put on bed rest until I deliver this baby." Taylor groaned.

"Is everything good?"

"Hypertension is getting the best of me, and my feet are swollen all the time. I have to keep them elevated, but everything is fine."

"I'll be there when he or she arrives. What about you Khai? Can you come hang with your best friend for a few days?"

"If you are buying. I am flying."

"No need to ask me. I'm not turning down a free trip." Shannon added. "Now go home and slurp on *dat* hummus, so you can swipe his card and buy these tickets."

CHAPTER 16

Red Light Special

Music from the studio blasted all the way to the garage when I arrived home. I was sure Mash saw me arrive on the cameras, but the music never paused, and he didn't come upstairs to welcome me home. *He was definitely pissed with me.*

I showered, then hung out in my bedroom texting back and forth with Khai while researching flights for the upcoming visit. The positive energy of my day compelled me to do as she instructed. I shrunk my pride and prepped an apology to end the feud.

Being isolated on what had become my side of the house during our fight, should never have happened. I felt silly for allowing the distance to grow between us, and even worse my own friends weren't on my side, subtly telling me to grow the fuck up.

My chest felt the pain of our discord the closer I approached the loud session in progress, deafening me once I entered the studio. The room was tinted blue from the borealis lights glowing from the corners, and Mash's face tightened at the sight of me. I rarely made an appearance in his workspace, which I assumed the reason he looked staggered as I stepped towards his station.

The music continued to thump as my heartbeat increased, and the hairs on my arms raised. I looked around the room, stepping over cords taped to the floor, and noticed Prano sitting on the sofa. He waved and I waved back, still watching my step, careful not to trip.

Mash was seated behind a slew of mixing boards and complex looking equipment. He stood and reached for my hand, and guided me into his station. His finger pressed against his puckered lips instructing me to be quiet, then he surprised me with an elongated kiss. The instrumental began to fade and the song stopped playing over the speakers. In my ear he mumbled, "Is everything okay?"

"Yeah," I answered, wanting another kiss.

I stood on my tipped-toes and took one more toke of his missed sweetness. He looked into my eyes and smiled as I leered in his face. He knew I wanted him, but did I deserve him was the question.

"This is wrapping up shortly. Okay?" He assured me, slipping his hands down to my ass. "You've avoided me for a long time. Is everything okay?"

"I don't want to fight anymore."

He grinned. "It's about time."

"And sorry for interrupting your work. I didn't know you were recording. I couldn't wait any longer to say I'm sorry."

The voice singing when I entered the room spoke through the speakers. "Did you forget I was in here?"

"Essence come out and meet my wife." Mash signaled towards the recording booth.

"Finally, I get to meet the woman who stole my party buddy. It's nice to finally meet you," she said, stroking the back of my hand.

"Nice to meet you, too." I inched my hand away from her grip.

"You are stunning. Prettier than Maxi led on."

"Thank you." I raised a brow, staring at her hair, unsure of which color to focus on.

"We hug around here. Bring it in. You're family now."

"Essence, keep it PG." Mash's voice deepened as he turned on the lights.

Essence smelled of fruity hair spray and day old marijuana. Her blonde, pink and lavender locks looked better than they did in the blue light— eye catching to the point I couldn't look away. She stood about my height, maybe an inch shorter, and her hug was lasting a little too long for my taste.

"Mash, play what we just created for these fresh ears." Essence continued to hold on to me.

"Oh no, I never get involved in his business. I was just poking my head in." I eased from her grip.

Mash turned the room back to blue with the push of a button. "I want you to hear it."

"I'm parched." Essence grabbed her throat. "Can I pour you a glass while I'm serving myself?"

"I drink red."

She returned with my wine, and I joined her on the couch, listening to the new song they recorded. The tune was catchy and upbeat, forcing me to hum along with the melody. When it ended, I stood and congratulated them on creating a hit, then excused myself.

"Don't leave me in here drinking alone with these two." Essence grabbed my hand.

"I suppose I can sit for a few minutes more."

Across the room sat Prano scrolling on his phone. He and I hadn't seen one another in weeks, so we chatted for a bit until Essence interrupted our conversation. "Mash, I think Nadia should go in the booth and do some adlibs." I stood again to leave and she grabbed my hand. "I heard you harmonizing with the melody. Go in there and give it some spice."

I declined and pried my hand from hers. Mash called me over towards the boards. "You wanna try?" His eyes gazed into mine.

"No." I aimed for the door.

His hand covered mine on the knob. "Let me hear what she's talking about, and we'll be done in here. Come on. For me?"

After failing to escape, I found myself slightly tipsy in front of a microphone, surrounded by darkness, with Mash's voice instructing me to hum the melody as I had before. Making a complete ass of myself, I repeated the words of Essence's melody singing through the headphones, missing the beat, and fumbling the words.

"Told you I was no good at this." I huffed.

"You're fine. When I point to you, give me what you got. And try to have fun with it." Mash winked at me.

As I waited for my cue, I goofed around in the booth, blurting whatever came to mind in the microphone— having fun with it. A few takes later I had done what was asked of me, and rejoined Essence and Prano back in the lounge area as Mash worked his magic.

Moments later, the music echoed over our conversation, and my equalized voice harmonized behind the lead vocals. I was mortified at the sound of my voice. Essence and Mash, on the other hand, screamed they loved it.

I sat on the sofa in horror. My face red from humiliation. My heart pounding at the sound of my voice. I placed my head between my knees, and rocked front to back, when the sensation of fingers stroked my ankles, slowly working their way upward.

"We could do so many things together. You, me, and Maxi," Essence whispered.

I jumped up and the music stopped.

"Essence, we are wrapped for tonight!" Mash shouted across the room.

"Are you sure we got it?" she asked.

"Oh, I'm sure." He chided. "Prano, thanks for driving Essence out tonight. Be safe on the road." He nudged her towards the front door.

"Nice meeting you." I waved goodbye, walking alongside Mash.

He secured the house and together we watched Prano's car disappear on the camera. I walked towards the hallway and waited for him. Briefly our eyes met when he turned the corner.

"She was a pit," I said.

"A what?"

"A pit. It's what we call aggressive women in the states. Like a Pitbull."

"Trust me, she's worse."

I scoffed. "Interesting choice of people you hang around."

"I've known her for years, and I don't hang. I work."

"You're right. Poor choice of words on my part."

"Come back downstairs. I want you to hear something." He reached for my hand then escorted me back into his sanctuary.

I hovered over him as he zoned out, squinting his eyes and curling his mouth as he tweaked buttons and pressed switches. The track we recorded played in the background, and near the song's end he pulled me close. "Check this out." He grinned on the side of his mouth, then kissed me.

'Deejay Mash you are turning me on.'

Shame overwhelmed me as I laid my hands against his chest. His grin grew into a huge smile as heat rushed to my face. I swallowed the gulp of air trapped in my throat. "Tell me that's temporary?" My eyes blinked more than a fading light bull.

"No. This is now my official tagline."

"I was playing around when I said that. You told me to have fun with it. Delete it, please?"

"I'm taking this to get mastered tomorrow. Now let me hear you say it to my face," he commanded.

I rose from the sofa. "I will do no such thing. Delete it."

"Say it." He pinched my ass.

I wiggled from his grip. "Un-uh."

Mash pulled me into his lap and sucked on my neck. Like ice on a furnace, I instantly melted from the touch of his hand at my waist, and his lips nibbling through the cotton of my tee arousing my breasts. "You've deprived me long enough," he muttered. "Tonight, I'm going in." He carried me to the narrow entrance of his work station.

"Says who?" I giggled.

"Says you. I can feel your pussy throbbing for me." He grazed his teeth on my ear lobe, laughing devilishly while placing his fingers between my legs.

I squealed as he grabbed my lower back and placed his hardness against my pelvis. "I missed you," he said, lifting my tee above my head.

"I missed you, too." I sighed into his mouth.

"Let's see how much." He thrusted two fingers down my yoga pants and parted my folds. "Ah, this won't take long. But I promise I'll owe you one."

"I keep score, remember?"

Foreplay was unnecessary. I had been wet for him the moment I inhaled his scent and he kissed me. My body needed his touch, and my warm embrace pulsed with excitement knowing he was about to be inside of me. "Yes!" I moaned as he roughly lowered my pants to my knees, bent my legs in the air, and plunged inside. Vigorous and steady.

I returned the favor and grazed his ears with my teeth gently, accepting the pain of the slight tear in my open wound. Mash clutched the back of my upper thighs from below, guiding me back and forth on his dick. I held on as I cursed, belted, shouted, and blasphemed. "Oh God!" I bellowed as my walls gyrated from the joy of his girth.

A day was too long to not feel his stiff, perfect timber. I was overdue for this thrashing, but as he said, it wouldn't take him long. His strokes grew wickedly intense, and his hands shifted to my cheeks, bounding me closer and harder on him. With growling obscenities flowing from his mouth and a trembling stance, his cock ballooned and exploded. "I'll never put you on punishment again," I whispered, caressing the arched muscles on his shoulders.

He found the strength to carry me back to the sofa while my pussy gyrated around his dick. Short breaths and weakened from his release, he held me up until I finished raining on him, then threw me on the sofa as he fell to his knees. "Get up here." I reached for him.

"There's no room."

"I won't have you on the floor."

He rose to his feet, and lifted me from the couch.

"I was under the impression that workout tired us both." I wrapped my arms around his neck.

He laid me on the sofa in the living room. "This one can hold us both. Let's sleep here tonight." He slurred, climbing behind me.

CHAPTER 17

Hit Me Baby One More Time

The sound of birds chirping outside woke me which meant I was late for work. Covered with the blanket resting on the arm of the chair, and snug in Mash's arms, I wriggled from his hold, quickly showered, blended the mix for the pecan waffles he loved, then ran off to meet my only appointment for the day.

It was off to a perfect start. My physical needs were met, my mind relaxed, Yohan extended an invite to Paris for one of his events, and a huge commission was in process as I ended my no sale streak.

I returned to the office to process the paperwork in high spirits, counting the money from the sale before it was complete— a bad habit I needed to break, but couldn't resist picturing the zeros dropping into my bank account nonetheless.

With the rest of my day clear, I proactively researched locations to present to The Stallworths. I scrambled from one task to the other, too busy to notice how fast the morning hours passed by. Noon was behind me when the chimes on the door jingled.

I stepped out of my office. "What are you doing here?"

Mash stood in the doorway. "I didn't know I needed an appointment?"

"Never." I smiled.

"I had some time to kill while my files are being mastered. Thought I'd treat my wife to lunch."

I beamed along the drive towards the West End of London, praying we would stay on good terms as we passed below the haloing angels. Our makeup sessions after a spat made discourse between us worthwhile sometimes, but seeing happy couples walk hand in hand along the upscale shopping district gave me a sense of guilt, and introspection to work on my faults.

Attentive as always, Maximus picked a quaint café on my list of dining options I'd recently mentioned. We ordered two appetizers and an entrée to share, taking turns dipping the chips in the queso.

"You seem lively today. What gives?" he asked.

"So much. I don't know where to begin."

"Lucrative morning?"

"Yes." I screeched lowly. "I made a sale."

"Congratulations. I was hoping you were glowing because of me." He smirked.

"You, and the commission I'm going to make once the I's are dotted and the T's are crossed."

"It's nice to see you smiling again."

"Love, I owe you an apology. I was done being mad at you a week ago. I don't know what I was waiting on to come to you, but I kind of felt like you weren't fighting for me. And somehow I became the villain in all of this."

"I texted *I love you* every day, and you never replied."

"I know. I was wrong for not responding."

The light in his eyes dimmed. "That's not good enough for me."

The rise of my cheeks sunk, and the weight of the previous weeks returned to my shoulders, shifting them south along with my mood.

His dark, sad eyes looked into mine. "Last night was great, but we need to have a serious talk."

The seriousness in his voice shook me. "I thought we were okay since..."

"What? We fucked and connected like a husband and his wife are supposed to? Nadia, we won't survive if you continue to behave the way you do."

I leaned forward. "How dare you bring me to a public place to chastise me."

"People have problems and shit happens, but it's how you handle them that determines whether you sink or swim. And you cut me off as if I mean nothing to you."

"So, I deserve whatever this is because I gave you the silent treatment?" I scoffed.

"You know I hate it, yet you do it instead of communicating. I know I love you more than you love me, but I would never act as if you don't exist. Life is short, and I need for you to do better."

"You do realize we were, or as it seems, are still at odds because of something you did. Right?"

"What exactly did I do? Not tell you about something to prevent you from being angry. Nothing happened. I need to know if you believe me or not?"

"I..."

I couldn't answer him honestly. Even when I hated him, I loved him, but in that moment I was cross— Heavily pissed by our conversation, horrified of his tone, and on the verge of going down the dark road of petty pride to hurt his feelings because he was hurting mine.

"Yes or no?" He badgered me.

"Yes, I believe you." I lied.

"Good." He adjusted his seat. "This is for you." He slid his phone across the table unlocked. "I paid handsomely to give this to you." He pointed to a picture of the hotel receipt from the weekend in Cardiff. "Slide right." He motioned his fingers as if I needed instruction of what to do when a video prompt appeared on the screen. "Press play."

"I don't want to see this." I sighed.

"I think you do. You needed proof, so press play."

"I said I believe you."

"And I thank you. Now watch."

The demanding tone of his voice led me to press the triangle. Footage of the night in question began playing— Mash walking into his room alone, and moments later shoving Nomi and her friend out into the hallway. Naked.

I stopped the recording.

"Carry on," he said, smug and righteous.

The video continued and showed him leaving the room shortly after the girls were thrown out, then cut to him in the lobby at the front desk, checking out like he said.

His eyes pierced mine. "I wanted you to see this so there would never be any doubt about my word."

"I said I believed you. What more do you want from me?"

"Your absolute trust. You say you trust me, but I don't think you do. I don't think you trust anyone."

"Trust is hard for me."

"Come off it, love. Trust is hard for everyone. Haven't I done enough to prove you can trust me?"

"But I do— trust you."

"Not completely. You doubt my word. You've left me, ignored me, and cut me off until you're ready to shuffle me back in. Frankly, I..."

"I'm over this." I cut him short and stormed away from the table.

In the midst of my theatrics, I left my jacket on the back of my chair, shuddering at the corner telling me to look left in bold print at my feet. As the breeze chilled my body, I was reminded of my earlier thoughts to think before I react. If I had I wouldn't have been cold, leaning against the front of the car for warmth in the parking garage.

The heat I felt internally as I fumed at the unexpected direction of the conversation, and the jabs delivered by Mash's words bleeding my heart did not provide me with warmth. Nor did the lingering curiosity of how he was going to finish his last sentence. *What was he going to say? Frankly? Frankly, he was what?*

Minutes later he walked up behind me with Styrofoam trays in one hand, and my jacket in the other. He placed my jacket around my shoulders. "Let's go," he said authoritatively. I shrugged away from him and slid near the passenger door, waiting for the lock to click.

Painfully I sat in his car swallowing every obscenity known to man. My eyes more than rolled. They cut him like sharp blades attached to a windmill. Before I knew it, a tear deceived me and fell. I wiped it away swiftly, then focused on the blurry cars passing by, and the hazy faces inside of them until I shut my eyes, praying for a moment of clarity.

The car twisted and turned then finally stopped. I opened my eyes, expecting to be parked outside of my office. To my surprise, we were parked in front of an old, brown abandoned building.

Mash wiped away the disobedient tear trickling down my cheek, embraced my hand, and frowned. He'd seen me cry before— at movies, or from stumping a toe on the dresser, but never like this.

"Where are we?" I exhaled long and deep.

He squeezed my thigh. "I know you're pissed at me, but I want to show you something."

"I'd rather you finish your sentence from earlier."

He let go of my leg and huffed. A few seconds went by and he leaned over and unfastened my seat belt. "Let's go inside."

"I don't want to. This place looks run down."

"It has character. You'll see."

I followed him inside the rusty building, wondering where we were, why we were there, and praying it wasn't an investment he was about to talk me into after the café cliffhanger.

"Smitty!" he shouted.

"Who is Smitty?"

"An old friend. This is where I trained as a boxer. Hello! Smitty! You here bud!" he yelled.

"I don't think anyone is here," I said under my breath.

"Someone is always here."

Dragging footsteps from afar caught our attention near a faded, painted hall at the back of the dingy room.

"Who's shouting in here as if they own the place?" A withered voice grumbled from a distance.

"Come see!" Mash shouted.

The frail silhouette made its appearance from the back hallway limping slightly to one side, swimming his arms through the air to help make way for him.

"I see a woman, but I heard a man's voice," he said.

"Over here old man." Mash chuckled.

"My eyes deceive me. Maximus?"

"In the flesh."

"Look at you with hair on your face. The boy is now a man." He patted Mash's back. "What brings you by son?"

Mash shook his hand and tapped his shoulder. "Nice to see you too, Smitty."

"Are you lost? I thought you gave this up?"

"Actually, I wanted to know if you could string us up?"

"Us? You and who?"

Mash looked at me with puppy eyes and kissed the back of my hand. "Where are my manners? Smitty, this is my wife, Nadia. Nadia, this is my dear old friend, Smitty."

"Nice to meet you sir." I waved, keeping my hands to myself. "But I have no idea why he asked you to string us up."

"Can you do it Smitty?" Mash insisted.

"I sure can. Get in there."

He led me to a set of steps and escorted me through the ropes. I took off my jacket and my heels, then gave Smitty my hands. He taped them, then tightened the strings on a pair of used black gloves. I wiggled my fingers inside the cushion, laughing internally at the seriousness on Mash's face punching a speed ball.

Smitty exited the ring. "She's ready for you!" he shouted at Mash, heavily engaged with the flow of punching the air ball near the wall. A few hard and final strokes later, Smitty praised him. "You still got it boy." Then he covered him with head gear, and a body pad.

Without taping his hands underneath, Smitty laced Mash's gloves, then held the ring rope open for him to climb inside. Mash moved around on the mat, showing off his footwork while punching the air.

I stood with my hands on my hips. "Why are we doing this?"

"Your job is to hit me." He danced and jabbed.

"I don't want to hit you."

"I think you do."

He was correct in his assumption as I had weeks of aggression to release. I posed to one side and lightly drove my arm to his chest. "Humph. There, I did it." I stepped backwards to my corner.

"Hit me like you mean it," he ordered. "Use all your might."

I swung again, this time using all of my strength while moving my feet. The punch landed on his arm and he grinned. "Much better. Hit me again." I took a big swing with my right hand, and another with my left, landing blows to the side of the padding, and surprising him with a jab on the tip of his chin. Mash looked at me as if he were proud. "Again."

I begged to stop, but Mash continued to encourage me to let loose, and hit him with conviction. "Use your legs and pivot when you throw." He instructed.

"How long do I have to do this?"

"Until you've got all of your aggression out. I know you want to kick my ass, so kick it. We aren't going home until you've got it all out of your system."

"You should have led with that."

I squared up and went in for the kill this time, imagining he was Nomi, Dylan, and even Isla. I swung wildly and paused, then punched him wherever the improvised blows chose to land. He blocked most of my shots, but I could feel the tension and anger in every punch I landed lift the load from my shoulders.

"Kick his ass darling!" Smitty cheered from the sideline once I found my groove, cornering him against the ropes.

"Why does your ex-girlfriend think she still has a shot!" I yelled, landing a punch to the padding on his headgear.

"She is delusional." His muffled voice added. "Don't believe anything she says. Please."

"Does a part of you still love her?"

"Absobloodynot!"

Mash still had the moves, blocking and dodging, dancing and ducking the majority of what I threw at him. The jabs and body shots I landed were mostly achieved out of pity, with one or two wild shots stunning him on the sly.

When I nearly passed out from exhaustion, Smitty rang the bell. "I've been at this long enough to know when it's quittin' time. Good job darling."

Mash held me in his arms so I wouldn't fall. "Are we good?" he whispered, taking off his headgear.

My face rested against the pad and I hummed. "Um uh."

"Still mad at me?"

"A little bit, but not really."

He laughed at my response. "No more fighting. Just love making from here on out," he said, kissing my forehead while I continued to catch my breath.

Smitty cleared his throat. "You two are always welcome to come here and work out your lover's quarrel. That was quite entertaining." He chuckled.

Slowly I crept to the car. The smell of my abandoned lunch hit my nose when the door opened, and I attempted to eat what I could before making it back to the office, only to shut my eyes before the fork reached my mouth.

The engine of the car turned off and I woke up.

"Carry me inside." I whined.

Mash leaned over and kissed my neck. "I'd rather take you with me."

"I need to put away my files and look over my schedule. I should be heading home in about twenty minutes."

"I can wait on you to finish. We can leave your car here overnight." He insisted.

"I'll be fine. Just don't take all night coming home. I have something to discuss with you."

"Tell me now."

"It's good news. I wanna tell you later so you can give me what you owe me. Remember?"

He kissed my cheek. "You do keep score."

I dragged my body inside the office and locked the door behind me. Sluggishly, I reviewed the properties for Yohan and his fiancé, then stood alert as the chimes on the door clunked and whistled.

"I could have sworn I locked the door." I mumbled to myself, then grabbed the baseball bat behind my office door.

Slowly I crept out of my office.

"I'm here to settle my debt." Mash kissed my open mouth.

The bat fell to the floor as Mash pushed me back inside the office. He nibbled on my neck, closed the door behind us, and pressed my back against it. I was previously aroused from our battle in the ring, but the sensation of his hands roughly rummaging under my blouse made me want him even more.

Fast paced motions burgeoned my breathing. My jacket was thrown across the room...My blouse slipped over my head, and tossed to the floor.

Mash slowed down the pace for a hot second, stood back, and surveyed me. "This looks new." His eyes gazed on my breasts so hard the clasp between my mounds loosened.

"I bought it in..."

"Shhh." He centered his finger across my lips, then pressed on the bottom to part them. "Anytime you speak you will be punished." He warned, sliding his finger inside my mouth.

I pulled on it and moaned. "Okay." I tested the waters, curious of the punishment.

"Un un uh. You spoke. Turn around." He commanded.

I turned towards the door with my hands pressed against the glass. He roughed me up by the waist and slid his fingers down my slot, slowly unzipping my skirt. While strumming his fingers over my bikini, he dropped my skirt to the floor. *Whapp!* His hand slapped my cheek.

The shock of it startled me. "Oh." I jumped and turned to look at him.

He stepped forward. "Who told you to turn around?"

"I..."

He twisted my face forward towards the glass. *Whapp!*

My pussy throbbed and my nipples hurt as they hardened against the glass on my door. A kiss where his spanking landed increased the heat bursting inside of me. I shivered, then melted like butter as a soft lick, and open-mouthed kiss wet my ass. Succulent licks mixed with a combination of sucking on my ass cheeks until his tongue popped had me climbing the walls, but in this case, climbing against the door.

"Now you may turn around." He decreed.

I obeyed and faced him, wired, full of flames, and in heat like a desert.

"On your knees." He directed the top of my head below his belt.

I knelt down like a submissive schoolgirl, and reached for it.

He smacked my hands away. "Do as your told."

I sat on my hind legs and waited for instruction, watching him meticulously unbuckle his pants, waiting for his smooth dick to spring forward.

A wicked laugh released above me. I looked up at him, catching a grin on his lips.

"You love this cock, don't you?" He rolled the tip around my lips.

I nodded yes, then remembered I would be punished if I spoke. "I do." I sighed.

He waved his finger side to side. "A simple nod would have sufficed." He lowered his briefs and his cock burst free, tapping against my forehead.

Mildly clutching a fist full of my hair, he rubbed the tip of his weaponry around my lips again. I gripped it with my mouth, fast and tight, making him call out to the heavens. While he sent worship past the ceiling, I turned my head sideways, and placed him in between the bottom of my tongue and the floor of my mouth. His cries of delight assured me I had him positioned in the right spot. He hummed sounds of maximum pleasure while I tortured his soul with my jaws and tongue swirling around him. A trick I learned to weaken his knees.

My willingness to make him feel like a man, and put forth extra effort to explore him sexually fucked him up physically and mentally. In doing so I nearly choked, pulled back, and went forth again after a minor break to catch my breath and recuperate.

"You like that, huh?" I smiled.

He grabbed a lock of my hair and stuck his dick down my throat. "I didn't give you the order to speak."

I gagged and he jolted near eruption from the way my wet mouth glazed his volcano. He lifted me from the floor, and placed me on the edge of my desk. My legs spread apart and he slid inside.

I lamented and leaned back, holding on to the cliff of my desk taking the fast and rough stabs, losing my grasp. My slippery palms grabbed the lamp, but it fell from my hands. The stapler dropped beside it— The desk slid closer to the file cabinet, gnashing across the floor.

"Your debt is paid." I muttered below strained breaths, earning the punishment of a hair tug.

"Someone likes getting into trouble." He groused, pulling my hair tighter.

"Ah yes!" I respired, groaning at the second tug.

"You-are-asking-for-it."

He stopped mid-stroke, turned my back to him, and lifted one of my knees on the desk. His wet tongue lashed against my orifice and I shuddered. My nails screeched against the wooden surface as I hollered of delirium when I felt him charge back inside of my warmth, slow and steady. As soon as I became comfortable where his cock resided in my pit, he plunged deeper with full force, and held it sturdy seconds at a time, repeating the offense until he felt sweat form down the line of my back.

My knee burned against the wood, but I endured the pain. Forgetting about the discomfort once Mash gripped my shoulder blades from behind, and drew moons inside my pussy. I pictured how his ass looked winding me in a circular motion, then clenched my canal tighter.

He screamed of ecstasy. "Ahh! Goddamn girl!"

Sweat nor air could seep through the tight hold he had on my body as he filled my cup.

"Now my debt has been paid in full." He declared.

"You forgot about the interest. You'll never catch up." I teased.

He whispered out of breath. "What am I going to do with you?" Soft kisses traced across the back of my shoulders as he caressed my hips.

"Love me." I reached back and played with his hair.

"I will forever."

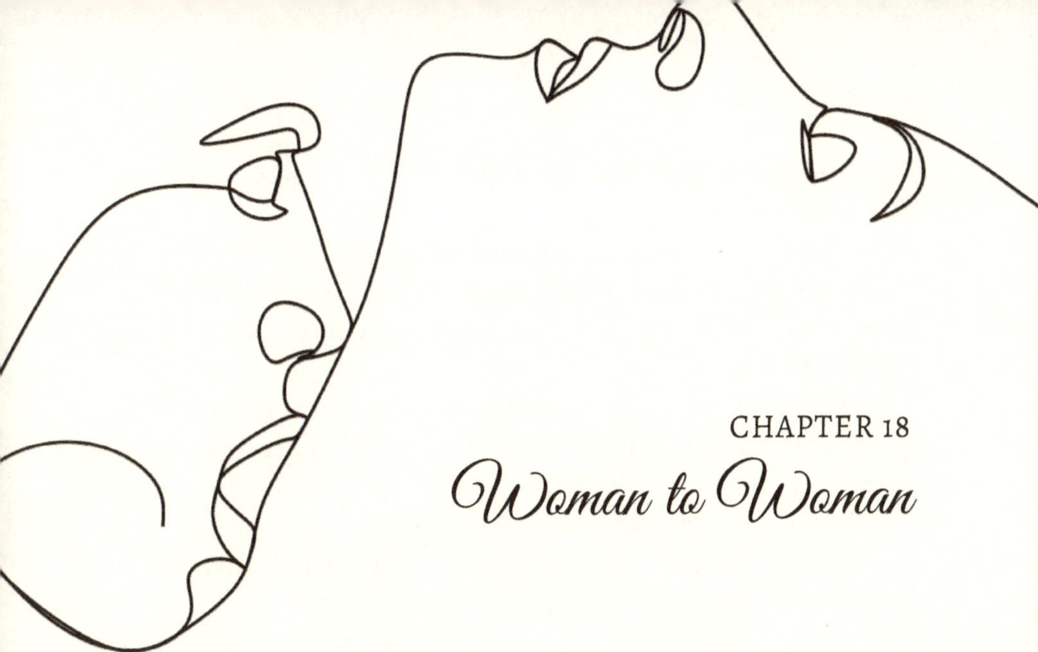

CHAPTER 18

Woman to Woman

The hour was late when Mash arrived home. I was stretched out on the sofa when the sound of the garage lifting woke me.

"Nad!" He called.

"In here!"

He waltzed and jiggled the drive in his hand. "Got it mastered." He grinned before leaning down to kiss my lips.

A slight gush of wind blew my way when he plopped down next to me on the sofa. Mash placed his hand on my thigh. "Sorry I made you cry today."

I looked at him unsure how to respond.

"But why did you walk out one me?" He wrapped his arm around my shoulder.

"What were you going to say after, "Frankly"?"

He took a long pause and scowled at me. "What did you think I was going to say?"

"Don't do that." I shook my head. "Answer my question."

Mash lifted his hands and pushed back. "I didn't come home to fight with you."

"Then don't."

"What did you think I was going to say? You walked out on me for Christ's sake."

"Answer my question first." I folded my arms.

"I was going to say frankly, I deserve better and I want you to do better. And you have to control your erratic emotions. Take a pause. For me...Please?"

I huffed. "I will make the effort, and what I thought you were going to say in that moment isn't important. I'd rather tell you my good news."

"You refuse to play fair, but I'm listening."

"Do you remember the yacht we went on in Cannes?"

"Yeah, it belonged to a film guy named Han. Why?"

"Yes, Yohan Stallworth. He came to see me yesterday. He wants to bring one of my scripts to life."

"I see." His eyebrows raised.

"I was expecting you to be a tad happier for me. You know this could possibly be my big break."

"I'm excited for you, it's just Han has a slight reputation, and the film industry is shady as fuck. Shadier than my industry."

"What kind of reputation? Like ripping off people's work, or not paying artists?"

"Nothing of the sort. It's been said to never leave your girl around him."

"Really? I didn't get that vibe with him. He was a complete gentleman. Talked about his fiancé quite a lot, and they might give me the potential sale on their next home."

"Trust me. He is not going to get married. Don't be naïve, okay?"

"I won't. One more thing. This morning he invited me to this writer's symposium and premiere event. Khai and Shannon are coming to visit in a few weeks, so I was thinking they could attend it with me since you have a show that weekend."

"So that's his play." Mash scoffed.

"This is a huge opportunity for me. I could really use your support." I stroked his shoulder.

"And you have it. If this goes well you can stop pretending you love selling real estate, and invest in some of your other talents. Like opening a restaurant."

"Are you still on that?" I pulled away.

"You have no idea what you are sitting on. No one cooks like you over here. And you won't be in the kitchen always. Just until the place takes off running. We could make a killing. I'm talking early retirement. Just think about it."

"Let's see where this opportunity takes me first."

We agreed to table the discussion of my cooking and called it night. In the morning, I dressed the part for my wealthy clients— Expensive high heels, A-line dress from Saks, and designer tote hanging from my wrist.

Since Yohan looked, smelled, and breathed money, I felt the need to keep up in his presence, and that of his fiancé whom I researched before going to bed. Olive Lapois, five-eleven top model, slim with curves hard to miss, perfect topaz skin, and highly desired.

Beautiful women have never intimidated me. I always held my own because I knew internally another's woman beauty didn't dim mine— that is until Olive walked into my office. One look at her, and I knew my working relationship was safe with Mr. Stallworth.

I couldn't compete with how well put together she was from head to toe. Tall and poised, the pictures of her I found online didn't do her justice. She maintained her model figure post her runway career, and her bronzed skin glowed as if she just walked out of an esthetician's office with a fresh facial. She was absolutely stunning, and I couldn't help but stare at how polished she looked without wearing any makeup.

Being in her presence was the first time I ever felt as though my light dimmed, and I couldn't comprehend my sudden loss of confidence. My voice changed, and I stammered in my words until Yogi took over the conversation.

"Mrs. Sharper, meet the soon to be Mrs. Stallworth, Olive."

"Forgive me for staring. You are more gorgeous in person," I stuttered.

"Thank you. How sweet. I look forward to seeing what you've found for us today," she said, pursing her lips.

"I have three properties I think you'll be pleased with. Mr. Stall-worth gave me a list of your preferences, so hopefully you'll fall in love with one of them."

"Yes. We'll see."

"Mervin, my driver will take us to the addresses if you don't mind." Yogi added.

"Perfect."

I watched how the couple interacted while we were driven to the first property, fixated on the fact Olive didn't compliment me in return. *Did she think I wasn't beautiful?* I wondered.

I sat quietly, pretending to look over paperwork, wondering why a sudden stammer took over my speech, and hated myself for appearing weak and subpar. I didn't like feeling inferior to her, and regretted not driving my own car where I could scream at myself in private.

The more she whispered to Yohan, the deeper my gut prepared me for a letdown. I kept my cool knowing beforehand I wouldn't be selling a house today, but carried on with the sales pitches I prepared.

Constantly smiling, and answering all of your majesty's questions, her distant stare proved my hunch to be true. Olive heavily critiqued the final house before we stepped inside. Yohan, on the other hand, never weighed in, or commented his opinion. Instead, he insisted we end the disastrous hours of house hunting to grab lunch, and discuss the hits and misses.

I wasn't looking forward to sitting down with Ms. Snooty Pants, but I remained hopeful a meal, and possibly a midday cocktail would adjust her attitude for the better. Sadly, I was wrong the pampered princess would be anything but herself. Not only was she cold towards me, she was also cold and rude to the wait staff, sending her plate back to the kitchen twice, and speaking to the poor fellow in a condescend-ing, obnoxious tone.

Once Yohan settled the bill, and he and Olive led the way to the car, I pretended I left my phone and returned to the table. Our waiter and busboy were changing the linen cloth and wiping the seats as I interrupted. "Sorry about my friend. She behaves uncouth when she skips too many meals." The waiter snickered at my joke, casing our surroundings. I placed a healthy tip on top of the one Yogi left for him in his hand, then joined The Stallworths to wrap up the afternoon.

I jotted down Olive's significant change of home requests and must haves, and promised I would find her the home of her dreams without any intention of doing so. Once she was out of my sight I sighed of relief, thankful my Grams and mother raised me better.

My foot was heavy getting home. The smell of marijuana led me to the man cave, where I found Mash hiding behind a cloud of smoke. I envied how relaxed he was, looking at me with smoldering red eyes, and a grin of not giving a fuck, bounded by orchestrated O's blown from his mouth.

I placed my feet in his lap, removed the joint from his fingers, and took one good toke of whatever special blend he was enjoying. I held in the hit for as long as I could, then choked out of inexperience.

"Rough day," Mash asked, taking the joint from my hand.

I coughed for nearly a minute, then lied back and ran my toes up and down his chest. He knew what I wanted him to do and gripped my feet, settling me down with intense strokes against my instep. His hands soothed me as he traced my vein lines with his thumb, later forcing me to giggle when his lips kissed the bottom of my feet.

"I gather you didn't make a sale." He inhaled.

I rolled my eyes and lied my head back on the armrest. "I doubt I will with these two."

"You are dealing with the high-class crowd now babes."

"I actually feel kind of bad for Yohan. Olive is drop dead gorgeous, but cold as ice."

"Most wealthy people are." His voice rasped as he inhaled again.

"Do you know what my commission would have been if they'd bought any of the homes I showed them today?"

He exhaled a cloud away from me. "I assume huge. Do you need another hit to calm you down? You are acting as if we are broke."

"I know we're okay, but what we have is from all of your accomplishments. I want to know what it is like to make a lot of money on my own. I've borrowed and lived off of my mother for years. I'm waiting for the moment I can send her a big check and say thank you."

"So, let's write her a check." He sat up.

"With money I've earned." I kissed his lips.

"Why does it matter where it comes from? She is my mother now as well. Is everything okay back home?" He offered me another toke.

"She's fine. It's just an image I've had in my head for a long time." I swatted at his hand, then stared at the colored lights above my head.

"Have it your way, but the offer still stands. Maybe you'll get a big check with this writing project, or from the sale of this house."

My eyes shifted from the ceiling to him. "What do you mean this house?"

Mash smudged the blunt into the tray on the edge of the table. "I was thinking we should sell. Build a new house from the ground up. We can look for land when you come back from your trip."

"I'm game."

"And do me a favor. Don't be intimidated by Olive. Yohan is a pretty big deal, so of course she thinks she is, too."

"She is gorgeous."

"She is, but so are you. The woman I saw dancing to my set had all the confidence in the world. And she is still the most stunning woman to me. Always be that woman."

I wanted to cry, but the buzz I had going led me to laugh instead.

"Yes sir." I saluted him.

"I'm serious." His eyes gazed into mine.

"Okay. Hearing you say such sweet words, and rubbing my tired feet might get you some afternoon delight." I winked.

"Is this putting you in the mood?" His hands drew circles from my ankles to my calves.

I rubbed my feet back and forth against his gray sweats, and signaled for him to come closer. "Make me feel like that woman you just described." I lured him in.

Always up for the task, he didn't hesitate to strip me naked, and I stood above him exposed. "Turn on your recording equipment."

He smiled at my request and went over to the boards. "What do you have in mind?"

The room turned red, the equipment whirred and buzzed, and I stepped into the recording booth. Low toned and seductive, I whispered into the microphone. "Come here."

He eased through the narrow entrance. "What has gotten into you?"

I freed his cock standing tall for me. "Nothing yet."

His hand grabbed my face, the other gripped me firmly around my waist. His tongue coiled around mine sweet and gentle at first, then within a breath owned my mouth as his dick twitched against my thighs. He was ready to enter my warmth. I was ready to welcome him inside.

"You will not toy with me and make me wait for you tonight." Impatiently I sighed heavy breaths.

He sat on the barstool, lifting me high enough to get a quick taste. I moaned and grabbed a hold of the narrow walls and low ceiling, holding my balance with strained arms. Maximus placed his lips perfectly against my portal, robbing me of my honey like a bee in the spring.

Incapable of controlling my moans, I bellowed out. "Don't stop!" Holding his crown, I hummed and called him several names. "Maximus. Mash. Mr. Shaper. My Love. I'm ready." I begged to be breached.

With my hips in his hands, he sat me on his tip. I inhaled his cologne and weed stench, then exhaled upon his entry, gasping from the soreness of his cut. Back and forth I rocked as he lunged upwards in my throbbing walls, grunting and hissing while I wound my pussy, gripping him tightly and drizzling on his stem.

"Mmm babe. You feel so good inside me." I throwed my slit so hard I felt him in my stomach and flinched.

"I can tell. You're wet as fuck," he said, squeezing my ass and spreading my cheeks east and west.

"Ah, guide it how you want it," I whispered.

He grunted. "I love it when you come home wanting to get dicked down."

My hair stuck to my face from the steam we produced inside the claustrophobic booth. The sweat from Mash's chest made it easy for me to glide up and down against him. I sped up my rhythm, giving him the ride of his life, enduring the pain in exchange for pleasure.

My pacing and efforts excited Maximus so much in the suffocating hole we were in, he finagled me to the wall. "Allow me." He placed my right leg over his shoulder, then pinned me in a vertical split with him excruciatingly close and tight inside my walls. Grinding slow then hard, slow then hard again, I wailed, braying his name.

"Maximus."

"You know what that does to me." He grinded harder.

Fucking me deeper, and rougher, his hands cuffed my ass, leaving no space for me to escape, scraping my pussy from side to side, clasped together like the hook on a wire hanger.

I jeered and jolted until he joined me on my high, nearly squeezing the life out of me as he thunderously came.

"I fucking love you," he whispered.

With what wind I had left in me, I breathed down his neck. "I love you, too."

CHAPTER 19

Power Trip

The next morning, I received a snippet of our recording. My cheeks beamed of fire at the visuals caught from the camera in the top right corner of the booth. "Damn I'm flexible." I giggled to myself.

The chimes on my office door sounded over the moans of love-making on my phone. I dropped it, frazzled a client heard me climaxing from my office. I shut down the message and poked my head out to the lobby.

"Am I interrupting something?" Yohan asked.

"No, not at all." I smirked, admiring his dapper attire. "I was just catching up on emails."

"Are you sure? You seem flushed."

"I'm fine. You caught me reading something hilarious from one of my girlfriends."

"One of the friends joining you in Paris, I presume?"

"Yes. One of them. She'd never forgive me if I blabbed. What brings you by?" I shuffled from behind the desk and sat with him in the lobby area. "I didn't think we were scheduled to meet again until after the symposium this weekend."

"I stopped by to have a word. If you have time?" He unbuttoned his jacket. "I saw what you did at the restaurant."

205

"I don't follow." My face wrinkled.

"I came back inside the restaurant to apologize, and leave a second tip to the waiter, but you beat me to it. Thank you, but you shouldn't have."

"I…"

"You don't need to explain. I also came here to apologize for my fiancé's behavior. She was out of line and behaved like a diva. If you were offended I totally understand."

"It's okay."

"Olive could learn a thing or two about being kind to people. What you did yesterday beguiled me. And if I know women, the way I think I do, I believe she is threatened of you."

"Me? Why? I'm sure you have plenty of mirrors in your house."

Yohan chuckled. "I do love that wit. I've spoken highly of you and your writing, and she doesn't like it when another woman has my attention."

"I really appreciate the compliment, but I— I, um, am lost for words at the moment. Actually, it was the other way around. I felt extremely nervous about impressing her, which is unlike me. I wasn't myself yesterday." I shook my head.

Yohan muttered. "Women and their competitive nature against one another."

I raised my eyebrows. "Excuse me?"

"Olive acted out of character. Now you are saying you weren't yourself. I don't know what brought on these different personalities yesterday, but to move forward, let's begin again. Olive really is a beautiful person. Inside and out. I think she may have sensed I have a slight attraction towards you, but I would never act on it. Our business is strictly professional."

"I'm glad to hear you won't cross any lines, and keep this new partnership professional. I plan to do the same. By the way, does Olive know I'm married?"

"She does now, but what does being married have to do with anything? People have affairs all the time."

"She wants a new agent, doesn't she?"

"You are quite instinctive. Olive definitely wants to hire another agent for our home, but she doesn't have any control over who I choose to do business with. I'd like to meet with you every day next week, except on Friday to get this project under way."

I exhaled and paused momentarily, shuffling through my emotions if it was worth pressing the issue of being fired as their realtor. *I shouldn't have counted those six figures before going into escrow.*

"How is four o'clock?"

"Four works for me." He grunted as he stood up and buttoned his jacket. "Also, I wanted to give you this for your time and trouble." He laid a white envelope on the counter.

My eyes focused on the bank label centered on the sealed packet. "I can't accept this. It wouldn't be right." I slid the envelope in front of him.

"You would have made a lucrative amount if we purchased a home from you, so please take it."

"I can't." I stepped behind the counter.

"You really are an impressive woman, Nadia. I don't take no for an answer. I'll see you and your friends on Saturday."

I locked the door behind him, and opened the envelope he left behind. A wad of crisp one hundred-dollar bills totaling to ten thousand dollars wasn't close to the commission, but the thought was impressionable. I placed the money inside the safe behind the picture on my office wall.

"Shit!" I exclaimed in a whisper. Thinking out loud, I paced my office talking to myself. "Mash would have a conniption if he knew Yohan gave me money. Is this what he meant about how people in the industry operate? Ugh. Keeping this a secret will end badly for me. I can't deposit this sum into our bank account, and if I send it to my mother, it would come up in a conversation somehow, and bite me in the ass."

Fully consumed by the distraction of the money, time quickly past, and I left for the airport later than I'd originally planned. I had come up empty with a solution by the time I heard, "Grandma Klump!" being shouted across the baggage claim area.

The arrival of Shannon and Khai satisfied my soul. We hugged and laughed on the terminal, made a spectacle bouncing like teenagers, and picked up where we left off as if time and space hadn't been between us.

I itched to blab about the ten stacks hiding in my office the moment we were secluded in the car. Khai could be trusted to keep the situation between us, but Shannon, the wild card, had a slip of the tongue from time to time.

They raved about the house. "Why are you putting this place on the market?" they both asked. I shrugged instead of going into detail, then showed them to their rooms, barely allowing them to settle in before forcing them out by the pool.

Shannon rolled two joints from Mash's stash I borrowed, and sparked a perfect doobie while we played catch up and pass.

"Did anyone else get the feeling Taylor was pissed we were coming over here without her?" Khai asked.

"Most definitely. She was short as hell with me when I called her last night," said Shannon.

"I'm worried about her," I added.

"This should be a happy time for her, but she has looked miserable since she's been on bed rest." Khai sighed.

Shannon nodded and exhaled a thick cloud. "She does seem miserable. I mean being held up in the house all day every day would drive anyone crazy, but like why aren't you happy? This is all you talked about before the wedding. Being a wife and having kids."

"Her hormones are all over the place." Khai mumbled.

We agreed with collective hums and head nods, passing the joint around until I giggled.

"So, what's going on with Isla? Is she still with my dreaded ex?" I watched the two of them share a look.

"Let me be the one to tell you, Isla thinks she is slick. She fakes like Evan is her end all be all, but I heard she was spotted out on a date with someone else. And guess what?" Shannon keeled over. "She's hummus shopping."

"Shut up!" I hollered.

"Yup. She still can't get over Mash checking for you, so now she is trying to match you white guy for white guy."

"I honestly don't know where we went wrong in our friendship. I mean Mash asked to meet me, not her. What was I supposed to do?"

"Exactly what you did. As a matter of fact, let me take some pics of this house to piss her off some more." Shannon cackled.

"Use the portrait filter." I smirked.

Mash snuck inside during one of our laugh fests. He walked out to the pool and gave us a simpering look, then grinned at us choking on his smoke.

Greeting me with a kiss he gloated. "Is everything alright out here?"

"Everything is perfect!" Khai shouted. "Why would you want to sell this house?"

Laughter flew from his mouth.

"She gets loud when she's high," I said.

He reached for the joint and pulled a short. "I can see that."

"Am I loud?" Khai looked at all of us.

Mash exhaled. "You can be as loud as you want. Consider yourself home while you're here."

"I was going to do that anyway." Shannon chuckled.

"And to answer your question, the wife and I are going to build a new home perfect for us. How have you ladies been doing? Seems like ages since I've seen you both."

"I'm doing fucking great over here in your land, chilling in your house, smoking on your shit." Shannon raised the joint with a hand salute. "Damn I wish you had a brother."

"It's always good to have you around Shannon." Mash snickered. "Well, I'll let you get back to your girl time. Luv needed this visit. Babe, I'm going to bed. You ladies have a good night."

"I'll be in soon." I blew him a kiss.

Once the coast was clear, we continued our conversation, sharing secrets, and giggling like school girls.

"In the morning, we are going for a power walk before our flight." I mentioned.

"Oh shit. Something's afoot." Shannon put out the joint.

"Did you say afoot?" Khai and I gasped then laughed.

"I knew you were holding back." Shannon shook her finger at me.

"It's nothing, but it's something. We'll talk— In the morning."

"I'm too excited to go to sleep. Living like you rich folks for a few days." Shannon danced.

"I'm not rich. I'm blessed. And a little lucky. Let's turn in. We have a full day tomorrow."

I double checked the girls had everything they needed in their rooms, then joined my husband sound asleep in bed. I cuddled under him from behind.

"What took you so long?" he asked.

I squeezed him tightly, and nudged my face in his back until I needed air. "I came as fast as I could. Go back to sleep."

"How is everyone, really?"

"Fine. Go back to sleep." I adjusted my feet under his leg.

"You're happy." He smiled with his voice.

"I am."

"I'm glad they came." He gripped my hand.

"Me, too. Love you."

"Love you, too."

We woke in the morning, quietly sneaking a thorough session in before Mash's flight to Berlin. I saw him off before the girls and I drove to the school a few blocks away to walk around the track. Shannon burned with questions and guessed random, ridiculous situations until her imagination drew a blank along the short drive.

"What's going on besides you and Mash making the bed springs squeak?" Shannon teased.

My mouth dropped. "I beg your pardon?"

"I heard y'all this morning." She snickered. "I was about to knock on your door to ask you how to work your weird coffee machine, but I turned around when I heard you trying to moan all cute and shit. "Yes Papi. Unh, unh, ah. Give it to me. Good morning Mr. Sharper." She laughed out loud.

"Shannon!" I screamed.

My face glowed of shame as I threw air punches towards her, landing one on her arm by accident.

"Don't Shannon me," she said. "I'm proud of you girl. I thought you might've been a lousy lay. I was wrong. You got a little spunk in you."

"You thought I was boring in bed?"

"You know how you can act boujee sometimes. And boujee girls can't fuck. They are too busy acting cute."

I stopped walking.

"But you're the good boujee kind. A fun, lovable boujee bitch." Shannon smacked my ass.

"Um, Thanks?" I questioned with a scowled face and picked up the pace.

"Never mind her. Now tell us what you obviously didn't trust talking about at the house. You scared Mash got the house bugged or something?" Khai asked.

"You never know." Shannon and I high fived. "Okay, so here's what's up. The Yohan guy I'm working with gave me some deep compliments— and ten thousand dollars in cash yesterday for my time, since his fiancé basically fired me."

"Ten thousand dollars?" Khai frowned. "Please tell me you didn't keep it."

"It's in the safe at my office. He wouldn't take it back. I told him I couldn't accept it."

"And why didn't you tell Mash?"

"Because he didn't want me to work with him in the first place. Claims he has a reputation," I mumbled.

"What man doesn't have a reputation?" Shannon preached. "But for ten thousand dollars all I hear is Jay-Z in my head right now."

"Which song?"

"Have an affair, act like an adult for once." She sang.

"I remember that line. But it's only a song. Not for real life situations." Khai reminded us.

"Or is it?" Shannon raised a brow.

Khai and I rolled our eyes at Shannon.

"What are we going to do with this one?" I asked.

"My mama has been asking that question since I was five and the answer is nothing. Y'all are worrying about the wrong thing. It's a free stash of cash sitting around in your office. What are we going to do about that?"

I sighed. "I can't put it in the bank. I can't tell Mash about it. I'm screwed all around."

"I think you should tell him." Khai slowed down. "Let him be the one to give it back."

"But then he will forbid me working with Yohan. My one shot at success will be over."

"Let's see how this weekend goes. If your boss turns out to be a creep, tell Mash about the money when we get back."

"Iyiyi. I don't want Mash to be mad at me. We've been doing good since we settled the dispute over what's her face. Which reminds me, check out the video footage he gave me as proof."

We huddled on the track and watched the clip. After viewing it, Khai nagged. "Have you ever acknowledged I was right?" I ignored her and walked a little faster. She sped up and pulled the back of my shirt at the neck. "Now do you trust him?"

"Yes, I do."

"Finally. Trust is everything in a marriage, and you struck gold." She pinched my forearm.

"You know I hate playing the fool."

"Who doesn't? But we all do at some point. Hell, he's playing the fool right now. His wife has ten stacks hiding in her office— From another man."

I hated when she was right. "I see your point."

"Everybody plays the fool, sometimes." Shannon sang.

I checked the time. "We need to head back to the house ole wise one and off key one."

"Ha ha." Shannon laughed. "Don't worry. I have your back. I'll make sure you don't get into trouble this weekend."

"I don't need a chaperone."

"Hmm. We'll see."

CHAPTER 20

No New Friends

Mr. Hunt took care of me and the girls, thanks to my better half. Yohan reserved a spacious, furnished apartment on the top floor of a hotel for the three of us with a breathtaking view of the Eiffel Tower from the balcony.

We checked in, and wasted no time heading out into the city. The saying, *funny how time flies when you're having fun,* proved to be the case for us roaming about town, forced to rush back to change into our first looks of the evening for a kickoff mixer inside a ritzy white tent in the hotel gardens.

Yogi and I acknowledged each other with a nod as he and Olive were inseparable for most of the night. I laid low with the girls until they became star struck, then found myself a corner to people watch with a libation in my hand.

Shannon being Shannon, found her groove and gained us an invitation to a few after parties. Before heading off to the first gathering, Yogi made his way over to meet the girls, and offer his staff's services during our stay.

Shannon sized him up. "Which after party should we attend?"

He blushed at her blunt and bold stare game. "Definitely the one at the Grand. I'm headed there myself. I can give you girls a lift."

"Will Olive be joining you?" I asked.

213

"No chain tonight. Models and their beauty sleep. What are ya gonna do?" He shrugged.

"Then we'd love to join you." Shannon grabbed his arm.

The tension rose between Yohan and Shannon in the car, and continued at the after party as the only conversation the two of them were interested in was the one amongst themselves. Khai and I sat quietly at our table, watching the two of them ignore us. She and I shared a look and excused ourselves from their company. Neither acknowledged when we stood and strolled into the crowded room.

Filled to capacity with a better turnout than the previous mixer, the scene felt less pretentious, and the selection of music made me wonder what Mash was doing. I wondered if he was thinking of me in that exact moment? I smiled at the thought until I skimmed the dance floor, and noticed Shannon grinding on Yohan. Khai left me stag and accepted the hand of a stranger to join our wild friend, so I found myself at the champagne tower alone, observing everyone have a good time until Maximus called.

"How is it?" he asked.

I excused myself to the lobby. "It's going well so far. The rental we're staying in is a dream."

"Yohan has the means. He wouldn't skimp."

"There is something I need to tell you though." I slurred.

Maximus sighed. "And here it comes."

"Let me tell you first, jeez. Anyway, Olive fired me. Yohan felt bad about it, and gave me some cash for wasting my time."

"What!"

"I told him I couldn't accept it, but he insisted. It's in the safe at the office."

The silence killed me on the line. My phone nearly slipped from my hand as my palms turned greasy.

"Didn't I tell you he was shady?" His voice echoed on the line.

"You did, but..."

Mash cut me off. "He knows you don't need his money. He knows I'm not broke."

"Maybe, but I honestly think he gave it to me as a kind gesture. He said he knew I would have made a lot of money if I had sold them a house. Anyway, you should be the one to give it back to him— After my project is released."

Mash scoffed. "Yeah. Okay. And when will that be?"

"Three to four months depending on how smooth casting and filming goes."

"I can't make any promises."

"Don't ruin this for me."

"I only agreed to this catastrophe because you want it so badly."

"Babe, hold that thought."

My nature of minding other people's business hadn't vanished since leaving the states, and the fact that Yogi had a sly look on his face, and getting keys from the front desk caught my attention.

He slipped into the elevator.

Mash diverted my attention back to him. "Babe, what are you doing?"

I whispered as if Yohan could hear me. "Not minding my business. I just saw Yohan get room keys, and slide into the elevator, but he and his fiancée are supposed to be staying in the same hotel as us. Oh hell no."

Shannon sashayed over to the elevator. The doors opened, and Yohan stood inside grinning at her. I waited until the doors closed, then sprinted to catch the floor number it rose to.

"Luv? I told you he wasn't going to get married." Mash snickered. "Does Shannon know about Olive?"

"She does. At least you know he's not after me and can stop worrying." I sighed.

"Don't be naïve. I love you. I have to go. Keep me posted on Shannon's Shenanigans." He laughed.

I took the next ride up and found an empty floor. I walked the hall slowly, listening for Shannon's exuberant voice echoing through the walls. Crickets. I double-backed towards the elevator. Still crickets. Then suddenly the sound of thumps brushed against the wall of room 517. I eavesdropped outside of it, pressing my tired face covered in makeup against the door, and there I heard the voice I was looking for.

"Oh shit, Daddy. You are working with a monster. That skinny bitch *don't* know what to do with all this dick. Let me show you how we do it in the dirty south." Shannon roared.

Then silence.

Seconds later I heard. "Uman! What ya do ta me?" Yogi's raspy voice and native tongue surged through the door. "Ya sure ya not Jamaican gal the way ya throwin' dis pus."

"Uh, Uh, you a got-damn horse!" Shannon shrieked. "Yes baby. I feel it in my back you rough riding motherfucker!"

I slid away quietly...Humored, upset, and intrigued. Shannon behaved exactly as I imagined in the bedroom, but choosing to do so with my new boss infuriated me. I didn't know whether to be amused at what I heard, or pissed in the moment while parts of me wondered just what in the hell was she doing to him.

I held myself, then covered my ears on the elevator ride back down. I could still hear them going at it in my head with the music blasting at the party as I searched for Khai. She was off doing shots at the bar with a group of men. *What the hell is up with my friends?* I wondered. I knew Khai worked hard, took care of her family, and rarely got time to herself, but being surrounded by a horde of men getting shitfaced was out of character. What Shannon was doing, not so much.

I made myself comfortable near a fountain trickling water from its base close to the entrance of the hotel. Alone at the party. Alone with my thoughts. A tap on my shoulder woke me from my daze.

"Hey. I've been looking for you." Shannon grinned.

I unfolded my arms and scrunched my nose. "Really?"

"What's wrong with you?" She shoved my shoulder.

"Nothing. I'm just ready to leave. If you guys want to stay I can take a taxi."

"We came together and we're leaving together. Where's Khai?"

I pointed to the bar.

Yohan ordered the driver of his car to lift us back to the apartment. Shannon adjusted herself numerous times during the drive. Khai was too inebriated to notice, but read me well.

"What's wrong, Nadia? You look sad." She hugged me. "I'm so happy we're together again.

"I told Mash about the money."

"What did he say?" Shannon asked.

"He wasn't happy about it, but agreed to play along until my project is complete." I bit my nails and stared out of the window.

"I don't think he has ill intentions. He appears to really be interested your work." Shannon added.

"So, you don't think the compliments and the cash were inappropriate?" Khai scowled.

"Think of it as an incentive. Or a bonus." Shannon suggested.

"I'm normally right about these things. It's a way of opening the door to wanting something— eventually," said Khai.

"I seriously doubt it." Shannon bragged in a singing tone.

"Let's table this until the morning." I huffed. "I need to make sure Mash doesn't act out and ruin this for me. He knows how these rich people operate, and can fly off the handle at times."

By morning, I had come to terms that Shannon was simply being Shannon, and the anger I felt towards her shifted to Yohan the more I thought about it. His actions didn't align with his speeches, and his flirtation had thrown me for a loop. I didn't appreciate the head games, couldn't figure out his angle, and saw him as Mash painted him out to be now that he had fucked one of my best friends, with plans to marry a woman who fired me.

The perplexity of it all created a weird vibe at breakfast. The girls and I ordered room service, and sat quietly at the nook with secrets between us.

"Are you in a better mood this morning?" Khai asked me.

"Yeah. Mash and I talked more last night. Everything is cool."

"You can tell Mash he has nothing to worry about. I took care of your problem last night." Shannon boasted.

"How so?" Khai stopped eating her croissant.

"I slept with Yogi last night. Nadia is in the clear."

Khai dropped the piece of broken pastry in her mouth into her lap as Shannon continued.

"While y'all were downstairs, me and moneybags were upstairs and voila— Afterglow." She waved her hands around and twirled.

Khai turned to me. "Why don't you seem surprised?"

"Because I saw them last night."

"Is this why you're acting salty?" Shannon scowled.

"I'm not acting salty. I'm just praying it doesn't affect my work dynamic with him. He's the ticket to my personal success. I need this project to go well, so I can be known for what I'm good at. Not for the person I married."

"Well Nadia, you should be thanking me. I did you a favor. He was skipping when he left last night."

I placed my fork on my plate. "Did you two at least set rules, or boundaries? And what about Olive?"

"What about her?"

"And Manny?"

"Manny is at home, and I am over here. Anything else?"

"Nope."

"Good, now let me tell y'all how Yogi is a Bear."

Khai and I jumped up from the table. "Spare us the details please, Shannon."

"He blew my back out. I know he is a heaux 'cause brother man got the goods. I recommend every woman have sex with him. It's a share piece. You get a piece, and you get a piece." She joked.

Khai and I looked at each other and laughed.

"Promise you will be on your best behavior today. I'm sure his fiancée will be watching him closely." I asked her holding up praying hands.

"I know how to handle these situations, Nadia. He isn't my first rodeo."

"Ya don't say."

~

As special guests of Yohan, we entered the screening before the red-carpet experience. I took notice of how the panels on stage were arranged, and learned questions were given to selected audience members beforehand. *Crafty.*

Seeing the writers and producers in action aroused my fear, and made me doubtful I belonged. They were poised and composed in answering the questions prepared for them. I was nowhere near ready for such a spotlight. "That's going to be you up there one day," Khai whispered, squeezing my hand. I turned my head to hide the tears forming in my eyes, recomposing myself before the lights turned on.

The main event concluded, and the crowd gathered down the hall at the after party— it was boring compared to last night's events. We mingled with the cast and crew of the film, learning most of them were pretentious assholes once they turned off their camera charm, bragging about who they were, why they were famous. From time to time, I tuned out of the conversation and searched the room for anything interesting to keep me awake.

Shannon and Yohan appeared to be having a moment from across the room, which caught my eye until an arm wrapped around my shoulder. A gentleman had eased between myself and Khai, placing his hand as if it belonged...As if we were familiar.

I looked past him over at Khai, stone-faced and still as night. "What the fuck?" I mouthed. To my rescue, a waitress infiltrated the circle with hors d'oeuvres. I grabbed the tiny fare, and removed myself from his unwanted advance.

My stomach turned as I exited the room, finding myself on a bench outside the arrival station facing the busy street buzzing along. Mash's words struck a chord deep within me. *The film industry is shady as fuck.* I hated he was right.

I was just getting my feet wet and already felt the pressure of imposter syndrome, harassment, and possible cash for favors. My skin wasn't thick, and my naivety didn't know how to deal with the vileness of this new world.

Sulking in front of strangers as the concrete pierced my skin through my dress, I stuffed my mouth with the quiche bite I took from the tray, gobbling it in public like I would in private.

The smell of rich bergamot travelled up my nose. "Can we talk?" Olive stood above me.

Please don't let this be about Shannon and Yogi.

I closed my mouth and nodded.

Of course, she would walk up on me while I was smacking like a pig, or a person with no home training.

She leaned over so her luxurious, flowing, long hair could fall to her side. "Firstly, I owe you an apology. I didn't feel comfortable around you, and wasted your time trying to find us a house. I should have met with you, and had a conversation before I told Yogi to find someone else. I'm sorry for the way I handled things."

"Thank you. I appreciate you sharing this with me. I was wondering why we didn't get on."

"Every woman knows their man. I wasn't sure if Han was dangling you in my face to get a reaction out of me. Men like him need attention. But I can clearly see you have no interest in him." She giggled.

"None. No offense." I held up my hands.

"I also saw what happened in there." Her eyes glared and eyebrows raised. "The hand on your shoulder? We women are often subjected to unwanted advances in this business. The behavior of the men in this setting is intolerable, but you handled it well."

"Do you know who he was?"

"No, but I'll see if I can get a name from Han."

Khai emerged with Shannon on her heels. "There you are. We've been looking for you all over the place."

I stared into Shannon's eyes. "Girls, I'd love for you to meet Olive, my boss's soon to be wife."

"Hi. I'm Khai."

"And I'm Shannon. Congratulations on your engagement."

Khai and I inhaled together. Our faces froze in suspense at Shannon's pleasantry. Olive smiled with curiosity, towering over the three of us.

"Thank you. Lovely to meet you both." She grabbed my hand. "Nadia, I'll be in touch. If I don't see you before we leave, have a safe trip back. Talk to you soon love."

"Thanks again for the kind words." I placed my other hand above hers.

Shannon waited for Olive to turn the corner. "Talk to you soon, love? What the hell just happened?" She sat on one side of me, and Khai the other. "Are you best friends with her now, love?" Her lips tightened.

I scoffed. "She was comforting me."

"For what? You know you can't be friends with her since I'm fucking her man."

"You'd know why if you weren't busy flirting with her man inside, and I doubt she wants to be friends with me. And what do you mean you're fucking her man? You slept with him once— so..."

Shannon grinned. "We'll see about that?"

Khai silenced her. "Does Olive know the man who got handsy? When you left, I heard someone refer to him as one of the producers."

"Figures. That means he has money, and thinks he can grope whoever he wants. You hear these stories all the time, but never thought it'll happen to me. You know?" I shook my head.

"Show him to me. I'll ask Yogi about him tonight." Shannon blurted.

I leered at Shannon. "Please don't screw this up for me. If Olive finds out about you and him she might tell him to scrap my project. Don't get caught up..."

Shannon cut me off. "I know what I'm doing. Let me enjoy myself before I'm on permanent lockdown. Now, allow me to handle my business."

I scrunched my face watching Shannon tip out for the night.

Khai whispered, "Wonder what lie your boss is going to tell your new friend to creep with your old friend?"

I sighed. "It's been a long day. Let's call it a night."

Under a starry, midnight blue sky and lights in our peripheral, Khai and I enjoyed trays of room service on the balcony. Over laughs, trading marriage stories, and tales of our days as roommates in college, I cut a deck of cards, and she dealt while reliving secrets we kept between ourselves. I laid down the first card and munched on fruit, waiting for Khai to play. Her eyes bulged and she blew from her mouth before throwing an ace to claim the book.

"Our *fivesome* became a foursome when you left, and now we're a threesome with Taylor on bed rest."

"I feel it when Mash isn't working at home, and I'm alone for days at a time. Not so much when I was traveling with him. Now you guys are here and we're supposed to be together, but Shannon is off some-where screwing my new boss."

We laughed out loud.

"But in all seriousness, I haven't made friends with anyone since I've been here. Olive could have potentially become my friend, but Shannon has ruined that from happening."

Khai nodded. "It wasn't intentional though."

"I guess. It's been difficult doing this marriage thing, this handle his ex-girlfriend thing without my friends. My sisters."

"We're just a phone call away. And I think you're handling it just fine. You've grown up since you've been here."

I blushed. "Have any of you figured out what's bothering Taylor?"

"I was hoping you had the *deets* and were about to tell me." Khai played her hand.

"Isla is probably the only one who knows. You should ask her. If not, I will in three weeks when we are all finally back together again."

We played a few more rounds until Shannon strolled in on cloud nine. In the morning we left Paris, forced to listen to Shannon's filthy night throughout the flight. Mr. Hunt chuckled to himself while Shannon's vivid description of her evening entertained and shamed us until we landed back in London.

"If your mother is as lively as you are, tell her I've got a set of wheels to park at her doorstep." Mr. Hunt helped her down the steps.

"I'll pass along the message, but you ain't ready for my mama." Shannon cackled as we said our goodbyes at Heathrow.

"See you in three weeks!"

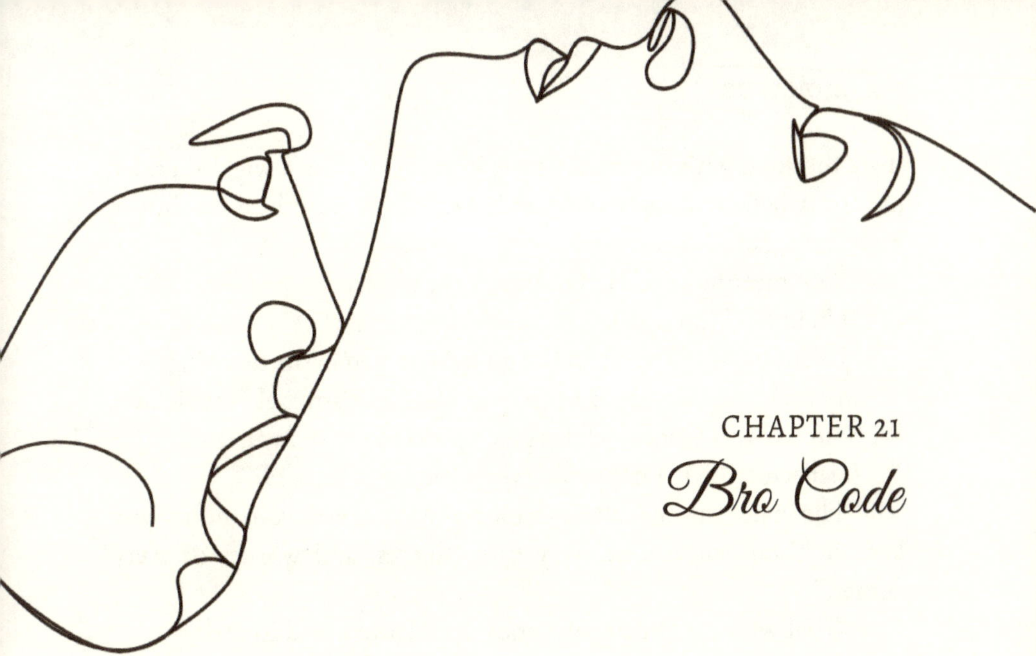

CHAPTER 21

Bro Code

Awakened by a kiss in the morning, Mr. Sharper returned from his weekend in Germany. "Morning. Kiss me again." He obliged. "Again." I held his lips longer, and he chortled in my mouth. "Thank you."

"What for?"

"You always smile at me when you come home. Don't ever change that."

He placed fresh orchids at my bedside, removed his coat, and tossed it on the chaise against the wall. With his hands in his pocket, he eyed me from the middle of the room.

"Would you like to go get breakfast, or are you taking the day off?"

I patted the sheets with my palms. "I'd rather lie in bed with you for a few hours."

"Tell me about Paris." He kicked off his shoes.

"The seminar was informative. Then overwhelming. I had a moment of imposter syndrome. Shed a tear. Shannon and Yohan hooked up. Twice. Khai had a blast. Overall, good times. Now come to bed."

While he showered, I wrestled with the idea of telling him about the man placing his arm around my shoulder. It felt like too much to share too soon with the money issue looming over us. I wiggled under his arm when he came to bed and opened my mouth, then shut it when he began to speak.

"Your meeting with Han is tomorrow, correct?"

"Un huh." I hummed.

"I went by the office. And I'm going with you in the morning."

My eyes opened wide as I lied speechless. His arm held me tighter. Without seeing his face, I felt his gaze upon the top of my head.

I deflected. "What happened when you went Vegas?"

"The same stuff that always happens. Money was won, money was lost, clubbing, alcohol at every turn, thieves, and whores in every corner."

"What whores? Did anyone hook up?" I attempted to rise.

"I'm not supposed to disclose such information, Nadia. It's a violation of bro code. But no, not to my knowledge. Why do you ask?" His arm refused to budge.

"Did Levi say anything out of the ordinary?"

Mash loosened his grip around me, and I rolled over to face him. "What's with the inquisition?" He squeezed my nose.

I pushed his hand away from my face. "I think something is up with Taylor. She hasn't been herself since she found out she was pregnant. I thought Levi may have told you if they were still having problems."

"The only thing I remember worth mentioning was something about their honeymoon. Apparently, he read a text message Taylor sent to someone that read she was married now, and to stop contacting her."

I jumped up in the bed. My mouth dropped wide enough for a golf ball to fill a whole in one. My hands covered my chest. "I knew she was being extra. It had nothing to do with being a bridezilla. Her questioning my decision to spend time with you was about her own issues. Now it all makes sense why Levi almost cheated with the girl on his job. He was trying to get back at her."

"Luv, it's none of our business, and they are doing fine now so let it go."

"Do you think he resents her?"

"His words not mine. "If I had seen her text beforehand, I wouldn't have married her." That's all I know. Now let it go."

"What else happened that weekend?"

Mash paused and propped his head on interwoven fingers. I raised my brows at him. He exhaled then smiled as he confessed.

"A few of the guys went heavy on me. Saying shit like I hit the jackpot with you. One claimed he had his eye on you. Another voiced he had an issue with couples like us, but gave me a pass because Levi spoke highly of me."

"Who said that?" My voice heightened.

"Doesn't matter."

"Yes, it does. I bet all of them have slept with a white girl before, but are quick to pass judgement on a *sistah* for stepping outside the color line. Damn double standard assholes." I nestled back in his arms. "Did I mention Olive and I settled our differences?"

"What brought that on?"

I hushed with ease from his question.

"Nad. What aren't you telling me?"

I squirmed in his arms and breezed by the incident, feeding him more of the story where Olive and I bonded. His heart pounded in my ear, and the temperature of his skin rose to a high level of heat.

"What did he look like?" he asked.

"White...around fifty I guess...bald...power suit."

"You can't say I didn't warn you. We'll ride into the city together tomorrow."

Nothing I said mattered at that point. He lifted himself and stretched for his phone, fiddling through his calendar while I rested on his chest. He put on his specks while replying to messages.

I looked up at him. "I accepting your invitation."

"My what?" He beamed with furrowed brows.

I climbed on top of him and placed his phone on the nightstand. "You know what those glasses do to me."

CHAPTER 22

You, Me, Him, And Her

The door closed to the wood-paneled room with Mr. Stallworth and Mr. Sharper on the other side. I sat outside in the hallway pretending to read my drafts, nervous of the discussion on the other side of the wall.

Mash appeared to be in good spirits all morning, but I was worried he would lose his temper when talking with Yohan. I had to trust he wouldn't ruin this opportunity for me, but only time would tell.

The wait was unbearable. After rummaging through everything in my purse, and clockwatching the time on my phone, I paced the hall and settled in an empty room next door to the private meeting amongst men. I spread out my paperwork to review my notes, making out some of the words as the bass of their voices travelled through the thin walls. Moving my chair closer to the air-conditioning vent helped me to better listen in, and as their words became clearer, I caught the tail end of what they were discussing.

When Mash spoke, my body tensed. "Was he at the party?"

Yohan hesitated. "He was on the guest list, but I didn't see him there, and I didn't see what transpired. Olive told me what happened."

"Do me a favor, will you?" The bass in Mash's voice deepened to a new low. "Tell him I know it was him, and I'm not amused."

"Mash, I honestly have no idea who the culprit is. If it were him I would say so, would have spoken up on her behalf had I seen it take place."

"Thank you for making sure my wife will work in a safe environment. She thinks highly of you, ya know. She's super excited for this opportunity."

"She has a fresh voice. Her work speaks for itself."

"On that note, my business here is done. Oh, one more thing before I go. Thank Olive for coming to Nadia's aid for me. It means a lot to the both of us."

"I'll be sure to deliver your message."

"And if you guys want to buy a home from my wife before she commits to this full time, great. But we are doing fine for ourselves and won't be needing any handouts. I believe this belongs to you."

The envelope slapped against the desk and the room fell silent.

"It was good seeing you again, 'Han. We should do this more often. You, me, and the ladies."

"I didn't mean to offend you in any way, Mash." Yohan's voice reeked of stammering guilt.

"You haven't. It was a nice gesture, but we're good. And let's keep everything we've discussed between us? I'll go get Nadia for you."

I rolled back to the table and waited for Yohan's secretary to show the men where I'd wandered. Mash peeped his head into the room.

"I'm done here. Go in there and make magic."

I collected my papers and smiled at him. "Is everything okay?"

He grinned with a twinkle in his eye. "Everything's fine. I'll see you later." He kissed me on the forehead then took off.

The butterflies in my stomach churned when Yohan stood from his desk. I entered the room with a nervous smile, shuddering on the inside.

"I can't believe I'm about to work with you." My voice shook. "I've wondered for so long how this process works, and now I am about to learn from one of the greats. It's so surreal."

"It's a lot of reading, rewriting, and reshooting, but the hard work pays off. I have my choice for the lead joining us later this week to table read what we come up with today. So, shall we begin?"

For hours we reviewed the original outline while creating a new one, tweaking the dialogue of the first thirty minutes of the film, and discussed different finale scenes to coincide with the meat of the story. Once we wrapped for the day, Yohan questioned my account of the incident.

"It's no big deal," I said.

"It is a big deal, and can become a great deal. I don't want a lawsuit of any kind to damage my company's reputation."

"I would never." I clutched my neck.

"You're not the villain here." He crossed his hands. "I'm just trying to find out who it is, so I can make sure they are aware this type of behavior will not be tolerated. There were several producers, camera men, and casting directors in attendance over the weekend, and it's not the way I run my business."

"Which is why I wouldn't have said anything." I mumbled.

"Which makes it even worse."

"Sure, I was uncomfortable, but it was a split second and I handled it quickly. I thought removing myself from the situation was all I needed to do. Others including Olive saw it happen, so I can't be labeled a liar which is what matters the most to me. I wasn't hurt, and I would like it if we could let it go. Please?"

"Are you sure?"

My shoulders slumped and head dropped. "Yes. I just want to move on and work."

"If you change your mind don't hesitate to speak up." Yohan rose from his seat. "Great work today."

"Thank you. My first day was fun."

"It won't be fun always. You'll see."

Three weeks in and I had yet to see a downside in my new career, but found frustration searching for land and available lots where Mash and I could build. A change of scenery could only do us some good as we fled dreary London for the states, where my return home was long overdue. If only I had known what I was returning home to.

CHAPTER 23

Goin' Back Down South

The true meaning of summer as I know it settled on my skin inside the plane before we landed. I could feel the temperature change from the heat seeping through the window, and my infectious smile travelled across Mash's lips. Two years was a long time to be away.

First stop, Taylor's house as a kind gesture since she was unable to fly over with the girls. Lying upright in bed with a swollen belly, and misery on her face, I lied about how pretty she looked. For half a second, she cracked a smile until the pain of her pregnancy wiped it away.

I rubbed her forehead and leaned down to hug her. "Are you sure you're going to make it until Monday."

"I hope not. I'm so uncomfortable right now. But look at you." Taylor grimaced. "You kept your word. I didn't think you were coming in until Saturday."

"I wanted to surprise you. We're spending a few days with my mom and Grams, then we're all yours."

"You should have jumped in here and scared this baby out of me." Her groggy voice grumbled.

"I hate to see you like this, Tay. Have you been like this for the entire pregnancy?" I asked knowing the answer.

She huffed. "Look. As soon as this is over, we are going on a girl's trip. I don't care where. Just take me away."

I grabbed her hand, waiting for a laugh, or any following statement she could offer to clarify her words, but silence bestowed upon us for too long.

"Let's get the baby here first before we start planning your push party. This is supposed to be a happy time, and I for one am ready to meet this baby, and love it, and spoil it."

"Nadia, it's been hell. So many complications. My blood pressure, the preeclampsia, the bed rest, the never-ending worry. Where is Mash?"

"Out back with Levi." My face scrunched. "Bosom buddies."

A second attempt at smiling crossed Taylor's lips. "You know you can make me laugh. How are you two getting along?"

"Good for the most part. We're selling the house and looking to build from scratch. It's stressful, but I'm excited."

"What's wrong with the house I came to?" She grunted, turning to her side in search of comfort.

I adjusted the two pillows propping her up and shrugged my shoulders. "Downsizing feels like the right thing to do. What time do we need to be at the hospital Monday morning?"

"Nine."

"We'll be there. I'm going to let you rest while we get on this road. Call me if anything changes." I tapped her arm.

"Bring me a candy apple back from the shop your grandmother took us to. Please."

Levi and Mash strolled into the room.

"She has been talking about a candy apple for a week now," Levi said, kissing Taylor's forehead.

"How are you feeling Taylor?" Mash asked.

"Like strings are being pulled inside of me. I see you've been taking care of my girl pretty well. She tells me you're selling that monster house."

"We are. Levi has already promised you three will be our first guests like last time."

"All I needed was an invitation." She smirked.

"And I'll see to it you get an apple or two." Mash grinned.

"Thank you." Taylor rolled her eyes at Levi. "Someone in this room wouldn't get me one."

Levi stuttered. "I would have, but she doesn't need it, and she knows it. My job was to make sure the two of them eat healthy and relax."

I interrupted. "Well it's a good thing you won't get it until after the baby is here. We have to get going, but we'll see you guys in a few days."

During the short drive to my mother's house, I realized driving on the wrong side of the road in London had become natural for me. Returning home and driving the way I was taught, the American way, suddenly felt odd until I took a few twists and turns down the interstate.

The arms of my mother felt like warm cushions inside a goose down coat. "So good to see my baby." She repeated numerous times before squeezing the life out of Mash. Her brown skin still glistened, and smelled of Camay and roses, and her joyful tears rolled down her cheeks while singing praises at the sight of us. "I can't believe it's been this long since my baby's been home. I wish you two would stay longer, but I'll take what I can get. My bags are already packed for the morning. You two get on in here and get some rest. We have an early day tomorrow, and I know y'all are tired."

We settled in, reminiscing about the last time we slept in the guest room. Spent from the trip, we fell asleep as soon as we hit the sheets, but recreated the passion years ago in the morning with a good, quick, quiet missionary stroke. I wondered, '*Why does sneaking to make love feel so damn good. Is it the holding of your breath, the risk of being caught, or the forced restriction of my mouth? Note to self, 'Explore this further.'*

I held onto him, feeling the closeness I normally experienced after Mash took care of me. Unfortunately, my comfort and desire to snooze came to a halt once the noise from upstairs, made its way downstairs to wake us up to hit the road.

After two and a half hours of mild South Carolina traffic, we arrived in Goose Creek when the doors opened at the home. I left

Mom and Mash chatting with the receptionist, and hurried to Gram's room.

There she sat in her rocking chair, staring out of the window in a comfortable sweat suit, and her hair pulled into a ball behind her ears.

"There is my pretty lady?" I said, as always when entering her room.

Grams jerked and threw her hands. "Why I didn't expect to see you until the party tomorrow." She pulled her fragile body up by the sides of her chair.

"You know how I do." I hugged her tight.

"And I take it my new grandson with the million dollar smile is in the doorway, or is he my birthday present?" She teased.

"Grammy!"

"Hello, I'm Maximus." He kissed the back of her hand. "It's nice to finally meet you."

"Oh no sweetheart, plant me one right here." Grams pointed to her cheek.

"Momma behave." My mother exhaled.

"Now you know I will do no such thing. Nadia baby, you did good I tell you what. Mmm hmm. So handsome."

"I'm thrilled you approve." I tapped her hand.

"Oh yeah. Grams lives on in you my sweet girl." She clutched onto my hand.

"How have you been doing?"

"Really good. Still here to see another birthday."

"How young are you tomorrow, if I may ask?" Mash interrupted.

"80 years young."

"You don't look a day over 50."

"Max baby, when you get tired of this one you give me a call. I'm the original. She's the remix."

"Yes ma'am." His face turned red.

Mom scoffed and grabbed Grams sweater from the closet. "Momma, what do you want to do today?"

"If you're not too tired, I'd like to go for a drive."

"Anywhere in particular?"

"You know the answer without asking."

"By the water." We said simultaneously.

We checked into one of many new hotel chains off the highway, and drove less than an hour to the beach at the Isle of Palms. An immense crowd beat us to the sand, and rented all of the beach chairs and umbrellas. To make the best of the drive, Grams and I held hands walking along the edge of water, sneaking in one of our private chats.

The breeze picked up and nearly carried her away, so we cut our time short on the water, and drove downtown to the city of Charleston for sight-seeing and shopping. For the first time, Mash witnessed the oppressing culture hovering above the city. He questioned the statues of confederate generals, reminiscent of how the good ole boys thought highly of their discriminatory practices. And after learning what took place below the bricks of the market, and the history looming above and below the city, he refused to walk inside of it.

We walked on the pavement parallel to the ghosts of slavery where well to do bakeries, cafes, and souvenir shoppes thrived from the tourism of people who either preserved history, or craved to relive it.

Mash stared at me in a manner he hadn't before. I avoided making eye contact with him, inhaling the smell of fresh pralines as I read his thoughts like a telepath. He had a plethora of questions, but kept them to himself, and I was grateful he knew I didn't want to discuss the past of Charles Town.

We reached the shopping district on King Street which lightened the mood with chain retail stores blended in with mom and pop businesses. The wind blew his hand into mine. He grabbed it and stopped walking until I looked at him, and spoke to me with his eyes. I refused to initiate the conversation he desperately tried to create, and leaned into him, accepting a kiss instead.

Grams spotted a pleated dress in the window of a boutique. Mash bought it for her birthday, along with a necklace, and sun hat for mom. After they were gifted with presents, we walked back towards the depressing side of the city, and grabbed a late lunch.

The freshness of the seafood satisfied our palette. It tasted as if it just came out of the water. We ate ala carte from every dish brought to our table, then headed back to the countryside to retire for the night with to go trays of shrimp, grits, and coconut cake.

Mash bombarded me with the questions and conversation I dodged earlier in the city.

"Have you ever looked up your lineage?" he asked.

"No, and I don't plan on it. I don't trust those DNA sites. My people's history is forever lost so..."

"How do you know it's not accurate?"

"I don't know for sure. It's a feeling I have. I can go as far back as my great-great-grandparents and that's it. Now can we..."

"For both parents?"

"Yes." I sighed. "Can't you tell I really don't want to talk about this."

"Yeah, which makes me wonder why." He moved in close.

"Because it upsets me!"

"It should. It's fucked up. Everything your grandmother taught me today made me think about how Taylor treated me because of the color of my skin. How she still sees me."

"The world has changed since then. We still have a long way to go, but at least you and I can walk hand in hand in public without being thrown in jail."

"It's so bizarre to even think we could have been kept apart. Come here."

I walked over to him staring out of the window. He turned to me and said, "Let the ancestors of this forsaken place watch me kiss you with nothing but love in my heart."

"You're being silly." I stepped away from the window.

He pulled me into him. "I'm being serious. If we lived back then, I'd go to jail for you over, and over, and over."

"You know they would have locked me up too, right?" I looked up at him. "Beat me. Violate me. Kill me."

Mash's face dropped hearing more of the dark history of the south. He closed the drapes, and carried me to the bed still covered in our filth from the day. Slowly, he removed the straps from my dress and caressed me from my hairline to my neck, beautifying every feature his fingers touched. He kissed me until I was covered in the trace of his lips. I trembled from the desire growing inside of me, wanting the animal, having to settle for the gentleman.

He slid inside and turned my face towards him by my chin. "Look at me." I stared into his brown eyes as they told the story of his love for me. "Do you see me?" he asked, stroking me hard before pausing.

"I see you." I gasped softly.

"It's you and me." He repeated over, and over, firmly stroking and pausing deep against the arc of my flesh.

"I know," I said, holding him tightly, failing to hold my breath to sustain the pleasurable pain of his strokes.

Faster thrusts stimulated my zone, then he paused again, holding his schlong in place against the top of my walls.

I squeezed him tight and pled. "Give it to me."

He poked every corner he could touch while his head rested upon my chest and softly whispered, "You're mine."

His grip, firm and perfect, held me close as together we and peaked to our destination. Heavy breaths warmed my chest, then he raised his head. Our eyes met, continuing the tale of affection he housed for me.

Lingering above my face, he brushed my cheek with one hand, and gripped my body with the other. We spoke without words. Bonded by our bodies and souls. Connected by his gratifying caress.

Fatigued and full, I relaxed in his hands, shifting my hips to lie beside him, falling asleep in his embrace, waking hours later still connected in the same position. Naked and cold, I slid from beneath him and maneuvered the comforter to cover us, staring at the ceiling with unimaginable thoughts of what if we were born in a time where our love would have been forbidden.

The thought saddened me into slumber, but I woke with a smile on my face, resting in the arms of love.

The natural alarm clock, also known as my mother, lit a fire under us to begin the day. She and Mash decorated the hall at the home before the guests arrived, while I kept Grams occupied, continuing our talk during a short private stroll around the town.

"Which one of your boyfriends will be at the party today?" I asked.

"Two of them will be there today. But I promised the third one I would save him a piece of cake."

I swallowed my laughter. "Which one do you like the most so I will know what to say?"

"I'm guessing Ernest. He still has his hair." She nodded. "Baby girl, do you have a boyfriend?"

"Grams, don't worry me now. You just spent the day with my husband." I placed the back of my hand under her neck.

"I don't have a fever gal. I know you have a husband. I asked if you have a boyfriend."

"Oh. Um. No. Just the husband."

"Don't be slow gal. Your husband is a good fella, but they can turn on you at any time. Be prepared with a back-up."

"Grammy?"

"Remember my words baby girl. It might not be for twenty years, but there will come a moment when you are going to wish you had someone else who loves you. And waiting for the day you come running."

"Did you wish you had a back-up plan?"

"Wish!" She laughed. "Hell, I had two. My mama told me what I'm telling you. Your mother is the slow one. She loved your father as if there were no other men in the world. Don't get me wrong, your dad was okay. He loved you and was a good provider, but he played out there in them streets, and your mother held her hurt inside and buried it. She had no one to turn to but me. By that time, she didn't know how to be with another man. Then when your father died she just gave up trying. She didn't get that weak shit from me."

"I've told her to get out there and start dating, but she won't do it." I huffed.

"I know. She has so much life left in her, and just wasting it doing nothing, and no one. There's no getting her back in the game." Grams shook her head.

"What do you know about the game?" I chuckled.

"Gal, my generation invented the game."

Sharply at four o'clock, a few family members along with my brother and his wife arrived to the home bearing gifts. We settled in the dining hall alongside Gram's friends from the village, and two of her childhood friends who made a surprise appearance. The look on her face was priceless at the sight of her guests, and there was more life in this room of retirees, than inside a maternity ward.

We listened to the lively bunch of elderly friends tell stories of their youth, share memories about the rebel we were celebrating, and laughed and danced until the moon was above us, and the chirps of grasshoppers drowned us in the garden.

"I see a lot of your grandmother in you." Mash snuck behind me and whispered in my ear. "See how she is so carefree and one with the world?"

"She is amazing, isn't she? Even now in her senior years."

"And so are you." He delicately wrapped his arms around me from the rear.

"Let's not get side tracked. We are supposed to be cleaning up." I squirmed from his embrace.

He reeled me back in and kissed the back of my shoulder. "Why are you running away?"

"Because everyone is staring at us."

"Let them look." He swayed me back and forth.

"The faster we get this stuff up, the faster we can get back to the hotel."

He pecked my lips. "You've won your case."

"Oh, get a room!" Ernest shouted, strolling to his room.

In the morning, we swung by the Sweet Shoppe to grab a few apples for Taylor, then said good-bye to Grams. She promised to get on a plane and visit us, and out of habit slipped Mash a twenty-dollar bill in cash. His face scrunched before he looked at me bewildered.

"Just take it." I mouthed.

He kissed her cheek. "Thank you."

Mash waited until we pulled out of the lot and held up the bill. My eyes met my mothers and we guffawed at the look bridled on his face.

"Why did Grams give me money like a magician?" he asked.

My mother tapped the back of his hand. "It's the way of black grandparents. Their secret passage of giving."

"Did she slip you money, Nadia?"

"We also don't tell anyone if they do."

I watched him grin ear to ear in the rearview mirror, happy to be welcomed as a part of my family. He folded the money like an accordion, tucked it in his wallet, and left it there. He called it his lucky charm.

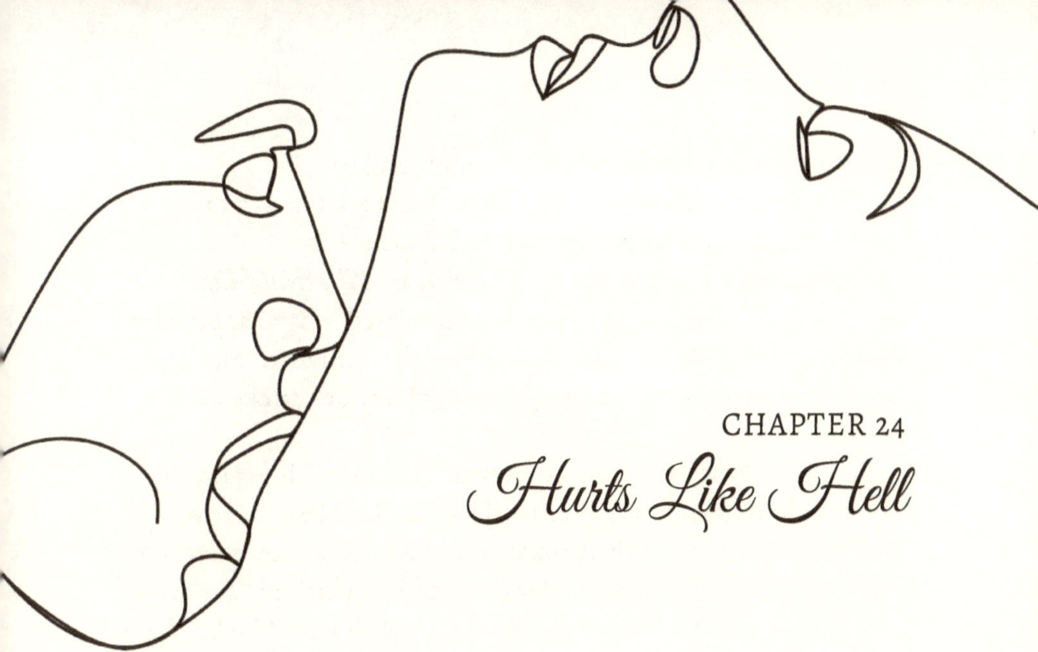

CHAPTER 24

Hurts Like Hell

ash stayed behind while I waited with Taylor's family in the waiting room. The grandmothers passed candy back and forth, the grandfathers tapped their shoes on the carpet, and Taylor's mother fiddled with the strap of her purse while her dad eyed the apples in my lap.

He grinned on the side of his mouth, then snuck a few more peeps at the treats. "You're guarding those apples pretty good." He sat back and chuckled to himself.

I smiled at him. "A pregnant lady gets what a pregnant lady wants."

Levi turned the corner. "It's a boy."

His announcement of the moment sounded different than I imagined, then I noticed his hands were trembling, and the look of shock in his eyes.

His mother hugged him. "Son what's wrong?"

A tear fell on his mother's shoulder. "Taylor suffered a light stroke during labor. She's stable and the baby is doing fine." He stuttered.

A collective gasp resounded in our corner.

"I need to be with my daughter." Taylor's mother darted toward the nurse's desk.

Levi broke his mother's hold. "I'll walk you back."

"When can we see the baby?" His mother asked.

"Should be in a few minutes. I'll take you back one at a time once I receive word." He charged after Taylor's mother.

Immediately I texted Mash. *'86 the cigar. I'll explain later. Call you in a few.'* Then, I ran outside and relayed what happened to Shannon and Khai as Isla approached the entrance. She and I surprised everyone with a hug. The news of Taylor's stroke killed the turmoil between us.

The girls went back inside to sit with the family. I hung back for a moment alone, taking deep breaths as I waited for Mash to arrive.

I prayed while I melted under the shade of a tree doing little justice, recalling what I said to Taylor when I first arrived. *'Everything is going to be alright.'* I never imagined the delivery could take such a horrid turn.

The sirens and the birds blended in the background as I cried for my friend's life, watching cars come and go in a daze. Loud music blasted from a car backing into a space in the lot. I turned towards it, catching a clear view of the car parked in the space next to it. The silhouette of the owner's head was easily recognizable. I walked over to the vehicle and knocked on the glass. "Dylan?"

He lowered the window, halfway revealing his perfect teeth and scruffy goatee. A few white specks had sprouted in his beard, but he looked exactly as I remembered. Still good looking. Still lust worthy.

"It's been a long time Nadia. How are you?"

"It has been a long time. Pardon me for asking, but what are you doing sitting out here?"

"I'm waiting for someone to come out. Life's been good to you I see." He squinted his smoldering eyes, and fully smiled this time. "You still look the same Cocoa Queen."

I pretended hearing his nickname for me didn't make me a little wet. I scoffed. "I forgot you called me that." I fought to hide any sight of blushing.

"You're still pretty when you cry. What's wrong?"

He still had a way of making me blush with a simple compliment, and tone that mocked he cared. Hearing him say those words made me wonder if that was part of the reason he kept me in tears for all of those years.

"I just got some bad news. You remember my friend, Taylor?"

"Of course, I do."

"She just gave birth and suffered a stroke."

"Aw man. Is she alright?" His grin disappeared.

"She's stable, and the baby is fine. It's just sad and unexpected you know." I wiped my eyes. "Actually, I should get back inside."

"I'm sorry to hear about your friend. I hope she pulls through. It was good seeing you Cocoa Queen. I heard you got married, and live out of the country now. You're big time huh?"

I pressed my lips together then parted my lips. "And I couldn't be happier."

"You look happy, besides the pretty tears. You take care of yourself."

I walked back inside with my head held high. I hadn't missed anything when it came to Dylan. Same old Dylan. Same old story. Vague in his responses, and elusive in answering questions. To think once upon a time I thought the world of him. The times had changed, and favor was on my side.

While waiting for Mash to arrive, I held Levi's hand for a moment. "Do you want to see the baby?" he asked.

I clutched his hand. "Of course, I do."

He showed me to the washroom where we covered in blue paper cloth gowns. The wet nurse opened the door to the baby ward where four new souls had been brought into the world. A boisterous baby girl broadcasted her presence as we entered, bringing a smile to my face. Next to her was the cutest baby I ever laid eyes on. He had a head full of hair which explained Taylor's indigestion, big sweet cheeks, and pouting lips.

"Am I allowed to pick him up?" I asked.

The nurse nodded yes.

Immediately, I inhaled the sugary scent of sweetness, innocence, and new life. A smell so special it has yet to be duplicated.

"Levi, I'm in love. What's his name?"

"Tyler, after his mother. I wanted to name him LJ after me, but of course his mother always gets her way."

"Either name would have been perfect like him."

"Thanks, Nadia."

"My flight leaves Wednesday night, but say the word, and I'll change it."

"I know you would, but we have more than enough family to help us out."

"When can I see Taylor?"

"They are saying only family can go back, so I'll tell them you're her sister. All of you will get the green light."

"We love you both, and are here for whatever you need." I squeezed his shoulder.

The waiting room was packed when we returned from the baby ward. One by one we took turns visiting Taylor's bedside. Mash checked on Levi, taking him outside for a breather away from the billion questions and commotion, and with the coast being clear, I filled the girls in on my parking lot coincidence.

"I ran into Dylan outside," I blurted, twisting my mouth.

"Oh shit." Isla mumbled.

"Of all days," said Shannon.

"Of all places." Khai added. "You okay?"

"Yeah. It was—well—it was fine. And brief. He said he was waiting on someone. And that was it."

"Do you think someone told him you were here, and he was out there hoping to see you?" Khai asked.

"I didn't get the sense he cared he ran into me."

"There is a GOD. That chapter is actually over." Shannon held her hands in prayer pose.

"That chapter was over when I dipped my toes in the waters of Lake Minnetonka."

My joke went over well, causing a stir that had to be silenced when Taylor's parents came back into the room. Isla jumped up and asked to join Levi's mother to visit Taylor next.

Shannon waited for Isla to leave, then whispered, "I'm proud of you girl. I thought you would fall back into your old ways if you ever saw Dylan again. That hold on you was strong." She fanned herself.

"I'm actually glad I ran into him. There were no fantasies of running off into the sunset with him, or anything. I got to see that I traded up." I smiled.

Khai chimed in. "Under normal circumstances, this would have been a reason to go out and celebrate, but..."

"It's not that big of deal, really. Just a little weird because it's like I felt closure, but I should have had closure before I married another man, right?"

"Usually. But in your case, you get to be an exception." Khai chuckled, tapping my leg.

It was soon my turn to visit Taylor. Seeing her unconscious, hooked up to machine after machine, and swollen with tubes attached to her body was surreal. I held one hand and Khai held the other, while we talked to her, knowing she could hear us and feel our presence.

Khai brushed her hair and braided it down, while I skimmed through the cards and flowers. One after the other, I read the kind words people wrote to her, hoping she would flinch from the overwhelming love she received. Unfortunately, it was I who flinched, as I read aloud one of the most beautifully written cards in the pile. My eyes jumped out of my head, and my chest concaved at the signature. *Dylan.*

Khai glared at me as I stared at Taylor. "Did you just say what I think you said?"

I was speechless. My pores felt wide open and my eyes saw red. Old feelings stirred in me, and I panicked, breathing as though I was the one who needed to be hooked up to the machines.

"He must have sent those after you talked to him outside?" Khai suggested

I shrugged my shoulders. "I'm going to call it a day and let someone else visit."

She pressed on my heels. "Nadia."

"I'm fine." I escaped to the parking lot.

Khai followed me closely.

"His car hasn't moved." I groused. "He said he was waiting for someone to come out. He meant he was waiting for Levi to leave, so he could go in."

"You're reaching, Nadia. It's all speculation." Khai chastised me. "You're letting your emotions get the best of you because it is Dylan we are talking about. He has always brought out the worst in you."

"Khai. I'm about to break my wife code and tell you something. When the guys were in Vegas, Levi told Mash Taylor was seeing someone up until the wedding. She sent a breakup text to someone on their honeymoon. That's why they've been fighting so much since the wedding."

"Brian didn't tell me about this."

"And I promised Mash I wouldn't say anything either. But now I've told you. That message was sent to Dylan. I know it. Think about how erratic she acted when Mash and I met. She questioned us being in love, and so into each other. My finding someone better pissed her off because she could no longer hold her little secret over my head."

"Speculation. Our friend needs us right now. I won't be a part of this. You can stand out here by yourself, and have a mental breakdown about a sketchy ass ex-boyfriend. Snap the fuck out of it." Khai snapped her fingers in my face. "Check yourself before you come back in."

Once Khai disappeared, I left a note on Dylan's car with the words, 'I know the truth.' I walked amongst the heavy traffic, and returned to the entrance when Mash texted he was looking for my whereabouts.

He met me outside and held me tight. His strong arms squeezed the frustration from my bones, assuring me everything was going to be okay, and assuming I was upset at Taylor's condition.

As I clung to him, confused and outraged, I spotted Dylan strutting to his car. I watched him read my note, and our eyes met while I was in Mash's arms. His shoulders sunk and he exhaled as I death stared him until he drove away.

I kept my cool by leaving the hospital. Betrayal at the hands of two people I loved ran circles around me, but somehow, I found the strength to return the next afternoon.

The commotion died significantly, so I was able to visit Taylor without waiting. I sat next to her, pouring my heart out of the pain she had caused me, hoping she heard every word I spoke.

I took a breather and spent time with the baby in the nursery as others stopped by to visit her, and returned once the

room had cleared. The nurse wheeled in her son, and I fed him for her, laid him on her chest for a few minutes so she could feel him near her, then read to Taylor after the nurse took Tyler away for his bath.

In my final hour of visitation, Dylan strolled in the room. I wrestled with having him thrown out. He knew from the look in my eyes he wasn't wanted, but before I could part my lips to lash into him, he sat opposite me across the bed.

"I wasn't expecting to see you on yesterday." He sighed. "I didn't know what to say."

The nurse rolled the baby back into the room. "He's already been fed, and is talking quite a bit tonight. I thought she might want to listen to him. I'll be back for him shortly."

I walked over to the sink to wash my hands, then picked up the baby from his crib. Like before, I laid him on his mother's chest, cooing and giggling.

Dylan stood and placed his hand on Tyler's back. "Have they said how long she will be in here?"

"No. They don't know yet. Do you think it's wise for you to be here?" I held Tyler back in my arms.

"Nadia." Dylan hummed.

"Don't."

"Let me explain."

I cut him off. "You know I always wanted to hold your baby in my arms. And look at me. I am. Not the way I imagined it, but here I am. Funny isn't it."

"We never messed around while you and I were together."

"Am I supposed to say thank you? Like what is your purpose in life? To go around and ruin people's lives? I mean you messed me up for years. Had me wondering why I wasn't good enough. What did I do to make you not love me? Or pretend to love me and waste my time? I prayed for God to fix whatever was wrong with me so you could love me. And when you didn't, I compared every man I dated to you. Trying to measure up to this false image I had given you. Now I see how stupid I was. You're worthless. And now here we are. Seven years later, and you are still doing the same old bullshit. You've ruined my relationship with my best friend. Do you know that? Probably ruined her marriage to a good man, too. He so doesn't deserve this shit. And now there's this innocent baby caught in the middle— of your shit."

Typical Dylan ignored my spill. "Can I hold my son?" He reached for the baby.

I gasped and held Tyler closer to me. "Your son. Ha! This baby's last name is Fields."

"Nadia, please. I came when Levi left so there wouldn't be any trouble." His hands twanged.

"But you're the trouble. Don't you see that?"

"Just let me hold him for one second." He begged.

The desperation in his eyes made me feel sorry for him. My pity overpowered the hate I felt for him. My love for Levi forbade me to place Tyler in his arms. "I'm going to put him in his crib and get the nurse. What you choose to do when I leave is on you."

I lied. I never went to get the nurse. I stood at the corner of the room, and monitored them through the blinds. Dylan picked up Tyler, and kissed his forehead, studying his features. As he searched for himself in the baby's beauty, he mouthed something in his ear, then placed him back into the crib. Tyler's finger wrapped around his when he laid him down, then he kissed him once more before hovering over Taylor. He kissed each of her cheeks, then her lips, and slowly exited the room looking back at her and the baby.

Upon his exit, our paths crossed one last time. With what resembled remorse written on his face he said, "I'm sorry."

I held back my tears in front of him, but bawled in silence after the nurse wheeled Tyler away. Before Levi arrived, I cleaned my face. He walked in as I was squeezing Taylor's hand. I hugged him goodbye before he stepped outside the room with the nurse for an update. Then I whispered in Taylor's ear, "I hope you wake up soon and find peace." And I left her and my past behind.

CHAPTER 25

Till Forever Falls Apart

It was easy to mask my hurt as sadness. Mash comforted me for days, tending to my needs and walking on eggshells as he patiently waited for the day a smile would return to my face. I grew restless tussling with the idea of fessing up the bombshell that dropped in my lap, but I feared the validation of my anger would be dismissed, and thought it was best to keep him in the dark, out of respect for his friendship with Levi.

Ruining Levi and Mash's bromance was at risk, so for weeks I carried the burden of truth on the edge of my tongue. The load was so heavy I could barely think straight, until I buried myself into my work.

I spent most of my time focusing on the film, viewing audition tapes, meeting with actors, and sitting in on the selection process. I neglected helping with the plot search, and shut off communication across the pond with everyone in Charlotte. Then, the universe decided to throw me a curve—

Olive invited me out for drinks.

Red always had my name on it, but I became obsessed with a cocktail Olive introduced to me called a lime elderflower. I ordered a second with appetizers, and as the hours went by I felt the most relaxed I had since returning from the states.

Early evening became night, and the night became my bitch. We were having too much fun to go home, so we went to a nightclub where we skipped the line thanks to her clout. I danced like I did the first night I arrived in London, except this time I was too inebriated to engage in a battle.

I ruffled my blouse back at the table. Some young boys sent drinks over and took it upon themselves to sit with us. I engaged in a game of flirtation with the cutest one until he turned creepy, studying my wedding band like a thief.

He gripped my hand. "What say we give the old ball a break tonight. Come back to my place, and decide in the morning if you want to leave," he whispered in my ear.

"Wow. I must really look tanked." I slowly pulled my hand away.

"Hot is more on the lines of what I was thinking." He winked.

Olive realized the heat was rising and our company was getting too comfortable. We shared a look, reading each other's minds, then she improvised.

"Sorry to end the party boys, but we've entertained you long enough. We can't be seen fraternizing with patrons all night long."

The boys laughed in a threatening tone, then the cute one sitting next to me said, "Who the fuck are you to call us patrons?"

Olive raised her glass and saluted the owner standing on the podium near the stage. Within minutes, he and a bouncer appeared at our table.

"Baby, my friend and I were just leaving. See to it these gentlemen receive a drink on the house." She looked both of the boys in the eyes. "Thanks for keeping us company."

The club owner escorted us safely to the exit, whispered something in Olive's ear, then passed us over to Yohan's driver, Mervin. Laughing hysterically like idiots, we hopped in the back of the car.

"That was brilliant back there. I was starting to get scared." I confessed.

"I picked up on a weird vibe with those two. Just goes to show you, looks aren't everything. The one talking in your face was cute, but had a temper. I sensed it when you turned him down. But enough about those losers, did you have a good time tonight?"

"A great time. You have no idea how much I needed this." I slurred, leaning against the door.

"I meant to call you sooner, but my schedule was full. I'm glad I ran into you today." Olive smiled to herself.

"The stars aligned for us to hang out. My plans for the evening were to drop by the radio station, and watch my husband host his guest spot."

"Is he still there?" Olive's face stiffened suddenly.

"I don't know. Can you ask Mervin to turn to 98.9?"

"I can do better than that. Mervin…"

"I'm on it, Ms. Lapois." He tipped his hat.

The car exited the ramp blasting the techno music in session at the studio. The bass thumped through the speakers in the trunk, and I zoned out waiting to hear Mash's deep voice speak to his audience. *Speak to me.*

Moments later he announced the artists he collaborated with on the song.

"That's my baby! Mmm, he's gonna get it tonight!" I shouted.

"You're so in love it makes me nauseous." Olive fanned her hands. "Look at you. You're smiling all goofy. I didn't believe real love still existed in this new age. You two are the exception."

"Yet you find us nauseating?" I frowned.

"I saw you two together a few years back in Cannes. I'm sure you know interracial couples stick out more than most, but what was eye catching was how protective he was of you. I also saw you in the hallway the day of your first meeting with Yogi. He walked you in. Kissed you on the forehead. Hesitated to leave."

"He did?"

"Yes, he did. I thought to myself, *'Damn, she has him hooked.'* But in all seriousness, what did you do to him?" Olive encouraged me with her eyes.

I chuckled to myself and hid my face beneath my palms. "I wish I knew. We had a surreal connection from day one, and here I am. I couldn't have found a better man to love me."

Olive scoffed. "I learned the hard way, it is better for a man to love you more than you love him."

"Oh my God Olive! You would get along great with my grandmother. She'd be so proud if she heard you say that."

The song on the radio neared the end and the beat continued to play. My eyes grew big, then I buried my face into my hands.

"What's wrong?" Olive asked.

I shrieked. "I can't believe he's going to play this entire song. I'm so embarrassed."

The tagline streamed and Mash's voice lit the airwaves. "Sup, Nad."

Olive's mouth dropped. "Is that you?"

I nodded. "I can't believe he played that on the radio."

Olive cackled. "See what I mean— love."

I blushed all the way to the station. Olive and I ended the night on a high with a hug.

"We have to do this again, Nadia."

"Most definitely. I haven't made any friends since I've moved here. You have no idea how much tonight meant to me."

"I'm not sure what kind of drinker you are, but I'm taking a cycle class in the morning. I'll send you the address. If I see you there, great. If not, I'll know you can't handle your liquor." She laughed.

"Well I guess you'll find out in the morning."

I went inside the studio of the radio station and watched Mash work through the glass. Something about the way he looks at me down his nose when he's working gets me going—

His hands mixing, his head held high, looking down at me with sexual energy while I was heavily liquored up made his gaze even more enticing. I could see us checking into a hotel in the city just to get one good fuck in.

Incessant calls from Shannon and Khai buzzed in my purse as I was daydreaming how I would jump my husband's bones. I sent their calls to voicemail, then was hit with urgent texts until I silenced my phone.

Mash stumbled into me. "You reek of prosecco. I take it this wasn't a red wine kind of night?" He smirked and held me close.

"Nope." I slurred. "Olive turned me onto something new."

"Olive?"

"Yeah, we hung out after we wrapped tonight. Turns out she's a fun girl."

"I see. Whatever you two got into worked. You seem lighter than you have been these past few weeks. Is everything okay now?"

"I don't know if things will ever be okay? Hey, I was thinking we could get a room in the city tonight and you know..." I purred, leaning on him.

"I'd rather get you home and give you what you're asking for. We have something to celebrate." He teased me with pecks on my cheek.

"What?"

"We were approved to buy three lots in Richmond. We can start building right away."

"So, it's time to put the Sor Fale sign up. I mean For Sale sign up."

"Wow." Mash snickered. "You are sauced tonight."

The spearmint in his cologne pervaded the car. Lost in his essence, I unbuttoned my blouse, and stopped him from cranking the ignition.

"Come on. Let's get the first one out right now." I begged.

He blew me off, then proceeded to leave the lot with a wrinkled face and sighed. "What's going on with you? And before you say nothing, I want you to know Levi told me you haven't called to check on them once since we left. Something's up. What is it?"

I hyperventilated at the salacious details about to pour from lips and yelled. "I found out Taylor was seeing my ex and he's Tyler's father!"

Mash's face stoned. "Why would you be worked up about her infidelity? I'm hearing you cut everybody off. Even Khai."

"This response is exactly why I kept my mouth shut. No one is going to see my side in this. Taylor was and is still fucking my ex-boyfriend."

"So, you've been sulking about him this whole time?!"

"God no! I'm not mad about him! I'm pissed at Taylor for stabbing me in the back all of these years. And I'm mad at Khai for not believing me, even though I read her the proof. You know I understand Isla doing what she did, but never imagined Taylor would be a throw them in the yard friend."

"A what?"

"It's when women don't trust other women around their man. Where I'm from the rules are don't come to my house if I'm not there. If you need to return something, throw it in the yard and keep it moving."

Mash snorted and choked in the same breath. "Is drunk Nadia making shit up?" He taunted me. "And who originated this rule?"

"I learned it from my Grams."

His mouth opened slightly followed with a grin. "Makes sense. What is Shannon?"

"Throw them in the yard." I scowled at him and my voice deepened.

"And Khai?"

I smiled. "I Trust."

His head leaned back. "Isla?"

"Don't even throw them in the yard, just keep it." I emphasized, turning up my lips and shaking my head side to side.

"Nadia, do you still have feelings for your ex-boyfriend?"

"No. I used to love him. I thought he was the one. And all of the girls knew it. They also knew how much he made me cry. How he killed my self-esteem. How bad he hurt me. I shared everything about our relationship with them. My so-called sisters."

"What am I missing here? You are married to me. Why would Taylor hooking up with your loser ex-boyfriend bother you?"

"There is a code amongst girlfriends. You don't have relations with your best friend's husband, boyfriend, or ex-boyfriend. Period."

"So, everyone in your past is off limits?"

"Yes."

"You're insane." He preached.

"So, hypothetically speaking, if we broke up and Prano asked me out. How would you feel?"

"I wouldn't like it, but there isn't anything I could do about it. I'd probably want to bash in his head, maybe even try, but I wouldn't because you two are consenting adults."

"I call bullshit."

"You're right. I'd hate you and probably kill him."

Hate was a strong word, but my inebriated mind, and sexual hunger ignored his response. I ran straight to the kitchen scouring through the snacks, munching on potato chips while the leftovers warmed in the microwave. Mash surprised me from behind and pinned me to the wall.

"Oh, now somebody wants a piece of me." I teased.

He lifted my top. "I always want a piece of you. If I could, I would relive our first time against this very wall." He pulled on my neck with his mouth.

"Selling the house has you feeling nostalgic?"

"Perhaps," he said, leading me to the floor.

Instead of standing this time, he sat me on his face while he lied on the floor, and sucked me like I was a peach. My eyes rolled back noticing the chip in a cabinet near the floorboard, then my attention diverted back to his elevated foreplay.

I rode him from above, delighted by the french kisses delivered below my crevice until it became too much, then rose to my feet and attempted to flee for a breather. He grew further enticed by the cat and mouse game I was playing, and caught me by my hair, lifting me to the wall.

"You miss this wall, too, don't you?" He grinned ear to ear, and then repeated those magical words from two years prior. "Breathe."

I softly gasped, grabbing on to the back of his head, listening to my body being plowed into the sheet rock as he plunged in my pussy going straight for the kill. Back to back I came, gyrating uncontrollably, causing him to celebrate himself with a cocky smirk.

He owned me. He knew he owned me. He knew I was his, and he was toying with me to satisfy his ego.

Suddenly, he exited my loins and led me to the pool table in the dining room. I expected him to position me the same as before, so I placed my foot in the socket. He laughed devilishly and turned me around. "You remembered, but we're making a new memory tonight." My chest pounded with wonder and my swollen womb throbbed, wanting him to get on with it.

Slow and steady he kissed me before elevating me onto the green velvet. "Lie back," he ordered. I did as I was told, and shivered at the touch of his hands caressing each foot before spreading them apart across the table. "Stay just like that," he commanded.

"What are you doing?"

"I'm going to score this eight ball in your pocket."

"What?"

"You know I wouldn't hurt you. Do you trust me?" He convinced me with hypnotizing eyes.

"I have in the past, but this..."

"I need to hear you say you trust me." He sharpened the bow.

I shivered. "Okay— I trust you."

Commanding and creative suited Mr. Sharper— what I like to call him when he took charge, which was often. I shuddered at the placement of the black and white ball atop the green. Trembling head to toe with my nook spread eagle, I exhaled and studied the flickering light in the fixture. *'What the fuck am I doing'* I thought to myself foolishly staying put.

He leaned down with his pointer in hand and positioned himself to strike the ball. Deeply I gulped, waiting to hear the clank of the ball in pursuit towards my brim, then flinched once it softly tapped me. The anticipation and sensation of the pat aroused me. "Ah." I expelled.

He climbed on the table. "What were you expecting?"

I opened my mouth to answer.

He placed his finger on my lips. "Why would I hurt that beautiful clit," he said, rubbing the ball against my soaked folds in circles.

"What the fuck are you doing to me!" I screamed, staining the velvet.

His dick stood fully erect and he drew himself down, placed his weapon back inside of me, and moaned at touch of my drip surrounding him. "I've dreamed of doing this to you, but never got around to it," he said, tonguing my neck and pulling my hair towards the carpet. The pace of his ride rendered me speechless. I was in full-fledged fuck me mode, mentally traveling into another dimension from the pillage of the beast staking claim on my body.

The only sounds to part my lips were those of gratification, which prompted him to thrust deeper and harder. "What's his name?" He dug inside of me.

I returned back to my reality. "What?" I asked, in between sighs of penetrable passion.

"What's his fucking name?" he asked again.

I raised my head, grabbed his face, and looked into his eyes. "His name is Maximus."

"His name is what?" He stroked firm and hard.

"Maximus!" I shrieked, weakened and eroticized.

"La petite mort." He groaned, clinching me tight as he released his load, blending it with mine.

Lifeless I laid beneath him, panting for uncounted minutes, and faded by his performance. I knew he was speaking French, but I didn't bother to ask what he said. Whatever it was I assumed meant something good, parallel to how I felt buried below him.

Somehow, he found the strength to rise, and pulled the half of my body hanging off of the green onto the table. He disappeared into the kitchen, and returned with the plate of food from the microwave I heated when we arrived home. We devoured the leftovers in all of our nakedness, silent and spiritually in sync. Words weren't need. Only the two of us. Properly fucked and coexisting.

CHAPTER 26

Girlfriend

S oul cycle was not the best choice for an amateur drinker of the elderflower like myself. Instead of being true to the current withered state I woke up in, I chose to leave the comfort of my bed to impress Olive as if I had something to prove.

I finagled from under Mash's arm, and promised to cook brunch when I returned from my mission to impress Ms. Perky Slim Jim across town.

It was obvious Olive handled her liquor better than me. I struggled to keep up, and regretted every minute of the tortuous class, while she peddled like a biker in the Tour D' France.

I wondered if she knew I was dying on my bike, and secretly reveled on the inside at my hideous attempt to keep up with the class. I counted the minutes until quitting time, and when the trainer congratulated us for completing our session, I was the first to stop peddling, and curled up in a ball on the floor.

"No time for naps newbie. Let's grab a coffee next door before the crowd beats us." Olive slapped my ass and held out her hand.

I grunted in agony lifting myself from the floor, and followed her next door. She ordered our drinks while I snagged us a table, just in time to beat the rush of other cyclers who took time to shower in the facility.

"I have to be honest with you Olive, I can't wait to crawl back into my bed." I sipped the sugar free brew, nearly gagging when I swallowed. "You're going to be that size forever, aren't you?"

Olive laughed. "Sugar is not your friend."

"It is where I'm from." I cringed at a second sip.

"I was surprised you showed up today. I could tell you were sloshed last night."

"I mainly drink red wine, but I did like whatever flower power you ordered me."

"Yes, the elderflower is amazing. I should have stopped you, but you appeared to enjoy it, and I sensed you needed to release some tension. Is everything going okay with the documentary?"

"So far, so good. Did Yohan put you up to this? I did mention I haven't made any friends here in our conversations."

"No, not at all. When I got in last night he wasn't too thrilled about our little flirtation at the club."

"Our, you say?" We giggled. "You were brilliant by the way."

"Those chums were going to babysit us all night. And the owner and I used to— well you can imagine. He was eyeing us all night, so I knew we were safe. I also knew word about my being there would get back to Yogi. Nothing wrong with a little shameless flirting to keep your man on his toes." She smirked.

Bravely, I sipped the unsweetened beans and studied the vindictiveness in Olive's eyes. *'She's not a slow one,'* I gathered.

I waited for her to stop smiling to herself and admitted. "I haven't flirted with a man since I met my husband."

"Well last night proved you haven't lost your touch. I worry I will lose my game with marriage. How much of myself do I have to give up? Like catching the eye of a man to know I'm still a catch. And the trust." She exhaled deeply. "I struggle with trust. Marriage is so different nowadays. Any advice before I walk the plank?" She raised her brows.

"I love being married. It's not easy every day, but I'm happy most days. Especially knowing Mash has my back and is protective of me. Are you having doubts about the wedding? Sorry to pry."

"I'm having doubts about everything lately. How long were you two together before you trusted him?"

I threw her off with a shy laugh and snort. "Trust is not my strong suit, and we aren't ones to follow rules by any means. We kissed on the first night, didn't hook up the second night because he had to work, and fucked like maniacs the third night. I stayed shacked up with him for three days straight, ignored all of my plans, dismissed my friends, and moved in with him after seven days. I don't know if it was love or lust, but after three months we were married."

"Wow. I mean damn. I mean whoa. Three months and married. And you're happy?" Her voice rose slightly in denial. "I assumed you were long distance lovers or something. Do you have to do special things to keep him interested?" She asked below her breath.

"No. We go at it pretty good." I chortled, thinking of last night.

Olive stirred her drink in a daze. "My concern is will I be enough? So many of my friends say things like they have to have threesomes to please their mate. Or they have these arrangements like one weekend out of the year they get to be single."

"Oh hell no. I'm not with the hall pass life. It can lead to getting you dicmatized or traumatized."

"Exactly. What is the point of being married if you have to do such things? I'm hoping he's getting all of his cheating out of his system now." She sighed.

"Why do you think he's cheating on you?"

"Men like him always cheat."

"Then why marry him?"

"Why not?"

I was stumped. And cornered. And suspicious. *'Did she know about Shannon and thought liquoring me up would make me blab?'* I wondered.

Our conversation paused nearly a minute when I blurted, "I am coming up blank with an answer to your question. I got nothing."

She laughed at my American use of language. "It's fine. My question was rhetorical. Sort of." she shrugged. "I've done well in my career and still turn heads. I'll always end up on the right side with

Yohan Stallworth, or another like him. A girl can dream that caliber of a man would be monogamous. But it doesn't exist."

The acceptance of secret affairs in Olive and Yohan's relationship reminded me love, honor, and truth isn't a factor for everyone. Money, status, and security played a huge part in some unions, and seeing the pain in her eyes she thought she was hiding made me grateful I had companionship and love in mine.

"I have a friend whose motto is until she says I do, she is free to spread it around."

"And what about after?"

"Then she'll be faithful. So she says."

"You know I thought about travelling down memory lane last night. If you weren't with me, I might've evened the score." Olive blushed.

"Well, if you listen to my friend's advice, you're free to do as you wish." I sipped my final taste of the bitter coffee.

"I'm so glad we took the time to get to know one another. I have friends, but none of them are this easy to talk to."

"I couldn't agree more. My friends back home aren't thrilled about me finding new friends. They think I'll replace them."

"Come to this luncheon I'm having. I want you to meet my girl-friends. They can sometimes be real bitches, which is why I can't talk to them like this, but you'll fit right in."

I seriously doubted I would fit right in with a group of girls who she considered to be bitchy, but I accepted the invitation graciously.

"Sounds like a plan." I looked at the time on my phone. "I promised the hubs I'd make brunch, so I'm going to head home and feed my man." I rose from the table, startled by Olive's arms wrapping around me.

"It was a pleasure hanging out with you. I'll be in touch soon." She released me. "Ciao."

Mash was still asleep when I returned home. I showered, then curated a brunch of his favorite dishes: a Dutch-oven blueberry pancake, country-fried potatoes, and cheese scrambled eggs.

I surprised him with breakfast in bed, waking him with the aroma of confection on the tray. He rubbed his eyes a few times before opening them fully, then smiled at the smell of heaven at his fingertips.

"To what do I owe the pleasure?" he asked.

"You were magnifique last night."

"Was I?" He reached for the fork.

"I like when you get creative."

He smirked. "If it gets me breakfast in bed, I'll defile you more often."

I playfully shoved him and he hid the grin on his face, exposing his mouth full of food.

He swallowed. "How was your workout?"

"Brutal."

"And Olive?"

"She's good. She opened up a little more today."

"Your first friend abroad." His brows raised, looking up at me.

"And perfect timing, too."

"Speaking of friends, Levi messaged again wanting to know why you're being distant. We need to get our stories straight."

I nodded. "Did I answer your question last night?"

He licked his fingers and exhaled as his eyes bounced between me and the plate. "Yeah."

I leaned forward and kissed his sticky lips. "Good."

We lied around for most of the afternoon, me in a t-shirt and no panties, him shirtless in briefs. By evening, my peace was disturbed with a phone call from Khai. Mash insisted I answer.

"It's nice to know you can still hold a grudge," she said.

"Ha ha."

"How are you?"

"At peace."

"So, we're down to short answers. I'd expect nothing less, than for you to make this hard for me. I thought you should know Taylor is recovering well, and hammering me about why you haven't called them. I don't know what to say to her."

"You can tell her I wish her well in all of her future endeavors."

"Nadia. I'm not saying that. What's up with you? You haven't contacted any of us, and yes it has been discussed."

"Because I was right, and you didn't have my back. You always have my back."

"Taylor literally had a stroke. Some things have precedence. Not some wild theory about who is seeing who."

"Well he came to the hospital before my flight, confessed about the affair, and the baby. I'm sure Taylor knows exactly why I haven't called by now. She should be thanking me for getting rid of the evidence before Levi arrived."

"My God. How do we fix this?"

"My friendship with Taylor is over."

"Unacceptable. We are too close for a jackass like Dylan to come between us."

"You know what plays over in my head. How fake she's been to my face. Throwing up the fact I couldn't get over him all these years and she's been fucking him the entire time. What kind of friend does that, Khai?"

Khai sputtered. "Come home. All of us need to hash this out. Face to face. At least come and see the baby. I know you love the baby."

I hung up emotionally drained after declining the request to come home. I sat on the sofa looking at the television on mute without realizing Mash had been watching me sulk. Also, listening to my conversation. I jumped at the sound of his voice.

"I overheard everything. Don't spend too much time being angry. And don't write your friends off just yet."

"Humph. Before we came to London, I broke up with the man Isla is currently dating. That very same night Taylor made me the brunt of her jokes, teasing I was still hung up on my ex, and all of my friends sided with her. All the while she was shagging him, and laughing in my face. Look at it from where I'm sitting. Do you understand how I feel, now?"

"Believe it or not. I do." He joined me on the couch. "Will this affect my friendship with Levi?"

"I hope not. Let's aim to get him in the divorce."

He brushed my cheek, and I captured his hand pressed against my shoulder. He finally understood I was mourning the loss of my friend and my pride, not the dreaded ex. But he was right, I didn't need to spend any more time being angry, when I could be living. And that was exactly what I planned to do.

CHAPTER 27

Lights, Camera, Action

S et life was intimidating. Experienced professionals and production teams ran circles around me in the fast paced, overwhelming, high stressed environment, but as time went on and the more I became familiar with the crew, the long days stopped feeling like work.

I shadowed Yohan closely, following his direction of repetitious orders and demands. Some days went long into the night, pushing Olive and I to spend more time together grabbing dinners and after hour drinks. Sometimes we joined the cast and crew on their late-night antics to the pub down the block. In doing so, the actors became approachable, and in turn I took notice of Chili, a thespian from the U.S. with a huge fan base.

Chili was sweet, fun, and full of life onset. One of the few men who held the door open for women, and made everyone laugh in between takes. He was often seen rehearsing lines to himself in a corner, or openly changing his shirt at the end of scenes. The ladies on set found him very easy on the eyes, and lingered around in-between takes to catch a glimpse of his abs and country boy smile. There was no doubt in my mind he knew what he was doing.

I was shocked to find myself watching him closely during his shirt changes as well. Maximus was hotter than him, and the only vanilla babe I'd ever been attracted to. So, to notice the American boy in such a way made me question if the blue-eyed cutie had come into my world as a test of temptation, or was I now an official hummus shopper?

Moments like this made me miss the girls. Once upon a time I would have ran to them with such gossip, taken the dozen jokes thrown at me, and thought nothing of it. Now, I found myself wondering if I should gossip about it with Olive instead, or apply the lesson I learned from the Taylor fiasco and keep it to myself.

A minor scene didn't receive Yohan's approval. "This looks weak." He complained. "Nadia, stand alongside Chili so we can wrap up this segment tonight." I shook my head no. He leaned over and whispered, "Word of advice, never say no when something needs to be done on your own project, or to the director."

"I'm not an actress, Han. I'm shaking right now. And I don't have on makeup."

"Your back will be facing the camera. Grace! Nadia is standing in as an extra next to Chili. Back facing the camera on the right side of the table."

Grace positioned me on the set.

Yohan screamed. "Roll'em!"

My legs trembled beneath me.

"My God. Stop shaking." Chili mumbled.

I froze and couldn't speak.

"Breathe," he said.

I locked eyes with him, thinking of the first time Mash spoke that very word to me. Suddenly I exhaled a sigh of relief.

"That's it. You're doing great. Just stand there while I pretend I'm having the time of my life. And don't make any sudden moves like toss your hair to take away from the main characters shot." He explained.

"Now I have the urge to toss my hair."

"Don't do it." He grinned. "I would hate for you to get yelled at."

"So, what should I do?"

"Um, can you do a fake laugh? Better yet tell me about yourself." He placed his hand on his chin.

"What do you want to know?"

"How long have you been a P.A.? That is what you do, right?"

"No. I wrote this piece."

"Seriously. You're the writer? I thought you were Yogi's personal assistant."

"No. Just the boring writer. Yohan is teaching me the ropes. This is my debut."

"Congrats, and I don't find you boring at all. I just realized you don't have an accent."

"I'm from the states. North Carolina."

"New *Jers* born and bred, but I live in between L.A. and N.Y. now. How did you end up all the way over here?"

"Cut!" Yohan yelled.

"Don't move." Chili warned. "He may retake the scene, and you'll need to be in that exact spot...You were about to tell me how a writer from North Carolina ended up in England?"

"Love." I smiled.

"Love of the city?"

"No." I shook my head.

"I see. It must be love if you moved this far for him. I hope he doesn't mind me saying he has great taste."

"I don't mind you saying it. He knows what he has. And thank you." I placed my hand across my chest.

"Something tells me you get compliments all the time."

"Not all the time. Men say things, but aren't genuine."

Yohan called out to the room. "Places everyone. Roll'em!"

Chili erased the look on his face from our conversation and returned back into his character. I stood still once again while he reenacted the same emotions as before for the camera.

"So, you do know what you're talking about," I said.

He flashed the top row of his teeth. "I've been doing this for a while. As you were saying."

I looked him in the eyes. "Men are unpredictable creatures. They say anything to get what they want and do whatever they please. So, when a man tells me I'm pretty, I say thank you. But I don't think they really mean it. They just see me as something they'd like to— you know, and then move on. You'd be surprised how many women suffer from self-esteem issues because of a man."

"Does this man of yours compliment you often?" Chili smoothed the baby hairs across his top lip.

"All the time. And he married me so..."

He smirked at my response and stared into my eyes. I knew then he was probing and sizing me up. I had to give it to him though. He was crafty.

"Ah, so you're off the market." He licked his lips. "Smart man. When you get a good one you better not let it slip through your fingers. Myself...I...ugh travel too much to settle down right now."

"Monogamy is hell for most men. The majority of them are bone collectors." I scoffed.

"Ouch. You did write this piece. Don't get me wrong, I want to settle down one day, but not any time soon. And she'd have to be the right woman."

"I hate when men say that— The right woman. As if women don't want the right man. We were all the right woman at some point, until some jerk came along and toyed with our emotions. I think men get high on pulling women's strings. You know what, my bad. I didn't mean to unleash my male bashing theories on you."

"It's cool. We're just vibing. And I got you to stop shaking on camera."

He was right. I got lost in our conversation and forgot the cameras were rolling. *Oh, he is good.* "Thank you for that. I'm totally not nervous anymore." I lowered my head and blushed. "Humor me. Why do men say they love..."?

"Cut! Okay we've got it!" Yohan shouted.

"What were you about to ask me?" Chili pulled on my blouse.

"It was nothing. Nice chatting with you. And thanks again."

I walked towards Olive arriving late on set.

She side-eyed me and spoke under her breath. "You looked like you were enjoying yourself over there."

We snickered.

"Yeah, watch out for him. He's a smooth one," I said.

"I sent you the invite for my brunch, but haven't received an rsvp.

Are you and your better half going to be able to make it? The elderflower will be flowing."

"We'll be there. I had to check his schedule before I sent you a reply. Now you and your better half have a good night. I can't hang tonight."

On the drive home I caught myself smiling at Chili's flirtation, picturing Grams applauding in my head. "Have a backup plan," she said, but I wasn't that kind of woman, and Chili wasn't the type to become entangled with. He had nothing to lose, whereas I had everything to fumble. And just like that, I stopped toying with the idea of him as a play thing. I went home and led Mash to our bedroom where he pounded any thought of Chili from my mind, and realized the long hours, loneliness, and hurt burning inside of me was creating a fire I needed to put out.

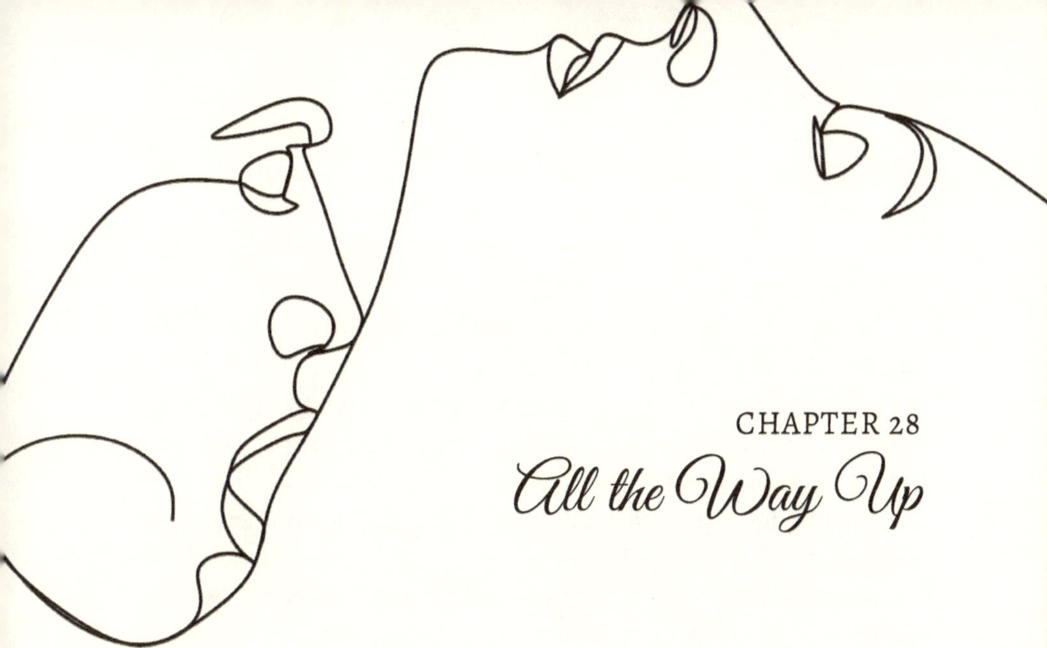

CHAPTER 28

All the Way Up

With careful maintenance, I had the best of both worlds—Interesting debates with Chili at work, and the delight of meaningful conversations with Mash at home.

In the meantime, ground was broken on the lot of our new home, while the sale of our current home in Virginia Water brought on anxiety. Stranger after stranger in and out of the house, violating our privacy with no follow-up, or offers to buy became unsettling. I loathed the outsiders walking through our personal space, touching our things, and seeing how we lived, so we moved into a flat in the city, leaving select pieces of furniture behind to be included in the sale.

Living out of suitcases, and being trapped between boxes and furniture tested our relationship. The temporary space was intimate, surrounded by everything imaginable from grocers, coffee shops, fitness classes, and the biggest change—

noise. Despite the latter, I enjoyed our new place. The ease and access of everything from shows, work, and shops had its appeal. It didn't beat living in the peaceful countryside, but the change was fresh and more importantly, necessary for our sanity and privacy.

The sanity part didn't last very long with the stress of designing a dream home. In terms of style, I wanted a mixture of the old world and the new. A classic exterior resembling historic England with a modern interior, and my personal lavatory. Mash loved the idea, but opposed one detail in the setup of my draft, causing strain between us.

"I maintain organization of my things better in the bathroom. Your side isn't as neat." I explained.

"Even as a single man, I specifically built a double vanity for the day I would share my life with my wife." He argued. "I like getting ready for bed together. You putting that goop on your face while I'm shaving. Me watching you primp to get ready. You want to take away something I couldn't wait to have."

Hearing his explanation filled me with guilt, but not enough to cave in with what I wanted.

I squeezed his lips. "That's very sweet, but I still want my own shower and vanity space. I don't like watching you brush your teeth, or being watched brushing mine. How could you have not picked up on that? Hell, I don't like watching people on TV brush their teeth. I'd also love it if I didn't sit in piss in the middle of the night, but fine, scrap my little piece of heaven from the plans."

"Do we at least agree on four bedrooms, a studio, a man cave, and an office?" He turned his head away from me.

I stared at him seething to himself. "And a pool."

He walked away flashing the 'Okay' symbol with his fingers.

I spazzed under my breath. "So, this is why couples bicker over building a house."

Mash stepped back into the bedroom. "What was that?"

"Nothing." I grinned.

Our disagreement suddenly made coming home the pit of my day, and going into work the peak. Having no space to find alone time forced us to deal with each other. And as time carried on without extra rooms to hide in, I realized I had changed. *Look at me being spoiled as if I hadn't lived most of my life in a starter home.*

Reshoots and overtime solved some of our problems, giving me a reason to come home just in time for dinner, after dinner, or near bedtime. And on the days we finished early and on time, I spent it hanging out with the cast and crew after work.

Mingling amongst them eased the sorrow I hid of feuding with my friends, and walking on eggshells in the flat. Serving the balance I needed as loneliness blossomed like a flower in the spring in my bones.

With my friends list shrinking, the weekend of Olive's brunch arrived right on time. I assumed her circle of cronies would be dressed in designer rags, and judge me from the texture of my hair to the nail polish on my toes. *Olive did call them bitches after all.* So, I made sure I was properly prepped, putting the husband's wallet to use.

We swung by the lot of our future residence on the way to Yohan's house. The progress was on target, if not further advanced. "We could be in here sooner by the looks of it." Mash clapped, smiling the blueprint was coming to life. "We did this." He emphasized. "You and I. Together."

"Yeah, I guess we did."

"I can't wait for us to move in. You have a surprise waiting for you inside. A few more weeks, we'll be christening every room."

A text in all caps from Khai popped up on my phone before I could respond. I muted my ringtone, and pulled Mash towards the car. "Come on. We're going to be late."

"Everything okay?"

"Yeah." I lied, covering my phone screen.

We left our future love nest, arriving on The Stallworth property minutes down the road.

Mash turned off the car. "It might be important. Go ahead and take it. You can't avoid them forever. I'll meet you inside."

I stood on the porch and braced myself for belligerence as I dialed Khai's number.

She answered. "Why haven't I heard from you?"

"I've been super busy. Is everyone alright?"

"You tell us." Shannon interrupted in the background. "That's right. She got you on speaker. I hear you have a new best friend. Are you liking your replacement?"

"Well, I can see where this conversation is headed, and since I'm at an event my new friend is hosting right now, I'll call you back."

"So, it's like that? Wow." Shannon fumed.

"We need to get together. Soon." Khai demanded.

"We can discuss that when I'm done here. I promise, I'll call you back."

I took a deep breath and regrouped before walking inside the chic, monochrome decorated weekend home of The Stallworths. It was beautiful. I suddenly understood why Olive said she would stay if he cheated. The perks, the homes, and the misery came as a package deal.

His house manager escorted me to the garden of paradise Olive called the sanctuary. The guests were assembled outside, separated by the sexes— The men gathered near the bar, and the women grouped by the courtyard's fire pit. I strolled towards Olive and her friends, suddenly taken aback at my name being shouted across the lawn.

"Nadia! Bring your cool ass over here! I was telling these guys about your man bashing theory! Come so I can prove you wrong!"

I froze in my steps and my shoulders tensed. Olive and I share a look of mortification, then I turned around on my toes to face the bar. "What in the hell is his problem?" I said under my breath. Mash's chest appeared still, and his face stern as a bull. A look I'd seen once in Copenhagen. My eyes roamed over to Yohan looking up at me behind his mug of beer, then over to Chili with an idiotic smile on his face.

In my mind the music came to a halt as I eased my path towards the group of gentlemen, praying the moment didn't lead to an altercation. I waltzed into Mash's arms and clamped my hands around his waist, then brilliantly improvised. "With everything going on in the world, you boys are over here talking about Venus versus Mars."

Mash placed his arm around my shoulder.

I asked him. "What have you been over here saying?"

"Just how lucky I am." He marked his territory with a kiss to my forehead.

"And you?" I turned to Chili. "Which one of my rants have you been over here getting twisted?"

"Hey, they were your words. Not mine. You know your theory about men really don't mean what they say when they complement a woman."

"I said men will say anything to get what they want, and do whatever they please. They don't mean half of the things they say to women." I corrected him.

"Now who wants to tell her she's wrong, besides me."

The men chuckled and sipped their beer until Yohan saved Chili from Mash's wrath. "Chili, you might want to quit while you're ahead. She has a point. Look at how many women we get with in a lifetime, and move on to the next. Can you honestly say you haven't said things you know a woman wants to hear, just so she will give you what you want?"

Chili stuttered. "We all have."

"Exactly my point. Men say whatever they need to get what they want. Case closed. Venus-1/Mars-0. Gentlemen, it was a pleasure. Now, don't sit over here and put nonsense into my husband's head. He's perfect the way he is." I tugged at his waist.

"Was everything alright with Khai?" Mash leaned in for a kiss.

I nodded yes.

Yohan chimed in. "How are your friends? Did they enjoy our presentation in Paris?"

Mash pinched my back and grinned.

I laughed internally. "Everyone is good. They enjoyed themselves and told me to thank you. It slipped my mind." My voice see-sawed. "Nice talking with you gentlemen."

I walked off looking back at Mash playfully, and toned down my strut towards the ladies, snickering to myself at Yohan's slick inquiry about Shannon. Olive and I locked eyes before I reached her. She lolled her head to the side and bellowed when I sat next to her near the fire.

"What the hell was he thinking?" She called for the waiter to serve me a glass.

"I wish I knew. Surely, he knew Mash was my husband. Right?" I scowled and rolled my eyes.

"Your days at the pub are done." Olive joked.

"You are probably right. Why are you and Yohan looking for a new house when you have this magnificent place? The landscape and the privacy are beyond breathtaking."

"He lived here with his ex-wife." Olive finished off her cocktail, then wiped the side of her mouth with her napkin.

"Say no more. I totally get it. I had to get used to the fact Mash has more than likely slayed a bitch, or two, or three in our house. I was so happy when he suggested we sell it and move."

"You understand me then."

I nodded. "So, who's who?"

She introduced me to her friends, Bianca and Nicola, and the wives of the men I'd just spoken with at the bar. They were all surprisingly welcoming and warm. I assumed they would be cold, and snooty like Olive on our first meeting.

After exchanging brief histories and discussing the way I pronounced certain words with my southern accent, we were seated to a table covered with teal linens and fuchsia florals. Olive arranged a seating chart, placing us at the table by name cards in front of shiny white dinner plates and sterling silverware.

Mash squeezed my thighs under the table, and I was less than inconspicuous with my reaction. The eyes of everyone in attendance were upon us until we settled down.

I complimented our hostess. "Olive this table setting is absolutely stunning."

Her brown cheeks turned rosy. "I can't take credit for it, but then again I will. Thank you, Nadia. I merely suggested the colors, and my party planner made the setting come to life."

A staff of hired hands entered the lawn every ten minutes with trays of soups, salads, vegan cuisine, and appetizers until the main course was served. Thirty minutes of boring business talk, taste tasting, and idle chatter ended with a smorgasbord of desserts to tide us over.

The conversation after dinner shifted to a unilateral discussion amongst everyone. Couples shared stories of how they met, creating a game of whose meet cute was the best. I sat quietly while Mash told our story, admiring his memory of small details from our beginning. The candlelight reflection in his brown eyes, and the way his lips curled when he said, "I knew she was the one when I let the track play all the way through," stirred me. We both blushed, recalling our kiss in the lobby the night before going to Glastonbury, and my insides tingled thinking about our trip to Ibiza. I never wanted him more in that moment, which was insane because I wanted him all the time.

I played with the hairs in his beard when he was done telling our meet cute story, and when he looked into my eyes I announced, "On that note we must say goodnight. Yohan and Olive, this was a magical evening and we thank you for inviting us into your home. It was lovely meeting you all and we must do this again."

We left the party and returned to our lot down the road, christening the Richmond air beneath the stars. I purred in Mash's ears as he rocked me sensuously in the backseat, feeling a connection of our souls travel between our bodies. Whatever the indescribable feeling was had to be love, because it was stronger than passion, and reminiscent of the morning I watched my friends leave me behind.

Weak from exertion, we opened the moonroof on the truck and stared at the stars in the sky, poking fun at our exit, and laughing at Yohan's obvious concern about Shannon.

"It kind of pissed me off." I confessed. "I mean Olive was only a few feet away. Men, I tell ya. Will one woman ever be enough?"

"I don't like the Chili fella. He's a prick and he likes you."

"He does not. He just thinks I'm cool because I speak my mind is all."

"I wanted to knock him on his ass when he shouted your name. It was embarrassing, and he acted too familiar with you. He had no idea I was your husband."

"Of course, he did. We've talked about you." I snuggled closer into him.

"What are you doing talking about me with him?" Mash scowled.

"Nothing personal like that. I'm just always saying my husband this and my husband that."

Mash huffed. "I don't like him."

"Point made. Tonight, was nice though, right?" My voice rose.

"The last fifteen minutes were." He kissed my head.

On set Monday morning, I raved about the soiree to Yohan. We shared a laugh at the highs and lows of the evening, Chili in particular, then he spoke candidly with me about my personal matter.

"I spoke with Shannon." He cleared his throat. "I wasn't sure I believed you when you said everything was okay. She told me you two are in the middle of a rift."

"It'll blow over I'm sure. My issue isn't with her anyways."

"She sent you a message. Or a joke. I'm not quite sure. Something about she'd be blue by now waiting for your call."

I chuckled.

"So, it was a joke I presume." Han glanced over his shoulder. "This poor fella." He kissed his teeth. "The young lad was quiet as a mouse after Mash cut him down like a tree with his eyes."

We snickered.

"Talk about embarrassing moments. For him and for me." I scrunched my face.

Yohan shook his head side to side.

Chili interrupted our conversation. "I hope I'm not interrupting anything. I just wanted to come over, and thank you for inviting me on Saturday. And Nadia, I realize I shouldn't have put you on the spot like that. I meant no harm."

His apology was overshadowed as the handsy man from the party in France fast approached our circle.

My stomach turned. "Everything's fine. My husband is cool." I lied to avoid reliving the moment.

The man from the party cleared his throat. "May I have a word with you?"

"Me?" I raised a brow.

"In private please. I'd prefer if we didn't speak family business in front of strangers. Besides, I don't think my son would like this one smiling in your face so much." He pointed to Chili.

Yohan brushed Chili on the shoulder. "Come on son." Then he turned to the strange man and shook his hand. "Senior, I didn't know you were dropping by today. Good seeing you. Have a word with me when you're done with your business here."

The stranger named Senior nodded. "Certainly,"

The familiarity in his voice shook me. With bright eyes I studied his features and knew when he said son, he meant Mash. He smiled in my face, and observed me from head to toe.

"Son?" I questioned him.

"Let me guess. He said I was dead. He thinks he can say it and make it true. That boy still has his mother's temper."

My heart fell to my knees.

"As you can see I'm alive and well. He's killed me off for far too long. I need you to get word to him for me. Tell him I've been unsuccessful in reaching him, and it's time we meet."

I stepped back. "I will not get involved in whatever it is going on between you two. Now if you'll excuse me."

Senior grabbed my arm. "Please do. And congratulate him on his upgrade."

I shrugged away from his grip. "That's the second time you've put your hands on me. I'm starting to get the impression you do whatever you like— Even when it's inappropriate."

"My dear, I was testing you and you passed. Maximus has selected well. And went all the way exotic this time. Tell him I approve and we need to speak. Lovely to meet you my dear."

I found my way to my chair and stared off into space while Yohan and Senior discussed their business near the exit. As I stewed over the now exposed lie Mash fed me over the years, I got lost in my own head. *'Why'*, I wondered, replaying our conversation on the plane with Mr. Hunt over and over, remembering how Mr. Hunt raised his eyebrows when Mash said his dad was no longer with us. '*Why would he lie about such a thing, and why was his father not bothered by it?*'

This bombshell put another scratch on our record, and feelings of being naïve, stupid, and gullible resurfaced. I wondered, '*If he was lying to me about something as sensitive as family, what else could he be lying about?*' Then, Nomi was the first image to pop into my head. Sure he provided me with footage of the one night I questioned, but then I went down a rabbit hole and wondered how many other nights should I look into?

I was too upset to stay on set. I lied and told Yohan I wasn't feeling well, and headed home hoping Mash would be there. When he wasn't, I kicked a few boxes around and made my way to the couch, opened my favorite bottle of red, and silenced my phone.

Drinking straight from the bottle, I fumed, formed scenarios in my head of Mash living the Rockstar life when I didn't accompany him on trips, and I placed him in the same category as the asshole who stained me with insecurities, and doubt. Dylan.

The light from my messages caught my attention. I clicked on the email icon, and opened up a message with Paid Writing Opportunity in the subject line, forwarded to me from Chili.

"Before I was rudely insulted and ran off earlier, I was going to mention a buddy of mine has this opening back home. I hope you submit. Hope you're feeling better and see you on set."

I drank to that and passed out on the sofa. Mash arrived home hours later, hammered and hot-headed.

He nudged my feet and woke me. "Nads."

I looked up and smart-mouthed him. "You found friendship with the bottle tonight, too."

"I had a few with Prano at the pub. I've been calling you for hours. What gives?" He stood over me with his hands tucked inside the pouch of his hoodie.

I sprung to my feet and stood in his face. "What gives is I met my father-in-law today. The father you claimed died. The mystery man who put his arm around me was your father. I think you knew that all along, and kept it from me. He sent a message. He wants to see you."

Mash tugged on my hip. "Let me explain."

I held up my hand to silence him. "He also said to tell you he approves, and you went all the way exotic this time. He's a real charmer that one."

"He said what!"

"Should I have been offended, or flattered?"

"Nadia, he's dead to me. Don't ever call him your father-in-law again. Am I clear? Stay away from him."

"How? He's a financial backer of my project."

"Listen. My... That man is not someone you want to get entangled with."

"Why would you lie to me about him?" I rose from the sofa.

"He's tied in scandal. He's untrustworthy. He's selfish and manipulates everything. It's his way or no way."

"I can see the father-son resemblance there." I stormed off.

"Don't..." He reached for me.

"Don't what? Point out the obvious control freak tendencies you share? For fucks sake, what did he do to make you lie about him being dead?"

"He slept with Nomi!"

Mash paced the floor and ran his fingers through his hair, then down his face over and over.

The rage in my eyes burned. "Ugh! I knew I wasn't done hearing that bitch's name!" I squeezed through the boxes, made my way into the bedroom, and locked the door.

Mash pressed against it. "You wanted to know why! Well there you have it! She is the reason I don't have a relationship with my father!"

I kept silent. So, did he. His footsteps rescinded down the hall then returned. The door suddenly opened, and he stood between the panels with a butter knife in his hand.

I rolled my eyes at him. "That is reason enough we have to get out of here." I pointed to the knife.

He sat next to me on the bed. "He always looked at her with lust in his eyes, then would preach to me "Son, she isn't worthy of our name. She's an opportunist.""

"You can spare me the details."

"Then I saw them having dinner in the city. I watched every move he made on her, how she responded, and how she went to his high rise with ease. They had no idea I was onto them, and I caught her in his bed. My father looked at me guiltless. "I told you son." Is all he said, and that was the last time I saw him."

I felt bad for him. He experienced something similar if not worse than I had with Taylor and Dumbass, but my anger and annoyance wouldn't allow me to comfort him.

I spoke without compassion. "That's a sad story, but I simply don't care. I'm sick of this woman being a part of my life. Our life. She has too much power over you. You've allowed her to disrupt us twice now, and ruined your relationship with your father. Is she the one that got away?" My eyes turned glossy.

"The one?" He scoffed. "How can you say this to me? I've done nothing but show you, you are the one. What else do I have to do to make you see how much you mean to me?" He held my feet in his hands.

"Sometimes I feel like I'm dreaming. Like this isn't real. It's too perfect at times, so I wait for something to go wrong, like this, to remind me nothing is perfect."

"Nadia, nothing's perfect. I'm not. Not even you."

"What other shocking revelation is out there waiting to punch me in the face? Do you have any children I need to know about? Tell me now if you do."

"I'm not hiding any secrets from you."

I teared up. "I think a part of you still loves her."

Mash's face turned red. He withdrew his hand and rose from the bed. "You're talking insane right now. I'm over her. I'm over my mother's sperm donor. And I'm over this conversation." He stormed out of the room.

I followed him screaming. "You don't get to turn this off because you're embarrassed! You know why! Because you lied! She was your girlfriend and you told me she was just a fuck buddy! And I think you still love her and don't want to admit it! But guess what! I forgive you for being stupid, and for falling in love with a dope-head heaux who was fucking you, your daddy and your friends!"

Mash walked out on me. He picked up his keys, slammed the door, and left without saying a word. It was our worst fight to date, but I was okay with him being gone. Him spending a few days at the old house gave me time to sulk, scream, and submit to every project I came across to deal with the shift in our relationship. Unfortunately, time and space didn't heal what was broken between us.

CHAPTER 29

Welcome to the Jungle

The couple of days we spent apart were damaging. My words went too far and bruised his ego. I hurt his feelings, though he would never admit it. We were back to where we were months ago when he threatened my behavior needed to change, except this time we both were having tantrums.

When he returned to our apartment, I was happy to see him walk through the door, but I didn't smile like usual at the sight of him. My love wasn't stronger than my pride when it should have been, and he was now giving me a taste of my own medicine. The silent treatment.

Two adults living on top of each other in a tiny flat, waiting for the other to crack became unbearable. I could have taken his return as an apology, but I needed to hear the words, even though hearing *I'm sorry* didn't really justify the lie he told.

Eventually I'd forgive him, but the analytic side of me couldn't let it go. The naïve side of me believed him when he said he no longer loved Nomi, but still I slipped into a place of desolation and imagination— Thinking the worst, because I was used to it. I wanted to hurt him before he hurt me, which would solve nothing, yet I couldn't resist the urge to strike the first blow.

A week of no communication turned into weeks of avoiding one another. Our newly built house was near completion and gave us a reason to talk, but the excitement disappeared, and I couldn't muster the courage to tell him I wasn't moving in it with him.

The torment of our disagreement led me to ask Yohan for a favor. After being passed over on the project Chili recommended, Han pulled a few strings with one of his friends in New York, landing me a gig as a Continuity Clerk for ninety days. Therein lied the first blow.

Even though we weren't talking, Mash was livid I would be away for three months, and demanded I decline the opportunity.

"How selfish can you be? The house is ready for us to move in." He fussed.

"I applied since we aren't getting along. You should move in. You hate this flat anyway."

"You're doing it again. All you know how to do is run." He exhaled deeply against one of the boxes in the living room.

I loved him. Missed him even, but something was off between us, and I couldn't move into that house feeling disconnected from him. He was also right. Running was what I did best and who I was.

"I can't move in that house with this bad energy between us. Hopefully we can work on us when I get back." I slipped past him.

He pulled me close and kissed me. "Turn it down for us."

This was the Maximus Sharper I knew. The man who'd been missing the past few weeks. I looked into his mesmerizing eyes and wondered where he'd wandered off to, and kissed him back.

"Where have you been?" I tapped his chest.

He leaned his forehead against mine and squeezed me tight. His pants tightened at the zipper causing my slit to pulse. I wanted to feel him fuck the frustration between us away, but refrained this time, knowing our problem would still exist after the pleasure of us bumping pelvises subsided.

"You always get your way. Not this time," I said. "I leave in the morning."

When I woke, Mash was asleep next to me in the bed. I expected him to play on my weakness for him. Looking at me with sad doughy eyes, and trailing me from room to room while I packed. He hit me with those four letters that made my heart flutter. "Stay," he said, when the taxi blew his horn.

Tempted and weak, my knees locked and my fingers trembled. With my back turned to him I paused in the threshold of the door. The leather from the carry-on slipped from my grip then I caught it. I turned around and stepped into my teary-eyed husband, kissed him passionately on his lips and whispered in his mouth. "I'll call you when I land."

Thousands of feet high above the Atlantic, I smiled at my reflection against the backdrop of the clouds. I no longer felt like the naïve, needy girl controlled by feelings and love, but a woman taking charge of her destiny and dreams.

As promised, I called home when I landed. Mash didn't pick up. The town car Yohan reserved for my arrival delivered me to the upper eastside of Manhattan to Olive's apartment.

Luxurious and very much to her taste, I felt uncomfortable living in her upscale pad. The layout was *decked* for a Grecian Goddess with gold fixtures and installed lamps on the walls covered with linen wallpaper, black speckled marble floors, and furniture that no one ever brushed against their cheeks.

I feared being accused if something went missing, or leaving a print on the beige sofa, a stain on the wooden coffee table, or a chip on the good china. Then, I entered the bedroom and knew I didn't belong. It was color coordinated in hues of grays and teal to perfection. The walls were covered with suede, and as I ran my fingers across a foot of the fabric, my handprint left its trace and I finalized my decision. I could not stay there. It was dust free due to the weekly maid service, and had a spacious kitchen I was sure Olive never set foot in, but not even the twenty-four-hour security, and doorman could bring me peace in her quarters.

I tossed and turned all night on the silk sheets, sliding to the edge and wrapped up with a pillow as the sounds of the neighbors, and creaks in the walls kept me awake. I checked my phone throughout the night, crying silently over the distance between my better half who still hadn't returned my call. No text, no missed messages, no communication whatsoever, and it felt like the beginning of the end for us.

I beat the sun, rising early to fix breakfast, cleaned behind myself, and questioned the doorman on availability in the building. Shortly after the leasing office opened, I signed a month to month lease for my own studio apartment, one floor above Olive's. It was smaller, cheaper, and empty, but it was mine. And inside my very own walls, I cried my eyes out on borrowed sheets from Olive's apartment on an inflated mattress in the middle of the living room floor.

At 5 a.m., the ringtone for Mash woke me. *"Day three seems promising,'* I thought, answering his call and exposing my puffy eyes and anguished face. We looked at each other through our screens and said nothing for more than half a minute.

Then, I broke the silence. "What is it? My appearance? Or are you still pissed I left?"

"I'm sorry."

"For what?" I rolled over and propped my phone against the pillow.

"Everything. My words, my lack thereof, my not seeing you off. The way I've treated you these past few weeks. Just everything." He dropped his head. "How are you?"

I sighed. "Fine I guess. As you can see I need to give myself a facial, and do something about de-puffing my eyes."

"You look beautiful from where I'm sitting." He grinned.

"And you're lying to me again."

"Nadia. I didn't call to argue. We've done enough of that for a lifetime in my opinion. There's ninety days between us. We shouldn't have let it begin like this."

"I agree. But I think we'll manage. We have before."

"Not for this long, but hopefully it'll go by quick. You know I love you. Right?"

"I know."

Leaving London was meant to hurt him, but I hurt myself in the process. Looking at his glum face, I knew I delivered a mighty blow. And him looking at mine, told him I regretted my hasty decision. But this was one of many storms we had to weather, and right now I needed him to be wet for a while.

I perked up a bit after hearing Mash's voice. I got dressed to do some home shopping, and walked a few blocks, familiarizing myself with the neighborhood. I stopped at the first hardware store on my route. Quickly, I learned I was on home soil, but not in the south. The clerk was overly direct, not too friendly, and never smiled when he made eye contact with me. He asked how he could help me, took my key from my hand, scorched my ears with his machine, and passed my set of keys to me.

While paying him I asked, "Is there a post office near here?"

He took my money and passed me my change. "One block up." Then carried on as if I wasn't still standing there.

The exchange left me staggered. I collected my feelings, used a search engine to find the post office, and stood in line to mail the extra key to Mash. A few of the customers hissed at me for not having my order together as I stood at the desk filling out the envelope. I rushed to sign my note and kissed it with my plum lips. As I passed the line on my way out, an elderly woman said, "He better be worth holding up the line honey."

I was culture shocked, having gone from the south where everyone says hello, to grand London where everyone judges you, now to New York where no one seemed to give a fuck. I often felt I didn't belong amongst the Europeans with my southern charm. Oddly enough, I felt the same in New York.

I wanted to race back to my apartment and hide, but I still needed to go shopping. I taxied about to a furniture store, ordered a bed and a sofa, and finished my day buying drapes and rods, pots and pans, kitchen utensils and one necessary wine glass for my short stay.

The city was loud, fast paced, and crowded. So was London, but this was a different type of crowded. It was fashionable, but not as posh as the places I'd seen during my short time living abroad, and less regal in a way.

The location of the studio wasn't in the safest area of the city, and with the long, late hours we worked, I racked up a plethora of taxi charges. One time riding the pissed-fumed subway was enough of the New York experience for me. Of all my grievances, it was the worst of them all with one good take away. I saw a woman sitting alone, dressed provocatively, but happy. She glowed in her seat, her fishnet stockings with random holes covered her crossed legs swinging her combat boots freely. Her flat stomach exposed by a cutoff baseball crop top, and flamingo pink hair cut low on one side. She smiled to herself, nodding to whatever pleased her ears through her ear pods, and I couldn't help but watch in wonder what her happiness looked like on the inside. Her smile was so infectious it made me smile from looking at her, and she winked at me before she swung through the open doors. I smiled even bigger from her notion, taking the exchange with me at the next stop.

Within a week, the train became the only thing I didn't fancy. I quickly adapted to the snaps, brisk tongues, quick wit, fast pace, crowded streets, loud fashion, colorful city of go getters. If I had followed my dreams and moved here when I graduated high school, I would be exactly like the city folk I feared. Remembering that made me fall in love with The City of Dreams in a New York minute.

The loneliness balanced itself with fatigue of working long hours. I missed the comfort of Mash lying next to me. How I slid my feet under his leg, and the warmth of his body behind me. To make up for his absence, I found a general store and purchased a heated blanket. Between that and the sound of waves on my computer, I slept like a baby high above the noise outside.

Flowers began appearing at my door every morning, bonding my only friendship in town with the doorman. He pitied me for my lack of a social life, which changed my third week in the city.

Chili came to town for an audition, and invited me to join him and some friends at a bar one Friday night. I jumped at the chance to be amongst people, familiar or not, and experience my first taste of the city that never sleeps.

On my way home from work, I took note of a massive street ad, and copied the look from the model. I dressed my fitted A-line skirt with a pair of sleek boots, a plain long-sleeved black tee, and a geo-printed belt with a wide buckle to tie in the two pieces. I dressed up the tee with a chunky brass necklace, and layered my wrists with brass and oatmeal bracelets, topping everything off with a form-fitting wrap trench.

The first to arrive of my party, I waited at the bar, and ordered a fuzzy navel to play it safe. The bartender and the gentleman sitting closest to me laughed at my drink of choice.

"Where are you from?" the bartender asked.

I knew he detected I wasn't from the city. "Long story," I replied.

"Tell you what. I'll make you a real drink, on the house."

"As long as it's not too strong, I'll try it." I flipped my shoulders to remove my coat.

Closely I watched him combine my peach schnapps with grenadine, vodka, pineapple juice, and either cranberry or cran-grape juice, and one other ingredient in a titanium mixing shaker. He poured it in a tall glass and topped it with a cherry, then presented me with his creation.

"Cheers. Welcome to the city newbie." He smiled.

The patron who laughed at my choice tilted his head slightly to watch me sip on the concoction. I swallowed a good bit, and raised my eyebrows as the flavors came to life in my mouth.

"Damn this is good. Thank you." I lifted the glass to salute him.

"A bartender loves customer praises." He smirked, wiping a glass dry with a cloth.

"I think you just made a new customer, Al. She looks like she'll be back for another one of whatever you mixed up," said the guy sitting closest to me.

"I hope so." Al winked.

"Al, my new friend, you should market this."

"I just mix the drinks, not copyright them." He teased.

"So, was Al right? Are you a newbie, because you look fresh to me?" said the guy next to me.

He adjusted his black and gray scarf which matched the hairs on his beard, and removed his navy-blue wool coat from his broad shoulders.

"You don't look like most of the women around here. Your aura is fresh." He added.

"Like I said, long story." I turned my head.

"I have time. I just got off of work and came down here to support my main man Al. Tell me your long story." He revealed one dimple on his caramel shaded face.

I pursed my lips and sipped. "My mother taught me not to talk to strangers."

He laughed. "We can change that."

Al watched our exchanged with a grin on his lips. I shook my head and sneered at the persistent gentleman.

"Can I get back to my drink now?"

He coughed. "Sure, if you'll let me buy you a second one."

"Is offering free drinks how you get what you want from women? Liquoring up the unsuspecting prize?"

"Not at all. I'm just trying to make a friend, but I think she is telling me to get lost the nicest way possible. I definitely know you aren't from around here. A New York girl wouldn't be as nice as you. She'd flat out tell me to fuck off."

"You're very perceptive."

"I am." He bragged.

"If your timing was right, I would tell you my name, where I'm from, and sit at this bar and be your friend all night, but I can't, so please accept my apologies."

"There's that nice girl again. I like you."

"You don't know me to like me."

"Right again, but I'd like to."

We stared at each other for a few seconds after his brilliant comeback. He tilted his head back and swallowed the shot Al placed in front of him, rubbed his robust chest, then looked at me and smiled.

"So friend." I interrupted him. "It's been a pleasure, but my party just arrived. Thanks for the conversation."

The guy looked over his shoulder at Chili, and lost the smile on his face. "Nice talking to you, too, lady whose name I didn't get."

Chili hugged me in a close, strange manner, and my face scowled. The guy at the bar noticed my expression and raised an eyebrow.

"You sure you know this guy?" he asked.

I nodded. "Yeah, Chili this is...ugh" I wound my hand in a circle.

"Lucas. Lucas Fleming." He ogled Chili.

"Chili Walker."

"I was just keeping the pretty lady here company. You two enjoy your evening." Lucas smirked at me.

"We will. I see you got started without me." Chili joked.

"Courtesy of my new friend, Al." I waved goodbye.

I followed Chili a few steps away to the booth his friends reserved. He introduced me to everyone, then ordered another round of drinks for the table. I asked our waitress to get the bartender to make his special drink for me, and raised my hand when she relayed the message. In turn, Lucas saluted me as if I was signaling him, and we shared a laugh together from afar.

Chili placed his arm above my seat. "Looks like you've made yourself a new friend."

I leaned away from him. "I wouldn't say friend. I never told him my name. But did you catch the pretty remark. I told you men use compliments all the time to run game on a woman."

Chili looked at me weird. "He wasn't lying though."

Bewildered by his remark, I turned to the stage as the band began playing a combination of new jazz fused with hip-hop and spoken word. I was no longer in Kansas anymore. After two years of being surrounded around techno mashups, and dancehall reggae, I found myself missing home, lost in the rhythmic sounds of Harlem.

The night turned out to be fun. I retired my bartender special after losing count of how many I had consumed, and recognized the dangerous look in Chili's eyes. His friends called it a night in the middle of the band's second set, and I followed their lead to make a clean getaway. Chili kept me trapped in the booth as they scurried off, gazing at me with that weird look again.

He slid close and I asked him. "Have you had one too many?"

Yelling over the music, he scooted closer to me. "Nadia, I've been meaning to ask if you like living out here?"

I remained facing the stage. "It's cool. And only temporary."

A purring sound rolled from between his teeth. "Temporary... Right. Are you eager to return to London?"

I took a deep breath and faced him. "Why the inquisition, Chili?"

Staring into my eyes, he smiled at me then angled his head forward. "If you ever find yourself in L.A. I have my own place. You could stay with me if and when you score a job out west. Unfortunately, when I come to New York, I stay with friends. If I had my own pad out here, I would have put you up."

"And I would have declined..."

He cut me off. "I dream about you sometimes. On an intimate level."

"And you're telling me this because?" I raised my eyebrows.

"Because I can't stop thinking about you. Your husband was crazy to let you come out here alone. I know I'm overstepping, but I'd be a fool not to shoot my shot."

"Chili you're cute and all, but I see you as a…"

"Don't say friend." He interrupted me again. "Kiss me and see if you still want to end your sentence the same way." He aimed for my face.

I curved him and pulled out my vibrating phone which read *'911'* from Khai.

"Who is Khai?" Chili inquired.

I pressed my phone against my chest, furrowed my brows, and sucked my teeth at him. "You have had one too many." I dialed Khai's number. "Hey, it's late and loud in here, what's the emergency?"

"I'm not supposed to tell you this, but Mash is in New York. Taylor overheard Levi talking to him. His flight just landed. I thought I would give you a heads up. You know since we are supposed to be friends, but you seem to have forgotten that." Khai sassed me.

"Thanks for telling me. I'll call you when…"

"Whenever you get the chance. I know." Her voice dragged. "Sounds like you're having a good time."

A sarcastic laugh escaped me. "We'll talk."

Khai hummed. "Um hmm. Good night."

Chili might as well have been on the call with me as close as he sat to eaves drop. I faced him to finish our awkward conversation. "Where was I?" I exhaled. "I was saying I see you as a good friend, but after tonight, I don't think we should speak for a while. And I lied to you before. My husband doesn't think you're cool. He detests you, actually."

I slid from the opposite end of the booth and skedaddled passed the bar to the exit. "Fuck," I mumbled at the traffic speeding by, preventing me from crossing the street to jump in an empty cab illegally parked.

I returned near the line of patrons waiting to get inside the club, ordered a car, and shivered for five minutes until the Lyft arrived. I hopped in and reached for my seatbelt when the back door on the other side opened.

"My man, can you credit her account and accept cash for this ride?" Lucas leapt in.

"No, I cannot," the driver answered.

"So where are we going?" His eyes stretched without blinking.

"I'm going home, and you are getting out."

"My man, drop me off two blocks ahead. Here is a fifty for your trouble." He handed the driver. "And here is a fifty for your ride home."

"I don't need your money." I smirked, pushing the bill forward towards him.

"If you don't take it, I'll tip my man right here." He smiled.

"Tip him."

Lucas dropped the fifty in the passenger seat. "My man that's for you."

The driver nodded.

Lucas looked over at me smiling wide, pleased with himself. The driver didn't fuss since he was paid off, and watched us from the rearview mirror.

"Hey guy, I don't know." I sat confused and flustered.

"Lucas."

"Look Lucas, I'm not impressed by your money."

"What is it about you? At least tell me your name?"

"If I tell you, will you leave me alone?"

"No."

At least he's honest.

"It's Nadia."

"Damn, that name fits you." He purred and closed his eyes. "Very sexy. I must admit when you walked away with that square at the bar I said to myself, *'She is a real woman. What could a clown like him possibly know what to do with a woman who is right under the hood?'* I saw him try to kiss you. Why'd you shoot him down?" Lucas chuckled.

"Because he's not my man."

"So, you have a man?" His eyes locked on me.

"I have a husband."

"Where is he?"

"Waiting for me to come home."

"Nah, you're bullshittin' me. He wouldn't let you come out and be with ole boy alone. Unless he doesn't know." Lucas gave me the side-eye.

"Ole boy is a co-worker, and my husband had to work so he couldn't join us tonight." I turned to the window, avoiding his eyes.

"I don't think "your husband" would approve of you having drinks with someone trying to kiss you, Nadia."

"Should I tell him?"

Lucas eye-fucked me for a few seconds and licked his lips. His fingers played with his chin hair as he pouted his mouth. "Nah. Save him the trouble."

I amused him. "If you were him, would you want to know?"

"Can't say." He shrugged. "I'd like to know you though."

"I belong to someone else is all you need to know about me."

"Why all the secrets?"

"It's complicated." I pressed my lips together.

"I'd like to hear about complicated." He stared at me until I smiled. "My man, right here is good."

Tapping on the back of the front seat, he broke his gaze, then gave me a once over. The driver pulled over to the side of the street, and Lucas reached inside his coat pocket.

"Ms., I mean Mrs. Nadia, here is my card. You see the sign above those lampposts? You can find me there. Second floor. Whenever you want to tell someone about your complication. Call me, or stop by. Either way I hope to see you again. Driver make sure she gets home safe. Good night."

Lucas jumped out of the car and tapped on the roof. The driver drove off looking at me in the rearview, leering at me as I threw the card in my bag. I pretended I didn't see him judging me, and hid my face from him as I smiled looking out of the window.

During the drive to my apartment, my mind raced about Mash's surprise visit. This opportunity was supposed to serve as a needed separation to self-examine, and heal from his lies. We needed to miss each other for a bit, and I was enjoying the courtship of flowers at my door, and messages of poetry, and song lyrics sent to my phone throughout the day. But then I opened the door of the car when it pulled in front of my building, and grew excited about his visit.

I raced upstairs and showered the club smell off of me, turned on my heating blanket, and threw on my pajamas. I read two chapters of a novel by the time I heard him outside of the door. I placed my bookmark between the pages and felt my nipples sharpen. "Is someone there?" I asked, loud enough for him to hear me. He turned the second lock and walked in, looking like Christmas morning. Before I could say what are you doing here, he rushed over and held me in his arms so tight I could barely breathe.

"I can't live without you," he said.

I clung to him, sniffing for his natural scent, and melting at the touch of his hands against my back. "What took you so long?"

"You took me so long. I tried to give you the space you wanted, but I had to see you. Then this key arrived, so I took it as an invitation. Did you really think I would let you spend your thirtieth birthday alone?"

"I told you, I'm not looking forward to it. It depresses me really."

"I still couldn't let my favorite girl bring in this big one alone. Babe, I may have fucked up and kept a huge secret from you, but it was for a good reason. I really hope these past few weeks has been enough time for you to forgive me."

"I have forgiven you." I pinched his chest.

"I see you haven't done much with the place." He took off his coat.

"This isn't home. Three months and I'm out." I snapped my fingers.

"What if you get more assignments here?"

"A bridge to cross later. Go shower so we can go to bed."

I waited for him under the sheets *pantyless*. He climbed in wearing a towel around his waist, and laughed at how warm the bed felt.

"Is this how you've replaced me?" He joked, feeling my prickled skin and kissing on my neck.

"It's cold here. Even colder without you to keep me warm at night..."

He shut me up with a kiss on the lips, wrapped his body around mine, and linked our fingers. "Sheesh your feet are freezing!" He jumped.

"You could rub them and warm them for me."

"I planned on rubbing something else."

His hands massaged my hips while we kissed looking into each other's eyes. He propped me on top of him and removed my shirt, fondling the curves of my breasts with a gentle brush of his fingers. Adoring me from below, he reached for my face and propped himself up with the strength of his abdomen to taste my mouth with a tender kiss, then gently bit my top lip.

I gyrated on his lap. "Somebody missed me," he said, fiddling in my wetness.

I opened the towel and traced the vein on his brick hard pipe with two fingers. "Somebody missed me."

Heat took over my body and I slid down his shaft, gasping from his girth, relaxed from his presence. I welcomed him and sat there taking it all in, carousing in the feels and remembering to breathe. The freshly spritzed cologne from his wrists ignited my senses as I sucked his fingertips, receiving all of him and the slow, hard pressed strokes he saved for me. Throttled and untamed tugs at my peak made my limbs shudder. My back went numb from the twitching of his head budding inside of me.

"Already." He grinned.

"It's been a while." I whimpered, gripping his bell-end between my legs.

"Allow me." He spun me on my back.

Submissively I ordered. "Do whatever you want with me."

I begged for a rough course of action than the gentle ride I gave him. But he ignored my command, and took his time with my pussy. Tending to my every need, my every inch, with plunges to remind my throbbing center who she belonged to.

My walls clung to his cock as sighs of relief released from my mouth, and the sides of my warm embrace curved to his delight. He felt just as I remembered. Maybe better. Distance did our bodies good, and Mr. Sharper came into town to fuck the nonsense out of me.

I listened to him whisper my name and confess his love. His craving for my folds brought out the passion we neglected. The desire we abandoned overflowed with me melting beneath him, capturing a moment to be remembered.

He was close when the perfected pounding paused in my pussy, and his hips thrust further into me. I grazed his shoulder with my teeth, and pulled his head back to see the look on his face when he could no longer hold it back. He hollered in delight, his elation read across his open mouth. I smiled to myself, proud to give him what he came for, and happy to receive the gift he carried below his belt.

He rolled me back on top of him and kissed my forehead, then my cheeks, then my neck, squeezing my thighs tightly against him to seep out his pearls.

"Can we do this all night?" he asked.

"I damn sure hope so."

CHAPTER 30

When Can I See You

O ur tanks were on empty by morning, but the courtship continued once we gained energy to roam the nearby streets for lunch. Inertly, we strolled hand in hand into a corner deli, ordering from every section of the menu, reminiscent of the many times we travelled abroad.

I choked on a sweet potato fry, completely won over as Mash asked me out on a date like he needed my permission. It was like a scene from an old movie, him pulling out two tickets from the inside pocket of his jacket to see a Broadway show. My cheeks beamed of flattery. Oh be still my beating heart. The planning he put into this visit made my body tingle, and I could feel myself falling for him all over again.

By nightfall we were witnessing Hollywood and New York legends work their magic on stage, followed by a late dinner in uptown. To finish the evening off, we strolled under the bright lights of Times Square with the other tourists.

In the midst of the hustle and bustle, I took Mash's hand. "Can we talk without arguing?"

His eyelids flinched. "What's on your mind?"

"Why didn't you want me to know Nomi was more than a friend?"

The tension in his hands tightened. "What did you think about me when we met?"

"I thought— damn he's fine...and I thought it was smooth how you sent for me...and I thought you had good energy."

"Now think back to my former management. Davie created the image of me as a "ladies' man" every woman desired. After hearing something over and over, you start to believe it. So here I am this "ladies' man", yet the one girl I thought I had a connection with sleeps with my father. Not a younger guy. Not another celebrity. The old man from which I came. What kind of ladies' man loses his girl to his father?"

"I get it's embarrassing, but trust me when I say it had nothing to do with you. When your dad said she wasn't worth your last name he proved it. She was a whore out for money."

"But I got played. If word got out, which is what she has been threatening to tell the media, my image would have been ruined. I'd be a laughing stock."

"Here's the headline. 'Heartthrob Loses Whore to Millionaire Father'." I grinned in his face.

"We know you're a writer. You don't have to show off."

"I'm trying to make you laugh. Lighten up. What they did to you is similar to what Taylor and my ex did to me. Betrayal is a bitch. I kind of know how you feel."

"You know they were the reason why I stopped getting high. Except for the bud." He explained. "I have nothing left for her, but my dad...I can't be a part of his life. Using the old I'm your dad and was trying to show you she was a gold-digger speech. I don't buy it."

"I say forgive him, but keep him at a distance."

Mash stopped moving his feet. "We're being kind here, so don't take offense to what I'm about to say. Stay out of it. Please. You don't know him."

"Then at least see what he wants."

"I'll think about it." He squeezed my hand. "Letting him in is like inviting the devil inside for tea."

"Well I'm from the south and we drink sweet tea."

He looked over at me and attempted to laugh, but something held him back. The worried look in his eyes told me to leave the conversation about his father right there on the street.

The ambiance of the city carried us into a risqué moment of passion, equivalent to a taxi-cab confession scenario, turning the driver's car into a make out mobile. "Please, no, not in here." The driver begged, watching our foreplay in his rearview mirror.

The mood for another wild fuck fest had been set. Mash tipped the cabbie generously for his trouble, then we ran inside my lease to finish each other off with a double play. For the first time in months, Sunday morning felt like a Sunday morning. I cooked breakfast, we lied in bed, watched a movie, did crossword puzzles, and napped until past noon.

"How is the house?" I asked him when I woke.

He turned to face me. "I wouldn't know."

"What do you mean?"

"I'm still in the flat. I'm not moving into the house until you come home." He caressed the side of my face. "I know when you left, you were telling me to fuck off."

"I would never." I smirked.

"I'll put a for sale sign up before I live in there without you."

"Tell me you've at least walked through it? Took pictures?"

"I did a walk through, and I have the keys, but the move in date is up to you."

"Mash, you hate living in the flat, and I'm going to be here for two more months."

He huffed and sat back on his pillow. I didn't have the heart to tell him he had to be rid of his demons before I would move in. We were getting along so well I changed the subject, and asked the other burning question on my mind.

"How long do I have you for?"

"Forever." He sighed.

"I meant when is your flight home?"

"I know what you meant. I leave on Wednesday. Are you tired of me already?"

"Actually, I don't want you to leave. We seem like us here."

He pulled me on his chest and kissed me on the lips. "I know what you mean. Feels like we've found our mojo again."

Before the city lost daylight, we took advice from one of his friends and checked out street performers on 42nd, then grabbed a pizza for dinner from a parlor two blocks away from my building.

I woke to an empty bed in the morning. A note rested under my arm with instructions to be dressed to impress by the time he returned. I played hooky for work, and dolled up like I was told.

Mash waltzed through the door holding a huge chocolate cupcake with a single candle stuck in the center, alongside a box of cronuts.

"It's not much, but I remember you saying you wanted to try these." He revealed the goodies.

"You remembered." I hummed.

"I pay attention. You have to place an order weeks in advance for these things. You should have seen the line. It was wrapped around the block. Happy birthday baby. Welcome to the thirties." He closed in and planted the sweetest kiss on my lips. "I love you. You want to open the cronuts first?"

I professed my love in return, and tore open the breakfast box full of sugary blend of donuts and croissants rolled into one. It was the perfect beginning to my day, followed by a morning full of laughs.

Then, he revealed my next surprise. A hired photographer curated a photo session of us in Central Park, prior to Mash shuttling me off to FAO Schwartz.

"You said you wanted that floor piano. When you're done jumping up and down on it, I hope you jump and down on me." He gently bit my cheek.

"You remembered that?" I gazed in his shiny, brown eyes. "You've thought of everything." My head rest on his chest.

"You'll get how much I love you one day."

For the next thirty-six hours, I nestled in his arms, ordered take out, and breathed the same air, consumed with the stench of one another, mixed aromas of food, and soiled sheets.

I cried when we said goodbye Wednesday evening. My feelings about my decision slightly changed about applying for the assignment now that we were back on good terms, but the little voice inside my head told me we needed the distance to get the resolve I was hoping for—for him to be free of the hold his ex had over him, and to mend his relationship with his father so we could move forward.

After spending a long weekend locked inside, I was happy to return to work and learn something new. The faster we completed the assignment, the faster I could return to London, and end my lonely nights in the city that never sleeps.

The week went by slow now that Mash was gone, and by the weekend, the loneliness and boredom crept back in. Monday morning, I volunteered to help setup for a seminar at NYU with the idea of keeping myself busy would help the time go by faster.

When the panel broke off for the day, I toured the campus, travelling down the road of what could have been my life if granted another choice. As I walked the grounds, I stumbled upon the library filled with undergrads.

An unattended phone at the check-in desk called to me. I convinced myself to make the most of the day when Lucas crossed my mind. I dug inside my purse and rolled the dice. The devil on my shoulder wanted him to keep me company. The angel on my other shoulder prayed he didn't answer.

"Lucas Fleming speaking."

"Damn," I mumbled.

"This is Lucas Fleming."

"Hey, I um. I wasn't expecting you to answer. It's the weekend. Figured you'd be busy, and not at work."

"Who is this?" he asked.

"I shouldn't have called. Sorry to bother you."

"Nadia, I'm playing with you. I recognize the accent. I'm surprised to hear from you."

"I'm surprised I called." I grew hot with guilt.

"The line says NYU?"

"Yeah, I on the campus wrapping up work, but I'm about to leave so."

"Where are you headed?"

"Home I guess. I don't know. It's a sunny day out, and I have the rest of the day off. I thought a local could show me some hidden gems in the city before my time here ends."

"I can be there in twenty minutes. Fifteen if the traffic is light. What are you wearing?" His voice softened.

"Why?" I questioned, searching for the gumption to end the call.

"So I can know what to drive."

I was overcome with relief. "Jeans and boots," I said.

"See you in twenty. Meet me out front."

Lucas drove up a few minutes late on a motorcycle wearing a black leather jacket, dark blue denim, and work boots. He removed his helmet to show me his one dimple, flashing a smile I recognized all too well. *The fuck was I thinking?*

"Hop on." He lured me over to the bike.

"This was a mistake. Plus, I have reasons to live." I backed away.

"So do I. I promise I'm a safe driver. Let me help you with your helmet."

He stared into my eyes on and off as he tightened the notch on my protective head gear. I broke his gaze, crumbling inside I lacked the courage to walk away. '*This is the most reckless thing you can do,*' I thought to myself. '*Well since you shagged a man unprotected in three days, married him, and changed your life.*'

Caught up in the conversation taking place in my head, I mumbled out loud. "That turned out just fine."

"What did?" Lucas asked.

"Oh. Sorry. I was thinking out loud."

He grinned. "Let's go."

I held on tight to his chest as he wiggled in and out of traffic. Twenty minutes later, he introduced me to Brooklyn. "Word is, women love coming to the botanical gardens." He parked his bike, then lifted me to my feet.

I walked ahead of him, admiring the scenery of florals, asking myself if I held on to him too tight, was there a Freudian reason I called him, and how could I get out of the mess I created.

He caught up to me and suggested we warm up a bit at a café down the street. Over a latte we shared light conversation about his work in construction, looking at pictures on his phone of the buildings he built in and out the city. He was prouder than I was impressed.

When he realized he had been rambling, he joked. "You don't look interested at all in what I am saying."

"I'm sure it's exciting for you. The finished products are nice though."

"You don't have to be nervous around me. I won't bite."

"I hope not," I said. "Thanks for taking my call and showing me this side of town. I should probably catch a cab home."

"There's more I'd like to show. Please. Don't run off." He reached for my hand after placing a twenty between the sugar packets.

I ignored the signs and hopped back on his motorcycle, enjoying the view of a newly built hotspot called Dumbo. Boutiques, cobble-stoned streets, market vendors, restaurants galore, and galleries brought in crowds of people from locals to tourists. It felt wrong I had stumbled on such a place with Lucas, and as we rode past a carousel near the Brooklyn Bridge on our way out, I created a speech to make sure Lucas and I never saw each other again.

He drove us to his place of work to defrost. A corner office over-looking the street from the third floor, well decorated with wood and plaques, with his name on the center of his shiny, chestnut coated desk. I studied his cockiness in his element, walking around as if he owned the place.

"Is it warm enough in here?" he asked.

"It's getting there. I'm thawing pretty nicely." I stood near the vent soaking up the heat.

"I ordered us some food. It should be here any minute."

"Thanks for showing me around today, but I really should get going. It's too late now, but I shouldn't have called you."

"I'm glad you did. I enjoyed your company this afternoon."

I scoffed. "When we met you asked me a million questions."

"And you refused to answer any of them."

"Now it's my turn. Why aren't you married?"

"I am. My wife lives in San Diego. Permanently, I hope."

"Trouble in paradise?" I teased.

"We're separated. There is no way I can leave this earth still married to her. She would get a pretty penny if my demise came before this divorce is final."

"What did you do to her?"

"I married her." He griped.

"Okaaaay. Why did you take me out today?"

"Because you asked me to."

"The real reason."

"I find you intriguing." He blushed.

"What is your intention with me, Mr. Fleming?"

"I think you know."

My eyes met his across the room. I grinned, folded my arms together, and looked back at the people and cars passing by on the street.

"I can help you get warm." He offered.

"I think the food is here."

Lucas sighed. "They would pick tonight to have fast delivery."

I laughed at his comment while he went downstairs to unlock the entrance and grab the takeout. He returned and laid the bags on the table near the heating vent. I avoided eye contact with him as he spread the food across the shiny wood, and poured us some wine in coffee cups from his cabinet.

"How many women are you currently seeing, Mr. Fleming?"

"I have a few friends. But no one serious."

"Are you really married?"

"Separated. Why would I say I was if I wasn't?"

"I don't know. To maybe keep women from trying to get too close."

"I'm telling you the truth. I would be divorced if my ex wasn't fighting it so damn hard. You think you know a person."

He was convincing regarding the disdain for his wife, but I smelled bullshit about his innocence in the friends department.

"Shall we," he asked, pointing to the spread.

I sampled the lo-mein and raised my eyebrows. "The rumor is true."

"What's that?"

"New York has the best Chinese food."

He raised his head and looked down at me. "Nadia, what happens with us after tonight?"

"I go home, lose your number, and pretend this day never happened."

"I propose I drive you home. You invite me in…"

"Not going to happen."

"Then meet me for lunch tomorrow. I'll send a car and take you to eat the best steak New York has to offer."

"How about I think about it. And if I call you we can meet."

He rose from the table and went into the drawer of his desk. "Take this." He handed me a flip phone. "I had to fire someone today. This was his company phone. It's been wiped clean and has a new number. Expect it to ring tomorrow around eleven o'clock."

I placed the phone in my purse and called myself a taxi— proud I didn't misbehave though Lucas's craftiness made it tempting to play his game. Stimulated by control yet detached from commitment, I shamelessly flirted with him, knowing it was wrong because it felt good in doing so. As long as I remained mysterious I held all the cards, but as I stepped inside my apartment, the excitement of him left. And I promised myself not to ever see him again.

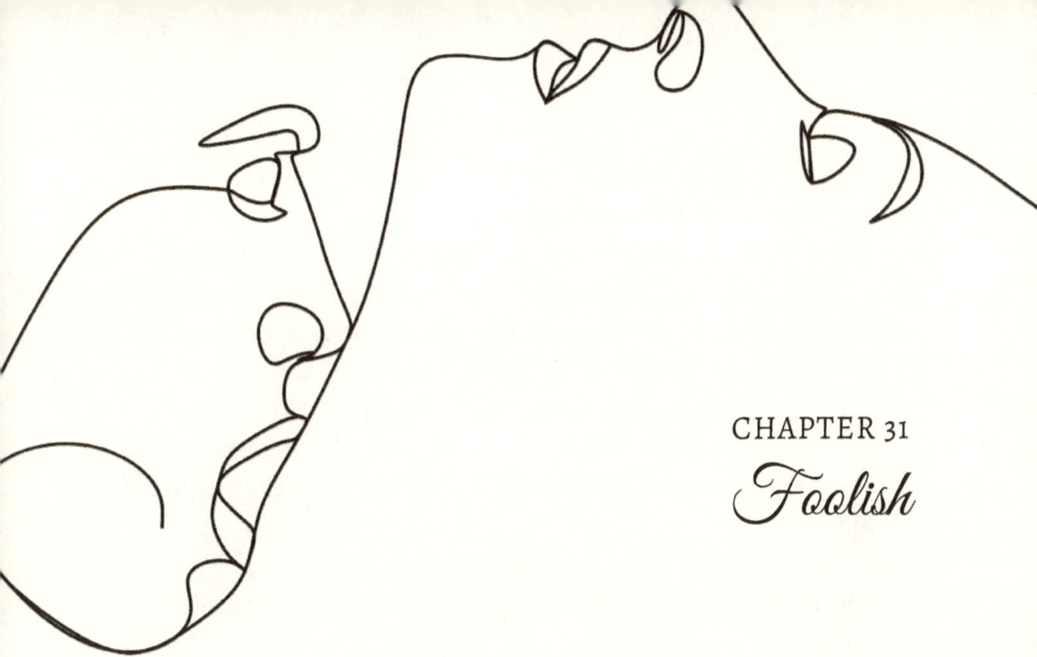

CHAPTER 31

Foolish

Walking down the hall of the studio a minute shy of eleven o'clock on the dot, the retro phone rang. I pulled it out of my bag and stared at it for a few seconds. A crew member I'd spoken to once or twice frowned at the device in my hand, then I laughed along with him until he turned the corner.

I let the line ring a few more times, then answered the call chuckling.

"What's so funny?" Lucas asked.

"The look on this guy's face when he saw I had a flip phone."

"I couldn't exactly call your phone, could I?"

"You're so relentless. Are you calling me to cancel, or give me an address?"

"I know this is a stretch, but tell me where you are. I'll send a car."

"That won't be wise."

"Then come to the office. We'll leave from here."

Lucas stood out front when the cab delivered me to another wrong move on my part. He opened the door of a town car for me, and whisked me off to a lunch date in style. He was a sight in gray. His broad shoulders perfectly filled the charcoal jacket he wore, and the imprint in his trousers was hard to miss. His big light brown eyes seduced me in silence, to the point I was forced to look away, peeping at him in spurts, blushing of nervousness.

We arrived at a restaurant on 57th street, with a huge wooden door and a sign nailed into it that read, '*Hours 5 p.m. to 1 a.m.*' Lucas made a call and the door opened, then locked immediately upon our entry. A short red-faced man shook his hand, and kissed the back of mine, then ushered us to a linen clothed table in the center of the room.

He returned with a bottle of champagne and placed it between us. I was impressed at the length he went to succeed in getting me to fall for him.

"A man of many connections, I see."

He held his head high. "In my line of work, relationships are important."

"Apparently. Any recommendations?"

"Whatever cut you select will be amazing. Feel free to try whatever you like."

I ordered the mignon medium-well with a side salad and baked sweet potato. He ordered the prime rib with mashed potatoes, and an appetizer of stuffed shrimp he insisted I try. The shrimp were so succulent and tender I wanted them all to myself.

"Amazing, right?" He grinned.

"The best I've ever had."

"Wait until the steaks arrive. I might get you to call my name after all."

I guffawed lowly at his inappropriateness. "I beg your pardon."

Lucas acted as if he didn't hear me and poured us both a glass of champagne.

I sipped a little. "I can't have much. I have to report back to work."

He raised his hand signaling he understood. "Say when."

Our lunch arrived and the room went completely silent, minus the sounds of us devouring our feast. Conversation picked back up between us as we sampled from each other's plate.

"If you tell me about your marriage, I'll tell you about mine."

He agreed.

"What went wrong?" I asked him.

He set his fork on the table. "So many things. I remember she grew upset on our honeymoon because I called her my girlfriend and not my wife. Easy mistake as a newlywed, but she went bananas. Completely shut down on me."

"What do you mean shut down?"

"No sex. It was our honeymoon, and she used an honest mistake as a reason to withdraw intimacy."

"No nookie on your honeymoon seems a bit extreme."

"Tell me about it. I called her my girlfriend for three years. Simple slip of the tongue. The next morning, I knew I had made a mistake, but I went along with the 'for better or worse part'. She woke up and acted as if nothing happened."

I held my hand over my mouth to cover the food processing inside. Gasping for air, and swallowing at the same time I snorted. "I'm sorry to laugh. It's not funny. But the way you tell it is funny. And I'm guilty of shutting down myself, but not for something as small as being called girlfriend."

"Good to know. The next nine months I was on pins and needles trying not to say the wrong thing. I was miserable. And let's not talk about me going to hang out with my boys. She would flip out. I was like where was this person before I wasted money on feeding people who didn't give a damn if we stayed together or not. Anyway, when we hit the one-year mark I filed for divorce, and she has hated me ever since. She won't comply with the terms, and is fighting me at every turn. I want out. Now tell me about you Ms. Full of Secrets."

"There isn't much to tell. My husband didn't want me to come to New York for this job I'm working."

"That's the complication you speak of?"

I nodded yes.

"I was hoping for a bit more, or a real piece of information about you. Like your last name. Where are you from? What movies do you like? Your favorite book? That sort of thing. Let me in a little. How long have you been married?"

"A little over two years."

"Still fairly new. They say marriage is an institution and they mean it. You learn something new every day like you're in school. About yourself and your mate."

"Spoken like a true person burned by the institute." I joked.

He laughed to himself. "You're witty. I know that about you."

He stared at me with ill intent written across his face. I was enjoying a meal with a man who wanted to rip my clothes off, feeling guilty every second knowing it by the way he looked at me. And I liked the torture. The desire in his gaze. The power I felt owning his attention.

He interrupted my introspection. "How are you enjoying married life?"

"I enjoy it actually."

"Have you and your mate figured each other out?"

"I'd say yes. I was lonely and heartbroken before him. Now it feels good to have someone to go through life with as an ally. We just have to work on straightening out a few wrinkles, but who doesn't? That's life."

"If I may, exactly where do I fall in line with what you have going on?" He stopped eating.

"I'm not quite sure. I thought we could be friends. But you've already expressed sleeping with me, and I'm not a cheating woman."

He wiped his mouth with the linen cloth, then leaned forward. "You're doing so in this very moment."

I swallowed a tiny sip of champagne and sat back in my chair. "I disagree."

"Cheating doesn't have to be physical, though in this case I would like it to. Very much so. And you won't admit it, but you want to sleep with me just as bad as I want to ravish your body into sweet submission and hear you call my name. But as you said, you aren't a cheating woman. And I believe you."

I was cornered. I had imagined what he would be like in the sack. How his lips would feel against mine, and if he had something new to offer I had yet to experience. I had no intention of ever finding out, but the images flashed before me as he said the words.

He grinned at me as if he knew what I was thinking. I grinned back at him as the server returned with a to go order of the shrimp prepared in a brown box, and a slice of banana fosters cake sitting pretty inside a clear tray.

"I knew you would love them so I ordered one for you to have for your dinner tonight." He spread five one hundred-dollar bills on the table.

"Thank you, my clever associate." I sampled the icing from the cake.

"Associate?" He mumbled, gazing at me hard as I licked my finger. "Oh, how I wish you'd call me lover instead."

We spent the remaining minutes staring at each other as the owner stood above with an invitation to return for dinner. The car arrived and drove us back to his office.

Lucas hesitated getting out. "Come away with me this weekend."

Tension in my legs rose and I stuttered. "I can't."

"Why not?"

"I have friends flying in this weekend."

"How about next weekend?"

"Lucas. I'm married."

"Think about it okay? And keep the phone turned on. I'll be calling you."

The car dropped me off a block away from the studio as I requested. I trekked down the concrete smiling to myself like the girl on the train I admired my first week in Manhattan. I didn't know her story, but I knew mine, and it was messy. '*What the fuck had I gotten myself into?*'

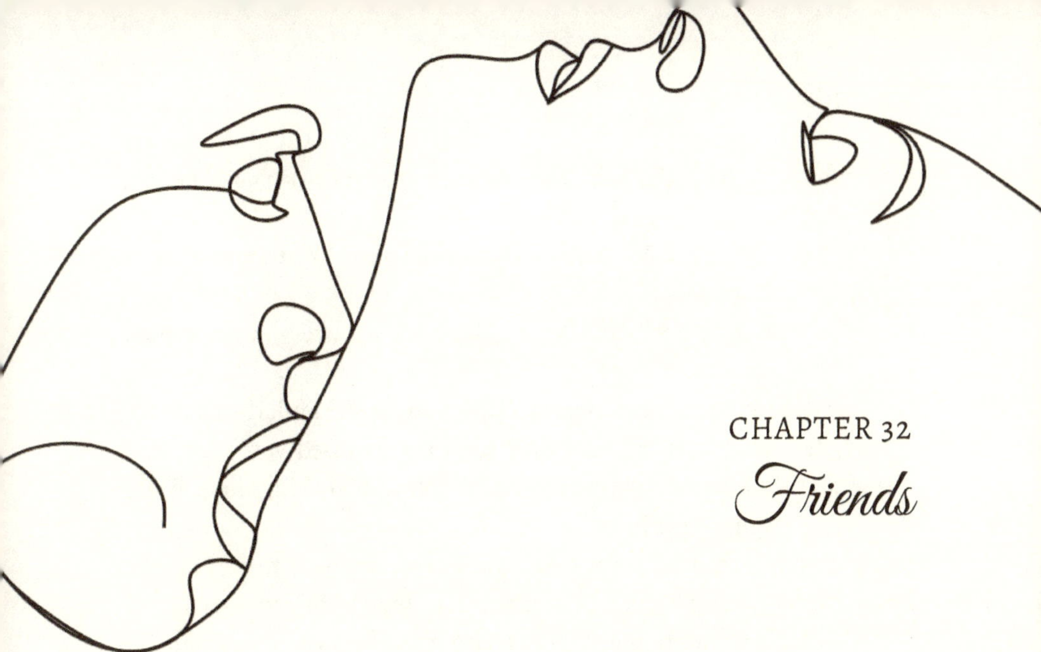

CHAPTER 32

Friends

The arrival of Khai and Shannon timed perfectly with my drama. Shannon, the devil on my shoulder, and Khai the angel, brought the much-needed camaraderie missing from my life.

Our sisterhood was cracked. I barely spoke to them for months, and found myself closer to Olive during the turmoil, but the minute they learned I was on home soil, they jumped at the chance to mend what was broken.

To prepare for their visit, I blew up the floor mattress and stocked the cabinets with liquor, wine, and snacks. I missed them so much, I met them curbside when they texted their cab turned on my block. We hugged and screamed on the sidewalk, easily picking up where we left off.

"Before we go inside, you should know the apartment is nothing like the house in London."

Khai looked around my empty space. "I'm not going to ask how much this small place costs because I already know it's a fortune with a doorman sitting downstairs."

"It's cute. And clean of course." Shannon critiqued.

"Now that the disappointment is out of the way, who's sleeping

317

with who? We have the sofa, the blow-up mattress, or someone can sleep with me."

"What's wrong with you?" Khai asked me. "Your eyes have a funny look about them."

"You guys just got here. We'll talk about it once you get settled in."

"Settled in?" Shannon laughed. "Bitch, we here? Spill the tea."

My face grimaced at Shannon's candor. "I missed you a lot. You know that?" I hugged her from the side. "Now, first things first. What do you two want to get into?"

Shannon surprised both Khai and I. "I am down to stay in the house tonight, hang back, and hear this tea. Thirty ain't so flirty."

Khai looked over to me. "This is who we've become. Scary right?"

I nodded in disbelief and slouched my shoulders, then plopped down on the couch. "Well, we can scratch off going to this nice bar I found where the music is on point, and the vibe is real mellow."

"Are you talking about the spot you were in the other night when I called?"

My face simpered of guilt.

"Were there any cute guys there?" Shannon asked.

"You won't find any Yohan's in there. Speaking of Han,

I can't be a part of your creeping with him. I'm cool with Olive now, and it doesn't feel right. Especially when he asks me about you using code language. I feel like I'm in on it."

Shannon sat next to me on the sofa and laid her head in my lap. "He's keeping tabs on me huh?"

I rolled her off of me. "Not like that."

She lashed into me. "I told you not to be friends with her. Should I gather my things and go to a hotel?" Shannon threatened.

"The last thing I need is to fight with you Sha. I have enough on my plate— But you know you and him were supposed to be a one and done."

"I can't help it if your boss prefers this Americanized ass over a boring stiff." She squeezed me and laughed. "Now, what did you mean by you have a lot on your plate? You and The Iceman Cometh having problems?"

"No. Nothing like that."

"Good. Because I'm walking the plank in six weeks, and you're both in the wedding. You'll still be in the states, so it all works out for my shower and bachelorette party. I also need you to fix this business with Taylor before I walk down the aisle so we can have a good time."

"I can be cordial to Taylor, but why are you playing around with Yohan when you've set a date?"

"There's nothing wrong with talking? Yohan is over there and I'm over here. And as for you and Taylor, being cordial is not good enough. I want things to be like they used to be, without the tension in the group."

I scoffed. "The best I can do is be cool. No drama."

Shannon raised her hand. "Do either of you hear a buzzing noise?"

My eyes grew big.

"It's coming from over there." Khai pointed to my purse.

"But your phone is in your hand." Shannon side-eyed me and we wrestled charging towards my purse. "Oh shit! Nadia you running the two-phone game?"

"Get your hands out of my stuff!"

Shannon pinned me to the ground.

"You've got Shannon on the line. Who is this?"

"Hi." Lucas's voice vibrated through the phone. "You must be one of the friends flying in for the weekend."

"So, you've heard of us." Shannon twisted her mouth.

"I have. Is Nadia available?"

Shannon held the phone next to both of our ears.

"Hey Lucas. What's up?" I sighed.

"I was wondering if you wanted to bring your friends down to the spot tonight?"

"Thanks, but we're staying in tonight."

Shannon talked over me. "We would love to join you, Lucas."

"Cool. I'll be there in an hour. See you then."

"You might not!" I shouted as the call ended.

Shannon giggled as she rolled off of me. Khai stood above us and reached for my hand. She pulled me from the floor, judging me hard like a school teacher in front of a class.

Shannon pinched me. "Bitch get dressed. You have some explaining to do."

I gave the girls the rundown on how Lucas came about, and how I ended up with the flip phone. Shannon did her normal routine of google searching people online, and checked out his profile.

"I'm glad he got to you first sis, because I would leave my fiancé for a man this fine."

"He's okay. Looks aren't everything." I rolled my eyes.

"Says the *sistah* with the white chocolate man giving her the world, and judging by these numbers a caramel macchiato who can almost do the same." Shannon reported.

Khai chimed in. "Self-sabotaging are we, Nadia?"

"It's all innocent. He's just a friend."

"Married women don't need male friends. What's really going on between you and Mash?"

On the way to the bar, I filled them in about the dreaded ex, his undead father, and our rift before I came to New York. As expected, Khai weighed in as the unlicensed group therapist.

"It's okay to be confused, Nadia. The backstabbing of a close friend, the ex-girlfriend who won't go away, and the pain Dylan caused you is still affecting you. Add on a misunderstanding with your husband, and your obsessive need to hold onto things, I'm not surprised you're up here about to fuck your shit up."

"Damn Iyanla. You 'gon call her beloved next?" Shannon joked.

I chortled. "Did I mention the man who put his arm around me in Paris is his dad?"

"Shut up!" Shannon shoved my arm.

"Nadia, you can stop this. You're using this Lucas person to prove a point." Khai stared me down.

"It's cool to look at the menu, just don't order from it." Shannon added. "Good morning Mr. Sharper is the man for you." Her tongue hung from the side of her mouth as she wound her hips on the seat, mocking me from her prior visit.

I looked ahead and held in my laugh. "You're not going to let me live that down, are you?"

"Never." She kissed my cheek.

Khai passed me a tissue to clean the lipstick from my cheek. I led the girls to the bar and introduced them to Lucas and Al.

"Remember me?" I flashed Al a smile.

"Good to see you. My friend here can't stop talking about you. He finally got you back in here for your special drink?" Al wiped the rim of a glass, glancing at my friends.

"Special drink?" Shannon pinched my ass. "You're like a totally different person up here."

"We'll have 3 specialties, Al."

"Bitch you keeping secrets like a *mufucka*. Who are you? Me?" Shannon questioned.

"Just shut up and tell me if you like it."

Shannon and Khai gave each other a once over, then sipped the mauve colored concoction.

Lucas smiled at Al. "Keep these coming, Al. Ladies, follow me," he said, leading us to a booth upstairs overlooking the stage. He looked at me. "I wouldn't put you in that hot seat."

Shannon whispered in my ear. "Bitch, I want all the tea."

I tittered to myself, grooving to the band, and table dancing with the girls, guzzling every drink Al sent to us. Khai cut off the final round of drinks.

"You've had one too many," she said.

"Why you say that?" I leaned on her shoulder.

"You're laughing at everything this man says. He's good looking, but not funny."

"He's not?"

She shook her head side to side.

"Ladies, I hired a driver for the night. Can I interest you three beauties in a midnight tour of the city?"

"We'd love to," I said.

Shannon sat in the front seat, flirting with the driver. I sat in the back seat between Lucas and Khai. We rode past The Apollo Theatre, admired the lights and billboards while stuck in traffic near Times

Square, then foolishly froze in the cold for a drunken photo in front of the bridge.

Lucas mentioned his apartment was nearby. Khai sat stone-faced in the car when Shannon and I agreed we wanted to see it. He gave us the tour of the recreation room on the bottom floor. Equipped with a jacuzzi, swimming pool, and fitness area. Then he welcomed us into his luxury pad.

"Why are we here again?" Khai asked.

"I hope it's so we can get in the jacuzzi?" Shannon asked.

"I think we should call it a night." Khai glared at Lucas.

"I have several rooms, and you're welcome to stay here for the night. We could order in, get in the jacuzzi if you like. The pool is also heated by the way."

"We don't have bathing suits," Khai replied.

Shannon in a drunken stupor didn't catch Khai's vibe. "I wish I had mine. I'd go downstairs and smoke on something in the jacuzzi."

"I'll send the driver to get you one." Lucas pulled out his phone.

"At this time of night?" Shannon raised her brows.

"You're in New York City baby."

The driver drove us to the closest general store. Lucas offered to pay for the goods.

Khai pushed his card away. "No thank you. We aren't broke bitches."

"I'm just being a good host," he said.

"Um huh." Khai hummed.

Back at Lucas's, Khai begged me not to get changed. "Trust me this one time," she said. And I did. I sat next to Lucas in the lounge chairs while she and Shannon soaked in the water and sipped champagne.

"Why did you change your mind about getting in?" he asked me.

"I'm a little tipsy. Not really up for it. Why don't you get in?"

"I would if you were in there." His russet eyes gleamed at me.

"Hey Lucas." Khai snapped her fingers. "Did Nadia tell you she's married?"

"She did."

"To a good man. A man we all love and approve of. I'm not

knocking you down to size, because you are undoubtedly doing good for yourself, and seem to be a nice guy, but her man loves her. Like a lot."

He looked back at me. "And she loves him. She's made that clear."

"Good, so what's the real reason you brought us here?"

He bowed his head. "Okay, you got me. I was having a good time with you ladies, and I didn't want the night to end. I brought you here to keep me company. There you have it. The truth."

"He's also married." I told them.

"Waiting for my divorce to be final." He corrected me. "And to lower any red flags, Nadia has been clear about our friendship from the beginning."

"Don't take this the wrong way Lucas, *but er ugh*, sis." Shannon waved her finger at me. "Don't sleep with this man. He is smooth. I sense trouble a-brewing between you two."

"We should go." Khai stepped out of the water.

While the girls changed in one of the spare rooms, I sat with Lucas on the loveseat in his living room. He picked up a remote from the coffee table and dimmed the lights above us, then reached down and placed my feet in his lap. He removed my left boot and ran his knuckles up and down the ball of my foot.

"Your feet are freezing."

"They always are." A tingle shot up my spine.

"Do you want a pair of my socks? They are thick."

"That would be nice." I kicked off my other boot.

He returned with a pair of fresh white knee socks and a blanket from his room, rolled the socks up to my calves and covered me.

"What's with the blanket?"

"Your friends are asleep."

"I knew they were taking too long."

"It's cool. I've wanted a moment alone with you all night."

'Dammit,' I thought to myself.

"I should go wake them." I kicked the blanket off of me.

"It'll be morning soon enough." His hands squeezed my feet.

"Lucas, a moment alone can lead to complications. Shannon's the single one. She should be out here with you. Not me."

"She's not my type." He bent my toes back and forth.

"But she's DTF." I gasped lightly.

He smiled at me. "Feels good?"

I nodded.

"A down to fuck woman doesn't turn me on. You do. A smart man knows when you lay with a woman, she is yours for thirty days."

"Thirty days? I'm afraid I don't follow."

"You know. Thirty days to see if you've planted a seed."

My cheeks rosed as I thought, *'That's some real heaux boy shit to say.'*

"Therefore, I choose wisely. I choose you."

"Do you have children?"

"A daughter back home in Seattle." He confessed, then deflected. "Are you comfortable?"

"I'm fine. I won't get any sleep tonight. Can't sleep in an unfamiliar place."

"I'm the same way. Looks like we're in for an all-nighter. Here." He handed me the remote. "You pick the movie."

I excused myself to the guest bedroom to shake the shit out of Shannon and Khai. One was half dressed with one shoe on, and the other still wrapped in a towel hugged up with a pillow.

I returned to the living room. "If we stay here, are you going to tie us up, and kill us in the middle of the night?"

"The tying you up part sounds nice, but other than that I wouldn't hurt a fly." He smiled, then passed me the remote.

Spoken like a true serial killer.

I strolled the lists on his apps and searched for a war movie to kill any romance vibes. He caught on to what I was doing so he switched to his monthly subscription channel, and suggested we watch a limited series. I chose one about crime. Murder and mistrust would easily kill the sexual tension in the room.

We sat through the first episode mesmerized at the storyline. By episode 2 he nodded off, and episode 3 took me down shortly after.

I jumped up an hour or so later when his hands gripped my feet. The program was now on episode 5, and I had no idea what was going on with the story arc. I escaped his grasp and snuck back into the room with the girls. I nudged Khai as I finished dressing her. She was out for the count. Shannon talked to me out of her head, pushing me away as I attempted to put her other shoe on. Then she snored like a bear, so I covered her with a corner of the comforter, and tiptoed back into the living room.

Lucas sat upright, changing the program to the news. "Is everything alright?"

I sat down on my end of the chair. "Yeah, just checking on my girls."

"I'm sorry I fell asleep on you. Come here. Sit closer to me." He patted the cushion.

I slid over an inch. "Who keeps you company at night?"

Lucas set the alarm on his phone and placed it on the coffee table. "Work. I haven't been able to focus on anyone with this impending divorce. I told you I have friends, but I'm not seeing anyone exclusively. If I were, she'd be here right now."

"I find that hard to believe."

The room fell silent. I placed my feet on the couch with both knees bent staring at the television, big-eyed and uneasy, struggling to stay awake. We watched the news, nodding off in shifts. Then, my head fell on his arm and I jumped. He wrapped it around me, and I squirmed. It felt strange to have another man's hands touch my skin. The hairs on my arm lifted as I sensed he was no longer asleep, and looking down at me. I kept my head turned towards the television, but that wasn't enough to deter Lucas from getting what he wanted.

He removed his arm and kissed my temple. I shivered and froze all at once. He leaned further down and gently kissed the side of my face, turning my chin towards him to taste his lips. I opened my mouth. "I can't," I said. He caught me on the inhale, and held his lips on top of mine. I puckered up and kissed him back, then pulled away.

He opened his eyes. "I knew it."

"You knew what." I turned my head.

"You wanted me, too." He grabbed my chin and turned my face towards him.

"Lucas, I'm not this woman."

"I know you aren't. I can tell. But I just couldn't help myself." He sat back on the couch, wrapped his arms around me, leaned his head back on the sofa, and this time went to sleep.

I removed his arm and slid to the opposite end of the couch, disheveled in my thoughts. One minute I was kicking myself, the next smiling. I listened to Lucas grunt in his sleep until the alarm rang. He turned it off, sat back and grinned to himself.

"Did I dream that?"

I didn't respond.

"Did you get any sleep?" he asked.

"Maybe an hour."

"I need to take a shower and get ready for a long day on site. You need anything?"

"I'm good. Can you ask the driver to warm the car? I'm going to wake the girls."

"Consider it done. It won't take me long."

I pinched Khai and Shannon until they woke up. They begged for five more minutes to sleep, dozing off regardless of my pricking their skin. Five minutes turned into ten minutes. Lucas hadn't returned to the living room. I knocked on his room door. "Come in." He granted.

I opened the door. *Have mercy.* "Kings and Queens," I mumbled.

"Say what?"

"Ugh, nothing. I was just remembering a lecture someone gave me." I couldn't look away at him standing in all of his glory.

"Sounds like you said Kings and Queens."

I did an about face.

He pulled me back inside. "Tell me what it means."

"Could you put some shorts on?"

He fumbled around in his chest drawer.

I hid my face below my palm. "The girls are moving slow. Can we hang back, and lock up when we leave?"

"If you promise not to rob me." He joked. "Of course. I trust you." He approached me with his undergarments thrown across his shoulder.

"Shannon was right. You are trouble."

He lifted me up and placed my legs around his. I felt like I was helping him maneuver me, but at the same time still as a broken clock.

He kissed me like he meant it this time. Tongue bathing my mouth until I exhaled the guilt mixed with desire rushing inside of me. I kissed him back, wanting to stop, but weak from the sensation tingling in my pussy now controlling my mind.

Lucas carried me around his waist to the side of the door and began to close it when I snapped out of delirium.

I hopped down and put my hand between the crack. "What the fuck have I done?"

He pressed against me and stared in my eyes, overflowing with lust I couldn't handle. "What needs to be done." He whispered. "It'll be great. You and I both know it."

I looked down and sighed at the monstrous, onyx lumber the constructionist packed. "Oh hell no, Lucas." My mouth watered.

"Kiss me one more time. Please." He begged.

In weakness, lust, and depravation of touch I agreed. "Just one more."

His dick nearly pierced my upper abdomen. I placed my hands on his chest. His heart was beating a hundred miles a minute as his cock contracted against my sweater. He reached to close the door again, and I stopped.

"Okay, that's enough. Lucas you will ruin me. I see why your wife doesn't want to let you go." I slid between the crack of the door.

"Don't ruin the moment talking about her. This is about you and me."

"There can't be a you and me." I pushed him off and walked out.

"Let me get dressed so we can talk about this."

"I'll call you later. We'll talk then." I rushed into the room with the girls.

I shook the shit out of Khai and Shannon until they woke up. Shannon cursed me, ready to fight.

"Grab your shit and let's roll now," I commanded.

Khai held her head. "What's wrong?"

"It's a code California." I emphasized strongly.

"California! Oh shit," said Shannon. "I said look at the menu. Don't taste from it!"

"I didn't taste, but I sampled the appetizer. We gotta go. Now!"

We scrambled for our things, jetted out of the front door, and fled into the car waiting out front.

"Nadia, what the hell man? Code California?" Khai shook her head.

"No talking in the car. Let's get home first." I shushed them, and instructed the driver to let us out a block away from my apartment.

We walked the short distance and entered the lobby looking like last night's havoc, napped for two hours, then woke for our brunch reservation at The Regent.

To mask my racoon eyes, I piled on makeup and wore sunglasses even though the sun wasn't out. The girls followed suit, and on the way to the hotel, I filled them in with what transpired.

"We haven't had to use code California since California," said Shannon. "When you say you sampled you don't mean oral transaction do you? 'Cause if you do, then you may as well have *ate* from every section."

"Jesus Christ Shannon, we only kissed. And I saw him naked."

"He kissed you, or you kissed him?" Khai asked.

"He initiated and I didn't stop him. Twice or thrice. It's all a blur. I'm so ashamed."

"How was it?" Shannon's voice lowered seductively.

"It was nice. Different but nice. It happened so fast and it was over quick, I don't know. Goodness I was dripping wet. What's wrong with me?" I whined.

"You're human. And I told you, you were self-sabotaging." Khai grabbed my hand. "But how did you see his dick?"

"When he was getting out of the shower."

Shannon fake coughed and cleared her throat. "Details please."

I smiled at both of them and took their hands. "The man could be on a poster. Face, body, and wood. I actually told him he would ruin me."

Shannon stared into space and Khai bit her fingernails while I smiled to myself. The driver grinned in the rear-view mirror, and shared a grin with me.

"If I had to say, the man has damaged many a womb."

Shannon slapped my arm. "We were in the house with a thick hog, and you cock blocked us from jumping on it."

"Shannon please." Khai hushed her. "These next six weeks can't get here fast enough. Nadia, I'm proud of you. You did good to walk away. Especially since I don't know if I could have. The man was tempting. I think I even dreamed about him last night."

"Whaaaaat!" Shannon and I blurted out together.

"Blame the alcohol." Khai tooted up her lips. "I mean I find other men attractive all the time. I just don't act on it."

Shannon's nostrils flared when I leaned up to look at her. Khai's confession shocked us into silence during the rest of the car ride.

Finding the eatery inside the maze of a hotel was a hard task for hungover, sleep deprived newbies to the big city. Once we found the café holding our reservation, Khai gave the maître de her last name, and he escorted us to our reserved table.

I stopped in my tracks and grunted. "You bitches."

CHAPTER 33

Talk About It

I was ambushed. Taylor and Isla sat with their backs to the wall, locking eyes with me the moment we turned the corner. I took a step back and the girls shoved me forward with whispered obscenities and threats.

"I'll never forgive you two for this. And not a word about last night." I gritted through my teeth.

"It's in the vault." Shannon assured me.

I clicked my teeth, then sat down across from the backstabbing duo. Taylor stood and extended her arms to me. I raised both of my brows and looked at her like she was crazy.

"As promised, we got Nadia here," said Khai. "She agreed to be cordial, so let's keep it rated G ladies."

Taylor sat down. "It's good to see you, Nadia."

"I'm glad you're doing well," I replied. "But I won't be forced into anything."

"I didn't think you would still be this angry with me. So much time has passed, I was hoping we could work this out. I truly am sorry for hurting you. If I could take it back I would."

"No, you wouldn't. It would be un-Taylor-like to not do whatever she wanted no matter the cost. I just have to know. Who pursued who?" I swayed my head and tucked my lips.

She paused and looked around the table. "He did. At one of the game nights. You two were having problems, and he said something I didn't take serious at first, but then you broke up and he approached me at a gas station saying he needed someone to talk to. He started calling me at work and then one day showed up at my job around the time I was pissed with Levi because he was still talking to his ex. I went out with Dylan to even the score, but you know how he is, and I gave in. But I promise we never snuck around when you two were together." She raised her hand to scout's honor.

I didn't believe her, but for the sake of us being in public I maintained my cool. "Here's my dilemma. I'm married so I'm in the position where I'm not supposed to care what, or who my ex-boyfriend is doing. My feelings are invalid in all of this, yet they are very real. Not for Dylan, but for one of my best friends making me look and feel like a fool."

"Nadia, I never..."

"I keep thinking about how you clowned me at your shower. Remember that? Teasing me. Saying I was still hung up on Dylan, and you were fucking him the entire time, and laughing at me in my face."

The girls mumbled and adjusted their seating.

"I don't hear anyone speaking up on my behalf. Have I said anything untrue?" I said to the table.

"You're hitting all the main points." Khai and Shannon cosigned.

"I don't trust you, Taylor. I will never think of you as my friend, and this ambush was a waste of time. But I wish you well."

"So that's it. You're just going to cut me out of your life?"

"You handed me the scissors." I pushed my seat back.

Khai grabbed my hand and gestured I sit back down. My shoulders slumped as I scooted my chair closer to the table.

"Wow, Nadia. You're sitting over there like you're all perfect." Taylor tapped on the table.

"I'm far from it. But looking at you, I see the kind of person I don't want to be. So, thank you, and know I forgive you. Dylan is your problem now."

I turned to Isla. "Since my ex boyfriends are the hot ticket item, how is Evan doing?"

"We're no longer..." Isla stuttered.

"You two are exactly alike." I added.

"Nadia, for my family's sake, we need to find a way we can get past this." Taylor pled.

"Family's sake?" Shannon questioned.

"Yes. Levi is on my case day and night wondering what happened between us."

"Well I'm not going to lie to him on your behalf, Taylor. It's why I have avoided speaking with him."

Eyes shifted from both ends of the table.

Khai asked the hard-hitting questions. "I thought everyone knew you had the affair with Dylan. But a moment ago, Nadia said he was your problem. If the affair is over, why is he still your problem?"

I raised my brows and scoffed. Taylor shook as tears fell from her eyes. She squeezed her hands together so tight they turned red.

"Yes, Dylan and I had an affair. But he is also Tyler's father." She confessed, then glared at me. "How did you know?"

"Your question confirms that Dylan is still a piece of shit and full of secrets." I chuckled. "I sat with you while you were sick. I read the card stuck inside the flowers he sent, and trashed it before Levi saw it. Yeah. That was me looking out for my friends. Then, he snuck into your room and told me everything. I love Levi like a brother, and won't ever tell him, because he's suffered quite a lot by your hands. You just better hope Dylan stays quiet."

"And everyone at this table." Taylor begged.

The girls locked their lips and promised not to expose Taylor's secret as our waitress finally arrived to take our order. As she walked away, Isla threw insults.

"Why do you three look like shit this morning?"

We eyed one another and burst into laughter, then removed our sunglasses to reveal the dark circles and bags.

"We went out last night and haven't slept," said Khai.

Shannon opened her trap as usual and said too much. "A hot guy flashed his shaboynka to Nadia last night, and it's all she could talk about on the way over here. You know it's been a few years since she's had a chocolate one in her face."

I looked at her like a deer caught in headlights as the entire table laughed at me like old times.

"What did it look like?" Isla asked.

"Like Michael Jackson singing on Christmas morning," I blurted.

The table roared, attracting unwanted attention and glares. We lowered our voices and snickered like we did when we were close.

"I miss this guys," said Isla. "Taylor isn't the only one who crossed the line. I did, too. Nadia, I'm sorry. I was jealous of you and Mash. And the joke was on me trying to date Evan. His ass was whack like you said."

I smiled at Isla for the first time in years. "I heard you were hummus shopping, too."

She blushed. "I tried it, but he didn't get our culture at all. I prefer being with a brother. They get me." She held her chest.

"Yes, my white chocolate is one of a kind." I boasted.

"Oh shit." Shannon leaned into the table and whispered. "Did y'all hear it?"

"I did." Khai and Isla tittered.

"So did I." Taylor chuckled.

"What?" I asked.

"You had a little British twang mixed in with your country grammar." Shannon teased. "Say it again."

"Y'all can go to hell."

"There it is again!"

We laughed together at my expense, and Shannon used the moment to unite us for her wedding.

"Doesn't this feel good y'all. We'll be doing it again in six weeks, and I want us to be just like this."

My phone interrupted her speech. "Excuse me for a second," I said, and left the table. "Hey. I'm with the girls. I have to tell you what happened."

"I have news also." Mash announced. "The house sold for fifty thousand dollars less than our asking price, but the new house in Richmond had an offer of $850,000.00 more than we invested from a buyer. You said you wanted to flip houses, so I accepted the offer. We'll be in the flat a little longer."

"I have no problem with that. Any chance I'll see you again before Shannon's wedding? It's in six weeks by the way, and you're in it."

"We can make it happen. Get back to your friends. Levi already told me Taylor was up there. I'm on your side, and I love you."

I returned to the table and suggested instead of clubbing, we all hang out together at my place, or their hotel room for the night.

"Does this mean you forgive me?" Taylor asked.

"It means, we're hanging out and we'll see where it takes us."

The night became reminiscent of the old days when we were five friends, and thick as thieves, figuring out our paths in life. It was the stepping stone to rekindling a fraction of my friendship with Taylor, and the first step in healing from the pain she inflicted upon me. Just what the doctor ordered.

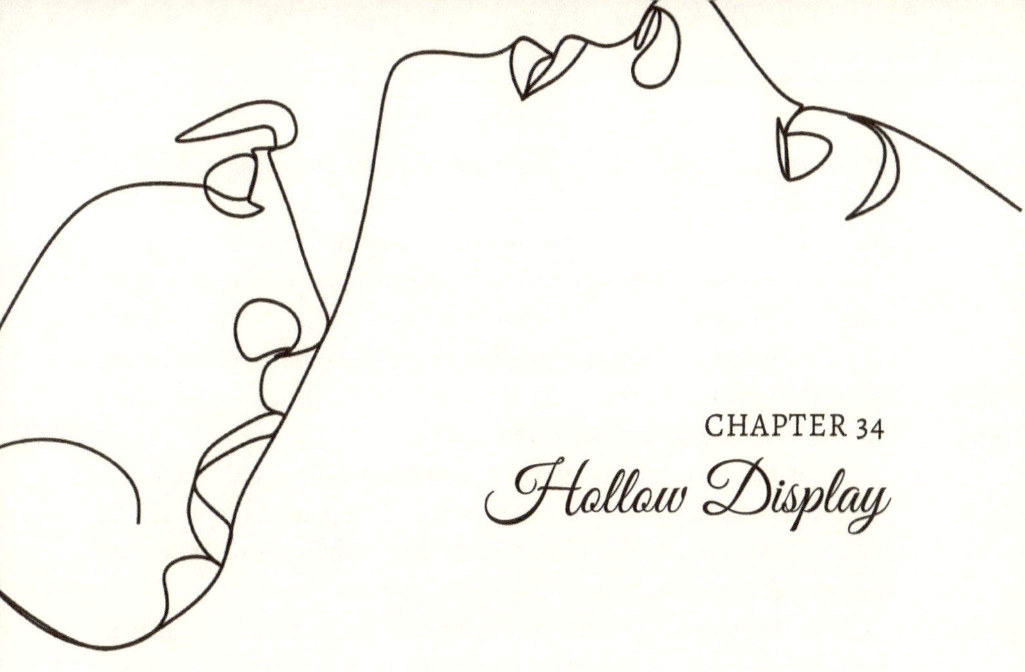

CHAPTER 34

Hollow Display

I lied to Lucas when I said I would get back to him. Flashes of his hands touching my face haunted me in the middle of the night, though there were times I found myself smiling at the thought of him.

The girls had been gone for two weeks, and in those weeks, I couldn't get him off of my mind. I powered down his phone, and placed it on the top shelf in the kitchen, all the way in the back. For damage control, I took matters into my own hands and surprised Mash at his concert in Berlin.

His song with Essence was charting big numbers, leading to nonstop shows throughout Europe, and with Gemma's help, I popped up on the side of the stage where I belonged.

Mash skipped the after show and we raced to the hotel. We stumbled, tripped, and staggered into his room, sucking on each other against the wall. I had to taste him. I needed to taste him. I kissed, licked, sucked and gagged on his shaft, erasing the image of Lucas from my mind until the scent of Maximus stained the tip of my tongue and nose.

Needing that hit of coital elation when our flesh collided, I suggested an act we never explored. "Choke me," I said. Mash looked concerned at first, but went with it in the heat of the moment. I accepted it as punishment for my wrongdoing, holding my breath when I climaxed with his hands around my neck. The peak of it was explosive and intense, bringing us closer through touch. The pit— it didn't feel like I was being punished. I thoroughly enjoyed it.

The exploration of our strangulation asphyxiation wore me down. Mash held me by the waist tighter than he did my neck. The guilt I carried with me led me to question him.

"Has what's her face been to any of the shows I missed?"

His grip around my waist softened, and he paused longer than I liked. "I saw her in the crowd once. She didn't approach me or anything though."

"So, the restraining order was a flippant threat, huh?" I squirmed from beneath his sweaty arm. "Were you going to tell me if I didn't ask?"

"I didn't speak to her, and we're not doing this right now. You didn't fly out here to argue with me about someone who is of no importance, and I didn't spend the last hour making you call my name to ruin it with meaningless conversation. I love you."

I took his answer as a no and gave up the argument. He assumed he talked his way out of having to confess he wouldn't have told me she was still hanging around on standby. I lied in his arms wondering, *'What is with those two? She threatens to go to the tabloids if she doesn't get what she wants, and he threatens a restraining order if she doesn't go away. But neither of them act on their warning. I'm truly sick of this shit.'*

Another round of mind-blowing sex I flew around the world for was enough to tide me over, and put the issue on pause. I threw my pussy on him so hard I thought I broke it the morning after my flight home, keeled over in pain from a bladder infection.

The matter sorted out with meds, and over the course of four weeks left in the Big Apple, I did everything to avoid making the same mistake again. I kept busy with Italian lessons and ballet classes through the week, and travelled out of the city on the weekends.

I flew into Charlotte and GSP for two weekends in a row. Getting fatter every day of my visits. I worked off the home cooked meals from mom, the dining out, and alcoholic binges with the girls in the fitness center on the basement floor of my building.

As the countdown was near its end, I took one final flight into Charleston to spend some time with Grams. I rented a car and drove her everywhere she wanted to go, including the beach in the middle of winter. The temperature wasn't nearly as freezing as it was in the north, but the forceful winds shortened our time spent on the shore.

Collecting sea shells stuck in the sand, Grams gave me more life lessons.

"I thought a lot about what you said on my last visit, Grams."

"I hoped you would."

"And I met someone." I confessed.

"I assume he is handsome. The devil always is." Grams clicked her tongue and winked at me.

"Very." I nodded. "And now I'm confused. How is it possible to be in love with someone, but thinking of someone else?"

"Easy. You love one, and you like the other. Just because you're married doesn't mean you won't find anyone else attractive. You still have eyes."

"So, what do I do?"

"Well your situation is different from most. In my day the majority of men were assholes. They felt entitled, because you know, women didn't have many rights. We were always looked at as maids, and property, and told to be submissive. Women like me who weren't putting up with the bullshit had it even harder. Nowadays, there are some men who actually respect women and see them as their equal. Even worship the ground they walk on. Like your husband. He calls me you know."

"I didn't know. Since when?"

"Since my party. But he calls me more often since you took this job you're doing. He loves you, and I don't think it's an act. He is afraid of losing you."

I looked out into the ocean while Grams shared her conversations with Mash. I felt bad for flirting with Lucas. Allowing him to place his arm around me on the sofa. Holding on to him on the back of his motorcycle. The kiss. That menacing gotdamned kiss.

"Now I know I told you to have a back-up man, but in your case, you're pretty enough to get one in your old age if you need one." Grams touched my nose. "Look at me. I have three, and I don't know what to do with any of them. Chile forget about what I said. My generation is my generation, and yours has evolved. Two different times, two different set of rules."

"Now I feel guilty. I mean things never got physical, but I have thought about it several times. I've avoided the other man for weeks because I'm afraid I'll give into temptation."

"And you haven't because you love your husband, and are loyal like your mother. I don't think this other fella could love you the way you are loved right now. Now if it were me, I would have jumped that man's bones, and went on like nothing happened. But I digress."

We shared a good laugh and headed back to the car. "Nadia, you did good gal. I'm proud of ya. Take heed to my word, and call it off with that other fella. Ya hear me?"

"Yes ma'am. I will. I'll call him when I get back and end it civilly."

"Civilly. Right. Now if you ever feel something isn't right in your bones, trust that feeling and do what you have to do. Remember a rat has more than one hole to go to."

I flew out in the morning and returned to the cold where I exercised two, sometimes three times a day. If I was too tired to exercise I wrote, or searched for submissions to find my next gig. Still mustering up the courage to face Lucas.

I stood on the edge of the counter and retrieved the phone from the cabinet. I powered it on and crossed my fingers that my ghosting him helped to kill the sexual tension between us, and revealed an ugly side of him to make him easy to forget. But I was wrong. There was no name calling, or derogatory messages on the voicemail. They were all pleasant, or empty with breathing and begging for me to give him a call. But I didn't call him. I went to see him.

I walked into his office and his head fell to the side. He looked up at me and smiled, holding his chin between his fingers, then sultrily parted his mouth to excuse one of his employees.

The gentleman left and he shut the door behind him. "You are a sight for sore eyes. I'm relieved you're okay. I must have left you a million messages." He hugged me.

"Yeah, about that...I'm sorry...I..."

"Don't apologize. I overstepped. But I don't regret it. I like you—a lot. And I'd do it again."

I pushed him away. "Therein lies the problem. I like you, too. But I love my husband, and I won't disrespect him any further."

"Look, I know I put you in an awkward position, but I am who I am. I wanted to kiss you and I did. I went for what I wanted, knowing I couldn't have it. And I still do. Even more so now in this moment." He stepped in closer.

I retreated to the window and he followed. "Lucas, I told you I'm not this person. I have wrestled with the guilt, and my part in all of this. I should have never called you, or allowed you to kiss me."

"Did you listen to my messages?"

"Yes." I sighed. "And I came here to apologize and tell you good-bye. Here's your phone."

He reached past the phone and caressed my wrist. "Keep it." He stuck it inside my coat pocket. "Since this is good-bye, can I have one final kiss?"

He grabbed my waist and pulled me away from the window, lowering his mouth to mine. He lifted my chin and kept his eyes open, planting his lips below my mouth, then to each of my cheeks.

I allowed him the pleasurable taste of my skin, granting him the request of one last kiss. It was soft, and gentle, and quick. I pulled back and he stole a second peck, speeding up the pace of my heart.

"Meeting you has changed me for the better," he said.

"I, too, have learned some things about myself since you came along."

"Like what?" he asked, seducing me with his eyes.

"That a rat has more than one hole to go to. And I'm not a rat."

An outburst of a chuckle moaned from his mouth. His hands fell to his side, and he watched me leave with a look of defeat written on his face. It was the look I aimed to remember of him. The face of what could have been my downfall. The face of temptation. The image of the disaster I would leave behind in New York, never knowing what would have been.

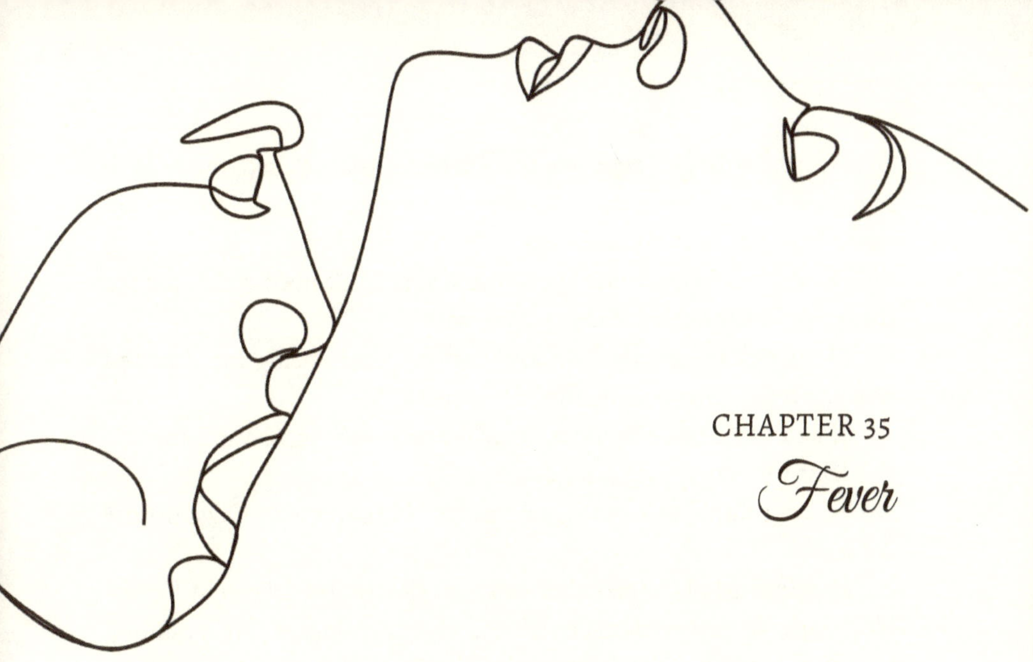

CHAPTER 35

Fever

The trial and tribulation of my stay back in the states finally ended. I made peace with my mistakes, and prepared to return to the U.K., donating my belongings to a nearby shelter after the doorman took all he wanted once I departed the premises.

I tied up all of my loose ends except the delivery of Lucas's cell phone. Hours before the car arrived to drive me to the airport, I packaged it with a note inside, and sent it to his office by courier.

The packing, organizing, ripping and running took its toll on me. I lied in the bed, waiting for time to pass before my flight to Charlotte.

While studying the design in the ceiling, my mind wandered from one thing to the next. I imagined what Shannon would look like in her wedding dress, if she was going to be a bridezilla like Taylor, and how much Baby Tyler was going to look like Dylan.

A knock at the door startled me. It wasn't time to leave for the airport yet, so I peeped through the keyhole for a clue. "Oh God no," I said to myself, staring at Lucas in the hallway.

I invited him inside. He walked circles around my near empty living space.

I paced circles of my own across the slick floors. "How did you find me?"

He slid a finger between the curtains, then closed them back together. "All of these months I could have been here keeping you warm at night. I would have even furnished the place."

"I told you I don't need your money. I didn't need much for the short time I was here. I managed well with little."

He posed against the window with his back facing me. I stayed near the front door waiting for him to speak.

"I had to see you one more time," he said, walking towards me.

"But we already said our good-byes."

"I don't think we said them properly." He cornered me against the door.

He outlined his fingers across my lips slowly and delicately. I trembled with desire, no longer fighting the yearning of my pulsating southern urges. I opened my mouth slightly and panted as his fingertips parted my lips.

"Nadia, can I make love to you?"

"Yes please." I shuddered.

We kissed reverently, stripping away our layers, and dropping them on the floor as he mounted me on the bed. The aching and longing of him in my thoughts, would now become tangible as his rough, un-manicured hands squeezed my body beneath him.

"I don't want to be a good girl anymore." I confessed, looking directly in his eyes.

"Yes, you do." His deep voice whispered. "You'll be my good girl."

He sucked on my neck until the blood under my skin felt like it burst. I heaved at the sensation as he moved to the other side, then to my breasts where he tickled my nipples with his tongue, clenching them with his teeth.

The satiable manner of his technique delivered sensations instead of pain. "Be back in one sec," he whispered, sliding his head between my thighs where it belonged.

"Mmm." I moaned, thrusting my core upward while he fondled my swollen lips with his, toying and tasting me. I jerked as my senses went wild with anticipation, then he licked my skin like an animal does when it's hungry. I cried out, "I can't take it anymore! I'm ready for you!"

He ignored my demand, caressing my ass while he fed from me, tongue twisting, and trilling my kitty as if he were rolling his r's in Spanish. I clung to the sheets as the vibrations paralyzed me. I could only lie there and wait for what was to come next. And I was not ready.

He penetrated the tip of his wood, but my rim fought his entry. "I promise I won't hurt you," he said, distracting me as he drilled his pipe inside.

I respired aloud to God while he stretched my walls. "Oh God!" I hollered.

"I knew you were holding heat." He growled in my ear, then gently bit my lobe. "Nadia." He purred. "I want you to look at me when you come."

I nodded okay, peeping at him through my lashes, witnessing the joy on his face for finally conquering me. He was a fiend atop of me, pressing his teeth firmly together, embracing me tightly so I couldn't escape. Relishing my nectar to the point I thought he would shed tears.

His hips swirled his manhood in and out of me so worthy I clenched his cock with my saturated treasure, making him woo and form a circle with his mouth. He lifted my legs and placed them above his shoulder.

I halted him, pressing my hands on his chest. "Lucas, I don't think I can handle you like this yet."

He stroked me once and I exhaled a sound of squeamish delight to his liking. So, he stroked again and again, faster and deeper. "Ahhh" I wailed, holding on to his shoulders with my eyes closed.

"Look at me." He ordered.

"I can't."

"Look at me, Love."

I opened my eyes as he demanded. He wiped the side of my face and swept my hair back, gazing at me without blinking and maintaining his rhythm. He ploughed and held his dick in place. I closed my eyes.

"No, my love. Look at me." He commanded.

I did as he wanted and looked at him while I climaxed, sounding off like a fire whistle. My mouth opened wide and he kissed me to muffle my roar. I could no longer obey his request and closed my eyes, digging my nails into his back. He orgasmed and rolled behind me, curling me into his arms, holding me close, and breathing heavily in my ear.

"He's not the only one who loves you." Lucas secured me into weakness and slumber.

A tapping noise woke me. I was still trapped in Lucas's arms. I wiggled my way free and looked on the floor to find the tapping noise. I saw nothing, then sat on the edge of the bed and held my face in my hands, covered in guilt, and confused by my actions.

I let out a sigh and heard the tapping sound again. I turned around to look back at Lucas sleeping peacefully in my bed, and choked on the air in my mouth.

Mash stood behind us, tapping his foot, and pointing a gun at Lucas. I waved my arms for him to put down the gun, incapable to form a word.

Mash wouldn't look at me. He stood there aiming at Lucas's back, zoned out in a rage.

My voice returned. "Mash don't do this. It's not worth it. Please put the gun down. Look at me please. I'm sorry. I don't know why I did this. It's my fault not his. Please, look at me."

His arm remained pointed at Lucas, but his eyes shifted to me. A tear dropped down each of his cheeks, and I fell to my knees, holding my naked body trying to cover myself.

Lucas woke up and called out for me. "Nadia. Nadia love, where are you?"

Mash's deep voice surprised him from behind. "Don't you dare say her name."

Lucas turned around and charged Mash from the bed.

I screamed. "No! Please stop! Both of you please stop!"

They ignored my cries and continued to tussle. The echo of the gun firing cut my ears.

I jumped up from the bed and held my chest. Thunderous knocking at the door woke me from my illicit dream. I peeped through the keyhole in fear my dream was about to become a reality, thankful to see the doorman standing on the opposite side.

"Your car has arrived ma'am. May I take your luggage?" he asked.

My blouse was wet with sweat, and my panties drenched from impure thoughts, but I still followed Paul downstairs, ready for a fresh start. I gave him the keys to the apartment, and we shook hands one final time as he opened the car door.

"Ms., Do you mind if I bum a ride with you?" Mash smiled at me from the front seat.

I stepped back on the curb. "I thought your flight was tomorrow?"

He hopped out and held me in his arms. "I changed it. I didn't want to wait another day to see you." He planted a wet one on me.

Inside the airport I grew nervous every time I saw a tall, slender, brown man walk near us in a navy coat. I breathed with relief when the wheels went up on the plane, happy the nightmare I had before the doorman woke me was in fact just a dream.

While overlooking the black ripples of waves below us, I vowed to forget Lucas existed, and to live with regret. Especially the regret of the words I wrote on the note inside the courier package I mailed to him.

'Leave this phone number in service.
It might ring one day.'

Book 2 Title Playlist

BRAND NEW ME
Alicia Keys
EX-GIRLFRIEND
No Doubt
GIN & COCONUT WATER
Calypso Mama
RED LIGHT SPECIAL
TLC
HIT ME BABY ONE MORE TIME
Britney Spears
WOMAN TO WOMAN
Shirley Brown
POWER TRIP
J. Cole, Miguel
NO NEW FRIENDS
Drake, Rick Ross
BRO CODE
Frenzy
YOU, ME, HIM, & HER
Jay-Z
GOIN' BACK DOWN SOUTH

Kings of Leon
HURTS LIKE HELL
Aretha Franklin
TIL FOREVER FALLS APART
Ashe, Finneas
GIRLFRIEND
Pebbles
LIGHTS, CAMERA, ACTION
The Lost Boys
ALL THE WAY UP
Terror Squad
WELCOME TO THE JUNGLE
Guns N' Roses
WHEN CAN I SEE YOU
Babyface
FOOLISH
Ashanti
FRIENDS
Whodini
TALK ABOUT IT
Etana
HOLLOW DISPLAY
Taj Weekes
FEVER
Michael Buble

Book Three

BLEND

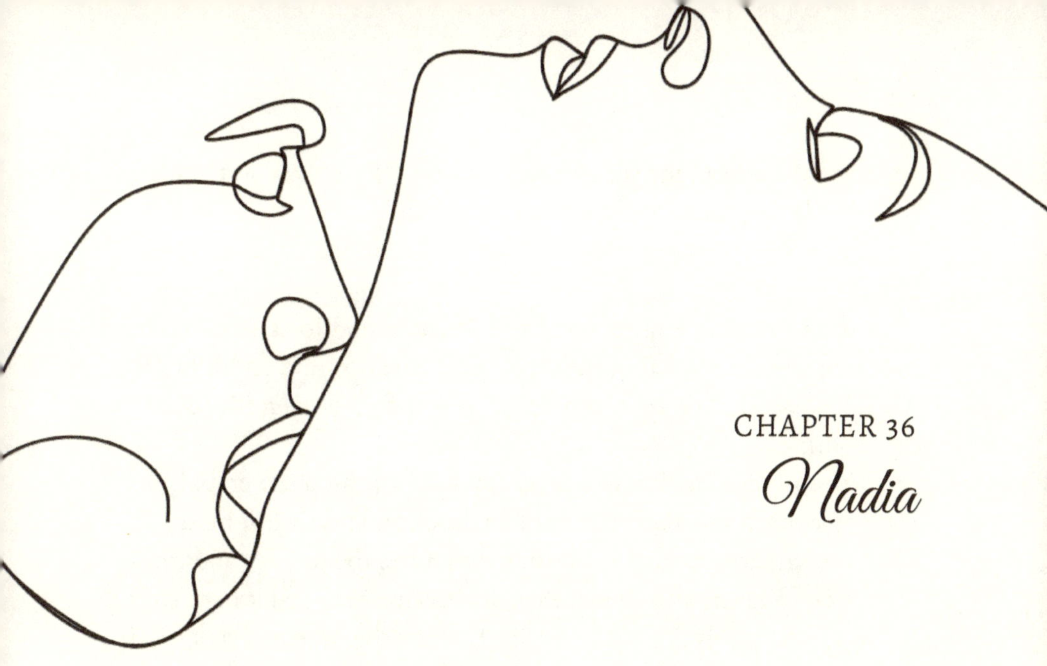

CHAPTER 36

Nadia

M y moans woke him. He watched me squirm and trace my inner thighs while I dreamed of his manliness, stroking near the verge of exertion. Deep inside of me. The wind from his nose tickled my neck as I grasped the back of his head, ravenously filled with intensity and gratification, when suddenly Lucas rose from behind me.

His mouth serenaded the small of my back up to the lobes of my ear; his fingers circled my shoulder. And I welcomed him. We welcomed him. Staring deep into Maximus's eyes, I smirked. I was having my cake and eating it, too. No secrets. No sneaking around. Pleasured by the two men who desired me.

Lucas's fingers travelled to my mouth, and I parted my lips to welcome them. The room shook as if it was being hit by an earthquake and faded to black. Then fervent kisses pressed against my cheeks woke me, and the insatiable nightmare came to an end.

My eyes widened, no longer bound by the fantasy of my inner desires, but enthralled in the reality of it about to happen. The man I married felt compelled to act without being asked. Grunting in my ear, "Your nipples pierced my back and woke me," he said.

He slid my hands from between my thighs. "Allow me," he said, smiling as he spread my slit and felt my heat. "Look how wet you are for me. Waiting patiently for your wakeup call."

I lured him in closer, rolled on top of him and said, "Then give it to me."

I didn't require a taste, but I was in the mood to taste him. His morning wood upended in the air through the opening on his briefs. My lips kissed it. "Good morning," I said before placing his cock in my mouth.

The sound he makes whenever my lips grip his shaft emboldens me, so I worked them upward until he shook and nearly lost his mind. I had become accustomed to pleasing him. Over the past few months I did a lot of pleasing and giving. Partially because of the guilt filled stint in New York, punishing me mentally. But also, because of the power I felt when I made him feel like a King. The way every man wants to feel.

Now that I was free from the burden of fear, and trusting him wholeheartedly, I breathed for the first time in years. I stopped holding back in our marriage, tried a few new things, and gave **ALL** of myself to him. *'It took me some time to get here, but finally I had arrived.'*

I caught a whiff of chlorine as the taste of salt pierced my tongue, so I retreated, careful not to cheat myself if I didn't hold back. Maximus suffered from my withdrawal and quickly mounted me, aware how badly I needed him to start my day off proper.

With full aggression and the right precision, the pressure of his circumference punctured his way to ecstasy. Uncontrollable pleasure took over my body and my mind, and a yearning for more throbbed between my thighs.

Mr. Sharper gave me what I wanted, and the aftershocks of his morning pillage were equally as hot as the steam from the shower. I smiled to myself in the mist, still feeling the work he put in, until the reverie of Mr. Fleming flashed before me, and wiped the smile from my lips.

As the water soaked my skin, the image of Mash, myself, and Lucas sharing a bed puzzled me. It was nice, but puzzling. I veered off into a daze, searching for reasons why he invaded my dream when I hadn't thought about him in months. '*Why rise from the crypt of my mind now?*'

Forgetting to lather the back of my body, the mistakes I made in New York rushed back to me: the motorcycle, the private lunch, the farewell letter, the first kiss, and the last. What I thought I buried across the ocean was wrapped in guilt, hurling about inside, now haunting me in exotic twisted dreams.

I fully regrouped and dressed before the morning rush was upon me. I saw Mash off and turned on my laptop for a virtual call with Yohan. Once our session ended, I dug into my latest edits for our second project, then met Olive on her side of town for a yoga class.

Conversation between us was light this morning. The most we chatted was during downward dog when the instructor couldn't see our mouths move. Then after class we scheduled a time to grab lunch, as both of us were in a hurry to tend to our mates.

I grabbed a salad from the market, and ingredients for a romantic dinner to reset the mood for an instant replay of the morning pillage. While massaging steaks, slicing potatoes, and slaving over the stove, I pictured Mash's perfect hard on pounding me into oblivion on the staircase.

It was our first night back from the states, and we were still riding high from Shannon's wedding weekend. The exhaustion from travel somehow disappeared once we landed, and we fucked like rabbits between, and on top of boxes stacked throughout the apartment. But the way we finished on the stairwell was epic.

I had him pinned against the rails howling, "Nadia, I fucking missed you!" He was helpless as I sucked on his cock like a banshee under his guidance with my hair in his fists. He liked that. Truth be told, I liked it, too. I was making up for the months I abandoned him, and the nights we spent apart before my departure. Just thinking about that night had me ready for him to come home. '*Yeah, I'm going to jump him as soon as he walks in the house.*'

Lost in my memories, the timer on the stove ticked, and the door from the garage slammed. I somehow missed hearing it lift on the other side of the house. Mash called out to me in a rage, "Nadia, where are you!?"

"Follow the aroma!" I shouted, whipping the potatoes into cream.

Mash entered the kitchen brooding and upset, but I did what came naturally, and flashed my teeth whenever I saw him. He didn't reciprocate. Instead, his face tensed, his eyes twitched, and he lifted a yellow package in one hand, and a flip phone in the other and asked, "Who the fuck is Lucas Fleming?"

CHAPTER 37

Nadia

I damn near dropped my prongs in the oven when Mash said his name. I glanced at the phone then back to him, afraid to breathe, blink, or speak. A rush of blood ran to his head and the package vibrated from his trembling hands.

My silence made the situation worse. My voice rattled, spewing unknown sounds as my lips formed to pronounce words but failed. My mind lost function, until it became clear last night's erotic nightmare was a warning.

I closed the oven, and answered his question with a question. "Lucas Fleming from New York?" Mash stood in silence with a blank expression on his face. I cleverly added, "He is a guy I met who gave me a list of the best places to visit before I left the city. Why do you ask?"

"He sounds like he gave you more than a list." His tone berated me.

I raised my brows. "What are you saying?"

"I'm saying there's something you're not telling me. There are over a hundred messages on this phone addressed to you for fucks sake!" He kicked the floor board.

"Okay, you need to calm down. You're getting way ahead of yourself. All this guy did was offer insight into the city. I wouldn't give him my number, so he insisted I take the phone you're holding to tell me about the latest happenings and special events. As you can see I sent it back to his office. As you can hear from his messages, I didn't communicate with him. End of story. Think! I honestly don't know how or why it was sent here." My chest ached with fear and guilt.

"It has a return to sender stamp on it. The building in New York forwarded it here. What aren't you telling me?"

I sighed and rested my hands on the counter. I couldn't look at his face covered in hurt and anger. "What are you accusing me of?" I asked, searching for a way to make this conversation end.

He scoffed and roamed the floor. "Nadia, did you cheat on me while you were in New York?"

"No. Why would you think that?"

"Because I'm holding a fucking phone with a man's voice begging my wife to call him!"

The phone flew across the kitchen as I screamed. "Stop yelling at me! I didn't have an affair! Jesus, Mash. You had a key to the apartment, and we talked all the fucking time."

His eyes cut me down and his voice cracked. "I'm going to ask you one final time, and I want the truth. Did you fuck this man?"

'*Only in my dreams.*'

"I said no! Go somewhere and cool off. We can discuss this later." I reached for the spatula and dropped it in the pot of potatoes.

"I don't believe you." He paused. "You need to leave."

"Excuse me?" I frowned at him.

"I want you out," he said with venomous eyes.

"Mash, be mindful of your words. There is no going back from certain things, and those words in particular I take personally," I said.

"You want me to be mindful of my words when you were... Humph, that's rich. I want you to take whatever you want and get the fuck out of my house! Tonight!" he shouted, and flung the canisters from the countertop to the floor.

I shook and held my chest, staring at him with the devil in his eyes. Red with heat and poisonous darts aimed for me. I had witnessed his temper, but never like this—And never with me.

I recalled when we met, he told me, "I say what I mean, and I mean what I say." And he meant those words. *'Get the fuck out of MY house!'*

I stood at the stove, frightened. Afraid to make a move. I waited for him to retract his statement. Say he was sorry for shouting at me. Apologize for losing his head.

The final timer for dinner buzzed, killing the silence between us. "Mash," I called out to him.

He turned around, fanned me off, and left me standing in my stupidity.

I died on the inside from the way he looked at me, and my heart broke when he fanned me off. It felt as though he was treating me like a fly and told me to *shoo*, or as he would say, "Bugger off."

What I had done in the dark came to the light, screwing me over tenfold. I hadn't thought about Lucas since I safely made it out of New York, yet he found a way to disrupt my happiness. But I couldn't put all of the blame on him. *Fucking guilt.*

I refused to allow a meaningless kiss to uproot my life. A kiss I stopped because I knew the hurt it would bring. A kiss I used to say goodbye and end an affair before it ever started.

I would not be dismissed from the man who constantly professed his love to me, and in an instant wrote me off. Feeling sick throughout my skin, I followed him, and begged him to listen. "I did not cheat on you. Do you hear me?" I pushed on his heels.

Mash shut the door to the studio and locked it behind him. I banged on the door, shouting through the oak, "Are you being serious right now! You know damned well I wouldn't do that to you!"

I pressed my face against the door. A loud thump, followed by glass shattering created a forceful vibration. I cautiously jumped back as music blasted from the other side. I held my chest and fell to the floor, whimpering silently for at least ten minutes. I thought, *'Surely, he would check on me and take back those vicious words.'*

He did not. The music never settled, and the studio door never opened. Distance grew between us a mile a minute. Angrily I pushed back to the kitchen, tossed the meal I labored over in the garbage, then heaved on top of it. When my stomach settled, I made my way to our bedroom and stood in front of the fireplace.

I cased the décor from wall to wall, unsure if I should pack my bags. The new house felt like my home, and I grew furious at the thought of leaving it after finally settling in. Six weeks of shopping, and ordering, and measuring and designing—all for nothing. Lost over a fucking kiss.

I sat on the edge of the bed and waited for Mash to calm down and talk to me. My nose dripped and my head ached, but I waited. And waited. One full hour went by and nothing.

Feeling silly and desperate, I lazily packed one bag. I didn't organize or select what went inside my luggage. Whatever my hands touched I threw inside, and the more I fumbled through the hangers, the more I became filled with rage. I stopped using suitcases and threw arm loads of clothes, purses, and shoes in the back of my SUV— filling every inch of the car to the point I couldn't see out of the windows.

I sat in the garage, still waiting for Mash to face me and say anything. "Sorry, don't leave," "I didn't mean what I said," "I love you." Anything to stop the pain burning in my chest. The longer I held out for reconciliation, it became clear he wasn't coming to check on me or make amends.

I pulled out of the garage and drove to the end of our street, put the car in park, and heaved again on the side of the road. My neighbors having a late evening run tended to me, offering to escort me back home. I lied to them moments after I composed myself. "My husband isn't home. I'll be fine driving myself to the ER."

I exited the gate, hoping to see Mash's silhouette appear in my rearview window, running to catch me like a scene from a movie. Wishful thinking on my part that didn't happen.

I sighed and slowly drove away from the neighborhood into the dark streets with nowhere to go. I roamed until I grew tired, finally stopping at a hotel I would normally never stay in. But the night was far from normal.

I checked into the lodging, unable to wrap my head around what was happening. I bounced from the chaise to the bed, holding myself while my mind ran itself crazy. Thinking of him, of us, and what was supposed to be— Crying in between the good and bad memories flashing before me.

Sometime in the night I made my way under the covers, and when the sun rose I was already awake, shaking in the poorly made lumpy structure. My eyes were swollen, and my hands shuddered in my mouth as I bit off my fingernails. My chest hurt as if I had been hit by a car, and my insides felt like a roller coaster. Waves of pain and quivering aches traveled through my body, and they were all too familiar. I had been here before. Dylan emerged from the hate pile of my thoughts — though this time I felt ten times worse -- and from there I blacked out.

With no master plan, backup plan, or indication what my next move was going to be, I foolishly assumed we were solid. And though I had money in my possession, I was clueless and lost without Maximus Sharper being a factor in my decision making.

Depression found its home in my mind once again. It seeped into its familiar corner, bringing with it the pain that flowed through my veins, weakening my body. I could barely move to wipe my tears soiling the bedding, and found myself held up in the low budget motel, sleeping incessantly from despair.

Every morning I beat the sun rising, until days later I accepted my time abroad had come to an end. I boxed my clothes from the car, and moved them into a storage unit near Olive and Yohan's house. I gave Olive the key to check on my belongings until I returned, and begged her to keep quiet about my dilemma.

She gave me her word and arranged for Mervin, their driver, to deliver me to the airport in style. I hesitated getting out of the car. My legs shivered, and my breathing skipped. Olive patiently consoled me in the drop off zone, and offered her cottage in France as a temporary getaway until I was ready to face reality.

Exhaling deeply, I declined and pretended I didn't experience a panic attack in front of her, though my flushed face told a different story. My words pacified my true feelings, and I convinced her the best place for me was home. "Call me if you need anything. Anything." She emphasized with a stern look in my direction.

"I will. I promise I won't be a stranger." I smiled.

"Now go let off some steam and find that pretty girl I was jealous of that *one* time."

We cackled hard at the first joke I ever heard her tell. She hugged and released me, then I bravely stepped on the console and faced my reality. I was done in London.

With nothing but time and space to comfort me in the air, I reflected on the past two and a half years. The night at the club where I met Mash, my work with Yohan, my friendship with Olive, the hate I felt being caught between her and Shannon, and then Lucas. The night I met him replayed over and over in my head until I became annoyed with myself.

I did my best to spin the truth, and pinned the blame solely on Lucas and not myself. I faulted Chili for inviting me out the night I met him. I faulted Shannon for answering the phone the night we went to his place. And in the end, I blamed the real villain. Me. I shouldn't have gone to the bar, and I should have tossed his business card out of the window, or left it in the backseat of the cab.

My sulk-fest lasted throughout my flight. By the time I landed in New York for a three-hour layover into Charlotte, I conjured the nerve to confront Lucas and thank him for ruining my life. I headed toward the exit with the burning question mouthing on my lips. *'Why did you do a return to sender with that godforsaken phone? Did you think I would want you after ruining my life?'*

As bad as I wanted answers to my questions, I cowered and listened to the voice speaking to me in my head. *'Don't go. Don't let his plan work.'*

I turned around and headed back to my gate, spinning out of control. Thriving off of impulse, I turned off my phone and changed my plans, purchasing a one-way ticket from a random counter, and ended up in Cincinnati.

Boarding the flight was better than sitting in JFK for three hours with the itch to seek out Lucas. The spontaneity of being wild as the wind increased my pulse, and spared me the embarrassment of returning home with my tail between my legs for a while. I was sure wagers were made of how long Mash and I would last. But I bet they never thought I would be the one to screw it up.

I landed in Ohio as a lost soul with nowhere to go, or direction of what to do. Following the other travelers to the turnpike, I hailed a taxi. "Take me to the nicest hotel in the city," I said.

As my luck would have it, the hotel the cabbie drove me to had availability. I made myself comfortable in a deluxe room where I ordered movies, and loaded up on room service, pinching from every plate delivered until boredom struck me. When eating became sickening, I entertained my sorrows at the lobby bar. Whatever the server suggested, I taste-tested and ordered until my vision became blurry.

The staff saw to it I returned to my room unscathed. It was way past noon when I woke with a hangover from hell, leading to my second day in town being spent in bed.

The next day I took recommendations from the hotel concierge and agreed to go on a tour of the city. *'Please let this sightseeing excursion help clear my head.'*

It didn't. As the guide read the history of sites such as the National Underground Railroad Freedom Center, Spring Grove Cemetery & Arboretum, and Taft Museum of Art, I managed to be at ease. But when she began talking about the novels based in Cincinnati, a sadness overwhelmed me. A brief mention of Toni Morrison's *Beloved* caused me to tear up, and melancholy knocked me on my ass when we arrived at Eden Park. "The famous novel *The Ghosts of Eden Park* is all about this place," she said.

It dawned on me as we toured the grounds, I was a single amongst couples. How I missed that fact on the bus, verified I wasn't in the proper head space to be amongst people.

The guide continued to read from her script, but her narration was no match for my emotions erupting in public. I turned into a mental patient, sitting at the back of the trolley, while the others continued to stroll in the park.

Unable to hide my tears behind my sunglasses, I softly wept in my corner of the carriage. The passengers took turns looking back at me. Few offered their help. "I'm fine," I lied. "I just learned of some bad news."

I suffered amongst them until the next stop, hailing a taxi back to the hotel. Humiliated and ashamed, I spent the rest of the day locked inside my room, repeating my drunken sorrow fest.

How unwise, drinking on an empty stomach. I paid for that mistake dearly over in the night. Migraines and stomach cramping painfully sobered me up, as the bed hugged me throughout the next morning and afternoon.

When the moon flew high in the sky, I took my bucket of tears to the airport and left Ole Cincy.

While standing in line to buy a one-way ticket home to Charlotte, I had a change of heart. Las Vegas called out to me.

I always dreamed of seeing the Grand Canyon as a little girl, but as a not so poor, not so middle-class family of four, such a trip was considered a luxury. Twenty years later, I was finally able to see the magic—alone on a helicopter tour, snagging a cancellation in two days.

The forty-eight hour wait presented me with time to unwind and be still. And this time, I regrouped without alcohol and a personal goal to not embarrass myself further in public.

While searching for my sanity, I took advantage of the hotel's amenities, splurging on a full day at the spa:

a facial, mani and pedi, body exfoliation, and a massage to relieve the knots of tension in my neck. The healing stones allegedly removed the negative energy, and cleared the rancid thoughts in my head. '*Temporarily.*'

I woke up the next morning rejuvenated, browsed in the boutiques in the hotel, and dined in one of the many eateries. Money and food were wasted yet again, as my appetite still hadn't returned, and another memorable meal was packed in a box to sour in my room.

To finish off the day, I rented a car and drove out to Area 51, curious to see what the hype was all about after watching a program of conspiracy theories on a local channel. The drive and the views of the mountains along the way briefly cleared my head. But the closer I drove to the sight, and read the danger and warning signs with the monotonous scenery of the red desert in the backdrop, disturbing images entered in my head.

I daydreamed I ignored the do not cross sign and jumped over the government-controlled fence. Bullets blew through me and put me out of my misery. Envisioning my death woke me from the horrid, dark fantasy, and I jerked the car to the side of the road.

Huffing and gasping for air, I teared up at the image of me lying lifeless in the dirt. *'I'm sad but not that sad. I don't think.'*

I drove back to the city, cursing myself for being dumb and weak, slapping the steering wheel to release my frustration. My body shivered, and my eyes watered continuously along the drive. I needed help. But not therapy help. I required check in a hospital and become sedated help.

Once the car was safely returned to the airport, I hopped the hotel shuttle, and relaxed on the feather stuffed mattress. Sleeping until the alarm woke me the next morning.

The helicopter ride to Arizona lifted off, and alas I was up in the air viewing the red and russet colored rocks of the canyon. The formation of grooves took my breath away, reminding me of Es Vedra in Ibiza. A single tear fell down my cheek, this time accompanied with a smile. The love I felt in that moment filled me from head to toe, and remembrance of those emotions somehow pacified me.

My veneration of the canyon soothed my aching soul, then the magic happened. We rode in the flat of the ravine during sunset and an unexpected, indescribable feeling came over me. I didn't know how to receive it or explain it, but I felt the presence of energy embrace me, and a sense of serenity took over my thoughts.

Something spoke to me and said, "Everything is going to be alright." I laughed to myself, thinking of the good times I shared with Mash, and also realized I had an interest in geology. I scoffed. *'My aha moment.'*

Here I was thirty years old, learning something of nature was important to me, as it guided me back to my true self. Back to me.

I felt anew and less dejected as the chopper flew back to Las Vegas, somehow balanced and filled with courage to finally fly home to Charlotte the next morning, ready to begin the healing process.

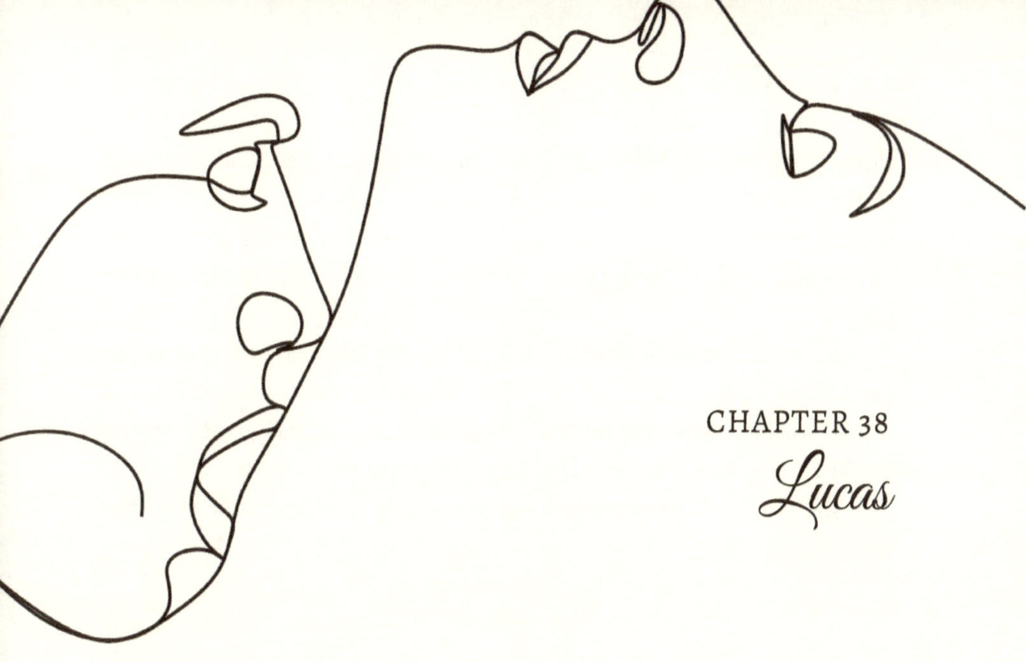

CHAPTER 38

Lucas

I ransacked my office, the mailroom, and my secretary's desk like a madman. *'Where the fuck is Nadia's package? I have the note, but what good is it without the phone? She could be calling me right now. Dammit! It has to be in here somewhere.'*

I couldn't get her off of my mind. She left me on edge like a message left on read and the three dots stopped moving— With no way to find her. No last name. No address. Nothing. *'How could I lose the one thing that could connect us?'*

A woman had never had such a lasting effect on me. I sat in my office for weeks imagining she waltzed through the door with those luscious plum lips slightly parted, and lured me over to sink into my arms. Every day the dream added something new to fill the void. No longer did I only envision her supple lips. Soon her breasts and mahogany nipples became clear, and real, and they were perfect, begging for me to kiss them. Then I'd wake just as my lips opened to taste her flesh. Hard as steel about to burst through the seams of my pants. *'God I hope she returns and puts me out of my misery.'*

For days I held my breath, waiting for the day to be graced by her beauty. We had something special, I know it. And in my mind, Nadia belonged with me. *'She will be mine.'*

The women I've dated couldn't light a candle to her. Her mysterious ways would keep any man guessing, and her resiliency and restraint disturbed my rest for many nights. Most of the girls I've encountered, begged for me to please them after seeing my endowment. But not Nadia. She wasn't a whore like most of the women I've slayed.

If I'm honest with myself, I fell for her the moment she sat next to me at Al's. I knew then I found what I had been searching for, but her stupid husband stood in my way. Never having met the guy, I knew he couldn't possibly treat her the way she deserved to be treated. If he did, she wouldn't have been alone in the city spending time with the likes of me.

~

Two months passed, and no sign of her. I gave up and accepted I would never see Nadia again. My memory of her was the only piece of her I'd ever have since the package was never found, and the phone was lost.

Out of frustration and despair, I burned her note in my sink causing the smoke alarm to sound. As I fanned the flames, I read her aching words for the final time:

> *'Leave this phone number in service.*
> *It might ring one day.'*

Her words gave me false hope, yet I wondered if she thought about me the way I thought about her—from the moment I wake, throughout the day, to whatever hour I passed out at night. The only way I would know is if she appeared before me. And I waited for that day.

To distract me of my agony, I took on new projects and worked day and night. My days were long, filled with investors and long pocket clients with the capital gains to expand my company's brand.

A newcomer to the city with big ideas on my calendar got me out of bed early one morning. I needed the diversion and the account. A big project with a mogul financially fit to take risks could have helped me restore my image in the office after months of outbursts and erratic behavior.

Normally, clients traveled with at least two representatives for the first summit, but my assistant escorted one gentleman into my office. *'Strange,'* I thought, expecting a team. I readjusted my pitch to the well-groomed gentleman standing opposite me across the desk with a serious demeanor, reeking of wealth.

I raised my hand to shake his and he refused. Again, catching me off guard. I cleared my throat and retrieved my hand. "Please have a seat." I gestured to the seat next to him. He unbuttoned his blazer and sat, staring at me viciously.

Wasting no more time, I began to sell the vision my partners and I discussed for the property in question when he abruptly interrupted me. "Scrap all of the plans you had in mind. I'll keep it brief. I'm here to advise you to stay away from my wife," he said.

"I'm sorry. I don't follow," I replied. My brows raised to my forehead in bewilderment. "I have no idea what you're talking about. Whom, may I ask, is your wife?"

"You prey on that many, *huh?* When's the last time you spoke to Nadia?" His eyes narrowed in on me.

And there it was. The name of all names to shatter me into pieces. When Nadia said my money didn't matter to her, I understood why. It was chump change compared to this family's generational wealth.

My research team found files on an older Mr. Sharper, who must be this guy's father, and who I was expecting to meet with. My net worth couldn't compete with this family, and judging by his suit, I had my work cut out for me.

I figured he'd only come to see me because there was trouble in paradise. I crafted my response carefully after staring at Nadia's husband with a grin on my lips. "So, you're the one standing in my way," I answered.

"You're the one who can't move me." He huffed.

"So Nadia's last name is Sharper?" I smirked.

"Mrs. Maximus Sharper to be exact," he bragged, tugging on his lapel as if his words intimidated me.

"To answer your question, I haven't seen Nadia in several months. How is she?" I asked, intentionally to agitate him.

"Humph. It seems you are a bit of a beggar, Mr. Fleming," he said, pulling out the missing flip phone from his pocket.

My eyes grew big, and the veins in my temple inflated. "The missing piece," I said, surprised to see it in his possession.

He laughed a rich man's laugh as if he pitied me. "A flip phone? Really? What kind of company gives their employees flip phones these days? And what kind of desperate man gives it to a woman who is clearly not interested?"

"Nadia does play hardball, but I wouldn't say isn't interested."

"Watch yourself carefully when referring to my wife, Mr. Fleming." His nostrils flared and his face turned flushed pink.

"What exactly can I do for you. Mr. Sharper?" I reclined in my chair and folded my arms.

"It's simple. Stay away from my wife. And don't ever try to contact her again."

"You seem nervous, Mr. Sharper. Trouble in paradise?" I laughed.

"You'd like that, wouldn't you? Unfortunately for you, my wife and I have a bond most couples don't achieve. I'm sure she's spoken of her loyalty to me, or did you not talk while you were shagging her?"

"She did mention something about her devotion to you, but unfortunately it wasn't while I was fucking her. If I had, she'd still be in New York. I mean, she wanted me to give her the goods, but you got in the way. I did, however, taste those succulent lips of hers, but again, you got in my way. It's a damn shame, too. I never got the chance to butter my potato, but I think that may be changing soon, once I find her— Thanks to you. I appreciate you stopping by and giving me what I needed. I finally have a name to put with the face. Nadia Sharper." I dragged her name to taunt him.

I pushed the button I wanted to push. He stood as if he was about to leave, but sucker punched me. He adjusted his jacket as if I was going to sit there and not retaliate. I sneered at him acting like he was the big man on campus, and shook off the blow, then rose to my feet. "If you fuck the way you hit then you've already lost, my friend."

He charged me with another blow I didn't see coming. He south-pawed me, and I had to give it to him— He was swift. I could feel the rage in that hit and rightfully so. I knew Nadia was holding honey in her Cheerio, and her husband was fighting to keep her sweetness away from me.

I stepped out of my professionalism and swung to return a lick; but he took a step back, causing me to send wind in his direction.

"If you fuck the way you miss I have nothing to worry about, my friend. Let this be the last time we meet," he said, and strolled out of my office.

I had never been more infuriated or annoyed by another man in my life. He ignited a fire in me I hadn't felt since my early days of bar fights in the city.

He also made me want his wife even more. I could already taste her sweet nectar on my lips. Feel her supple skin pressed against mine. Her ample ass in my palm. Our union was long overdue, but surely Nadia Sharper was about to be mine.

CHAPTER 39

Mash

The image of another man's hands on my wife caused my temper to flare, and I threw the phone against the hardwood. I wish it had shattered into pieces like my ego, but I only managed to crack the battery casing and bend the antenna.

I couldn't stand to look Nadia in the face, so I locked myself inside my studio until the morning. And like I demanded, she was gone.

It was the last time I saw her. She was disheveled and scared, and I showed her a side of me that terrified her. I couldn't live with myself knowing I put her in such a frantic state. I also couldn't live with knowing she would betray me and take a lover, especially after learning about my past.

She knew how damaged I was from the deceit Senior and Nomi caused me. *'How could Nadia hurt me like this?'*

With her gone, I was stuck with the memory of her bawling her eyes out uncontrollably on the floor, when I promised I would love her forever. A total hypocrite I proved to be.

'What the bloody hell was wrong with me? Why didn't I believe her?' A man knows when his woman has let another play in his house, and I knew Nadia loved me enough to never violate my trust, or allow

another to destroy what we had. I should have listened to her, but I didn't, and now I've lost her.

Three days passed, and she hadn't turned up. I barged into Yohan's office making an ass of myself, demanding he call Olive and question what she knew. He denied my request, and I couldn't blame him. I was out of line and would have denied him the same if he'd acted as I had.

Frustrated and embarrassed, I apologized with my head up my ass. Han offered to notify me if he heard anything. We shook hands, and he patted my shoulder sympathetically. "Women. What can you do?" he said, shaking his head.

Nightfall was upon me as I sat at my low point of despair. When my phone rang, I answered on the first ring, hoping it was her. It wasn't. "Olive drove Nadia to the airport, but doesn't know where she was heading," said Yohan.

"Has she heard from her since her departure?"

"She has not. I'll touch base if I hear anything," Han promised.

My Nadia was gone. A waif somewhere out in the world alone. Unreachable and unattainable, and it was my fault.

The suspense of her whereabouts drove me insane. I called her phone numerous times, receiving her voicemail on the first ring. The laugh in her greeting stole a piece of my soul, but I dialed her number incessantly to hear her voice. I needed her to know how sorry I was for my behavior. For my words. How disgusted I was with myself for not believing her.

Wanting to apologize in person, I only breathed when the line beeped to speak. My body ached, but I feared she was in more pain from my verbal blows. I longed to hold her in my arms and beg for her forgiveness, smell the pomegranate scent in her hair, and taste her delicious lips to heal my open wound. *I should have never told her to leave.*

The days rolled into a week with no word from Nadia. Her absence destroyed me. Her unknown whereabouts led me to the edge of my sobriety and on the brink of buying an eighth to have a minute of peace. Four years off the white, and there I was remembering only the good it did me. The brief high and gift of blissful short moments of not giving a fuck about anything. *'Don't do it,'* I convinced myself.

She left me no choice but to track her phone. When New York appeared on the screen, my insides damn near fell to the floor. *'If I've run her into that wanker's arms I will kill myself,'* I thought. I threw her to the wolves, but couldn't fathom the thought of never getting her back. It would truly be the biggest mistake of my life.

Before Nadia left, she wanted me to reconnect with my father. Her disappearance led me to his doorstep. Forcing me to make amends with the man I despised. I went to him and asked to use his resources and connections to locate her as I had failed. He sensed the severity of my need, and didn't torture me with questions. A simple nod, and it was done. "One more thing," I added. "Find out what you can about a Lucas Fleming in New York."

He nodded. "I'll call you when I have something, son."

Senior called me son as if he had been waiting years for the right time to use it. I denied myself to find joy in the moment, and headed over to Prano's place to ask for a favor.

He made a run to the yard for me, and I left without explanation. I took my package, contemplated throwing it out of the window on the drive home, but the addict in me wouldn't let it slip from my fingers. Tiny bits of sweat formed with it in my palms as I slipped down a slippery slope I swore to never skate on again.

It comforted me back at the house, where I walked room to room, haunted by Nadia's ghost. Her spirit watched me make the tragic mistake of reacquainting my nose with candy, searching for a moment of relief.

I lied back on the couch and thought I felt her climb on top of me. I smiled at the thought she'd forgiven me and come home, and I imagined I pressed my lips against hers. For a moment, I was relieved she was back where she belonged. Her supple breasts pressed against me, her flowing hair tickling my chin, her dark brown eyes summoning me to mount her.

The morning I foolishly told her to leave played before me during my flight. Her smooth, perfect dark skin glowing in the stream of moonlight which crept through the shutters, while I had her pinned against the sheets. Her curves thrusting up at me, receiving all I had to give. I loved looking at her when we made love. Watching her enjoy every stroke I planted inside. The way her mouth moved when she called my name, and how she slightly opened her lips when she came like she was ashamed. It was as if she held her breath when she climaxed. What a perfect morning we shared. She wanted me before the sunlight hit our window, moaning as she yearned for me in her sleep, and damn near swallowed me whole— sucking me the way I taught her. I loved when she was on one.

Suddenly, her image faded into thin air. I became embarrassed with myself for thinking she was really in the room. I never thought she would see me like this. She didn't know me when I was on blow years ago, and I would never bring her around such disgrace. But her ghost saw me. And that was bad enough.

I sat on the couch and let my high mellow itself out. When I woke, I packed a bag and caught the next flight to New York. I was determined I would find her, and Lucas Fleming was where I started.

I posed as a potential client and had his secretary squeeze me in for an appointment at the end of the week. He was taller than me but posed no threat. I could take him if he tried his luck, plus I had sheer determination to punish him for the trouble he caused.

It took everything in me not to strike him as soon as I entered the room, but I enjoyed his little clown dance— tap dancing for me to earn a buck. The look on his face when I interrupted his spill was priceless, and when he learned who I was, I sensed an urgency of desperation.

He did his best to taunt me with words, claiming he could sit in my seat, but also confirmed there was no indiscretion on my baby's part. But when he disrespected Nadia, I jabbed him in his mouth. He didn't know what hit him. I dazed him and felt my blood rising, waiting for him to talk slick out of his mouth again, and when he did I punched him a second time. *Bloww!*

He rose to his feet ready to tussle, but I moved too quickly for him, dodging his fist. He realized he was no match for me and didn't dare take a second attempt to lunge at me. He stood in his stance and struggled with a final smart remark, so I finished him off and left him holding his jaw. He learned he didn't want any smoke with me.

I left his office kicking myself. *"BOLLOCKS!"* I muttered, agonizing over the biggest mistake of my life. Losing Nadia. The bastard confessed she never laid with him, and rejected his attempt after he violated her sweet lips. And I let her down. I let her go. I pushed her away.

Her disappearance reminded me of her past battles with depression. In a panic I called Senior, hoping he had an update. "Still no sign of her. It's as if she fell off the face of the earth," he said.

"Well, I have no reason to be in New York. Call me when you have word," I replied, and headed to the airport.

With New York being her last known stop, I was sure she ran to this *pissant*. But after learning she didn't swing his way, the strings lessened around my heart. All I had to do was find her and bring her back where she belongs. Next to me. Hopefully, I'd find her in Charlotte. *'I hope I'm still welcome.'*

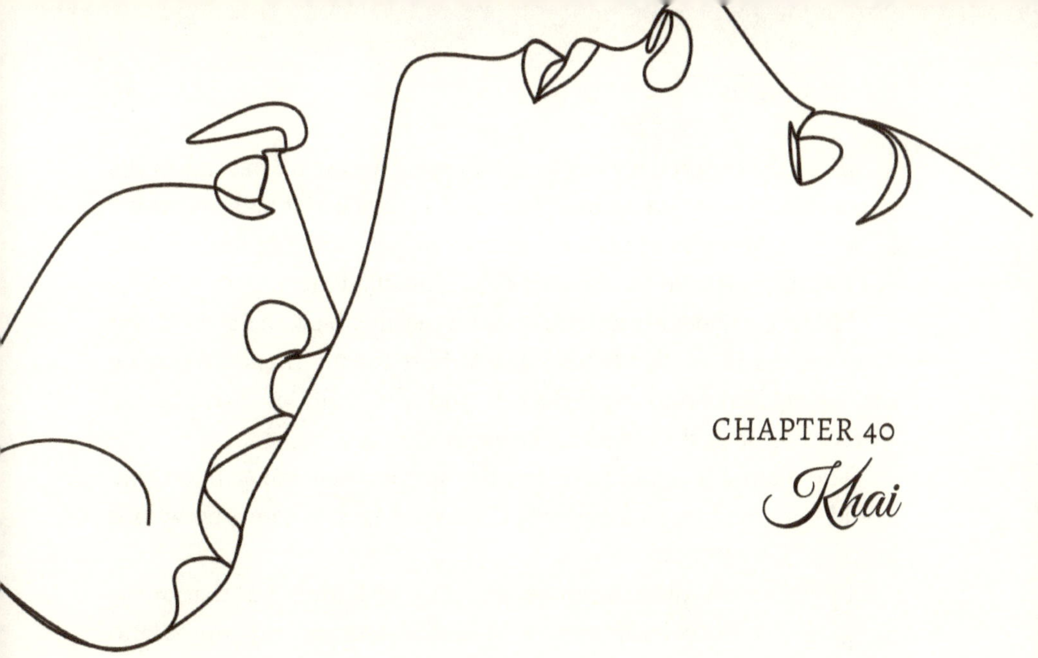

CHAPTER 40

Khai

adia was known for her surprise visits, so when she called and said, "Bring your keys outside," I sprung to the exit.

As always, we hugged when we saw each other, but didn't spend too much time on the sidewalk because the heat was sweltering. Immediately I recognized something was wrong. Showing up out of the blue on my job hauling luggage around. Red flag.

The two of us were kindred spirits, but I didn't pry. I let her beat around the bush for a bit, then showed her to my car to load her luggage. I clocked out early for the day, sensing she needed her friend. "You are just what the doctor ordered. A good reason to use some vacation time," I said.

"And here I thought I was *gonna* have to convince you to play hooky."

As I wheeled us out of the garage, Nadia's face was flushed with tears. She wiped her nose with one hand, and held a burner phone in the other. "What are you doing with one of those?" I asked. "Where is your phone?"

From the corner of my eye I saw teardrops fall onto her blouse. Quickly, I pulled over to the curb, and we sat until she was able to talk. As she cried, I patted her shoulder to console her, and turned the air conditioner on to full blast to cool us off.

Patiently, I waited for her to calm herself and share the reason she uncontrollably sobbed without warning. I suspected it had something to do with Mash, hence the amount of luggage and unplanned visit, but I wasn't prepared for the load she dropped on me.

Hearing the details unfolding from her lips blew me away. I was disappointed in Mash's behavior, and hurt for my friend. Watching her losing her mind was surreal, and the state of hysteria she descended into as she talked broke me into pieces.

The wound was too fresh to offer words of encouragement that would comfort her, so I said what everyone says to someone who is hurting. "Give it time."

I preached, hoping to restore an ounce of faith in her that everything would work itself out in time. She received my words and slightly perked up, but still offered no explanation of why she was carrying a burner.

I passed her a pack of tissues from the glove compartment, and checked my mirrors for the clear to merge back into traffic. She twisted her lips while drying her eyes and nose. "Wait. Hold up," she said, then opened the door to vomit.

My hands covered my mouth and against my stomach. Nadia closed the door and sat back in the seat. "Are you???" I raised my brows. She turned to face me. "I mean you look smaller than I remember but..."

"I'm not pregnant," she interrupted. "Whenever I think about him and realize it's over between us, it comes up. And I didn't pack my medicine," she said, wiping her mouth.

"What medicine?"

"My iron pills. My hemoglobin was a 7 the last time my physician checked."

I shook my head. "First things first. Let's get you healthy. You're staying with me."

"I appreciate the offer, but I have a hotel room reserved. I don't want to stay with anyone," she emphasized.

"This isn't a good time for you to be alone," I argued.

Her face stiffened in seriousness, and her voice lost its normal casual tone. "I also don't want anyone to know I'm here. Understood?"

"You aren't thinking straight. Have you eaten?"

"I try, but I can't. And I know how hideous I look. Can we swing by a store? I need to grab a few things before we go to the hotel. By the way, I made the reservation in your name."

I put the car back in park and stared her up and down. "Why did your luggage have a Vegas tag?"

"I spent this past week in Cincinnati, then Vegas. I finally saw the Grand Canyon. It was divine." She praised with her hands.

"By yourself? Like this? For an entire week?"

She nodded.

"You're all over the place. Let my doctor put you on something for a little while." I held her hand until she jerked it away from my grasp.

"For what?" Nadia argued.

"Anxiety. Depression. I say this with love. You don't look so good. The sudden weight loss, low iron, your marriage. Why would you deal with this alone when you have friends and family who are here for you?"

"Look, I'm not ready to face everyone. This fiasco is embarrassing for me. My heart is broken, and a pill is not going to fix it, Khai. I came to you because I trust you the most. And I need you to do something for me," she said in a higher pitched tone of voice.

"What? Call Mash and talk some sense into him?"

"No, please don't tell anyone I'm here, especially him. I'm going to give you some cash to get me a car."

I stared at her in black disbelief. She stared back at me straight-faced and didn't flinch or blink. The silence in the car became awkward until she pulled a wad of cash from her purse. "Nadia, are you in hiding?" I scowled.

"Sort of, but not really. I doubt Mash is looking for me after the way he treated me, and even if he is I don't want to see him. He can never know how badly he has hurt me. I can't lose that kind of power again to a man." Her voice deepened and her eyes pierced mine.

"Same *ole* Nadia," I huffed. "We all fall down at some point. Even you."

"Just say you'll help me buy myself some time to get my shit together. When I'm ready, I'll face the music. Right now, all I need is your name. I found a place in Atlanta. I'll pay you for a year's rent all up front. Same with the car." Her eyes dilated and scared me.

"Say I agree. What's down there?"

"Work possibly. I'm confident I can land a job writing for someone. If not, I can ask Yohan to make some calls to help me get my foot in the door."

"I can't be a part of this and not tell Brian. You can trust him to keep quiet. But what about your mom? You're nuts if you think she won't know something is wrong."

"She doesn't need to know what I'm dealing with. She'll tell Grams, and they'll both worry, and I don't want them to. This is what I want. Can I count on you?"

I agreed to go along with her cockamamie plan if she let my doctor do a workup. The next morning, she was squeezed in while I plotted how to check her into a mental rehabilitation facility. Not really, but it did cross my mind.

Her tests confirmed her iron level dropped to a 6, she was dehydrated, and also suffering from panic attacks. I begged her to stay with me until she was well, but my stubborn, proud, fragile friend refused. "Your doctor is referring me to a hematologist in Atlanta for an infusion next week, so let's head to that car lot." She bossed me.

I don't like authoritarian Nadia. She was exactly like this when she and Dylan broke up. Running around high strung with a crazed look in her eyes. Then the next minute crying. Then the next minute pretending to be tough. Treating everyone like they owe her allegiance, until she crashes, and someone needed to be with her to pick up the pieces.

As I dealt with the bossy, strong woman persona ordering me around all afternoon, and throwing cash around as if it grew on trees, I waited for her to burn out. She didn't. She test drove and purchased a used sedan in cash, gave me a lump sum for a bank account to use for the rent, and before I knew it we were on our way to Georgia.

We surprised her mother in South Carolina on the way to Operation Disappearing Act. Sadly, I was her accomplice in lying to her sweet mother. I was hopeful Mrs. Melton would see through Nadia's facade, and talk some sense into her. "My Lord, why are you so frail?" Her mother asked when she placed her arms around her.

It took everything in me not to blab. I screamed on the inside. *'Tell her Nadia isn't eating or holding anything down.'*

The good friend in me was torn to keep my word, or abandon our agreement and lose her trust. I held my lips tight.

It sickened me to watch her fib to her mother's face about some made up diet to lose weight for an audition. "I thought you were writing the stories, not acting in them?" Mrs. Melton asked.

"I'm trying to do it all. The women in the industry are toothpicks, so if I am going to compete I have to look like them," Nadia lied. Easily I might add.

'How long has she been planning this charade?'

"Well I don't like it," said Mother Melton.

"Neither do I," I cosigned, and rolled my eyes at Nadia.

Mrs. Melton appeared to buy her daughter's story, but didn't let go of it easily. She scolded Nadia about her weight, and repeatedly placed food in front of the both of us during the visit. She fussed, "I'm upset you girls won't at least spend the night. I can't believe you came all this way, and you can't spend one night with your own mama."

"I'll be back in a few days to spend some time with you. I'm going to hang with the girls this weekend, and then I'm all yours," Nadia promised.

"You better."

Not once did Nadia mention she moved back to the states to her mother. I thought about that during the drive to Atlanta and assumed her pride was controlling her. Her lack of mentioning her return also gave me hope Mash still had a chance to fix this ridiculousness.

Being an accomplice to Nadia's escape made me shaky on the inside, but it didn't stop me from munching on the goodies Mrs. Melton packed for us. Hours later, I signed a twelve-month lease on a townhouse rental. It wasn't the luxurious house in the hills outside London, but at least it was new.

Once we received the keys to the unit, we shopped for necessities during our first night stay. Nadia kept it simple and bought an air mattress and linens, curtains and rods, towels and soap, and a few dishes. She ordered a bedroom and living room set for delivery the next morning, and worked with a burst of energy all evening setting everything into place.

The night reminded me of our college years. "Shit!" Nadia exclaimed. "We forgot to get a TV."

"It would watch us instead of us watching it tonight. I'm tired," I said.

She stood peeping outside from behind the curtains. "If you're having second thoughts, I can break the lease with no problem. You can spend a few days with your mom, or stay with me so you won't get lonely," I offered.

"That won't be necessary. I'll be fine. It shouldn't be too hard to settle back into my old ways of living alone." Her voice withered.

"Has he called you?"

Nadia shrugged her shoulders. "There are a few breathing messages on my voicemail." She sighed.

I was too exhausted to continue trying to break her. I rolled over and went to sleep, awakened in the morning by the delivery workers knocking on the door.

As they set up her furniture, we cleaned the cabinets, the fridge, and bathrooms, then hit the streets for more shopping to spruce up the bare walls.

"Does this remind you of our college days?" she asked.

"I was thinking the same thing last night. Roughing it out with no television in the room."

"Driving down here for the parties." She added.

"And the cute, stupid boys we chased."

"Please don't name them. I've erased those jerks from my memory and want them to stay forgotten forever."

We laughed.

Traveling on a familiar street, we came across our old favorite

Mexican restaurant. "You'll be happy to hear this," she said. "I'm hungry."

"Thank God the meds are working!" I shouted.

We sat in a corner off to ourselves. The mariachi sounds over the speaker were loud enough to offer us privacy, and hide the sounds of our stomachs rumbling.

As the smells of the cantina played with our noses, I played twenty questions, testing Nadia's headspace. "How long do you think this little plan of yours is going to work?" I asked.

"Hopefully six months to a year," she said, not batting an eye.

"You are *trippin'* if you don't think Mash is going to find you before then. There is facial recognition technology everywhere. No one has privacy anymore. And he has money. Rich people make things happen."

"The only way he will find me is if someone tells him where I am. My phone is off. He can't track me. I'm using cash only when I need to spend. No one will find me unless I want to be found. Stop believing what you see in the movies."

"You're delusional," I sang in a fun tune. "If this turns into a missing person's case, I will tell your mother everything. And you better cover my ass."

"It won't come to that. Promise you won't mention anything to the girls. Taylor will tell Levi, and he will tell Mash, and he needs to sweat while I prepare how I want to proceed."

"I won't say anything as long as you check in with me so I know you're okay."

Finally, a breakthrough. She turned away from me and wiped a tear forming in her eye. "You don't have to shut out everyone who loves you," I said.

"I have to do this my way," she cried softly. "I can't heal with everyone giving me their opinion, or asking me how I'm doing, or suggesting how to fix this. I want to deal with this privately."

Her eyes watered, and her shirt vibrated heavily near her chest as she spoke. Somehow, she magically regained her composure. *'Is it strength or determination she is pulling from?'* I wondered.

"Let's talk about something else?" She sniffled and folded her arms.

"It's better to get it out than leave it in. The man loves you. You know that's him breathing on the phone."

"You didn't see how he looked at me." Her voice cracked. "How he sounded, and to tell me to get the fuck out was..." She took a deep breath. "You know how I feel about those words."

I nodded. "Yes, I remember."

"The fairytale is over, Khai. He threw me away like trash. Maybe I am tra..."

"Stop it. You are not trash."

Nadia stared out of the window, still able to control the water glistening in the corner of her eyes. I overstepped, "Don't hate me for asking you this, but have you talked to Lucas?"

"No." Her face scowled at me. "And I don't intend to."

The waiter returned and placed the heavenly scent of refried beans, cumin, and peppers in the center of the table, creating a better vibe between us. We spent the night in the townhouse, then drove back to Mrs. Melton's house in the morning. Brian picked me up from her house, and I slept peacefully in my own bed knowing Nadia was with her mother for a few nights.

As I expected, the secrecy of Nadia's break-up didn't last long. I resisted the urge to call London once the rumor started circling amongst the group. Instead, Brian and I maintained our loyalty and respected Nadia's wishes.

I feared how she would react if she heard the gossip was making its rounds, so I carefully sugarcoated the situation when I checked in with her, days after she left South Carolina. "How are you feeling after the infusion?"

"My legs are a little sore, but I'm not in any pain," she stammered.

"You sound drained."

"I am tired. And in one of my moods."

"Then you're not going to like what I have to say." I briefly paused. "Mash is in town. Have you dialed into your voicemail?"

"No, I haven't. What does he know?"

The sound of panic echoed through the phone from her end.

"From what I've gathered, nothing. He showed up in town without warning and met Levi and Brian for drinks. Brian says he is a wreck and got pissy drunk. Levi took him back to his house."

"Fuck! That means Taylor knows."

"So does Shannon. Taylor called the both of us, asking if you were in town and avoiding her. And Shannon shared Yohan called her, questioning if she knew of your whereabouts. They are both on my ass."

Brian walked in the room and stole my attention. "Get dressed. Levi invited everyone over for drinks."

"It's a setup," said Nadia, fuming and gritting her teeth. "Levi and Taylor are getting you all together in one place to snitch."

"I knew he would come looking for you. This is so romantic!" I squealed.

"Um, it's not. He put me out, remember? Keep your *fuckin'* mouth shut. I gotta go." She closed her burner phone violently in my ear.

'I'm going to pretend she didn't hang up on me.'

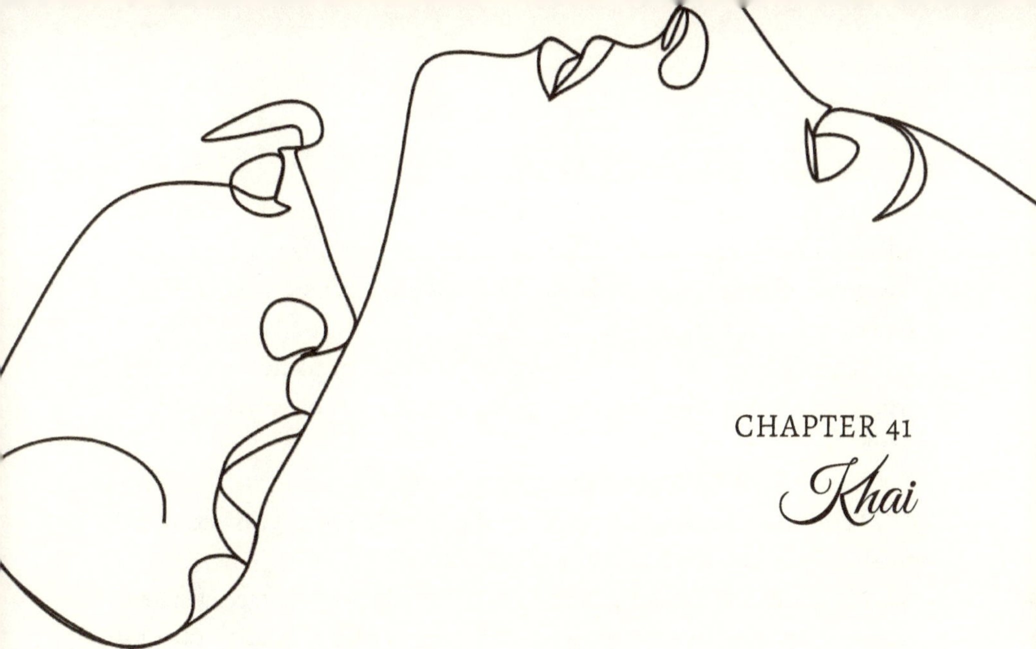

CHAPTER 41

Khai

aylor answered the door and widened her eyes when Brian and I entered. Under her breath she mumbled, "He's real shifty acting," then led us into the living room with the rest of the party.

I greeted Mash. "Just the person I want to see," he whispered in my ear while hugging me. He leaned over to Brian and asked, "Do you mind if I borrow your wife for a second?" Brian gestured his approval, and we eased off into the dining room.

He was good looking, but not looking good. Worry was written in his eyes, and his face appeared lifeless behind his grin. "What are you doing here, and where is my girl?" I asked.

His sad eyes twitched, "I was hoping you knew."

His bottom lip disappeared under his teeth, and he wiped his face with his palms. "So you haven't heard from her?" he asked. I kept my word to Nadia, crumbling at the look of defeat on his face.

"Mash, why don't you know where she is?" I fished.

"I feel like an idiot coming here." He sighed.

"Talk to me. What's going on?" I asked, luring him to tell his side of the story.

"I fucked up. Royally. I lost my temper and told her to leave." He dropped his head.

"No, you told her to get the fuck out." I sneered.

His eyes grew big like the hole inside of a doughnut. "You have talked to her." His face lit like those commercials when a light bulb has gone off in someone's head. "How is she? Where is she? Khai, please? Take me to her now," he begged.

"I can't help you there. She called to check in so no one would worry about her. She said she's going to do a bit of traveling for a while."

"How did she sound? Is she okay?"

"The last time I spoke with her she sounded fine." My stomach twisted. "She says she has her moments, but she's fine."

My shoulders tensed at the look of anguish on his face. I hated lying to him in such a frantic state, and being a part of Nadia's plan to punish him into an early grave. These two belonged together. I knew it from the night I met him at the grunge fest where they put on a shameful public display of affection. I didn't agree with Nadia hiding from him, but I also didn't agree with him throwing her out of their house in the most demeaning fashion either. *'I should be lashing out at him right now.'*

I opened my mouth to insult him. Then he bit his fist, and his eyes turned watery. His display of self-inflicting pain forced me to hold my tongue. I patted him on the back instead. "Everything will work itself out. I told Nadia to give it time. So, you do the same. In time you two will find your way back to each other. I suggest letting her have her space and let things cool down."

"You think I still have a chance?" His eyes flashed a tiny bit of hope in them.

"Why wouldn't you?"

"Because I accused her of cheating with some prick she met in New York. Khai, he left her so many messages begging her to call him. **My wife**. And when I asked her who he was, she flinched. The way she looked when I called his name tore me apart."

"How did she look?" I pried.

"Guilty. Like she was hiding something."

"Well nothing happened between them. You do know that. Right?"

"I do now. I need to tell her I was wrong, and I'm sorry, and I want her to come home. I need her to come home."

I felt sorry for him. The hopeless romantic in me said drive him to Atlanta, but my loyalty stopped me from betraying Nadia's wishes. "There is something you probably don't know. The words you used have a negative history with Nadia. When we became friends in college, she lived off campus with this girl who couldn't keep a roommate. Long story short, one night they had a disagreement, the girl told her to get the fuck out of her apartment, and because it was in her roommate's name there was nothing Nadia could do but leave. The police were called, the girl threw her stuff all over the lawn, except Nadia's things she chose to keep for herself. She was so distraught, she failed a major test the next day. I came across her crying in the student lounge during my work study. She was looking at the bulletin board when I clocked in, and was asleep on the sofa when I left. The next night, she slept on the sofa in my dorm. Shannon and I moved her into our room, and she crashed on the bean bag for the rest of the semester. She resents anyone who utters those words to her."

"I'm fucked," he mumbled.

"Personally, I think it'll blow over because I know you two are crazy in love, but it's going to take some time. What you also don't know is her ex did this to her as well. She opted out of getting an apartment off campus with us when he convinced her to move in with him. A few months later she found out he was cheating, and he said those very same words to her when she confronted him. She vowed to never live with anyone ever again. Think about how she was hesitant to stay with you."

"I'm kicking myself right now. I have to make this right. Where do you think she is? I'm going to her mother's in the morning. Hopefully I'll find her there."

"You won't. She doesn't want her mom or her Grams to worry. I'm the only person who knows about the separation." My thumb pointed to my chest.

"We're not separated," he emphasized. "How is she calling you?"

"She's traveling with a prepaid phone. I have to wait to hear from her."

"Next time she calls, connect us, please. You have my number. I'm not going back without her."

I nodded, and we rejoined everyone in the living room. I remained sober to avoid a slip of the tongue as the girls eyed me. I knew they wanted to inquire about my private conversation with Mash, but the only person I repeated it to was Nadia, smiling on the other line, pretending not to care.

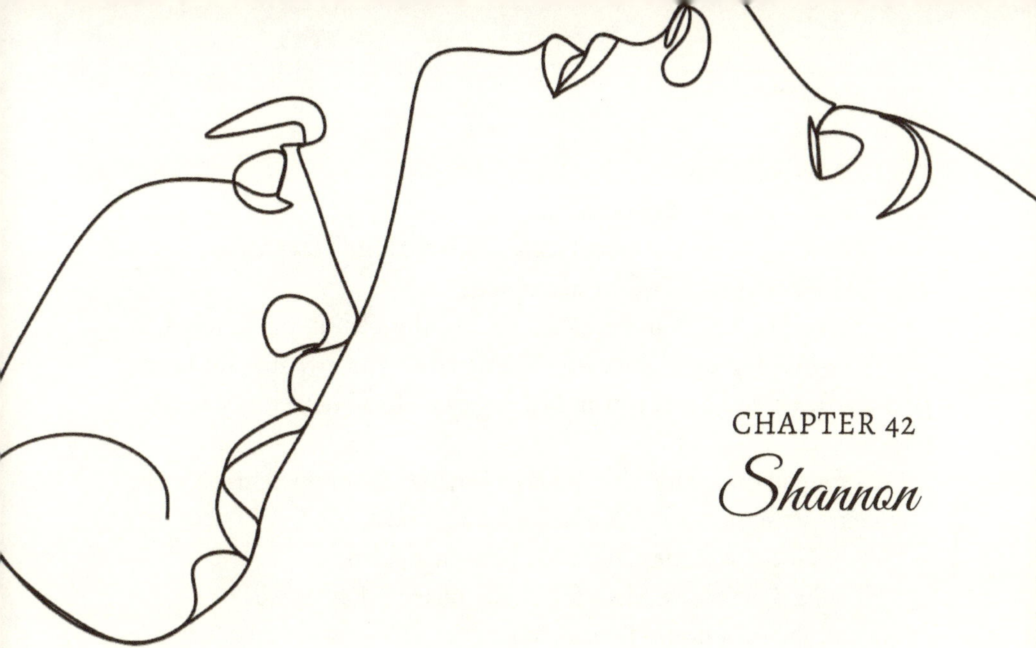

CHAPTER 42

Shannon

The jig was up. Something was going on. I knew it when Yohan asked me about Nadia. We've never talked about her before. And when Mash popped up in town without her, it was time Khai was put on Front Street.

She slipped out of the dinner before I could catch her, so I woke Taylor early in the morning and headed over to her house. We rolled up on her doorstep without notice. "Get dressed. We're going to breakfast," I said.

She threw on a pair of leggings and an oversized tee and hopped in the back seat. "Why are we sitting here with the engine turned off?" she asked.

I turned around and locked eyes with her. "I'll start the car when you tell us your secret. What were you and Mash talking about last night? And before you lie, Yohan told me Nadia left him."

She sucked her teeth and looked out of the window. "Well, if you know that much, why are you giving me the third degree?" She stalled.

"Cut the shit, Khai, do you know where she is?"

"I do," she sassed, threatening me with her eyes.

"Why didn't you tell us what was going on?" Taylor asked.

"Because she asked me not to." Khai sighed.

"Well, what happened?" Shannon continued.

"Lucas happened."

"Who is Lucas?" Taylor asked.

"Noooo. I know she didn't leave Mash for him!" I screeched.

"Who is Lucas?" Taylor interrupted.

I turned to Taylor and exhaled, tired of this ordeal, and annoyed at Khai for keeping us in the dark. "Remember when we met for lunch in New York, and I told you and Isla a guy flashed Nadia his penis?"

"Yeah."

"I fudged that story a bit. It was more like he whipped his dick out trying to get some ass and Nadia code *Cailfornia'd* us."

"Ah! Good ole code California," Taylor giggled.

"Nadia didn't leave Mash for Lucas, okay," Khai huffed.

"Did she fuck him?" I inquired.

"No! She didn't sleep with him!" Khai exclaimed. "Yeah, she's too vanilla to do something I would do. But he was tempting if you ask me."

"Let's be clear. No one had sex. Nadia and Mash are in the middle of a serious disagreement. Things got heated, Nadia is on her vengeful trip, and now he's looking for her. End of story."

"I wouldn't leave my house. His ass would have to leave," Taylor chimed in.

I couldn't contain my laughter. The situation wasn't funny, but I imagined Nadia packing up her shit and leaving poor Vanilla Ice clueless. "I'm sorry, but finally getting the details, and thinking about how sad Mash looked last night has me tickled. She's worrying the hell out of that man."

"If he didn't know before, he knows now not to dare a *sistah*," Taylor joked.

"Nadia ghosted him and he's walking around questioning where he went wrong. This shit is classic," I added.

"And we all know Nadia is going to ride this out for as long as she can." Taylor shook her head, smirking.

"We've seen how they're living. She's most definitely going back," I said. "She's probably in New York giving Lucas a whirl right now. Then she'll go back. At least that's what I would do anyway."

The car grew quiet with all of us in deep thought. Taylor broke the silence, "I don't know who this Lucas person is, but I do want to go home, and tell Mash to get the hell out of my house now."

Khai and I snickered. "Go easy on him," Khai suggested.

Taylor turned up her lips.

"So where is Nadia?" I asked.

"I promised not to tell," Khai answered.

Taylor and I gave her the death stare.

"Atlanta."

"Nadia is in party city, and you didn't tell us!" I reached over my seat and pinched Khai.

"Road trip!" Taylor hollered.

"If we all get missing with Mash in town, he is going to know something is up, and last night he said he isn't leaving without her," said Khai.

"With all due respect, his feelings aren't my concern at the moment. Go pack a bag. We'll be back in an hour and ready to ride," I declared.

Mash called Khai during the drive down. Taylor turned down the radio and signaled for her to place the call on speaker. "Have you heard from her?" he asked.

"Not today, no," Khai answered.

Mash grew quiet.

"She is checking her voicemail. Maybe you should leave her a message." Khai proposed.

"I'd rather talk to her directly. If you do hear from her, tell her I love her. I'm checking into a hotel for a few days, hoping she turns up. Call me if you hear anything. Please."

"Will do," said Khai, then sighed once the call ended.

We sat speechless for a while after his sadness transferred into the car with us. "She's really sticking it to his ass," said Taylor. "You sure she didn't cheat?" Khai didn't respond.

The phone call and the silence in the car killed the vibe we had going. To liven things back up, I turned to the radio station we used to listen to whenever we traveled to Atlanta to party. Worked like a charm.

We arrived at an upscale apartment complex north of the city, shy of a four-hour drive. "These units look new, but there is no way Nadia is serious about giving up her life over there to settle for this," I said.

"She must really be pissed at him," Taylor added.

"Before we go in I need to tell you two something. I have seen Nadia, and she didn't look so good. Be nice. Be gentle. And don't judge her when you see her. Okay?" Khai warned us.

We agreed to the terms and stood outside her door with zero conversation happening. Nadia took her time answering the buzzer. I couldn't believe my eyes when she opened the door. My friend with glowing, brown skin and vibrant personality wasn't standing before us. This person let herself go down in the shitter. Her hair hadn't been combed, her appearance was frail, her skin dull and dry, and her spirit defeated.

Normally, I would provide comic relief, but the sight of her rendered my puns and wit. She moved aside and gestured for us to enter. "Yohan spilled the beans. Not me," said Khai.

I followed Khai inside. "Where is my hug?" I asked, grabbing her fragile body.

Taylor came inside behind me. "How are you doing?"

"You be the judge," Nadia answered.

"I don't know what's going on with you, but you'll always be pretty," said Taylor.

Khai and I gasped quietly at Taylor's response. "Maybe there's hope for them after all," I whispered, then followed Khai into the living room. The space was cold, halfway empty, and tragically different from her pad in London. So was our interaction with one another.

After too many awkward silences to count, Taylor broke the ice. "Nadia, this isn't you. Look at your hair, and where did you get this grandma looking track suit you're wearing?" Nadia stared at Taylor with an evil eye, but didn't respond. "Do you have shampoo? I can at least make you look decent until we get you a hair appointment down here," Taylor offered.

Khai and I sat quietly, waiting for Nadia to light into Taylor. She said nothing. "Then it's settled," Taylor announced. "Shannon, go find her something to wear, and Khai give her your hat. We're getting you out of this apartment and putting you back together. This is unacceptable. Let's go, y'all," Taylor ordered.

Khai brushed her hair back into a ponytail, and loaned her hat to Nadia, while I dressed her in a pair of baggy jeans and a tee. We were no strangers to The Peachtree City, our old stomping grounds for parties, and a trail of broken hearts. We knew where to shop and what boutiques to tag.

We pitched in and bought Nadia haircare products, a few cute outfits, and groceries, even though she had more than us in the bank.

To fatten her up, we tried a trendy café and ordered appetizers a la carte, and liquored her up to ease her sorrows. The trick worked, giving her a light buzz. She dug into the plates, moaning over every savory bite. "Is it good?" I asked.

"Um uh," she hummed.

"Did you enjoy today?" Khai asked.

Nadia nodded.

"Now please tell me why Mash is at my house acting all shifty," Taylor blurted.

Nadia placed the chip in her hand back in the bowl of salsa. Khai leaned towards me and whispered, "And you thought they weren't going to bump heads."

The waitress returned with more of our order. Nadia waited for her to leave the table and scoffed. "I appreciate you all coming down here, but I'm fine. Really. I may not look the part. But I'm dealing with this my own way. If you don't want Mash in your house, put him out. He has no problem doing it."

"Nadia, I have to know. Did you sleep with *ole* boy in New York?" I asked.

"Nope, but I should have."

It was hard to tell if she meant that, or if the liquor was talking. "You still can," I said.

"I don't want to." She burped and giggled. "Why don't you sleep with him? At least one of us will have been on that ride to make this all worth it."

'It's definitely the liquor talking.'

"You did say he had a weapon of mass destruction. Why pass up the chance to get some decent action when technically, it's owed to you now?" I suggested.

"Then I wouldn't be any better than you and Han?"

I smirked at her smart-ass comment and nodded my head at her verbal dagger. "You still *gotta* problem with that I see. You and Miss Thang must have gotten close over there."

Nadia huffed and turned her head away from me.

Khai intervened. "It's been two weeks, and your husband is calling me nonstop. He's sorry. And he loves you. Can you at least call him?"

Nadia shook her head no. "I'm starting to make my peace with it. Getting out of the house today did me some good. I admit, I lost control this week because everything was going wrong."

"Like what?" Khai asked.

"Like I fell asleep and missed an application deadline. That led to a crying spell. Then I got a note from the complex manager that my music was too loud. Then I stupidly went for a walk at night, got chased by a dog, fell and scraped my knee. I haven't been out of the house since. Go ahead and laugh. I can laugh about it now since the damned dog didn't bite me."

What began as snickers turned into a roar. Our cackling put the first smile on her face since we arrived. "I wish I could have seen you outrunning a dog!" I hollered.

Nadia finally laughed. Seeing her light up eased the tension and mood, and gave us the clearance to speak freely like we normally do. "How long are you going to punish that poor man?" I asked.

"Whose side are you on?" Nadia rolled her eyes.

"Yours, of course. But you know your life over there was better than this. I mean is Lucas worth coming back to live like us common folk?"

"Lucas has nothing to do with what is going on in my marriage."

"No shade, but I think you liked this Lucas person more than you're letting on," Taylor stated. "And it's okay. It happens. You're married. Not dead."

"I enjoyed the flirtation. That's it." Nadia scowled.

I chimed in. "Lucas liked her. He definitely wanted to hit it, but the question remains, would he have quit it?"

Back at the apartment, Taylor shampooed and braided Nadia's hair into a bun. She twirled around the room, showing off the finishing touches, and we applauded her fresh look before streaming movies and teasing each other.

Nadia fell asleep before the credits rolled, snoring, wheezing, and grunting—getting the rest she badly needed. Hearing her exhausted pipes saddened the three of us. Our eyes shifted around the room, speaking without words, mutually feeling her sorrow.

"Nobody looks like that after a breakup if they didn't love the person," I whispered.

"I hope she forgives him," said Khai.

Taylor sneered, "Yeah right. Nadia and forgiveness are like oil and water."

Khai and I giggled. If anyone knew what it was like to be on the receiving end of Nadia's wrath, it was Taylor. "I bet you thought she'd never forgive you?" I asked.

Taylor exhaled, "Has she forgiven me?"

The three of us wrinkled our faces at each other, unable to answer Taylor's query, and ended the night with the flaming question in mind. '*Has she really forgiven Taylor, and what did that mean for her and Mash?*'

CHAPTER 43

Nadia

Once again it was silent. With the girls gone, I was reminded of my loneliness. Stuck with my pride and racing thoughts, I followed Khai's suggestion, and dialed into my voicemail.

It was filled to capacity with his voice. I saved and replayed the messages saying, *"I love you,"* and *"Please call me,"* and *"Come home,"* but the messages with shrill silence and no words, I felt the most. Desperate, jarring breathing, and regret transcending through the quietness.

All night I tossed and turned, waiting for the sun to rise. As I stared at the ceiling fan, I considered my next moves, then I heard his voice call my name. My mind was playing tricks on me, but I found comfort in the prank and welcomed it, happy to reminisce about the morning of the day I left.

I could taste the food I cooked for him, which never made it to my mouth. I felt the sex injuries that were worth the sting in my bones—a minor bruise in the small of my back from the bathroom sink, and a carpet burn on my knees from the studio floor. I also felt my pussy throb thinking of the erotic nights we created.

One night, I told Mash to blow his ganja while I blessed him with my best lip service to date. He looked so damn sexy as his mouth released puffs of thick circles, telling me I would be the death of him as he almost blew my head off. '*Why did I have to be so stupid?*' I wondered, before drifting off.

It was nearly three weeks, seventeen days to be exact, since I saw him last. The dry heaves and panic attacks stopped, but the loneliness continued to occupy my every breath. I was nine pounds lighter, living in a temporary condo in my third city in over two years. '*I never saw any of this coming.*'

As daylight cast a shade of beige in my bedroom, I opened my eyes and couldn't move. Just like the morning I learned I was anemic. As if turning thirty wasn't bad enough, my knees were starting to feel the strain of high heels, and my health decided to add a low blood disorder in the mix.

To top it off, I was a total fucking mess mentally. Not just physically. I was unemployed, newly single, surrounded by strangers, and comfortable with self-loathing.

Haggard and restless, I reported to the doctor's office. The nurse stuck me, filling my veins with the second injection of oxblood and black colored iron. I sat with her for half an hour to make sure I felt fine, then dropped by an electronics store for a new laptop. Feeling the soreness creep up on me, I grabbed two entrees from a Mexican spot by my condo — one for now and one for later, then hurried home before more side effects kicked in.

A slight headache began to form near my temples as I pulled into the lot. I parked my car and rubbed my head then scoffed before nearly shitting on myself. There he sat on the cemented steps to my apartment.

I considered driving off, but I couldn't take my eyes off of him. The hate I felt for him the past few weeks somehow left my bones. My sight was locked on him, curious as to who gave me up, and secretly happy he was there.

He didn't know I was in the Camry watching him sit with his legs spread apart, and his head bowed down on his suitcase. I stayed put and waited to see his face, suffering through the pulsing aches above my forehead. Moments later, he lifted his head, and I smiled internally. He was still as gorgeous as the day I left him.

He looked in my direction as if he sensed me lurking, then he rose and grinned at me with his dark circles and rugged beard. I didn't smile back. I sat in the car unable to move, unnerved and exultant all at once.

Mash made his way over to the car, and I cranked the engine. Stretching his arms and holding his hands out, he raced to my window. "Please turn the car off," he pleaded.

I kept it running and yelled through the window, "Who told you where to find me?"

He pressed his hands against the glass and stared at me with his sad walnut eyes. "Please. Turn it off and I'll tell you."

I wasn't ready to confront him or hear his incessant apologies, but I did as he asked, refusing to lock eyes with him. Even when I hated him I loved him, so I stared straight ahead, careful not to let his eyes captivate me into submission. My conflicted mind and heart reached to crank the car again. "Please, Nadia," he begged.

Hearing him call my name weakened me. My chest pounded with immense confliction of love, anger, and hurt, but I longed to hear his voice call out to me. So, I refrained. "Get out so I can hold you in my arms," he said.

I looked at him like he was crazy as my neighbor pulled into his parking space beside me. He saw the look on my face and intervened, tapping on the passenger window. "Is this man bothering you?" he asked.

"No, we're fine. Thank you for asking," I replied and curved the side of my mouth.

"Are you sure?"

"Yeah," I explained. "He tells bad jokes."

"I'm her husband," Mash replied. "And you are?"

"Husband? Are you now?" My neighbor questioned. "Is he your husband, 43?"

"Yes. Everything's fine." I nodded.

My neighbor took his slow time walking inside his place, as I took my slow time getting out of the car. Mash squeezed me and felt the enormous bandage wrapped around my arm. I eased away. "What's that for? Are you alright?" He worried.

"It's nothing," I answered.

"You're smaller than I remember. And you look... different. Let me help you."

He grabbed the bags of food from my hands and brought his baggage inside. I waved at my neighbor still spectating, and leaned against the door behind me. Mash stood near the sofa staring at me intensely. "Are you ever going to look at me?" he asked. I looked up and our eyes met. "Do you hate me?" He sighed.

"A little bit," I said, then turned away from him.

"I wasn't expecting you to say yes, but I don't blame you," he admitted.

My eyes returned towards him. "How did you find me?"

He stepped closer to me. "I had help from a few people. My dad was one of them. What's with the bandage?"

I stepped towards the sofa and sat down. "It's good you two are speaking. And this is nothing. My blood dropped, and I had the iron infusion done today."

"Can I hug you?" he asked, hugging me before I could answer him.

"I answered your question, now answer mine. How did you find me?" I fought my hands to hug him back and wandered to the other side of the room.

"Levi."

"I ought to call Taylor and..."

"She didn't tell him. He has tracking on her phone after he found out about— you know."

"Wow. Ha! Good for him. Guess I can turn this back on now." I pulled my cell phone out of my bag.

Mash huffed from across the room. "You don't seem too thrilled to see me."

"Should I be? After the whole spill." I blazed him down with my eyes. "What hotel are you checked into?"

"I was planning on staying here," he spoke with conviction.

"Why?"

Our eyes locked.

"Because I'm your husband. And we have a lot to discuss," he said, hovering over me.

I hummed to myself and leaned my head back on the sofa. "There's a slew of hotels a few blocks from here. I'll drive you over there in a few minutes. Just let me rest for a second," I said.

"Can I get you anything? Is there anything you need me to do?"

"You can tell me why you're really here since you believe I had an affair and put me out of what I thought was our home."

"I want you. I know you didn't..." he paused. "I was out of my mind to think you would ever betray me. I acted out of anger, and you have every right to be pissed at me. But I know you love me. How do I fix what I've done?" He stole a kiss from my forehead.

I didn't respond.

"Can you at least look at me?" He pleaded, rubbing his face against mine. "Nadia. Look at me. I'm sorry. I made a mistake. I'm a fool. The worst person in the world. And I'm miserable without you."

I opened my eyes and looked at him. He meant every word he spoke, but my stubbornness and lack of energy prevented me from jumping into his arms. "Say something," he implored.

"I hear you, but I'm too tired to have this conversation. Can I close my eyes for a few minutes? Please?" I asked, and drifted off before he answered.

When I woke I was covered with one of the blankets the girls left behind on the sofa. Mash sat at the opposite end with my feet in his lap asleep. I watched him for a short while, then closed my eyes again to nap a little longer.

The second time I woke up, it was evening. Mash was awake, reading my medical instructions, warnings, and side effects list from my doctor. "How are you feeling?" he inquired.

"Tired and sore, but I can manage." I removed my feet from his lap.

"Will you tell me if any of these side effects occur?"

"Yeah sure," I answered, shaking my head at his concern.

"This pamphlet says you go back for a reading in a week. What is the reading supposed to tell you?"

"How my body is reacting to the iron. Nothing major," I maneuvered best I could.

"I have some shows coming up, but I'll cancel them so I can go with you."

"No need. It's only a reading." I struggled to stand.

"Let me help you."

"*I got it*. I'm going to take a shower. I don't feel like driving, so I'll bring out some sheets and more blankets. You can have the couch tonight."

He scoffed. "I wasn't going to a hotel anyway," he said.

I rolled my eyes at him and headed upstairs. Mash was on my heels. "Your food is cold, and I didn't see a microwave in the kitchen. I was thinking about ordering a pizza. Do you mind?"

"You have the address. Do as you will." I sighed.

My mind got lost in the shower as my thoughts jumped from one to the next. I had no real recollection of me bathing, yet I was covered in soap with warm water tapping on my back. "Nad, I don't mean to hound you, but you've been in there for a while. Are you okay?" Mash asked.

I snapped out of my daze. "I'm fine. Be out in a second."

I dressed in the spaghetti strap pajama set Taylor bought me and covered in my robe. I removed my satin scarf from my head to dry it from the shower steam and studied myself in the mirror. I didn't recognize the person looking back. *'Thank God I'm getting my hair done in the morning.'* I smirked to myself. *'He thinks he's slick calling me Nad.'*

I curled up on the bed, listening to Mash interact with the delivery guy. The wood on the stairs creaked from his footsteps and he knocked on my bedroom door. "The pizza is here. Do you want a slice, or do you want me to bring your food up here?"

"Is the pizza good?" I mumbled.

"I'm honestly impressed. Wait right here."

He returned with the box and cups of ice, and a two liter of pop.

The box sat between us on the bed, and I took a slice and placed it on the inside of the top lid. "This is good," I said. "What made you pick this place?"

"The name. Little Italy. I figured the pie must be good to name their shop after the homeland."

"I'll add this place to my list."

Mash stopped eating. His head dropped and he placed his slice back in the box. "Add to your list? Are you planning on staying here?"

"I signed a twelve-month lease," I said.

"We can break it," he replied.

"It's already paid for."

"Then sublet it." He raised his brows.

"And go where? London? To your house?"

"Home. To our house."

I wiped the crust from the sides of my mouth and prepared to be badgered from my response. "I had my own house, and no one could tell me when to come or when to get the fuck out. You reminded me of that. I like being in control of my life and need to have my own shit from here on out. I can't trust..."

"How long am I going to pay for my mistake? We've had weeks to cool off and reset, but you act as if you don't miss our life together."

"I miss us. But look at me. I got sick behind you. I couldn't eat, couldn't sleep, or keep anything down on my stomach. I'm worried about what direction my life is headed in. Not you. You weren't rejected and tossed out like old socks. You didn't have to find somewhere to sleep in the middle of the night, or figure out how to start over. You cut me deep," I explained.

"I know I did." He approached me.

"I will **never** put myself in this position again."

"So you hate me." He dropped to his knees.

"I want to hate you, but I don't. More than anything I want to hurt you the way you hurt me. I can never call your house, home again."

He grabbed my face and kissed me on the lips. I fought the urge to reciprocate. "I love you," he said.

"Love is not enough. Look where love got me." I pulled away.

"It got us here. Together again. You tried to hide from me but I found you. Love keeps bringing us together no matter how many times you run away."

He had a point. I had a good run of hiding from him. I covered my tracks well and he still found me, but he didn't earn any points with me because he showed up at my doorstep. I leaned back on the pillows. "Can we clear the air? Get everything out in the open and address all of our issues."

"I don't need to know anything else," he said. "I know enough and want to move on from this. With my wife."

"And this is why I live here and you live there. It's your way or no way. We can't move on if we're carrying baggage from our pasts." I threw the crust of my slice of pizza in the box.

"Nadia, I reacted erratically because of how that douche was calling your name." His face shriveled. "Images of you with him made me lose my shit."

"I owe you an apology," I admitted. "I'm not one hundred percent innocent in all of this."

Mash's shoulders stood erect, and his face turned a pinkish and reddish hue. He pushed the pizza box out of the way and placed his head at the foot of the bed. "What do you mean?" he mumbled.

"Make sure you listen this time. The night I met Lucas, I was meeting Chili and some of his friends at a bar. He witnessed a weird interaction between Chili and me, and followed me out of the bar to see if I was okay. I told him I was married, and he threw his card in my purse in case I needed anything."

Mash covered his face and asked, "What happened with Chili?"

"Nothing happened, per se." My voice rose. "We're cool, but I did tell him you never liked him."

"And the wanker in New York gave you his card, and you called him?" He grunted.

"I did. One day I asked him for references to check out, and he offered to show me the new development in Brooklyn. I thanked him, but he wanted to keep in touch with me. I refused and wouldn't give him any information about me. So, he gave me that phone to keep me updated about things going on in the city. I mailed it back to the address on his card. The messages you heard *was* me avoiding him.”

Mash stared at me with anger and confusion across the top half of his face. “What I’m hearing is you went on a date with him.”

“Not a date. A tour. And it was innocent. He knew nothing about me except my name was Nadia. No last name, your name, nothing.” I crossed my hands.

“Well, he knows it now. Have you talked to him?”

“No! Why would I?” I frowned.

“Okay. Okay. Sorry I asked. He told me he kissed you.”

My heart skipped and my eyes popped wide. “When did you? How? Wait. What? He told you what? When did you speak to him? Why would you speak with him?”

“Your phone was last tracked in New York.”

“And you thought I went running to him. Wow.” I jumped to my feet and left him in my room.

My face burned from his assumption. My head roared with a headache. “Maybe you should stay at a hotel!” I yelled from the stairs.

“What else was I supposed to think, Nadia?!”

I stormed back up the stairs and threw my new house shoes Khai bought me at him. “Did you realize I was telling the truth before, or after you spoke with him?”

“Before I clocked him a few times.” He reenacted what he did by punching the air. “Trust me, he had it coming after how he disrespected you. But he confirmed what I already knew.” He smiled.

“My word should have been good enough.”

“Terrible mistake on my part. It won’t happen again.” He placed his hands on my shoulder. “By chance did he tell you he has three children, whom he abandoned because of a domestic violence charge?”

I shook my head no. “I should have never asked him to show me around. This is all my fault. And for that, I’m sorry.”

Mash looked at me with those brooding eyes and grin I found hard to resist. He fidgeted with his phone and placed it on the bed, then reached for my hand pulling me in closer.

My favorite song began to play from his playlist, and he swayed us side to side. I placed my head on his shoulder as Sting belted out the words, "*If he loves you, like I love you.*"

"You're not playing fair." I smiled.

"I know I'm not." He sneered.

"What if I were to say turn it off?"

"You won't."

We chuckled.

He tightly squeezed my lower back, and I reclined in his arms. My sore legs wavered with the tempo, and my arms clutched him firmly. His hands ran up and down my spine, and I wilted further in his grip, nearly collapsing from weakness as everything felt right with the world.

The touch of his lips nibbling on my neck, exhaling deep breaths of exhilaration invoked my hidden arousal. I lifted my head from between his strong pecs, and he caught my lips as if he'd been waiting for them.

I, too, was eager to feel his lips against mine, and joined him in a tender lip lock. "I miss you," he said, moaning in my ear.

I mumbled, "I miss you, too."

"Forgive me, and say you're mine again."

"I need time," I whispered.

"What if we don't have time? Say I'm yours, and you're mine, then tell me I can have you."

I backed away and observed the lust mixed with adoration in his eyes. My chest pounded with force I could hear in my ears. *'Don't be so easy,'* I thought.

I released his hands and placed mine on my knees. Breathless, I bowed down. "I'm not ready to do this."

"You don't want me anymore?" He teared up.

"I do. But not like this."

I crawled under the covers and turned my back to Mash. He stood over me fuming with his hands on his hips, then closed the box of pizza, and packed up the drinks. "I'm going to hop in the shower and let you relax. If you change your mind, need me, or want anything, I'll be downstairs."

"Good night," I said.

The temperature in the house was perfect, but my fatigued body was burning up. A known side effect. Also, a reaction to my gorgeous houseguest asleep on my couch.

I craved his perfect weapon inside of me, rekindling the fire only his spark could ignite, and make me feel like a woman. But forgiveness was my kryptonite. I struggled to get past him making me feel like a desperate bitch out in the street weeks ago— a real life version of the song by Oran Juice Jones telling the woman to leave with only the things she came with.

The hurt and humiliation he handed me surmounted his words of "I'm sorry." But still I checked the clock every two minutes until an hour had gone by, wanting a piece of him.

I threw the covers to the other side of the bed, desperate for a waft of cool air to breathe over me from the vent. It was quiet downstairs. I assumed Mash was sleeping off the tension and travel.

I tiptoed down the steps, crept into the kitchen, and jumped at his silhouette standing near the window. "You startled me," I gasped.

He was sexier than I remembered. The moonlight illuminated his shaved bare chest with a few hairs attempting to stubble free. I was a sucker for him when he walked around in Bruce Lee mode, barefoot and shirtless in pajama pants. "You couldn't sleep either?" he asked.

"Nope. I can't seem to get comfortable."

"You think it's one of the side effects?"

"Perhaps. You're really concerned about those side effects," I sassed.

"I don't like seeing you ill." He turned towards me.

"I'm okay. It got a little hot upstairs, so I came down to get one of my cubes. What are you doing in here?" I asked, reaching for the tray in the freezer.

"I was hoping you had a beer or something stronger to help me wind down, but this place is damn near hollow. You don't even have crisps. What do you have there?"

"This is a Kool-Aid cube."

"A what?" His face wrinkled.

"We ate these when I was a kid. Grams would make Kool-Aid, which is terrible for you by the way, and pour some into empty ice cube trays. Before they were completely frozen, she would stick tooth-picks in them, and we would eat them like mini popsicles. Try one." I held out my hand.

"A second ago you said it's terrible for you. Why are you eating it?"

"Because they're delicious," I answered, humming as I licked it.

His judgmental face switched from wrinkled to humored. "Maybe I will try it," he said, taking the cube from my hand. He held the toothpick upside down and ran it across my lips, causing it to melt a trace along the path he drew. He leaned in and sucked the melted juice. "This is good," he said, "The best thing I have ever tasted."

Gazing into my eyes, he inserted the cube into my mouth briefly, then asked, "Can I have another taste?" I nodded yes, and he kissed me gently, then pulled back. My chest pounded violently as I stared at him. My loins screamed, *'Please take me,'* as he traced my neck from east to west with the flavored ice in his mouth.

I held my breath and gasped for air. Reaching for my shoulder, he slid my strap down to my biceps, then traced my nipples with what was left of the flavored ice.

I *peaked* a little in my panties as my breasts saluted his mouth, inviting him to play with them longer. He read my body's needs and cupped them with his tongue, pinching them delicately the way I liked. "Mmm," I moaned, feeling the cut of his abs and dip right below it.

Face to face we stood staring at each other, panting of what was to come. Knowing I yearned for him he said, "Don't deny me," then slowly ran his hands from my cheeks to the back of my hair, tonguing me like ice cream.

My lower back held firmly pressed against the island, and his hands unfastened my pinned hair while his fingers rummaged my scalp. He guided me back with a fistful of my tresses, and licked me from my neck down to my slit.

My shorts fell to my feet along his path, "No panties," he grinned, then pressed his nose against my landscape and sniffed. "Mmm, that's it," he groaned. I looked to the ceiling while the sensation of his tongue ran across my skin then inside to my flesh. I shuddered from the relief his lips gave my pussy, and whined in ultimate reprieve. "I've missed this pussy," he whispered.

"It missed you, too," I hummed.

My thighs grew limp, and my hands played in his hair while he licked and sucked and kissed and flicked and tongue twisted my labia. I trembled in his mouth as his hands clutched my ass towards him, eliminating any space to creep between us. My body grew weary, relying on his strength to hold me up by my thighs to stabilize me in position.

Finally, he came up for air and inhaled sharply, ending his tongue's caress, and lunged inside my oval house of pleasure. I exhaled a painful squeal mixed with notes of bliss. He exhaled a rigorous grunt of delight, plunging deep into my abyss, "You still love me?" he panted.

"Yes," I whispered.

"Tell me," he demanded, stroking stronger.

"I still love you."

He grunted and grumbled with every stab, sinking his teeth into his bottom lip. I rose up the side of the island from his jabs, shrieking when he lifted my ass to the edge hanging halfway off.

He pointed my legs towards the light fixture above, carving his outline into my walls while kissing my thighs and my calves.

"That's right. Rain on me, baby. I'm sorry I've got you all backed up. Get it all out," he ordered. "Come for me."

I purred and pulsed around his dick, quavering in delight from the much needed maneuvering and stabs delivered to my cave. Without warning, he slanted his cock and pressed tightly inside, exuding unsteadily inside of me. He shook, clutching onto the back of my calves as support while I gripped my pussy around his dick tightly, selfishly wanting him to stay inside my lubed warmth.

I was on the cusp of my second rain, and didn't release my hold of his cock until I spritzed on him once more. Kissing my calves, he moaned quietly, wanting more of me. And I the same. My legs remained elevated atop the linoleum, while he raided the fridge for water.

He placed a plate on my stomach and stacked slices of cold pizza from the box on top. He handed me the bottle of water, and carried me upstairs to the bed with the plate securely in tow on my belly.

Carefully, he laid me on my side of the bed, then climbed over me and the pizza, placing the plate between us. We shared a slice— him feeding me whenever I opened my mouth until we finished off the pie.

We shared the bottle of water, and he held me face forward in his grasp, huddled in silence. Words weren't needed. We spoke with our eyes and watched each other blink until we fell asleep. Me in his arms and my hand in his. Finally, I was at peace.

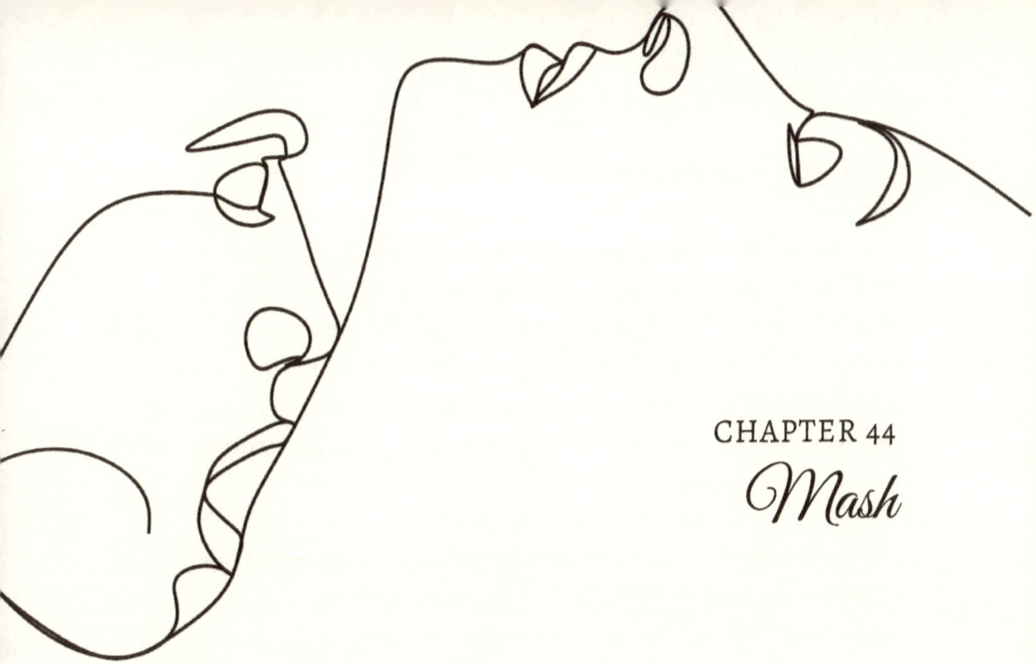

CHAPTER 44

Mash

The dark sky was on the verge of turning misty blue. The lack of drapes allowed me the privilege to see her from the light which crept between the shades. My sweet was where she belonged, lying in my arms, sleeping peacefully, and beautiful as ever.

I didn't disturb her as she appeared to need the rest. The agony I felt waiting for her to wake, felt as horrid as not seeing her face these past three weeks. I slid below the sheets and draped her cocoa legs over my shoulders, and woke her with sensuous kisses to her supple folds.

I yearned to taste her, mount her, and feel her. I savored her sweetness on my tongue, readier than ever to put my cock inside her once more and hear her call my name.

Alas, she gasped and woke. We hadn't spoken since she dripped mercilessly on me downstairs— Which was fine for me as her body intertwining with mine was all the talking I needed.

I held her thighs and pressed my mouth against her vertical smile, sampling her pussy first thing in the morning like I did back home. She jittered in my hands, sighing of ecstasy above me. I finished worshipping her and gazed into her glistening sandalwood eyes, hoping she realized how much I needed her.

I brushed my nose against hers. She blushed in my caress, and we locked lips with our desires in sync. Her intoxicating scent powered me. I spun on top of her and pressed my hardness against her thigh. She placed her arms around me, ready to receive my morning wood.

I stared down her nose and swept my hands against her temple, then down past her navel, feeling her wetness slick my fingers. I wanted more of her. I slipped back below the sheets and hard licked her north of her orifice. Pressing my lips against her hot spot with force always got her going, so I rolled my tongue into her hole making her squirm, then made her folds disappear into my mouth. "Maximus!" she screamed.

'That's it, my love. Call me. I'm yours.'

Surprising her in the middle of my service, I gripped her ass and rolled on my back bringing her with me. I didn't need to tell her what to do. She rode her perfect brown ass on my face like a cycle, and I grew harder from the respirations she panted.

Her thighs clenched my cheeks, blinding me. Her tight pussy vibrated on my tongue. I didn't need to see her rubbing her nipples with a light touch in circles. It was a given she was pinching them as she rocked. She always did. "Unh," she belted, warning me she was ready to slide down my dick and rodeo me like a bull until the sun made the darkness disappear.

I loved looking at her fuck me. I loved her. Period. I wondered what she was thinking about while I was inside of her. *'Was she going to forgive me? Was she coming home with me? Did her body ache for me as mine ached for her? Did she know how lost I felt with her gone?'*

The rest of the world ceased to exist when she was fucking me. She moved her hips side to side, then around in a rhythm of her own I never figured out. She drove me crazy, and this time I would last way longer than before.

Whenever distance was between us, I never lasted long. She was the only woman whose touch affected me in such a way— so much to handle, I lived to be inside of her.

I had to look at her. I missed her gorgeous face. The way her tits bounced around when she really got into it, and how she guarded them when she came. Jackpot. Right on cue.

I removed her palms and kissed the curves of her breasts to enhance her climax. I grinded her from below with two deep thrusts then paused against the back of her wall. She gripped the back of my head while she screamed, "*Supaman Luva!*" Man, when she spoke in street talk I damn near lost my mind every time.

I rolled her over and plowed her ass into peril— I was her assailant. After she vibrated on me, I pulled out and went back down on her for a few kind licks, then slid back in for more punishment. She hollered my name, "Maximus!" Good grief she knows how that excites me.

I whispered in her ear, "The one and only Mrs. Sharper," drilling her to bits. I wanted to remind her she was mine, and her gold belonged to me and me only. I stamped my name on her ass and her brain, and I held back my climax by pulling out and rubbing it against her clit— a move she begged for.

"Maximus!" she implored, yearning for me to put it back inside.

I resisted. I paused and tasted her luscious lips until I couldn't resist her warmth anymore, gliding back inside to finish her.

I pounded my baby intensely into the bed. The box spring shifted and the headboard sounded as if it were damaging the sheetrock behind it. Her hands around my neck, and her legs wrapped around my waist, "Ah!" I exerted and trembled inside of her.

"Don't take it out," she commanded.

I happily obliged, lied on top of her, kissed her shoulders, and ran my fingers up and down her face until she drifted off to sleep. I fell to her side and followed her lead, a whole man again, hoping she didn't break my heart when the sun lit the sky.

The alarm on her phone woke us a few hours later.

"Good morning, sweets. Do you have somewhere to be?" I asked, kissing her cheek.

"I have a hair appointment in an hour." She rolled her fists on her thighs.

"Care if I come with?" I removed her hands and rubbed her legs. "Are you feeling alright?"

"My legs feel sore," she answered. "You want to come with me to the salon?"

"Why not? I can treat you to lunch after."

"If you insist." She rolled out of bed.

I followed her inside the brick building, and the hostess escorted me to a waiting area. I had an hour and a half to kill, so I stepped outside for a stroll of the plaza.

The shopping village was quaint with coffee shops, off brand clothing boutiques, bakeries, cafes, and a one of a kind furniture store. I spotted a carved wooden table with jagged edges in the window. *'Nadia would love that,'* I thought.

Inside I inquired about the piece and bought it, unsure of the message I would be sending if it were delivered to her apartment. Fearing she might think I was in agreeance of her living there, I paid a ton for the owner to ship it to our house in London. *'She's gonna freak when she sees this.'*

After an hour of killing time, I made my way back to the salon. The hostess was absent at the front desk. I walked towards the area where Nadia was being serviced, and the room fell silent. "Excuse me. I'd like to have a word with my wife." I cleared my throat with every eye in the room upon me.

"Come here." Nadia signaled.

I kneeled down. "How much is your tab?"

"Ninety dollars," the stylist answered.

I pulled out a one-hundred-dollar bill wrapped with a fifty-dollar bill inside of it. Nadia took them both and handed them to the woman. "She brought me back to life, so she deserves a big tip" she said.

I grinned. "As long as you're smiling."

I made eyes with the stylist and thanked her. "I'll be waiting for you out front." I kissed my wife on the cheek, and returned to the front of the salon.

Moments later, Nadia walked out with her hair flowing and a huge smile, beaming with the confidence I remembered.

I showed her the shops I walked through in the village, and a café I thought we could try. We sipped margaritas while narrowing down our order. "The Mexican food you had yesterday makes me want to try this cilantro hummus," I said.

Nadia chortled and chuckled unlike before. "Say what now?"

"What's so funny?" I questioned.

"Nothing," she answered, tapping the front of her throat and giggling under her breath. "I'm fine."

"Should I order it or not?"

"I don't want any, but please help yourself." She laughed softly.

Sitting across from Nadia glowing and happy, made my world shine. I watched her talk with her mouth full, her almost crooked smile, and her bosoms teasing me with her perfect posture, feeling like the luckiest man in the world. *'This is how it should be. Always.'*

"Are you happy?" I asked her.

She swallowed the last bit of her meal and answered, "Not really."

"How can I change that?"

"I don't know if you can. I was contemplating seeing a shrink. I need to sort my shit out. Make sense of this predicament. Fix whatever is broken with me," she confessed.

"You're not broken. We've both made mistakes, but I'm ready to move past them. I was hoping you were ready to move on as well."

"I'm not there yet. I do want things to go back to the way they were, but it can't happen with the snap of a finger." She gestured.

"It's been three weeks," I huffed.

"And? I wasn't ready to face you. I wasn't ready to face anyone. I was wallowing in my sadness. Giving myself the time I need to think, feel, cry, scream. The me you saw yesterday was a vast improvement from the weeks prior. I'm not loving myself right now, so how can I love another person?" she explained.

"You don't love yourself?" I reached for her hand.

"I'm a mess. I make terrible decisions, and I would like to be a better person. I struggle with forgiveness immensely, and it weighs me down. I've hated myself these past weeks."

"We have that in common."

She paused and scowled. My admittance of hating myself stopped her rant. She raised her hand forward and finally accepted mine, giving me hope. "I don't want to be with anyone else. I want you. I had you. Then I lost you," she said.

"You never lost me. Come home with me," I begged.

"I told you, I need to be on my own for a while."

"Where, Nadia? Here?" I released her hand.

"Wherever I decide. Here. Charlotte. Maybe London. Maybe anywhere." She looked away from me.

"Most of those options are away from me. What about last night?"

"Last night was mind blowing. It always is, but can you honestly say we're meant to be with the fuck-ups you and I have made?"

'This is a new side to her.'

"Our good outweighs our bad," I said.

"This ordeal made me realize I lost myself in you. I've become dependent on you." Her face scrunched.

"Am I being punished for providing for us? I don't get what you're saying?"

"The house is not mine. I could never afford it, and I was thrown out of it. I'm never going to be comfortable in there."

"We'll sell it and move again. Khai told me what happened to you. If I would have known I wouldn't have said what I said."

"Maybe. Maybe not. My point is I shouldn't have put myself in that position again."

I sighed. My apology was not being accepted. Her forgiveness I'd never receive. I looked at her differently for the first time after our exchange. I was far from the dog house. Nowhere near the yard. And I was afraid I'd never be allowed back in the gate. "Nadia, what's your plan?"

"What was your plan?" She sassed me. "Come down here, throw me some good dick, and have me following you around like a puppy?"

"Throw you some good dick?" I raised my brows and repeated slowly.

'Who the fuck is this person?'

"Sorry for being brash, but it's how we operate."

"No, we coexist. We fight. We make up. We love hard. We fight some more. We make love. We laugh. We live. We fuck like rabbits and do it over and over again." My voice carried.

A woman sitting at the table next to us looked our way and smirked. I regained my composure and sat quietly while Nadia continued to be ridiculous.

"What happened, happened. I'm working on moving past it, but until you showed up, I've been planning my next chapter in life. Since you've been here, I'm having to rethink everything to your liking. You're trying to control how and when I forgive you, but it's not up to you. It's up to me," she argued.

I apologized again. "I don't mean to be controlling. I want to right my wrong."

She rose from the table and left me with the check. I watched her from the table, standing outside staring into the sky as her hair blew along with the wind. I paid the tab and joined her on the curb. She walked a few steps ahead of me, strutting and turning heads.

A car blew the horn at her, and she stopped and waited for me to catch up, making my heart sing. She stroked my ego while we walked the block. "The women in the salon fancied you," she said. I didn't respond to her flattery. "Did you hear me?" she asked.

"I heard you, and I couldn't care less," I replied.

We went back to her place and occupied different rooms. I stayed on the sofa and searched for a flight home, crying on the inside as she avoided me upstairs doing God knows what.

As time went on, I lost focus on finding a flight. I burst into her room to demand she come home. She was curled on the bed crying. "Nadia love," I called out to her. She put up her hands, motioning me to stay back, and I obeyed.

Watching her suffer from the pain I caused her tore me to pieces. It hurt even more there was nothing I could do or say to make things right. She turned her back to me, but I didn't leave her side. I stood there listening to her cry, wanting to console her, but respected her wishes and left her alone.

In that moment, I came to terms how conflicted she was feeling, and accepted how controlling and how much of an asshole I was still being. The poor little rich kid toying with the affections of the woman he loved more than life.

When she appeared to settle down, I disobeyed her wishes and wrapped my arms around her until she fell asleep. But I didn't follow suit. I stayed awake and held her with one thing on my mind. *'Do whatever she asks of me to win her back.'*

CHAPTER 45

Nadia

The look on the girls' faces in the salon made me chuckle on the inside. Often when a woman walks into a barbershop, the men stop talking and the room is hit with a sudden silence. When Mash walked inside the salon, the ladies zipped their mouths shut. Their curling wands stopped clicking, and blow dryers turned off.

I inconspicuously skimmed the room to see their reactions when he approached me. Murmurs softly echoed as the stylists stared at him up their noses, clients peeped above their books, and the shampoo girls stationed near the sink listened in on our conversation. I enjoyed that moment.

Mash kneeled down to my eye level to ask what I needed. Something about him looking down at me reminded me of the night we met. How I swooned over him, the same way the ladies in the salon were, but still he only had eyes for me.

When he returned to the front of the shop, my stylist and I whispered and laughed at how thirsty the women were. But I was no fool. She was thirsty, too.

I said some not so nice things at lunch, but I spoke my truth. I was happy Mash searched high and low and found me, but I masked my excitement because of my pride.

As much as I desired to be in his arms and erase the past few weeks, I couldn't pretend it didn't happen and forget how easily he threw me away like an expired carton of milk. Forgiving him was where my problem lied, and I would in time, but I couldn't rush it, and neither could he.

I dismissed him, but he wouldn't leave. He watched me come unglued until I laid in his persistent arms, and fell asleep in the comfort of them wrapped around me. When I woke, his side of the bed was empty, his bags were gone, and the only trace I had of him being in the house was dirty towels and a note left for me on the kitchen counter.

> *I stole a lot of kisses before I left.*
> *This isn't goodbye. I'm giving you your space.*
> *You know how I feel and where I'll be. I'll*
> *call you in a few days. Take care of yourself.*
> *All My Love,*
> *Mash*

I felt dejected after reading his letter, but also relieved. I was no longer under pressure to make a sudden decision about what I was going to do, or having to include his feelings while sorting out my own.

It was a new day for me, and I didn't want to spend it wallowing in my loneliness. I dressed in one of the outfits the girls bought me, and drove my fresh new look around the city, open to whatever possibility came my way.

I stopped on the side of the road and grabbed a free *Creatives* paper from the bin. From there I selected random places to go and events to attend, such as standing in a long line for free ice cream because it was National Ice Cream Day. Then I cheered on marathon runners downtown, baked in the sun at a food truck park, and closed the night at a happy hour intended for the work crowd.

The next day I reacquainted myself with the kitchen and stir-fried a home cooked meal, power-walked in my neighborhood, then read the reviews of therapists online.

Seven days later, I found myself in the office of Dr. Jouer, the therapist with the highest recommendation on Doc.com. The reviews mentioned he was attentive and warm, exactly the type of comforting spirit I needed to help me sort out my issues.

His aura was inviting when he welcomed me into his office. I couldn't help but return his smile, and stare at him as he resembled a middle-aged version of Mr. Robinson with early signs of crow's feet, dressed in a maroon cardigan.

In my head I sang, '*Won't You Be My Neighbor*' as he introduced himself. The temperature in his office was perfect. Atlanta was blazing outside and freezing everywhere you went to escape the heat, but Dr. Jouer's office was cool, comfortable, and cozy.

I lied back on the chocolate suede chaise, introduced myself, and jumped right into my song. "Okay here is what you need to know. I'm only in town for a few weeks, so I need quick therapy. Nothing drawn out over time. I'm married, currently separated from my husband. He's kept secrets from me, nothing sexual, and I recently engaged in a non-sexual relationship with another man. I have a good marriage so what I need to know from you is, did I subconsciously engage with this other man as revenge, or were my intentions something deeper? Was I acting out of character because my best friend was secretly sleeping with the man I initially thought I'd marry? Did I do it because I am somehow threatened by my husband's ex? Or did I do it because my curiosity about something new and shiny dangling in my face intrigued me when it shouldn't because I'm crazy about my husband?" I exhaled.

"May I?" Dr. Jouer asked.

"Sorry. I totally took over." I covered my face then pulled my eyes out wide.

"It's nice to meet you, Mrs. Sharper. I'm not familiar with quick therapy. Have you received previous counsel prior to today?"

"Um. Yes. Kind of. It was group therapy."

"I see. I'll need a little more information before I can help you sort out what it is you are seeking advisement for."

I filled in the blanks for the doctor with a rundown of our timeline, the magic we shared, the dilemma with his management, the lie he told me about his father, the secret he kept about his ex-girlfriend.

I told him about Dylan and Taylor, Isla and Evan, and Khai's theory that those instances created insecurities within me and led to a string of bad decision making on my part.

"Is your friend a clinical therapist?" he asked.

"No. She's a loan officer." I perked up.

He scoffed and wrote in his notepad. "How many weeks will you be in town?"

"Maybe a month. Maybe longer?" I alluded, with hope he wouldn't attempt to drag out our sessions for years without resolve.

"You have provided some thorough information, but unfortunately our time is up. Can we meet again on Thursday? Same time?"

"See you then, doc." I clicked my tongue and winked at him. "I don't know why I did that. Sorry."

I left his office doubting I would keep the appointment. A weight had been lifted off of my shoulders as I spewed my troubles out loud to him. Hearing myself say it all in one breath, I realized I didn't want anyone else's opinion on my life. I wanted my own.

I sat in the parking lot and dialed Mash. His voice skipped and cracked when he answered. "Babe? How are you?"

"I saw a shrink today," I blurted, assuming he was shocked to hear from me by the sound of his voice.

"I'm not sure what to say to that?"

"I honestly don't know why I told you." I frowned.

"I don't know much about shrinks, but I'm sure it doesn't work with one visit."

"I know... I don't know. We'll see."

"How are you getting on? Say the word, and I'll hop on a plane."

"Don't you have upcoming shows?" I asked.

"Is that your way of saying no?"

"I didn't say no. How are you?"

"I've been better." He sighed.

"I didn't call to upset you. I called to hear your voice and check in. And finish our conversation from the café."

"Nadia, I'm following your lead."

Mash's voice sounded distant and distracted. I grew worried he was slipping away from me, and wondered if I should cancel the reading of my blood results and fly to London. Possibly revisit Smitty's gym and duke out our demons in the ring. *'Slugging it out worked the last time.'*

By the time I made it home, I convinced myself to call the office for my results and catch the next flight out of the states. As I exited the car, the mail carrier startled me. His bag knocked my sideview mirror. "Sorry, ma'am." He smiled. I nodded. I sped in the heat from my car to my door, as he trailed behind me. "I believe this is yours," he said, handing me a box and certified letter. "Sign here, please."

"I'm sorry. You have the wrong address," I argued.

He pointed to my name on the package, "Are you headed to 43. Last name Sharper?" He poked out his lips.

"That's me." I sighed, and signed with the stylus.

I went inside and opened the letter first as there was no sender information listed. My mood shifted south when I saw the name of the signee. Lucas Fucking Fleming.

Nadia, Nadia, Nadia, (Sharper)
It took a lot of bribery and favors, but I finally found you at
this address. I haven't stopped thinking about
you and would love to see you. Actually, I need to see
you. Here's an open ticket to New York. Seeing your
face walk through my door is all I can think about.
I'll be waiting for the day you show up and put me
out of my misery.
Lucas Fleming

I was convinced the devil was sitting on my shoulder with his foot pressed on my neck and having a laugh at my expense. I wanted to run. Anywhere I couldn't be found, or tracked down, or harassed.

Lucas wasn't going to go away easily. He possessed the stupid, damaging note I wrote, and I could feel he was going to be the end of my marriage. Talking to myself I screamed, "You should have never given him false hope!"

His letter caused me to spiral out of control. I pushed the box aside, uninterested of its contents until it ate away at me in the middle of my shower. I left wet footprints on the carpet as I bounced downstairs in my towel and opened the box. Inside was a stunning handbag, surprisingly my taste, and a handwritten message on a card.

> *The best for the best.*
> *All my love,*
> *Maximus*

I breathed the heaviest sigh when I read his name, dropped to my knees, and cried happy tears clutching the bag hanging from my arm. I hid my face and snapped a photo, then sent it to Mash with the caption:

> *The best from the best.*
> *I love you!*

He called within seconds. "Why can't I see your face?" He sounded aggravated.

"Didn't want you to see me crying. Your gift was right on time. You have no idea. You sound a lot better than you did when we spoke earlier."

He deflected. "Did my gift upset you? I didn't send it to persuade you. Or make you cry."

"These are happy tears. I love it. I love you."

I managed to survive our call without telling Mash about the letter and the ticket. Talking with him swayed me to keep my appointment with the hematologist, and fly out to London after I had been seen.

My fingers twitched while I observed the other patients in the waiting room. An elderly couple sitting across from me held hands in silence, a baby to my left stared at me until I smiled at him, and the woman at the end of the row beamed as she whispered on the phone. The rosiness in her cheeks matched the cheeks of the baby, who lifted my spirits by simply showing me his toothless gums.

"Sharper!" called the nurse.

Down the ivory hall I followed her, into the lab with my arms being prepped to be stuck yet again. My veins were a nurse's dream. Ripe, plump, and easy to pierce.

In went the needle, and the extraction began. My dark red blood streamed into two tubes, then a ball of cotton cleared the spot of blood before the bright pink tape sealed the hole. "Follow me," the nurse said.

She led me to a small room with an ugly orange chair, observation table, and portable computer on wheels. My thoughts carried away lying on the white paper, and counting the dots on the tile ceiling. I hardly slept the night before, thanks to my mistake from New York looming somewhere in the wind, and despite having the infusion done, I still felt tired.

I drifted off into a nap, and jumped up when Dr. Oliver walked in. "Nice to see you again, Mrs. Sharper. How are you feeling today?"

"Still a little tired. But I didn't get any sleep last night, so it's nothing a nap won't cure," I answered.

"Painting the town red?" he teased.

"I wish," my voice elevated. "A night on the town could do me some good."

Dr. Oliver pinned the right side of his mouth together, "Well, before you go wild in the streets, be mindful of the heat. And continue to take care of yourself. The infusion was successful. You didn't reach a level 12, but your numbers did increase significantly to 11.5, which is good. Now if I remember correctly, you recently moved here from..."

"London," I said.

"Yes. I knew it was from somewhere pretty far. Your results show an HCG level that indicates you're pregnant. That could explain why you feel tired. There are a few OBGYN offices in this building I can refer you to since I assume you don't have one here in the states."

"Pregnant?" My eyes enlarged. "Are you sure?"

"The numbers say so. Would you like for our office to schedule an appointment with a referral?"

"Can I be seen today?"

"Wait here. I'll have the nurse come back in with that information. Congratulations and we'll speak soon."

The short time I waited for the nurse felt like an eternity. I couldn't believe I heard the word pregnant come from his mouth. *'He must be mistaken.'*

I sat there in disbelief, recalculating the timeline of my last period, wondering how far along I was, and sadly questioned what I was going to do about it.

The nurse returned to the room. "Two floors up, you'll find the Women's Care Center. Dr. McGrath can see you in one hour if you would like the appointment."

I nodded as the words, "I do," spewed from my mouth.

The nurse handed me paperwork to complete for the visit. "I'll let them know you are on your way up. You may not have to wait a full hour," she said. I thanked her and skipped riding the elevator to the office. Instead, I walked the two flights of stairs to kill time, and sat on the steps in a daze talking to myself in my head. *'What am I going to do with a baby? Why now?'*

Time seemed to slow down, but the heat didn't as a sweat bead dripped down my nose. Failing to compose myself, I exited the corridor and entered the Women's Center looking like a deer trapped in headlights.

Impatiently I waited for my name to be announced, studying the pregnant women coming and going. Petite, tall, short, and huge women waddled around and put the fear of God in me. I was raised religious, but strayed away after reading several books with different perspectives about faith and spirituality. Yet the idea of becoming a mother led me back to the path of believing in an instant. *'God, I am afraid.'*

I never truly saw myself as a mother and was never sure if I had a maternal bone in my body. Sure, when I was serious with Dylan I imagined having a family one day, but it was what you do when you think you've found the one. I loved my nephew dearly, and smiled at little babies whenever they passed by, but never have I ever pictured me giving birth— and especially not under circumstances like this.

"Sharper," my name sounded from the double doors. I snapped

out of my troubling thoughts and followed the nurse into an ultrasound room. Once I stripped off my shorts, I found myself in stirrups, shivering while I stared at a poster of a monkey with the words "Hang in There" below it.

The lab tech asked me to relax, but I couldn't. My legs shook uncontrollably. She buzzed for an assistant to bring me a heated blanket to calm my nerves, and made small talk to distract me from the intrusion about to follow. The speculum wand entered between my legs and I hysterically burst into laughter. "This shit is not happening to me."

I placed my hands over my face, and the tech asked, "Are you doing okay up there? What I'm doing right now is measuring the fetus. It looks like you are coming up on six weeks. I'm turning the sound on now, and I'm going to move around a little bit. Ah, there it is. That's your baby's heartbeat."

An hour prior I didn't know what I was going to do, then the simple sound of two beats continuously thumping inside of me changed my world. My downward spiral no longer had importance, and a little person I'd never met had complete control of my thoughts. Giving me a new purpose to carry on, and become a better version of myself. He or she had been a part of me for weeks, experiencing the lowest point of my life at the start of theirs, and chose to stick around. I was impressed.

I dressed and met with Dr. McGrath afterwards, nodding along to every word leaving his mouth about vitamins, sonogram pictures, and the calculation of the first day of my last period. My face confirmed I had no idea what he was talking about. "I'm sure you have questions," he smiled.

"Several. I saw blood the other day after having sex." I blushed.

"A little bleeding is normal after intercourse," he confirmed.

"So I shouldn't have sex?"

"Sex is fine. I wouldn't get too wild though."

"Is everything normal, and will travel be a problem?"

"Your baby's heart rate is strong. Traveling now shouldn't be a problem, but not recommended at the end of your cessation. Take care of yourself and we'll see you in four weeks, but don't hesitate to call if you have any concerns or further questions."

I left the center with every concern and question in the world crossing my mind. *'Is everything going to be okay? Will I be a good mother? Am I ready for this? Why me? Why now? Am I crazy? And how am I going to break this news to Mash?'*

CHAPTER 46

Lucas

The delivery confirmation verified Nadia's address. I wasted no time booking a flight out of LaGuardia. I had to make my move while she and her husband were at odds, and convince her to free herself from his strings and explore life with me. After all, my sources risked their careers tracking her and her husband's phones for me. It would be a waste to let their efforts be in vain.

The redeye was steep at the last minute, but seeing Nadia's mocha skin illuminating in the night sky was worth every penny. I checked into a hotel overnight and waited for mid-morning to work my way over to her place.

Along the way, I saw many attractive women with wide hips, long hair, bodacious booties, and non-existent waistlines throughout the city. Turns out Atlanta wasn't the country town I pegged it for. But as tempting as those women were, I held out for the one woman on my mind, Nadia. None of them were as stunning as her, and the way she controlled my thoughts these past months, no other woman would ever be. My only hope is this trip down here goes according to plan and she agrees to run off with me.

I stood outside her door for an hour. No one answered when I knocked, so I waited for her to show. I circled the building to see if a

433

light was on inside her unit, and listened closely for her voice inside. The sound of silence assured the apartment was empty.

The heat was blistering, and my clothes reeked of sweat. This wasn't exactly the presentation I had in mind to woo her into my arms. I planned to surprise her and treat her to an expensive lunch, similar to the one we had on 57th, but not in soiled clothing and smelling like outside.

Then hunger struck me, and I was forced to leave against my wishes. I tucked my card under the door knocker and wrote on the back:

I'm in town. Call me when you get this.
Lucas

The following day I faced the same feat. Still no answer at the door. Still no Nadia. I was convinced I had chased a false lead, and wondered who signed my letter with the airline ticket inside.

It was clear Nadia would never stand before me again, and be a memory I'd forever fantasize in my mind. Being so close to seeing her once more and failing, troubled my soul. *'I need a pick me up.'*

To ease my mind of my plight, I found myself at one of the famous strip clubs in Atlanta. And I must say, not only were the women perfectly embodied angels, but the lemon pepper wings were out of this world.

Though I enjoyed the scenery of beautiful black women jiggling and bouncing before me, I still couldn't get Nadia out of my head. My dick grew hard looking at the naked women sliding down poles like angels, and grinding against other patrons. I couldn't wait for Nadia to be in their position. I would make her pay for making me wait so long to taste her, then make it up to her with the best stroke game north of the Mason Dixon.

I needed sexual relief. I called over the dancer eyeing me the moment I sat down. She strutted over from a few feet away and kept me entertained. "I can take you in the back for a few hundred if you like," she offered.

I grinned at how well she read me. "Lead the way," I said, following her down a dark hall.

We passed an open room of *heauxs* hard at work on a *jon*, then slid in a fluorescent purple room a few doors down. She closed the door behind us and I made myself comfortable in a black leather chair.

She circled me, dragging her fingernails around my shoulders and back. "No need for the teasing," I said. "Just get to it."

She looked at me and smiled. I assumed she either liked taking orders, or was ready to alleviate me of my demons. Leaning over me, she slowly lowered her body and rubbed her hands against my chin and licked my lips. I grabbed her by the neck, "I don't kiss *randoms*," and pulled a rubber from my wallet. '*The nerve of this whore trying to kiss me in my mouth.*' I was wasted in that shithole establishment, but not out of my right mind.

She rested her hands on my knees while I *latexed* my johnson. "Go ahead. You know the job," I said, imagining it was Nadia's full lips slurping up and down my dick. When she finished, I kept the bag on my pipe until I left the lot, and tossed it out of the window on the freeway.

I showered back at the hotel, still unable to get my dream girl out of my mind, and hauled ass to the address hoping she was there this time. "I've seen you lurking around here for a few days now! Get lost or get cuffed!" A woman's voice shouted from above.

"I want no trouble, Miss! I'm looking for the young lady in 43! Pretty brown girl, about five-four in height, gorgeous. Simply gorgeous!"

"You don't look like her type!" She chuckled.

"So you've met the husband!" I replied.

"Who are you, the boyfriend?"

"I wish!"

We shared a distant laugh.

"She left with a suitcase, so you're out of luck. But I'm single!" The neighbor cackled.

"I might have to take you up on that offer!" I joked. "You have a good night!"

"You too, sugar!"

I was flattered by the feisty woman in the window. And grateful she verified I had the right address. My ego was bruised with the news of the husband though. '*He must have intercepted my letter,*' I thought, because I was confident Nadia would have reached out to me.

My fight was far from over as I planned to return and try my hand again. If I was lucky, I'd get the chance to lay one on her joke of a husband and even the score. If not, taking his woman would do.

CHAPTER 47

Nadia

I promised Mash I would call him when I left the doctor's office, but I didn't. I placed my phone on airplane mode, and went to the mall instead. I walked inside every baby store I crossed, fumbling through clothes and scoping nursery furniture.

I couldn't resist this yellow two-piece set with the matching hat and socks. I contemplated mailing it to Mash as the announcement, but decided against it as I wanted to see the look on his face when he heard the news.

After I window shopped for a few hours, I headed home to have my joy stolen. I trashed Lucas's card and followed my initial instinct to skip town. I raced inside, threw a quick bag together, loaded the car, and drove to my mother's house in South Carolina.

My plate was full. Mash was acting normal, a baby was growing inside of me, and now Lucas was back from hell. The anxiety of it all led me to the side of the interstate before I reached the South Carolina state line where I cried hysterically, and had to wait half an hour before merging back into traffic.

I screamed to the top of my lungs while simultaneously singing along with the music blasting, unsure if my outbursts were signs of another breakdown, or pregnancy hormones.

I arrived at my mother's house puffy faced, snot nosed, and red eyed, but as always, her arms eased my pain. My surprise brought a smile to her face briefly. "What brought you to tears?" she asked.

"Nothing," I lied.

"Um huh," she moaned.

She led me to the kitchen and began cooking. "Call your brother and tell him you're here." I did as I was told and cleaned myself up before he and his clan arrived.

We caught up for old times sake, ate until our bellies were full, and I hid everything about my personal affairs.

In the morning, Mom and I drove to see Grams. Three generations with a fourth on the way. We spent the evening dining at a white table-clothed eatery, and on Sunday morning attended church service.

I envisioned the door bursting into flames when my foot crossed the threshold of the Baptist halls. I checked the time on my phone countless times during the sermon until a peaceful spirit surrounded me. *'Grams must have said a silent prayer to ease my anxiety and be present in the moment.'*

After church, the three of us enjoyed what was left of the hot sun on the beach. "What's going on with my gal?" Grams asked.

"Nothing," I lied.

"You lie bad like your daddy." Grams scoffed.

"I thought if anyone could get the truth out of her, it would be you, Mama," my mother added. "She gave me the same answer."

"Nothing's going on," I emphasized.

"Umph, umph, umph. Never thought you'd shut me out gal. It must be something big." Grams stared at me.

"I'm working something out, but when I know for sure I'll tell you two everything. I don't want you to worry if there is no need to worry. That's all I can say right now." They both stared at me until I shouted, "The sun is about to set!"

We quieted down and ended the evening under the umbrellas enjoying the breeze, opposite the sun sinking into the water, and said goodbye.

I waited until Tuesday to return to Atlanta, under the assumption Lucas would have returned back to work. My neighbor called me from her window. "Hey 43, a handsome young man was camped out here looking for you some days ago," she said.

"Are you sure he was here for me?" I asked.

"He didn't call you by name, but he described you to a tee. You in some kind of trouble?"

"No. Why do you ask?" I sassed.

"I don't know many husbands who would like another man staking out his wife's place."

"How do you know I'm married?"

"People talk."

"Thanks for telling me," I said aloud, then mumbled to myself, "I bet she knows everybody's business."

The news of Lucas still lurking around worried me. I had spoken with Mash briefly over my long weekend, and didn't like how he sounded. It seemed only right to share what the neighbor told me—run to him even. But I couldn't resist making him sweat a little and teach him a lesson about not getting what he wanted when he wanted it.

I needed to be firm and prove I could stand strong on my own, so I put off calling him and tackled the dirty laundry from my trip instead. While sorting my load, Gemma, Mash's assistant, popped up on my screen. Chills ran down my spine when I answered.

"Sorry to bother you at this hour. I wouldn't call if it wasn't important," she said.

"You're fine. Is everything okay?" My voice cracked.

"I'm out of line and overstepping right now, but I wanted to mention something to you and hope this conversation can remain between us."

"Okay..." My words dragged.

"Mash has the team concerned. They don't know I'm calling you, but I thought you should know his behavior has been questionable lately. He's been

flying pretty high if you know what I mean."

"Does anyone else know he's...?" I questioned.

"If they do, they won't say. I normally wouldn't either. I'm crossing the line here." Gemma's voice lowered.

"I won't mention this, and thanks for calling. Can you send me his schedule, please?"

"Done. We're in Manchester Arena this weekend. I'll have a car and pass ready for you."

The doorbell rang, and I jumped. "Thanks, Gemma," I whispered, then eased over to the window. A sigh of relief escaped my lips, and I opened the door for the parcel delivery guy.

"Sign here, please." He held out his stylus pen.

Quickly I signed for the package and double locked my door. *'I can't live in fear like this,'* I thought to myself.

I placed the box on the sofa. I was crossed between sadness of the news about Mash, and annoyed at whatever guilt gift he sent to apologize for using again. I never saw him as an addict, but the picture he painted of those days were vivid enough, I didn't want to experience that side of him. The smoking weed I could handle, but heavy narcotics was a road he would travel alone.

The more I replayed Gemma's words in my head, the more I felt he relapsed because of me. My mind was frazzled, my heart ached, and peace seemed like a dream to never come.

It was clear I was needed in London, so off I went, running to help the man I swore to teach a lesson and make suffer, only to falter when he needed me.

Mash was already in Manchester by the time my flight arrived. The car Gemma arranged for my pickup drove me to the house I vowed I would never step foot in again. I took a deep breath, went inside, and checked out every room to kill time.

They were exactly as I left them except for the dishes in the sink, the crumbs on the counter, and my closet. Mash cleaned the mess I left behind. He hung up the clothes I'd thrown to the floor during my rage-fest, restacked my shoes in the squares, hung my bags on the shelves, and placed my jewelry and scarves back on the prongs. *'He truly was waiting on me to come home.'*

I walked to the other end of the house and entered his studio. It was a war zone compared to the other rooms. Completely wrecked. I had never seen it in such a disarray. Wires unsecured, records outside of the covers, microphones lying around out of their sockets, and pizza boxes smelling of old cheese left behind on the pool table next to the residue of a trace of cocaine.

I didn't dare touch his tracks. I left it as is, questioning if I made the right choice to come back and deal with him, and this situation I knew nothing about.

I had more than him to think about now, and I was unsure if I should check into a hotel and never let him know I had returned, or stay and do what Gemma asked of me.

I double backed upstairs and tripped on my steps when I passed the dining room. It was the one room we hadn't decorated because we couldn't decide if it should be formal, or furnished to Mash's signature style—with a pool table in the middle of it.

A big red ribbon caught the corner of my eye, causing me to misstep. I caught my balance with the wall and entered the once empty space, now furnished with a beautifully hand-crafted maple wooden table.

The edges were cut with a precisive curve, and captivated me with its uniqueness and beauty. It ornamented the room to perfection and felt to be made with me in mind. *'Nice play.'*

Caught up in its details and artistry, my mind temporarily eased in the moment. Filled with forgiveness and hope, I decided I would stay and ran to the store before the car picked me up for the show.

I organized my few ingredients to cook breakfast in the morning. *'Red velvet waffles are a good way to start over,'* I thought, then prettied myself up.

My heart skipped a beat when I entered the coliseum below deck. Gemma met me at the side door with my pass, and handed me off to security who escorted me through a horde of drunks, druggies, and *heauxs* to Mash's dressing room.

When I entered, I knew I made the right choice by staying. Our for better and for worse was being tested, and it was my turn to take care of him, the way he had taken care of me.

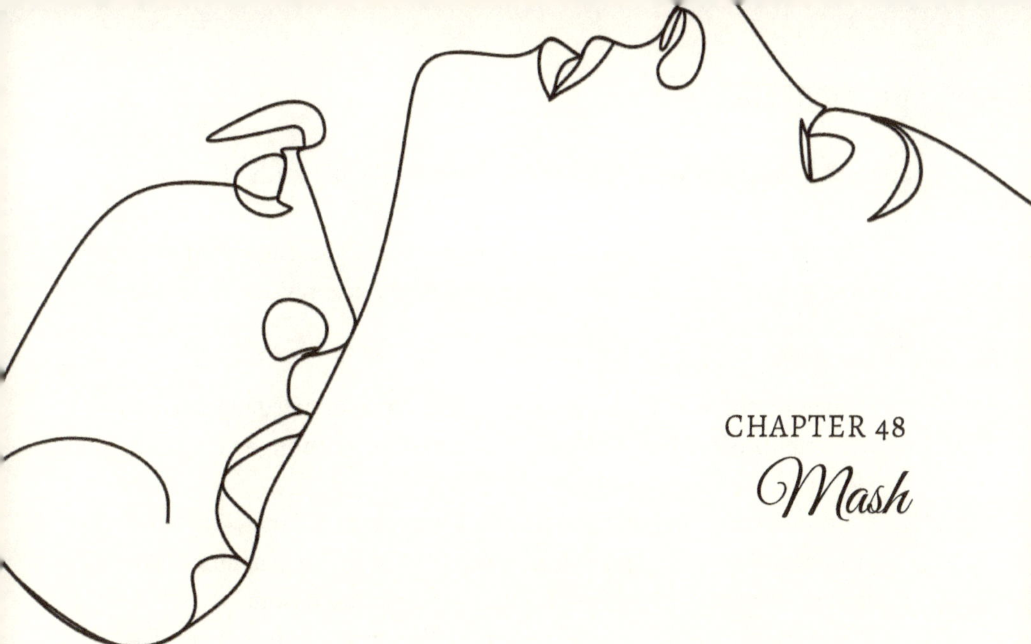

CHAPTER 48

Mash

I needed a good hour to myself before the show started. I hadn't felt like mixing lately, which threw me off of my game. My personal life never interfered with my money in the past, but Nadia and this itch had my world spinning upside down in a pool of descent.

The door opened to my dressing room. "I said don't let anyone in." I fanned my hand.

Footsteps approached closer.

"Even me?"

Her voice raised the hairs on my forearm.

"You showed up quick this time. You must know how bad I need you right now," I confessed.

"What the hell are you talking about?" she asked, then ran her hands across my beard.

"Damn, you feel real this time."

"What are you on? And how long have you been off the wagon?" she questioned me, now running her hands through my hair.

"You normally don't talk to me," I replied.

"Say what?" Her country twang spilled.

"Last time you gave me your look of disappointment when you

appeared, but you've never spoken before. What's with the questions?" I asked.

She sat down in my lap, reached for my face, and turned it upward to look at hers. She took her fingers and wiped the residue from my nose. "How long, Mash?" she asked.

"I'm tripping hard," I said.

"Snap out of it. It's me. I'm here." Her hands squeezed my face.

Staring into her eyes I exhaled, "Thank God. I thought I was on top."

"I'm not sure what that means, but I think I get it," she said.

I hugged her waist and sniffed the gardenia in her perfume. "We bought that in Paris, didn't we?" I hid my face in her bosom.

"You have to pull yourself together. You can't go out there like this," she whispered.

I rolled my brows against her bosom. "I have thirty minutes until my set. Does this mean you're back for good?"

"Sort of. I have a few appointments I need to keep. You should come back with me."

"I've never needed you more than I do right now." I kissed her hands.

"Why'd you fall off?" Her face scowled. "Never mind that. We can fix this. Let's make it through tonight and start from there. We'll go home, relax, maybe swim a bit, then have a conversation."

"Have you fallen out of love with me?" I asked.

She flashed her pretty smile and kissed my lips. "Baby, Cupid's arrow is so far up my ass you needn't worry about that ever happening."

I smiled back at her. "You say the wildest things at times."

The stage hand knocked, and Nadia gave me a once over. She planted a big one on me then sent me on my way to handle my business. I put on one hell of a show knowing she was there, and counted down the minutes to get her home and play house.

To my surprise, Nadia wasn't as eager to let me make love to her. Normally we would have left our mark in the dressing room, or jumped bones on the side of the road, but she was hesitant coming to bed.

She cooked and cleaned at three o'clock in the morning. Obviously avoiding me. I offered, "Do you need me to rub you down? Help you unwind from the trip?" She shook her head no and stretched for a bowl up high in the cabinets. I stepped behind her, slid my hands underneath her silk gown and ran my chin against her shoulders. "Do you need some help?"

"I know how you want to help," she answered in a coy manner. "I'm almost done prepping."

"You're driving me crazy in this thing you're wearing. Let's go to bed. Leave this. I'll take you wherever you want to go for breakfast," I begged.

"I promise I'll be done in a sec."

"You're stalling. What is it? The time zone? Whatever it is, we can talk about it." I pressed against her back.

"Not right now." She slid away.

"I can tell you're uneasy. Is it me? Is it the house?"

"Mostly," she answered.

"Isn't what I sent you enough to make everything alright again?"

"A handbag?"

"No. The second package with those Kendall Miles boots you wanted that were sold out."

"I haven't opened it yet. And why would boots make everything alright again?" She huffed.

"I put something else inside the shoe box. Since you have no clue what I'm talking about, what made you come home?"

"Your voice didn't sound right on the phone."

I pressed my palms on her shoulders and applied pressure to help her relax. "You do still love me." I smiled. Massaging my fingertips against her bones she moaned, "Mmm."

"Allow me to release this tension," I crooned.

"You were really high tonight." Her words cut me.

"You've seen me high before."

"Not to the point of hallucination. I saw what you left in the studio. How often are you doing it?"

"Maybe once a day. Here and there."

"So, what I walked in on tonight..."

"Won't happen again," I promised.

She was pissed, and I didn't blame her. I needed to prove I wasn't an addict, but I wasn't ready to quit. My stash was stocked for at least a month, but she was the drug I needed right then. I could control my use while she was home, and I needed her to curb my appetite.

I followed her every step toward the bedroom. The aroma of her perfume dragged alongside me as we passed the dining room. She paused. "Where did you find this masterpiece?"

"I have been waiting to have this conversation. I saw it in a store when you were at the salon. I knew you would love it so I had it shipped here."

"Damn. You did all of that for me? Thank you." She looked surprised and I didn't know why. "So where do you want to put the other pool table?"

"Wherever you tell me to put it. Now about this table. I think it wants to be broken in," I said, stroking her back.

I pulled her in close and she buried her head into my chest. "Mash, I don't know," she whined and shied away. "I've never been with you like this."

"Like what?" I asked.

"High on lines."

"I'm not high right now. This is me, baby. Say you want me." I nibbled on her face.

"Mash, I..."

She didn't say she wanted me, but she didn't stop me either. I strolled my hands up and down, tracing the line down to the small of her back. She was the missing link to making me feel whole again, and I had to have her to feel complete.

I caressed her gently this time and told her I needed her. She knew I did. I could tell she was aware of how bad her withdrawal was shattering me. "Do you want me, Nadia?" I had to hear her say it.

"I always want you."

"Do you touch yourself thinking of me?" I asked, putting my finger on her g-spot, making her wiggle in my arms.

"Every night."

"See how I know your body so well," I said, now sliding my fingers inside real slow.

"Promise to be gentle," she said, worming about.

"Did I hurt you last time?" I asked, pausing my finger play.

"No. It's been a while since you've slow-whined me." She whirred and wiggled, trying to make me move my fingers.

She was ready.

"Did I make you feel good last time?" I squeezed her labia in between my two fingers.

"I can't think of a time you haven't." She gripped my shoulders.

I loosened my grip, and rubbed her outer layer, not too soft, not too rough. She tightened her thighs when my palms kneaded them. "I'll do you however you want tonight. You want slow, you got it." I bit her bottom lip and tapped on her southern set below.

"Make love to me," she begged.

My fingers left her tunnel and moved back to her g-spot. I thumped it the way she liked me to, stroked it slow, then swiped her clit from side to side. She held on to me and exhaled to Heaven until those lips of hers barely parted, and she grabbed onto her breasts.

"That's one," I said.

"Your turn." She sighed, and pulled for me to slide inside of her.

"Do the thing I taught you," I said, making her wait for me.

"Brace yourself, cowboy."

I steadied myself. My early morning wood stiffened harder than the table I leaned against. When Nadia fulfilled my requests, the magic was inconceivable. Without a fuss, she dropped to the floor and licked her lips. "Is this what you want?"

I jolted in my stance. "It's what I need."

Her swift licks caused me to quiver. I could feel my cock extend further down her throat. She slid it halfway out and played with the tip in between the front of her teeth, and inside the top of her upper lip. I nearly oozed before we fucked.

I slowed her down, painfully retracting my spear from her mouth. "Did I do it wrong?" she asked.

"God no," I breathed out. "I'm trying to hold back. Trust me, I don't want you to stop." I confessed.

She took control and went back in full throttle. Stroking my cock with the inside of her jawline, hard and tight. I called out to the heavens, knowing I wouldn't last a minute if I didn't stop her.

I jerked back and took my shirt off, then covered the chair with it. She placed me back inside and tickled her throat with my pipe and no gag. I retrieved. "Get on top and show me how much you've missed me."

"I thought I did a second ago," she grinned.

"Ooh, you know I like when you talk shit to me."

"You owe me," she said, throwing her leg across my thighs.

My sweets craved me and slid down on my dick nice and slow, then stopped once she got it all in and took a breath. *'She remembered.'* She squeezed her walls around my wood like a long time no see hug, and damn did *we* feel the welcome.

She told me to be gentle, but didn't follow her own request, riding me like an old western flick. I was her horse and she was an outlaw hunted for murder finding justice for her magic carpet ride.

Snug and firm, she gripped my wood. Every now and then she threw her head back, but she always ended up looking back at me. Gripping my shoulders like a headboard, rolling her soft ass on my thighs. She rocked me so hard I thought we were going to break the brand new chair. I could hear the wood roll and the legs creek against the floor, surely scratching it as the chair grazed with her moves. Then she quickly turned and gave me a back shot. I was about to lose it.

I had to hold out a little longer, so I stood up in her pussy while untying the red ribbon from the center of the table. Pressed against the back of her tunnel, I held her in place feeling the gyration of her flesh for a few seconds, then I pulled out. I laid her on the floor and tied her hands to the leg of the table. She watched me in wonder yet intrigue.

Once I had her in bondage, I kissed her body from north to south, then back north to taste her chocolate entrance. She squirmed as she couldn't do anything but take the tickles my tongue slowly delivered.

I wondered why I had never done this to her before as she begged me to finish her, and I was going to, but not before I flipped her over and planted my full face in between her ass.

I took my time and traced her perfect round cheeks with my palms as she crawled to her knees, then I went in for the finale with one deep stroke followed by three more to the left wall, and another curved jab to the right. "Mash," she whimpered below me. I poked and scraped for as long as I could hold out then she screamed, "Maximus!" And it was over.

"Yes, Sweets!" I echoed in return, pressing her skin closely against mine.

"Hold me," she said.

I fell to the floor and untied the ribbon from her wrists. She placed her head upon my chest, and I wrapped my arms around her, kissing her forehead and sweeping her hair. "You're a *gotdamn* animal," she whispered out of breath. "But I loved every minute of it."

Whenever she praised me, I felt like a king, and though I was far from it, the way she stroked my ego was all a man could ask for.

In the morning, I asked Prano to come over and take my stash off my hands. With Nadia showing signs she was coming back to me, I didn't want to take a chance and ruin it. I needed to go cold turkey, and avoid the temptation of sneaking in a toke with her in the house.

He took the package, and Nadia accompanied me to my show, followed by doing what was normal for us. Getting one in, in the back of the truck.

She finally cooked the meal she had been preparing, and on Monday she broke free of me for a few hours. I had the urge to toot while she was out, and there I realized I was an addict. I sparked a joint to kill the impulse, but in addict fashion I compiled the residue she found in my studio and inhaled.

The smell of my joint masked my other high, and Nadia had no idea I betrayed her trust. I hated myself for what I had done. It triggered me to want more. And when Tuesday rolled around, I stupidly let her leave without me, and found myself back on the prowl and yearning for more white.

CHAPTER 49

Nadia

My time in London was coming to an end, but I managed to squeeze in a lunch date with Olive before my departure. I looked like shit the last time she saw me, so I spruced up for our outing, and dressed in some of the higher end pieces I left behind to compete with whatever fashion trend she was going to arrive in. Denim leggings, ankle boots, a white fitted tank, and a cropped khaki jacket layered me fashionably.

She hailed me when I arrived with her signature sultry smile. "Kiss kiss," she said, air kissing my cheeks before we sat down.

"Did you miss me?" I asked.

"I was worried about you more than anything. Why didn't you call me?" She gave me a stern eye.

"Trust me when I say, you didn't want to be bothered with me these past few weeks. I was a total mess, and went into hiding from everyone."

"Not cool, Nadia. I almost didn't show today. I was pissed you didn't call when you said you would." Her eyes rolled.

"I apologize. Forgive me?" I looked up at her like a chastised child.

"Of course." She tapped my hands resting on top of the table. "You seem to be bouncing back to normal. Good for you."

"It's all a façade. I'm a work in progress, but I'm getting there. Last time was all about me. What's been going on with you?" I hunched my shoulders and placed my elbows on the table.

"Where do I begin?" Her brows raised. "Yohan is slipping. He left his phone unlocked one night, and as soon as I went to pick it up he barged in and locked it."

"What did you say?"

"Nothing. I told you I'm riding this out. I figured it was time I level the playing field."

"Noooo." My tongue dragged.

"Yes," Olive smirked. "Let's just say there is truth to the grey sweatpants rumor. If this guy was half as rich as Yogi I would marry him instead."

"Olive, you have your own money. Why does your partner need to be rich?" I asked.

Olive chuckled under her breath and shook her head. She found amusement in teaching me rich girl codes to live by. "I realized a long time ago, I'm a person who always wants more. Yohan provides me luxury. Sweatpants can't."

"So... does he know he's your dirty little secret?"

"I think he's turned on by it."

"Careful. He might catch feelings." I pursed my lips from experience.

"True. I'll have to make sure he remembers it's strictly physical. I tell you. I don't know how men do it. It's a lot of work lying, hiding, and showering, and pretending. And Yogi has at least two, maybe three he's juggling."

"How do you know?"

"I cracked his code. Listen to the names he calls them. Thick Thighs, Blue Moon, and RT3."

"What's my name?" I questioned.

"Worker Bee," she snickered.

"And yours?"

"Second Wifey."

"Ouch," I mouthed.

"Exactly."

"I do need to reach out to Han for work. Once I decide where I'm going to live," I added.

"You're here. I assumed you two worked things out."

"Not officially. I don't feel comfortable in the house. I'm being a brat I know, but I can't help it."

"Oh, I get it. Now you know why I still have my place here, the cottage in France, and the apartment in New York." She sipped her tea and twirled her eyes.

"Speaking of New York. Lucas tracked me down in Atlanta. He left his card on my door."

Olive placed her glass of tea on the table and stared at me. "How?" Her face wrinkled.

"I don't know. I haven't spoken to him. He even sent a plane ticket begging me to come see him."

"He sounds so basic. I hope you were telling the truth about not sleeping with him." Her chest fluttered as the disappointment rolled off of her tongue.

"I didn't sleep with him. I'm regretting the whole ordeal. Don't get me wrong. He was charming, but nothing special."

"So what did you do with the ticket?"

"I upgraded it to come here."

"Good girl." She clapped her hands. "How does Mash feel about him stalking your place?"

"I haven't told him yet. I couldn't. He went to his job and assaulted him."

"Shut up!" Olive exclaimed in a whisper and enlarged eyes.

"I know right," I muttered. "The whole exchange surprises me."

"Two grown men brawling over you." Olive twisted her lips with a smile. "Very Victorian. I love it."

"I'm told Mash did all the punching."

"Now come on. You have to admit Mash deserves a second chance."

I roamed the café and caught my breath. "What would you do if Yohan told you to get out?" I asked her.

She moaned with an exhale. "*Yeesh*, I don't know. I would definitely leave, but I can't say if I would go back to him or not. But Mash isn't Yohan. He's going around beating up guys for you. He made a mistake. I doubt he will ever make it again. And if you could have seen how he stormed into Yogi's office, you would know how passionate he is for you. You'll do what's right and move back here and be my bestie."

I left our lunch date swayed in the direction of moving back for good. I returned to the house and smelled the *loud* before fully coming in from the garage. But I didn't complain. I was excited I had reached a decision, and was in the mood to confess all of my secrets and make a fresh start.

I tested the waters slowly. I told him I was coming home, and asked him to come back with me a second time. He considered it, but didn't give me a definite answer. Then I eased in the hard part. "Lucas sent me a letter and left his card on my door at the apartment."

Mash punched a hole in the wall and lashed out at me for not telling him sooner. "I can't go back with you, so you need to cancel whatever it is you have scheduled and stay home," he demanded.

"What I have scheduled is important. I can't," I explained.

"I'm not letting you go back without me."

"Letting me?" I questioned.

"What if he does something to you? I'm all the way over here. I'm telling you, he is a dodgy fella that one."

"I'll go to my appointments then stay with my mother, or in Charlotte with the girls until I've settled my affairs. Plus, the group trip to Miami is coming up. We can meet up there."

"You're staying here, and we'll both have to miss the trip," he said with his chest.

"I gave Shannon my word we would be there."

Mash paced around the studio, now clean and in order from when I arrived. His blood moon colored eyes looked at me. "I warned your little boy toy to stay away. I'm going to have to..."

I cut him off, "Do nothing. And don't you ever call him my boy toy again."

Our conversation died briefly, and I pointed to him. "This is exactly why I didn't want to tell you."

"I don't trust him." He gritted his teeth.

"Neither do I. But if you're so worried, come with me. I promise I'll make it worth your while," I hinted.

"I can't."

We were at an impasse. He wouldn't reveal why he couldn't come with me, and I didn't reveal I wanted him to be present for the next pregnancy appointment.

Mash saw me off for the airport. I couldn't shake the feeling that what he couldn't discuss with me, had something to do with his sobriety, or missed contractual engagements due to his habit. His secrecy occupied me as the driver maneuvered through the thick traffic until we were stuck.

Barely moving gave me time to think about my choice to return to the states alone. Mash's concern caused me to suddenly fear Lucas's passion for me. The desperation in his letter led me to wonder, '*Could he hurt me and the baby for rejecting him?*'

Impatient with the traffic and a sudden change of heart I asked the driver to take me back to the house. He rode the median to the next exit, and returned me where I belonged. I used my key to the front door and ran inside of the house, bursting through the studio door where I knew I would find Mash. "I don't want to be without you another minute," I said.

"Nadia, it's not what it looks like," he stuttered.

"It looks like you couldn't wait for me to leave."

"This was the last of it. I swear. I can't go back with you because I'm going to rehab. I sign in tomorrow. Please don't look at me like that," he begged.

"I don't know you!" I cried. "I won't be hitched to a junkie."

His face sank and his chest pounded intensely through his shirt. "A junkie? I'm not on the street begging people for money. I'm in the privacy of my home." His voice trembled.

"You've got a little something on your nose," I said and slammed the door.

I ran back to the car and ordered the driver to get me to my flight by any means. I replayed Mash's rehab confession over and over in my head as I boarded the plane, but the image of him sniffing made him unattractive in my eyes. And leaving him behind on the verge of tears hurt like hell, but I meant what I said. I **could not** and **would not** be attached to a junkie.

CHAPTER 50

Nadia

My world was in *The Upside Down*, and though I left the man I vowed to love for better or for worse thousands of miles away, he was still with me when I arrived back in the states.

His gift sat on the coffee table staring at me when I walked through the door of my condo, taunting me before I could settle in. It haunted me for two days after ignoring it and him, until I made the mistake of listening to his sad voicemails.

Hearing the grief and stress in his voice broke me. He was suffering, as was I, and avoiding his calls accomplished nothing. I felt his pain through the phone and could no longer be mad at him, when I realized what I feared the most was his disease.

Overcome with compassion and clarity, I stopped pretending I didn't care and answered the next time he called. "You worry the hell out of me," he said when I picked up.

"I apologize for not taking your call. I needed some time to process things."

"Call me selfish, but I need to know you are okay? Are you being careful? And aware of your surroundings?" His voice dragged.

"I am. I shouldn't have left you like that. I want you to know you aren't in this fight alone."

"You might love me after all. I thought I would have heard from you once you opened the box."

"It's still sitting on the table," I mumbled.

"Please, open it while I'm on the phone." He insisted.

Inside were the stunning boots I fancied over for months, along with a copy of the deed to the house, solely in my name. I held my breath as he called my name on the line. "It's yours. All yours. I'm a tenant living in your house," he joked.

"I've seen the bank statements. Nothing reflects a purchase this big."

"Stop playing detective. You said you wanted to be a homeowner — Have security. Now you have it. If anyone has to leave it'll be me."

"I'm coming home."

"I won't be out of here for a few weeks. I want to get well for you."

"Don't do it for me."

"I do everything for you."

"I know."

～

I began organizing the little I had in my apartment after our call. Still terrified of the unknown territory of addiction, but excited to finally be on the same page again.

For a second I contemplated leaving everything behind, flying back to London, and skipping the weekend with the gang. While wrestling with my decision, I ordered a pizza from the place Mash discovered, and called Khai to share the latest. She was rooting for us after all.

We agreed to sign the car over to my brother, keep the apartment as a weekend getaway for the group until the lease expired, and discussed how to divvy up the furniture when that day arrived. She convinced me to stay and allow Mash to do the work in the clinic. "You being so close by is only going to make him want to sign himself out early," she said. "I'll rally the group, and we can make it a party weekend in The A. Sit tight. We'll come down and keep you company."

"The couch isn't going to be enough. I'll pick up another floor mattress later on tonight," I added. "Hold on, my pizza is here."

I went upstairs to grab cash for a tip and looked out of the window before opening the door. "You cannot be here!" I shouted.

"Who are you *shouting at*?" Khai asked.

"Lucas is at the door," I whispered.

"I have to talk to you, Nadia!" He exclaimed.

"I don't want any trouble. Please, just leave," I begged.

"Are you alone?" he asked.

"Say no." Khai whispered on the phone as if Lucas could hear her.

"No. Jesus, Lucas. Get a clue. I haven't spoken to you in months. What do you want?"

"You." He sighed.

"Not going to happen. Now please leave."

"Is he telling you what to say? This doesn't sound like the girl I remember. It sounds like the flake who came to see me to size up his competition."

"You might have to call the police, girl," said Khai, still whispering.

"Did your soon to be ex-husband tell you he sucker punched me? I owe him one. Tell him to come out here and fight me. Winner gets you. Go ahead and kiss him goodbye. I didn't come here to lose."

"Lucas, go home, okay?"

"Do you know how long I've waited to hear you call my name?" He placed his palm against the door. "At least let me see you."

"I'm not opening this door." My brows raised.

"Then come to the window." His voice seductively lowered.

"No."

"Then I'm not leaving. But it's cool. I'll wait out here. Go ahead and pack a bag. You already have a ticket to fly out of here with me."

"I'll mail you a check for it. What do I owe you?"

"I don't take money from women. I'm a man, sweetheart."

My palms grew sweaty, and my chest pounded with pain. Nerves filled my stomach as I fought the urge to hurl. "I owe you an apology," I confessed. "I made a mistake and was wrong to get entangled with you. My note sent the wrong message. Do you still have it?"

"Let me see you, and I'll answer your question."

He must have heard the desperation in my voice, or sensed the fear flowing in my veins of the damage he could cause if he showed Mash my words when I bid him farewell.

I went to the window and let him see me through the screen while Khai continued to listen through the speaker. "Damn I wish you'd let me have you. Do you know how many nights I've dreamed about this moment? I can make you happy and forget about this clown you call a husband. He must not be home, or he would have come outside by now," he baited me.

"Do you still have my note?" I raised my voice.

"Not anymore. I burned it. I got upset you hadn't called and *swish*, I lit it in flames." He gestured an implosion with his fingers. "Why won't you admit you felt something for me?"

"I liked you, Lucas. As a friend. But nothing more."

"Bullshit. You saw we had chemistry, got scared, and cut me off."

He wasn't lying. *'But I was also being stupid and reckless in New York without knowing anything about this man.'*

"I thought you wanted to be my friend. Until you didn't. I made it clear I love my husband. You took advantage of my loneliness, and I almost fell for it."

"You can love two people, Nadia, and I think you do. If I have to share you with him, I will."

"Khai, this motherfucker is crazy," I whispered into the phone.

"Do I? Have to share you?" His voice shook.

"Why did you tell him we kissed?"

"He rubbed me the wrong way. I said it to get under his skin at the time, and it worked. You could have done better than him." He gloated and tugged on his beard.

"goodbye, Lucas."

"I'm not leaving."

"Okay. That's enough. You tried. He isn't responding to you being nice. Call the police, Nadia!" Khai yelled through the phone.

"I'm dialing 911 now," I said.

"Wouldn't be the first time I've been to jail. I'll go for you." He smirked.

"Fine. Sit out there and wait on them to cuff you. I'm done with this," I said, lowering the shades.

I walked away and he yelled loud enough for my neighbors to listen in. "Have dinner with me, and I'll leave! I promise. Have dinner with me tonight."

"I told you I'm not alone. I can't do that." I lied.

"Tomorrow night then. My hotel."

"Hell no." I laughed.

"You pick the place then."

"City Kitchen in midtown. Look it up. Nine o'clock. And no funny stuff."

"Tomorrow night it is." He smiled with hands in a praying pose, then walked off to his car with his chest poking out.

Khai scolded me as I wrote down the make and model of the car he was driving. "Have you lost your mind?!" She lashed out at me.

"Not completely," I replied.

"Why did you agree to meet up with him?"

"To get rid of him."

"And if he comes back?"

"I won't be here. I'm packing up now and getting the hell out of here. Tonight."

"Thank God!"

"I'll be at my folks'. Guess you all will have this place to yourselves for the weekend. I'll call you from the road after I've run a few things by Levi."

CHAPTER 51
Mash

Hearing Nadia call me a junkie felt like a slap to the face. I wasn't blowing near as much as blow as I used to. Then I heard myself. I sounded like an addict. And snorting the residue off the table was my wake up call.

When she left, I could tell she was done with me. The hatred and redness in her eyes I felt to my core. She was calm in her words, but her face couldn't disguise the disgust and contempt she felt for me in that moment. Her lack of emotion almost neared repulsion, and when she didn't answer my calls, I knew I fucked up. The silence was loud and I heard her.

The challenge of rehab was difficult without Nadia's support. My one phone call a day went unanswered for days, and having no communication with her made my nostrils itch. I was on the brink of checking myself out early to go find her, then she finally took my call.

Her forgiveness gave me hope I could beat my demon. She was returning to me, and knowing she was coming home in a matter of days gave me the strength and determination I lacked before to beat this setback. *'This time we were going to be as close to perfect as possible.'*

The walls were closing in on me close to a week inside. I had had enough of the facility and had to get out of there.

The receptionist summoned me to the office to take Nadia's call as

I contemplated signing myself out. "Are you able to have a serious conversation right now?" she asked. I sensed trouble in her tone.

"Something is up. Are you alright?"

She hesitated and let out a deep sigh before answering. "I want to make sure we are on the same page," she said. "It's time we grow up. We've been dysfunctional long enough. Do you agree?"

"Yes. I fell off the wagon for the last time. I hope you know that. Wait a minute. I thought we already had this discussion."

"I'm just making sure we're in sync from here on out. We have to be," she emphasized.

"You called me a junkie. That's all I needed to hear to get my shit together." I huffed.

"How are you feeling?"

"Almost back to normal. And you? I can tell something's wrong. You haven't changed your mind about coming back, have you?"

"No worries, I'm coming home," she said in a strange tone of voice, then took a deep sigh. "Um, you should also know I moved out of the condo, and will spend a few days with my mother before the trip..." She paused. "Because Lucas came by the apartment, and I didn't know how to tell you. But don't be upset. I left before there was any trouble, and I'm fine. I told you I could take care of myself," she blurted quickly in one breath.

"I warned that mother...I'm on the next flight."

"No! Levi is taking care of him."

"I appreciate Levi having my back, but this doesn't concern him. This is exactly why you need to be here. With me."

"You're right."

My anger left momentarily at the sound of words I had never heard spring from Nadia's mouth. "Did you agree with me?" I choked.

"I did."

"Make sure we mark today's date and time on the calendar when we get home."

The sound of her laughter temporarily deescalated my rage. A maniac stalking her infuriated me, and I lashed out at the doctors who confused my outbursts and behavior with withdrawal symptoms.

They refused to believe my rage stemmed from wanting to punch Lucas in the face again. But I knew my heart.

Completing the program was no longer my main focus, and I found myself at a crossroads— do what Nadia asked of me, or do what came naturally. Protect what was mine.

CHAPTER 52

Nadia

s I packed, my emotions ran high, fearing Lucas knew I was alone. His behavior rattled me. He seemed obsessed and unstable, and his domestic past made me fear for my safety when he didn't get his way.

As Olive said, he proved to be basic. I questioned everything he told me, and saw him for what he was—A random, serial pussy hound, avoiding commitment while suggesting he and Mash share me. *'Damn he almost had me.'*

As I tossed my bags into the car, I looked over my shoulders, and reflected on my stint in New York, and felt like a complete idiot. My bullshit was no better than Mash's bullshit, and I came to the realization, forgiveness has forever plagued me and served as my downfall.

Dr. Bartley told me years ago I needed to learn how to forgive myself for the mistakes I made, as well as forgive others. I purposely let her advice go over my head. I had forgiven Taylor and Isla, and reclaimed our friendship. I had forgiven Dylan and got over him, but I never forgave myself for all of the bad decisions I made.

I wasn't at peace internally because I regretted the years I spent pining after Dylan. The years I would never get back. I let his indiscretions give me insecurities because I felt he discarded me, and wasted years continuing to love him while I neglected myself. And when I learned Taylor was the reason he casted me aside, I allowed them to make me feel less than my worth, and carried the weight of their inflicted pain on me. Doubting myself, making poor choices, and most importantly forgetting who I was. *'No more.'*

I left one of my plants on the doorstep of my meddlesome neighbor, and placed the box of delivered pizza on the passenger seat. I cranked the car and left my lonely apartment in the rearview, with a new mindset to move on. I forgave myself for giving those who hurt me the power to change me. It felt good to finally arrive, as I let go of all of my baggage, and set myself free. Free to love, free to flourish, and free to be me.

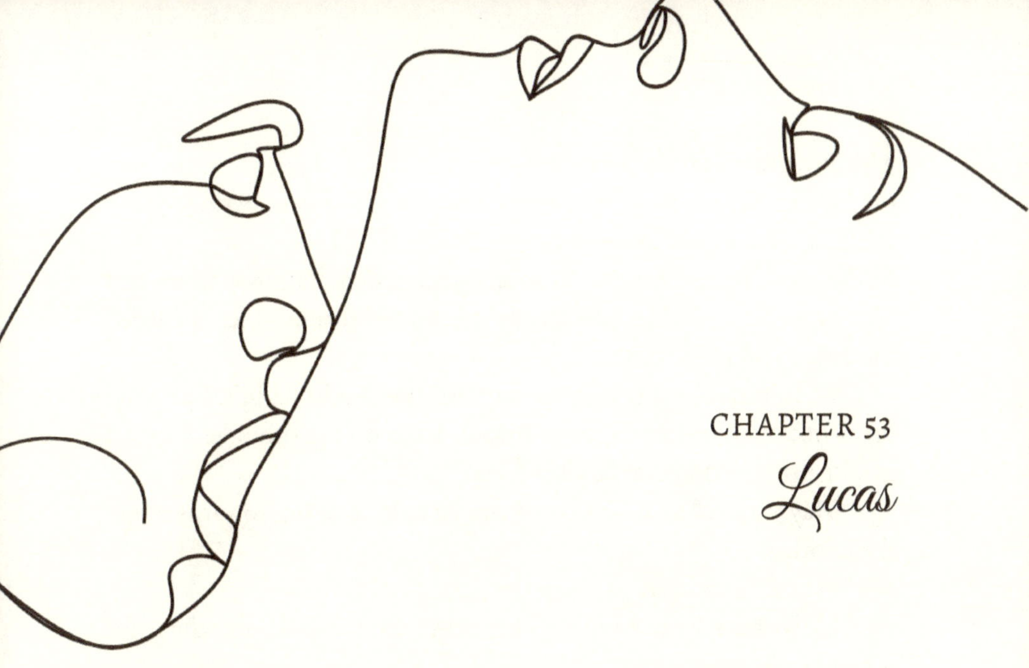

CHAPTER 53

Lucas

Nadia was destined to be mine once I found her. We could have avoided this whole song and dance if she had stayed in New York, and not fled from her feelings for me. I felt the rush of blood flowing inside of her when I had her pinned against my wall. She was scared because of how her body responded to me. I heard the same in her voice last night.

She sounded nervous and afraid to be seen with me, but I wish her husband could see how she lights up when I'm around. Bubbly and playful, yet somehow shy. He wouldn't be able to deny our connection if he saw what she and I shared

The long months I dreamed of her pretty brown eyes staring into mine nearly happened, but I didn't plan for a screen to be between us. Refusing me access into her world when women normally give themselves to me made her stand out from the rest. Won me over, in fact. She turned the tables on me and left me hanging with a stiff rod, and I planned to show her what she was missing out on.

～

The hostess looked back at me twice, and heads turned when I walked into City Kitchen. I could have added many more ladies to my roster without effort, but my heart was set on Nadia. Judging from the way the ladies were on me, I was a sure thing, and I was hopeful it was a good sign she would follow suit.

While I waited for Nadia to arrive, I ordered a screwdriver and appetizers for the table. Specifically the stuffed shrimp since she loved the dish so much on 57th.

Ten minutes later the shrimp arrived, but Nadia hadn't. I finished my drink, then ordered a second when a tap on my shoulder aroused me. I turned to find two familiar faces.

"May we sit?" asked one of them, already scooting towards me in the booth.

"Please." I scowled.

"How have you been?" The other one asked, signaling for someone to come over.

"Shannon. Right?"

"No one can ever forget me," she teased.

"And you're Khai." I parted my lips.

"How have you been?" Khai coldly replied.

I responded then inquired of Nadia's whereabouts. Before they answered, a group of people squeezed into the booth. "I'm confused. Where is Nadia?"

"What's up, man? You must be Lucas." One of the fellas held out his hand.

I leaned across the table and gave him a firm handshake. "Lucas Fleming, and you are?"

"Levi, and this is my wife Taylor."

"And this is my husband Manny, and Brian, Khai's husband," said Shannon.

"Nice to meet you all I guess. Can someone tell me what is going on, and where is Nadia?"

"Nadia is...Wait a minute. Let's at least order. I'm starving. And I hear the chicken and waffles are a must have here. What did you order, my man?" said Levi.

I sat astounded by the audacity of these people turning my intimate night with Nadia into a group function. The Levi character lifted his arm and signaled for the waitress to come over.

He placed a huge order for the table, damn near everything on the front page of the menu. I sat quietly waiting for my question to be answered, and observed these people while they waited for the waitress to return with their drinks.

The Taylor woman studied me hard while the others whispered amongst themselves after tasting their concoctions. They avoided giving me an answer and included me in their small talk.

We ate and drank for nearly an hour, then Shannon asked me, "So how did you find Nadia?" The chatter at the table died down. It was then I realized I was in the lion's den.

"I know people who know people. I take it this is a test of some sort, or she isn't coming? Which one is it?"

"Be cool, man. You were real chill when we hung out before," she added.

"You all have me cornered in here, and I don't want any trouble. If you will, let me out, and I'll be on my way," I said.

"There will be no trouble. I give you my word," said Levi.

"Why are all of you here?"

"Because our good friend asked us to be." Levi replied.

"And where is your 'good friend?'"

"With my best friend. Her husband."

The waitress brought shot glasses to the table, and Levi slid one towards me. "And which one sent you? Your best friend or Nadia?" I swallowed my shot with one gulp and eyed him.

"Does it matter?" He swallowed his shot and flinched.

"It does to me. Tell your good friend I don't ever give up on revenge. If you'll excuse me, I'll be on my way."

I rose my brows for Brian to get up so I could remove myself from their company. He didn't budge.

"Everybody leave us. I'll take care of the check," Levi ordered.

The party removed themselves, and Levi and I sat across from one another testing who would be the first to blink. "Look, I know I'm the bad guy here. And yes, I'm in the wrong, but my affairs are none of your business."

"You're one hundred percent correct. But Nadia is my business. She's practically my little sister. She asked me to speak on her behalf.

She wants you gone. Your persistence comes across as threatening, and so I'm asking you to please respect her wishes and leave her alone."

"She knows I wouldn't hurt her." I assured him.

"She knows about your priors. You know the domestic violence case against your wife," he said with a smug look on his face.

'Careful. You can easily catch a fist for your best friend.'

"Enough with this bullshit. Where is Nadia?" I rose my voice.

"See. You're not listening. Let my family enjoy their peace."

"Man to man. You wouldn't let another man snuff you and walk away."

"I might if I was trying to push up on his lady. You kissed his wife and he put hands on you. You had it coming. Don't lose everything you've worked hard for, over someone who wants nothing to do with you. A businessman with stalking and harassment charges— not ideal in this climate. And we all know money is power. You come nowhere close to her husband's family influence."

"His money doesn't intimidate me." I scoffed.

"It should." He warned.

I rose from the table and shook Levi's hand. "Tell Nadia if she ever changes her mind, she knows where to find me." I threw a Benjamin on the table for the tip and left.

My ass had been handed to me via third party, but I smiled on my way out of the restaurant. I had to give it to Nadia, she did her dirt classy and smart. Having me bombarded in public. What a strategist.

Every kiss we shared, including the ones I stole flashed before me as I drove away from the restaurant. I wasn't ready to let her go again, and though I said I would respect her wishes, I drove over to her place to see her one last time. "I see you came back!" Shouted the old woman in the window.

"Hello again, I don't mean to disturb you!" I shouted back.

"She isn't in there. She left with a bunch of bags. Didn't look like she was coming back if you ask me. Plus she gave our neighbor one of her plants. Didn't leave me anything!"

"I'm sure she didn't mean anything by it. I tell you what. I have some flowers in the car. I'll leave them down here for you. You take care of yourself!"

"Thank you sweetheart. If you ever need a shoulder to cry on you know where to find me!" she humorously offered.

"I sure do! Good night!"

Nadia forced me out of her life. A foreign fool was living the life with my woman, and the agony of defeat ate away at me. I drove away bursting with anger and energy, and found myself at the strip club from the week before.

I paid the whore who serviced me last time three hundred dollars to leave and be mine for the night. We went back to my hotel room, and I took my frustrations out on her gush. She dug her nails in my back while begging me not to stop. She needn't worry. I had months of built up aggression to deliver to her womb.

After I had my way with her, I threw her to the side and told her to grab her things and go. I went to the bathroom and removed the filled bag from my wood, took a piss, then turned on the water to wipe the whore off of me.

In the reflection of the mirror I noticed her rummaging through my pants. *'Typical whore, searching for more than what she earned.'*

I let the water run and snuck up on her, then held my hand out to strike her for the violation she had no time to commit. Thank goodness I wasn't completely shit-faced, or I would have gone through with it.

I lowered my hand and gave her a look of death instead. She grabbed what she could before I threw her out of my room. Half-naked on her walk of shame.

For the remainder of the night I lay wide awake, stroking my pipe, thinking of Nadia. Her sweet lips and perfect hips, unapologetically teasing my thoughts. I may not be the best man in the world, but I would have been to her. *'Damn I lost.'*

CHAPTER 54

Mash

Twelve days clean, and I was thinking clearly. It was too early to say I had gone cold turkey, but it was true. Nadia needed me, and that was reason enough to quit besides the fact how badly I yearned for her and her only.

With that wanker Lucas roaming about, I needed to be at her side, and out of this program. Talking once a day wasn't good enough. I worried about her safety every second I wasn't there to protect her until anxiety got the best of me.

I struggled with the notion if I was healthy and strong enough to leave every night. Then the front desk said I had a call, immediately sending my thoughts to think the worst. "How is it going in there?" asked Grams.

The biggest smile appeared on my face. Hearing her angelic voice was the sign I needed to know I was going to be okay. "It's coming along," I said, nervously nodding, her call was for the greater good.

"That makes me happy to hear. Nadia and her mother came to visit me. She told me what's been going on."

"Yeah we're working it out." I sighed.

"Good. I told Nadia no one is perfect and life always has speed bumps, but you have to keep on driving."

"Your granddaughter is in the driver's seat. I don't plan on getting out of the car if you know what I mean."

"Listen to you." She chuckled.

"How are you handling the heat?"

"Oh I'm doing mighty fine. I plan on hanging on as long as I can. Especially since my great-grandbaby is going to need me. Someone's *gotta* make sure the *youngins* coming in know the real secrets to life. You folks are too much into these computers and your devil music. It took me forever to figure out how to call you on this thing Nadia gave me. Slide up and right and foolishness."

"Nadia didn't mention her brother had another one on the way. Must have slipped her mind."

"I'm talking about you and Nadia's baby. She didn't tell me she was with child, but I dreamed I was catching fish on a lake. One look at her, and I knew."

I couldn't believe what came out of Gram's mouth. "Are you sure?" My face frowned, and my heart rate increased.

"A grandmother knows. No one can tell me different. I've been here a long time, you know."

"I love you, Grams. You're a real angel. Did you know that?"

"I've been called some things in my day, and angel ain't never been one of them." She cackled.

"Well, you are to me. I'll be seeing you real soon."

"I better." She hummed and ended the call.

Prano picked me up that evening as my busy mind jumped. I was chuffed to bits knowing my days of coming home to an empty house were numbered. News of Nadia giving me a lad of my own had me spiraling. I couldn't think of a time I was happier besides the morning I woke with her in my bed.

I prepared the house for her arrival, and as I cleaned I thought about the night she asked me to be gentle. *'I should have known then. No wonder she said it was time for us to grow up.'* Cupid really was far up her ass. With my arrow.

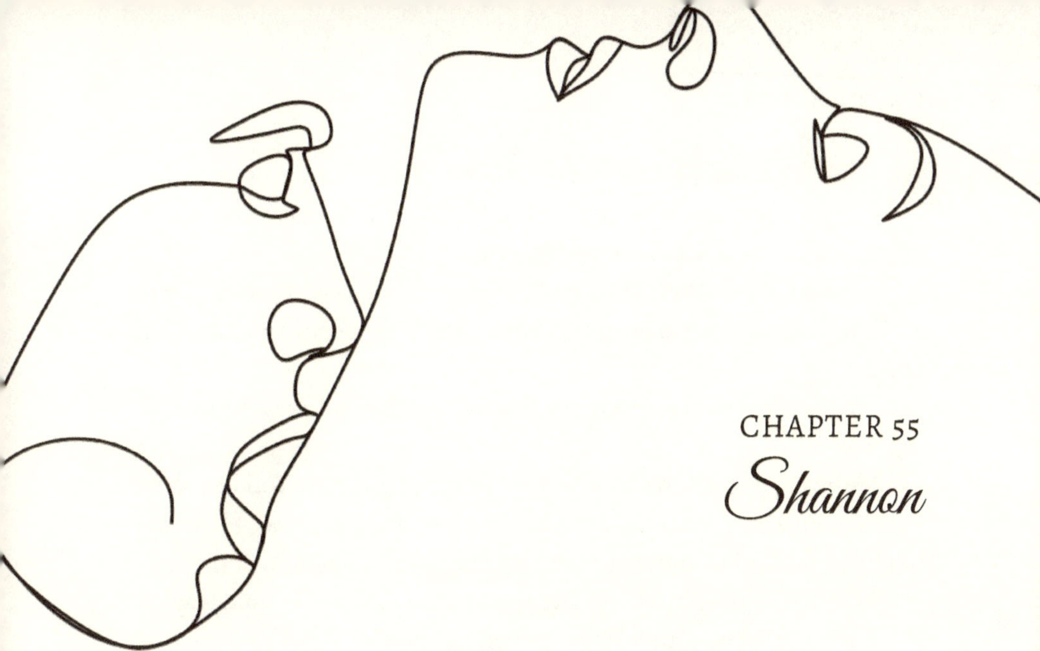

CHAPTER 55

Shannon

The pressure was on me to make this weekend perfect. Every time we went on vacations and getaways the trip went smoothly, except for California, and I wasn't about to be the one to fail.

Our home team was playing their season opener away in Miami, a *poppin'* city with much to do, so the planning was easier than I anticipated. Especially with Yohan's influence, making calls to his connects to get us on the list of the hottest venues.

We were shacked up on a beachfront luxury home, equipped with everything imaginable— two XL SUV's, swimming pool, enclosed deck, jet skis, and a secluded bonfire setup.

By sunset, just about everyone had arrived. We laid out near the bonfire while the guys barbecued on the pit, and roasted S'Mores. Not a good mix with alcohol.

The fire kept us warm from the cool breeze flowing in from the ocean. I popped in an old hip-hop mixtape to set the perfect mood of reminiscing about old times, and share stories of the good old days when we were wet behind the ears. "Throw some steaks and corn on the grill," I ordered the guys.

"Baby, we got this," Manny assured me. "You girls sit over there and let your weaves blow in the wind," he joked.

"You like pulling on this weave though." I rolled my eyes.

"Okay, you two. The night is still young and that's too much information," said Khai, calling time-out.

I ruffled her feathers further. "I'm sure Brian would love it if you let him pull on your hair, girl?" Khai glared at me and pointed her finger.

"You let me worry about my husband and mind your business," she replied.

"Why are you always so private? It's called girl talk. You can share a little something once in a while. You never contribute. Hell, you might be the OG of the group and teach us something new."

"The quiet ones truly are the freaky ones. I'm told," said Taylor. "Nadia is a quiet one, too. How are you doing over there?"

"I'm tired as hell." She dragged. "Travel takes a lot out of me these days."

"Levi was looking forward to Mash joining us. He was happy as hell y'all worked things out. Are you ready to give up all of this and abandon us again?"

Everyone listening in laughed, knowing Nadia's answer before she spoke. "Hell yeah. I miss my life over there. The fashionable yet grey vibe. Traveling in style to new places with my man. The TV shows. I almost didn't come this weekend."

"You miss your tea and crumpets," said Isla.

"She misses her hummus." I teased.

"I do miss him," she said. "Oh my God. I forgot to tell you all this. We were at lunch one day and he asked if I wanted to try the cilantro hummus on the menu. I legit had shits and giggles." Nadia's faced beamed in the light from the fire.

"Did you tell him?" I asked.

"No." She snickered. "But he kept looking at me strange because I couldn't stop cracking up."

"Why are y'all talking about hummus over there?" Manny interrupted.

We giggled as he stared at us dumbfounded.

"No reason. I forgot to buy some earlier. Is the food ready yet?" I answered.

Girl talk took a pause as we merged with the guys around the fire to eat. The songs on the mix tape brought up old memories, and created a flowing conversation allowing everyone to enjoy themselves. Until Isla opened her mouth.

"Let's play Taboo," she suggested.

"*Nooo*. You are the only here with no partner so you can't embarrass yourself," I said.

"Then how about Truth or Dare?"

My eyes shot darts in her direction. I thought to myself, *'Is this bitch dumb or something?'* "How is Truth or Dare different from Taboo?" I asked.

"Let's do it." Levi chimed in.

"How about Never Have I Ever?" Isla added.

"They are all the same. This trip is my baby. Those games start shit," I said.

"So Truth or Dare it is." Levi decided.

Sweat beads formed on most of our foreheads before the game started. We all had our fair share of secrets, side clicks, and besties, so playing an intrusive game was fifty percent fun, and fifty percent reckless. "Here are the rules," said Isla.

"We know the rules," we said in unison.

"Okay. Shannon, you are the host this weekend, so you ask the first question."

"Truth or Dare, Isla, did you break up with Evan, or did he dump you?" I demonized her with my eyes.

"Truth. He broke up with me." Isla lowered her head.

"What?!" we all screamed.

"He said he didn't want to be around our group because he felt like everyone was judging him for dating Nadia's friend."

"Please say you told him the real reason we were judging him," said Taylor.

"Which is what?" Levi asked.

The banter came to a halt while the girls and I collected ourselves. "I didn't have the heart to tell him we call him little meat," Isla said.

"Y'all call him what?" Levi stood up and ran in a circle. "You better not *say nothing* like that about me!" He pointed to Taylor.

"Enough about pencil dick. My turn. Manny, truth or dare. Is Shannon submissive when we aren't around?" Isla asked.

"Truth. She's not as boisterous at home," he answered.

"Really, babe. You were supposed to take the dare!" I chastised him.

"So you want everyone to think you run me like some chump? Nah. Now you answer a question. Did your mother tell you not to marry me?"

I looked at him dead in his eyes and grinned. "I'll take the dare." Our circle *ooh'd* and booed in between laughs.

"Wow," said Manny. "I dare you to tell Isla what you said about her the other night."

My eyes widened at the betrayal. "You must not want any action tonight." I threatened him. "I'll answer your question and still do the dare. My mother loves you, but she did not want me to marry you because athletes are known whores, and she feared I would be looking over my shoulder for the rest of my life. There. And now for the dare. Isla, I said you could find a man if you weren't so hateful. You get what you give. I still love you, though."

"Hateful?" She questioned me.

"You know you can be a certain way at times is all I'm saying. Like suggesting this game." I blinked my eyes at her nonstop and sipped on my drink.

"This is becoming toxic. Let's quit while we are ahead," Khai suggested.

"Not until we have a full round," I answered. "Khai, I pick you. Who is the breadwinner in your house?"

"Un uh, too personal. I'll take the dare."

"I dare you to drink two shots back to back."

I could have gone harder on her, but Khai was sweet. She also couldn't handle shots. "Chug chug chug chug!" We chanted.

"I hate this game." She choked and swallowed the shot.

Brian stroked her back until she caught a second wind, then whispered in Khai's ear. She called on Levi. "Levi, this one is for you. Truth or dare, what were you and Mash whispering about in Vegas?" Levi turned to Brian and lifted his hands.

"B. What kind of question is that? Your wife wasn't with us in Vegas, so why would she ask me that? New question!" he shouted. "I'm not breaking bro code," he added.

"Sounds like you are taking the dare then." Khai folded her arms.

"Go easy on me," Levi begged.

"I dare you to sit in the waves until you're soaked."

Levi headed towards the water as we cheered him on. "I thought we were cool, Khai!" he yelled, removing his shoes.

"I'm sorry!" Khai shouted.

The game took a fun turn. *'Thank God.'* Instead of sitting on the beach so the waves could soak him, Levi went in knee deep and dove into the water. We squealed and laughed as he returned to the circle completely soaked and shivering.

Khai covered him with a blanket and begged for forgiveness. Levi shook her hand and faced Brian.

"Brian, my man. The husband who will pay for the sins of his wife. Truth or dare, would you trade lives with anyone here, and if so who?"

"Truth. I would trade lives with Khai because she has it pretty damned good," Brian answered.

"No fair. You can't say your wife!" Levi mocked.

"Too late!" Brian argued.

"Group vote— I get a do over."

"As organizer of this trip, I say Levi gets to ask another question since Brian punked out with that answer," I intervened.

"New question. Who would be the worst person to date in this group?"

All eyes shifted in Brian's direction. "I'll take the dare this time," he said. Levi rubbed his hands together and grinned.

"I dare you to kiss Khai's feet with the sand on them."

Brian walked over to Khai and did more than kiss her feet. He licked both of her legs until he reached her feet, and kissed the top and bottom of them, then licked her big toe. "Don't get turned on out here," he teased his wife.

"Just ask your question so this stupid game can end," said Khai.

"Uh oh. The wife is ready to get to the bedroom." Brian joked. "Moving on. Taylor. Truth or dare. Would you give Levi a hall pass?"

"Truth. No. I'm too selfish," she answered.

"That's for damn sure," a few voices whispered.

"Last question!" I emphasized.

Taylor turned to Nadia. The circle grew quiet knowing the history of these two was bound to bring drama. "Nadia, truth or dare. Did you sleep with the guy in New York?"

"Seriously, Taylor! What is your problem?" we all yelled.

"What?! I don't think she is telling the whole truth about that situation. That whole hiding out in Atlanta fiasco has never sat right with me. Why would that man like her so much if they didn't do anything?"

Mumbles, grunts, and teeth sucking travelled around the circle. I replied to Taylor's question first.

"Because he's vain. She's beautiful. And refused him. That's why. Some men love a challenge. He was determined to win a bet within himself."

"And like a kid, he wanted what he couldn't have," said Khai.

"And he wanted to even the score because Mash kicked his ass," said Levi.

"Thanks, y'all. It's cool. I'll answer her question. I didn't sleep with him, so you can stop wondering about it. I sure have. And don't ever bring that man up again."

"Thank God you said no," added Brian.

"Sorry to disappoint. I didn't cheat on my husband. There's no breaking news here," Nadia replied.

"That man was adamant about knowing your whereabouts," said Taylor.

"Did anyone else catch on how he never answered the question on how he found her?" Manny asked.

"Guys, I really don't want to discuss this. I've moved on with my life."

"Everybody has had a turn so let's end this game and head inside," I said.

"Oh no. I get to ask a question, then it's over," said Nadia.

The look on her face was one I recognized. The look of petty and vengeance. Her eyes sparkled, and her lips curved on one side. Nadia's question was sure to be a kill shot.

I was sure Taylor felt the heat before the words left Nadia's mouth. We all did. She fidgeted in her seat, aware of the loaded weapon we all had against her.

The waves roared, but the beach appeared to be silent as all of our faces watched on in fear, waiting to see if Nadia was about to reveal Taylor's biggest betrayal, and finish her for good. "Taylor. Does Levi know?"

"Oh boy," I said.

"Know what?" he asked.

"Nadia," Khai whispered.

"Does Levi know what?" Taylor answered.

I shook my head side to side and muttered to Nadia, "Please don't do this now." She looked at me with sympathy, then a grin returned to her lips.

"Does Levi know what code California means?"

Myself, Khai, Isla, and even Taylor exhaled a sigh of relief. Nadia went with one of Taylor's shameful moments, and not the truth of Tyler's birth.

"You didn't say Truth or Dare," said Taylor.

"Do you really want me to start over?" Nadia threatened.

"No," Taylor replied, jittering in her chair. "Truth, the answer is no, Levi doesn't know what it means."

The sound of the waves coming ashore returned to my ears following a chorus of sighs. I told Manny the secret about Tyler's paternity, and apparently Khai had leaked the secret to Brian, too. "What is code California?" Levi asked.

"Since Isla suggested we play this ridiculous game, I think she should explain it." Nadia insisted.

"I overheard you say it once on the phone, and always wondered what it meant," Brian said to Khai.

Isla avoided eye contact with the group and stared into the fire. Nadia tapped her feet and ended the awkward silence. "Well, if Isla doesn't want to, I certainly can," she cattily remarked.

"Sorry, Taylor. So, during our last year of college we took a trip to L.A. Taylor met this guy during Freak-Nik who promised to show us a good time if we ever came out west. He was some rich kid whose parents lived in Beverly Hills, and their main house had a guest house in the back. Taylor stayed in the main house with him, while the rest of us huddled together out back. Until things turned weird. The guy came in our room over in the night and licked Khai's face and mine while we were sleeping. I was so shook I couldn't go back to sleep. In the morning, Khai and I told the girls. Taylor swore we were making it up because we were jealous."

"That sounds about right," said Levi.

"The next day he took us shopping in this ritzy area. Nadia was pressed to go in this expensive store and try on a dress she saw in the window. She got stuck in it and couldn't get it off. We all took turns tugging at it until it became comical. You had to be there to see how bent over she was. Anyway, we came up with code California if we ever got into a situation we needed help getting out of. Little did we know we would be using the code word sooner than later. We went back to the house, and the crazy dude promised he had friends coming over for a pool party he wanted to throw for us. Khai and myself refused to sleep another night in that house, so we packed up everybody's stuff."

"And left I presume?" Brian asked.

"Not quite. Taylor and Shannon took some pills the guy gave them and lost their minds. They were so out of sorts, they didn't realize hours had went by and not one of this guy's friends ever showed up. So Khai asked him, "When are your friends supposed to get here?" This fool said, "They are already here and pulled his dick out."

"What?!" the guys shrieked.

"No lie. The joke is, when he and Taylor would talk on the phone, he kept saying he had a dick of gold. We all thought he was bragging like most men do. But he literally meant it. This nut job had a glowing gold penis and said to us, "Meet my friends Willie and his partners Dingle and Dangle. Which one of you bitches is hopping on first?" All of us screamed, "California!" and hauled ass to the car. Except for

Taylor. She was so high we had to wrestle that weirdo to let her go. We found a cheap hotel, huddled up in one room, and got the hell out of California. That is how code California came about."

"Do me a favor. Don't tell anyone else that story. It takes away the sexiness of the group," Manny joked.

"A glowing gold penis?" Brian asked.

"We don't know if he spray painted it, or dipped it. All I know is we didn't talk for a long time in the car until Shannon's high came down and said, "Was I the only person to see a gold penis today?" We laughed like hyenas.

"Weirdest trip ever," said Isla.

"Are we even now Nadia?" Taylor asked.

"Never," she replied.

I rerouted everyone inside to cut the tension and noticed everyone was laughing about *goldie* except Levi. "I'm going to take a walk. I'll see y'all back inside," he said.

"Take a walk where?" Taylor asked.

Levi walked off and didn't answer. I pulled Isla to the side. "Don't make any more suggestions this weekend." She shrugged free from my grip and scoffed.

The damage was done. By the time I made it inside, Manny and Brian were in the den watching sports news, Nadia and Khai turned in early, and Taylor and Isla sat at the bar whispering near the kitchen.

Levi found his way back to the house and gave Taylor a dirty look. "I'm calling it a night, guys," he said. Taylor followed him into their bedroom and closed the door, but we could hear their argument through the walls. "I feel like I was duped," he said. "I have no idea who you are!"

"How can you be mad at me for something so long ago? It's called being young and stupid for a reason."

"You're a big liar, Taylor! You lie so much, you have no idea why that story pissed me off! Do you?!"

"A liar?"

"I remember your trip to California. I gave you money to go on that trip. And you used it to go see a dick painting freak!"

"Like you didn't *do shit wrong* when you were young!"

"Of course I did! But not scheme money out of you to go fuck some other girl! You should be mad at yourself right now. Your envy is showing. If you hadn't asked Nadia such a dumb ass question, what happened in California would still be a secret among you and your friends. And I'd still be walking around like the sapsucker of the year. And why does it seem everyone was relieved Nadia didn't ask that second question?"

"What am I a mind reader now?"

"No. Just a liar."

"You holier than thou motherfucker!"

"I'm not holy. Everyone has a past, but you…You…Yours has a lot of color in it. I wish I knew this before…"

"Before what? Before you married me! That's what you're thinking, right?!"

"Let's call it a night."

Taylor continued to yell, but Levi remained silent. I turned to Isla. "Thanks for ruining the weekend before it ever started," I said, and joined Manny in my quarters. Khai knocked on my door and I followed her into the hallway.

"I totally forgot Taylor was dating Levi when we went out west," she whispered.

"But Nadia didn't forget."

"Let's go check on her."

We barged into Nadia's room and shut the door behind us. "I heard everything all the way up here," she said.

"I'm so pissed right now. I had this weekend planned perfectly and now it's all going to shits because of a stupid game," I complained.

"I thought you were about to reveal Dylan was… you know. I totally forgot they were seeing each other back then," Khai admitted.

"I'm tired of Taylor *punking* me. She had no right bringing up Lucas. What if Mash was here?"

"Nadia has a point. I'm going to check her. But not tonight because Levi is doing a pretty good job of it."

"I'd bet money she wants to pursue him. She just doesn't know how."

Khai and I shared a look. "You agree with me don't you?" Nadia smirked.

"She was studying him hard at the restaurant."

"If I didn't love Levi like my own brother, I would have brought up the baby, but I don't want to hurt him like that."

"I was relieved you didn't." I sighed. "I could ring Isla's neck right now. Tonight is a disaster because of her."

"Shannon, don't be mad, but I'm thinking about flying out in the morning," said Nadia. "I should be with my husband."

"Nope. You can't leave."

Isla and Taylor waltzed in Nadia's room. "What are y'all talking about in here?"

"The noise complaint going on my renter's record," I said.

"I'm sorry the weekend got off to a rough start, but we can turn it around in the morning," said Isla. "To make it up to everyone, I'm going to cook breakfast, mix mimosas, and give a formal apology to the entire group."

"I'm good on apologies. I'm leaving in the morning," said Nadia.

"Why is that necessary? Since everyone is upset with me, I'll leave," said Taylor.

"It's not a competition," Nadia added.

Taylor looked as if Nadia snatched her wig and ran off with it. "What do you mean by that?"

"I think you know. And don't push me further." Nadia's face turned to stone. "You're lucky I kept my mouth shut out there. And don't act all tough. You were scared to death I was about to tell your little secret. And I should have. You slept with Dylan behind my back, tried to sway me into not being with Mash, and now you bring up Lucas for no reason at all. I should have asked you Truth or Dare, do you want to fuck Lucas?"

"Nadia! What has gotten into you?" said Khai.

"I do not want to sleep with your stalker!"

"Then why would you ask me that question? Go ahead and admit it. You want to add him to your rotation. Right? Be real with me for once. You either secretly hate me, or secretly wanna be me. Which is it?"

As I clutched my fake pearls, I met eyes with every one of us present for this lashing. One of Khai's hands draped her chest and the other held onto Nadia's arm as she sat with her mouth open. Isla's eyes were so big they nearly popped out of the socket and her hands covered her mouth. Nadia sat stone faced and surly with pressed lips and narrowing eyes. And Taylor stood next to me at the foot of the bed with eyes zeroed in and stuck in headlights like a deer. "Girl, the devil has gotten into you!" Taylor screamed, and lunged towards Nadia on the bed.

Nadia lunged forward and swung upward as I pulled Taylor back. Khai grabbed Nadia and pinned her to the bed. "I am not the jealous type!" Taylor screamed continuously.

The guys burst into Nadia's room and broke up the feud. "Taylor!" Levi screamed. "Stop shouting. Let's go to bed," he said, and removed Taylor from the room.

"I don't know what happened in here, but let's break up the *Bad Girls Club*," said Manny. "You all are ruining my baby's hard work. Sleep it off. We'll reset in the morning."

You could hear crickets on Taylor and Levi's side of the house. Not the case on my side. The football coach came and rectified the mess and deserved to be rewarded. We sounded like a Midwestern compound with headboards banging against the wall, mattresses squeaking, and screams of passion from our room.

Khai and Brian attempted to keep up, but the surprise came from Isla's room. Manny and I laughed ourselves to sleep at how good she was handling her business—herself.

In the morning I greeted her in the kitchen. "Make sure you wash those hands before you cook our breakfast." I teased. She nudged me and blushed of embarrassment. I raised my eyebrows to let her know I was serious.

Nadia came downstairs with her bags in tow. I convinced her to eat with us, and had Manny take them back up to her room.

As promised, Isla delivered a lengthy apology and fed us a mediocre breakfast which explained why she was still single. The tension was still present amongst us, so before we headed into the city, I pulled the girls out to the deck to talk things out. "If I have to buy sage sticks while we're in the city, say so now because we have to fix this disconnect. It's gone on for too long," I said. "Isla and Taylor, you both started this. Isla we accept your apology. Taylor, you instigated this feud with your question. I can't make you apologize. But you were wrong. Nadia..."

"I have a flight to catch." She interrupted my spill.

"I was going to say, You retaliated with the California story within reason, and also, I hope you got everything off of your chest last night because whew." I wiped my forehead. "That was a lot to take in."

"Everyone asked personal questions last night," Taylor said.

Accountability, Taylor. Look it up," said Khai. "Your question was out of line. You need to apologize so we can move on."

"As always, the room is against me."

"The only way we are going to solve this is to get to the root of the problem. What is it?" Khai asked.

Nadia folded her arms and Taylor bit her nails. I looked to Isla and Khai. "Do either of you know?" They both shrugged their shoulders.

"Nadia thinks she is better than me, and frankly I'm sick of it. She's gotten worse since London. You all didn't see how she was acting at his house, and frankly I didn't think it was fair of you to steal the spotlight on my wedding weekend— Hooking up with a stranger, all lovey dovey, when I was going through what I was going through."

"I didn't tell you to hook up with my ex."

"There it is. The judgement."

"You can't blame me for your guilt. You're miserable, and it has nothing to do with me."

"I also think you and Levi are a little too close for my taste."

"That is rich coming from you of all people."

"There it is again. The *judgey* face."

"Because you sound crazy. Levi is like a brother to me. You are creating shit about me in your head, and I don't know why."

"Because I'm not happy, like you said. Okay. Levi used to say Dylan wasn't good enough for you. I wonder if he would say the same thing about him not being good enough for me."

"Taylor, no one told you to fuck that loser," Nadia whispered with a sarcastic grin on her face.

"I don't know what I'm doing. I'm not happy."

"Because you love Dylan. Am I right?"

"I do."

"Then be with him, and set Levi free to find the happiness he deserves. He's too good of a man to be treated this way. I meant what I said in New York. I have no feelings or concern for Dylan whatsoever. He is your son's father. Go be a family if that's what you want. Just know what you're doing, *'cause* going from Levi to Dylan is going from sugar to shit."

"But please don't do it this weekend," I begged.

Taylor looked aloof with tears in her eyes. A breeze floated upwards to the deck, and we all exhaled. "If I leave Levi for Dylan, I'll be alienating myself from you all," Taylor confessed.

"No shade, but Mash and I said we would get Levi in the divorce."

"There it is. The holier than thou attitude."

"I said no shade. I was trying to be funny but also tell the truth. You're worried about the wrong things. You should be focused on your son."

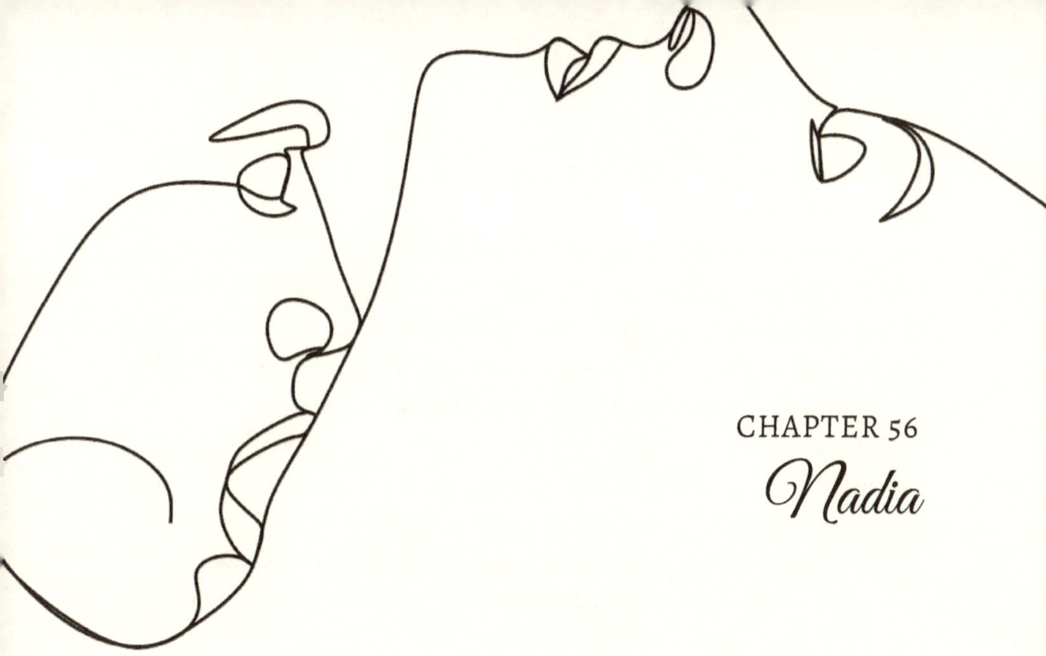

Nadia

Shannon convinced me to stay against my wishes. We went into town and explored the city, enjoying a spa day at the grand opening of To The Max.

I was pampered like the name of the salon, then had my makeup done by a lovely girl named Jen Carson, an artist whose talent hid the bags under my eyes, and brought out the glow buried beneath the stress on my skin. "Your secret is safe with me," she said when I sat in her chair.

"I beg your pardon?"

"I overheard your friends talking about going out later on. I can tell from the way your neck is jumping, you'd rather be off of your feet and taking it easy." She winked. "Don't worry. I'll make sure you look better than them tonight. I'm the best artist in here."

"Is that so?"

"Well, I should be. It is my place after all." She gloated.

"Congratulations. I admire successful women. Make sure you give me your card. I'm venturing out and could use a makeup artist with your skills the day I hit the red carpet."

She slipped me her card and escorted me to the lounge where Shannon revealed her big surprise. "When we get back to the house, put on your shades of blue you were asked to pack. We are going out on the water tonight."

We followed our orders and met downstairs. The path outback was lit by glass covered candles, leading the way in the weed covered sand and seashells to the pier. Squeals of excitement were drowned by the sounds of the ocean as we crossed the gangway and boarded a yacht Shannon rented for an evening tour of Miami's coast.

She led us to the top, fully catered with a spread of the many flavors of Miami, and another surprise on the outer deck. "Oh My God!" I shouted, jumping into the arms of Mash.

The sight of him sent me into my own private world. We made out like we were behind closed doors. "Do you have something to tell me?" He raised his brows and smiled.

"How did you know?"

"Grams called me, and I immediately came to be by your side. Tell me it's true." His eyes never looked happier.

"Yes. I'm having your baby," I said. "I never could get anything past Grams."

"Do they know?"

"I haven't said a word to anyone. I thought you should know first."

"Give me those lips one more time." He kissed me, filling me with a burst of energy. "She's having my baby!"

Congratulations came from all aboard minus one, but the different shades of blue outweighed the minor green. The mood on the water was serene as we circled a small distance not far from the house. We danced, we ate, we drank, and we laughed, then scattered off into sections while the men smoked cigars on the balcony.

Isla pointed out yet again, she was the only single person on the boat. "I'll ask Levi to hook you up with Drew," I suggested.

"He was going to come this weekend, but something happened with his company. He may show up to the game, but honestly, I hope he doesn't. I'm going to need a partner to live the single life with," said Taylor.

"You two didn't make up last night?" Isla grabbed Taylor's hand.

"We haven't said two words to one another all day. It is what it is.

But enough about me, let's talk about this baby. I should have known something was up. You were way harsh last night."

"Blame it on the hormones."

'That would be Taylor saying congratulations.'

"How far along are you?" Shannon asked.

"Three months this weekend."

"Which one of us will be the godmother? You better not say Olive." Shannon pouted.

"All of you, of course. And speaking of Olive, she

knows about Yohan's philandering ways."

"Does she know about me?"

"Only by moniker. You're either Thunder Thighs, Good Good, or RT3."

"Did he really put RT3 in his phone? I'm so flattered." Shannon blushed.

"You're RT3? What does it mean?"

Shannon giggled to herself. Shrieked to herself. And rocked her shoulders side to side. She looked over her shoulder then confessed. "Yohan does this thing that drives me insane. I've been trying to get Manny to do it, but he won't budge. Let's just say, he gives the best oral care I've ever experienced." She held up her finger. "But also, he goes back down on me after we've arrived, and licks me from the Rooter To The Tooter. RT3."

I fanned myself while Isla verified the details. "He does it every time?" she asked.

"Every time." Shannon grinned.

"I might mention that to Brian." Khai rose her brows and grinned.

We laughed at Khai's sudden freaky freedom flag blowing in the wind, then ended two hours of treading in the water. Still wound from the cosmic energy of the ocean, the house felt serene when we returned, and the night was spent filling the house with screeching mattresses, muffled pillow moans, and relentless orgasms coming from all of the rooms. Especially ours.

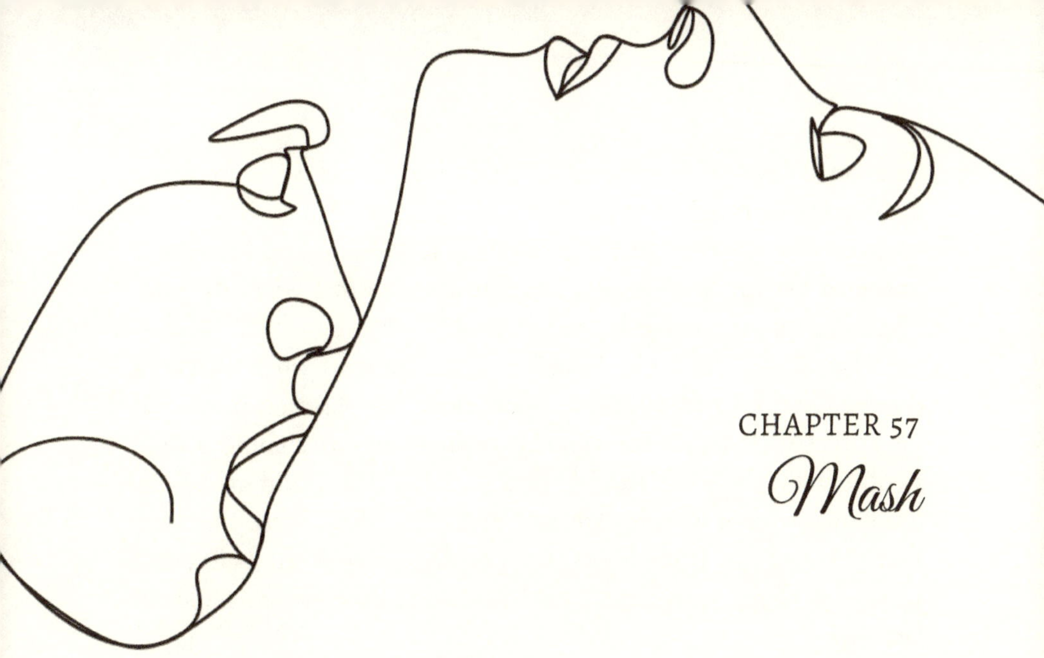

CHAPTER 57

Mash

My time in the air felt like a lifetime. I was in a hurry to feel Nadia's stomach, look into her eyes, and see myself in them when she confirmed a part of me was growing inside of her.

During the layover I grew anxious, but my nerves eventually settled once the plane took off and circled the Miami skyline.

The end of summer in the southern U.S. was significantly different than it was back in London. I had to peel off layers before we landed, then took a cab to the house. The driver studied me in the rearview as I appeared crazy, smiling on and off to myself. But I didn't care who stared or judged me. The past few months had been shit, and I was in need of this reunion.

I checked the time incessantly, waiting to see them march from the house onto the pier. Nadia was close, and I could feel her in my arms before she arrived on the boat. I couldn't wait for her to see me sober.

Her silhouette stuck out to me as soon as she stepped onto the deck, and the shade of blue she wore reminded me of our first date. I envisioned the way she looked the night we stood outside of Buckingham Palace and grinned to myself. She knew she was irresistible in blue. She knew wearing that color that night would make me desire her. And she was right.

Her skin glistened in the moonlight that night, and in rehab I imagined her lips kissing mine, and how she looked when she said, "We can go to your house."

The air was cool, but I wasn't. I was nervous when footsteps echoed aboard. I waited on the upper deck like Shannon instructed me with sweaty palms the closer high heels tapped coming up the steps. Finally, there she was. Me in these navy khakis, and my Nadia, luminous in cobalt. Pure radiance bottled in the silkiest chocolate skin. I could smell her fragrance sweeping towards me before she jumped into my arms, and I held her close, listening for a second heartbeat.

The breeze was steady but we embraced so tightly, our skin formed sweat beads from the heat between us. I kissed her honeyed lips then showed her off to everyone aboard and announced, "She's having my baby!"

Our friends applauded and interrupted our embrace with their own, then I made my way back to her. I wanted to keep my hands on her tiny hardened bump, but the fellas pulled me away to celebrate.

Levi congratulated me and passed around cigars for all the guys, but I could tell he had other things on his mind. "Look at you planting seeds." He tapped my chest with the back of his hand. "This is what you two needed. You were about to throw away a good thing."

"A magnificent thing," I added. "I'm so happy, man. What about you? How are things going?"

"Terrible. Be glad you got here a day late. I'm sure Nadia will catch you up. By chance do you know what code California means?"

"Ugh, yeah. Nadia told me during pillow talk one night." I sighed.

"Well, I learned about it last night."

We both raised our eyebrows and puffed our cigars. "Speaking of codes, do you know why the word hummus is so humorous?" I asked.

"I can't say I do." Levi sucked his teeth. "These women and their secrets. If it wasn't for Tyler, I would have filed for divorce a while ago. I have no idea who I'm married to. A new start might do me some good."

"Nadia and I go to the gym and box. You two should try it." I suggested.

"We would kill each other," he said, then led us in laughter.

"Then spend some time on my side of the world."

"I just might. You owe me one anyway. I dealt with ole boy for you." He shook his head.

"He's a prat." I seethed through my teeth.

"If that means a motherfucker, then you hit it on the nail. I see why you clocked his ass. He had it coming."

We finished our cigars and headed back inside with the ladies. I pulled Nadia away, and we tucked in a corner on the upper balcony. Her hair tickled my nose as I kept her warm, draping my arms around her.

I was on a natural high, following her around like the puppy she once claimed to be, and pounced on her with lightning speed when the boat docked and brought the evening to a close.

We had some making up to do. I was wild with desire, but afraid to unleash like the beast inside of me. Nadia, on the other hand, begged for the savage to come out. "I've been waiting for this all night," she said, gripping my wood at the tip. I caved immediately.

She mumbled indistinctly, but I wasn't listening. Her swirling tongue had all of my attention, sucking me front to back, up and down, and around my shaft to the bell-end. She bodied me intentionally so I wouldn't take long, and when she rose, she turned her back to me, spread her ass open, and invited me inside her warm walls. "I'm ready," she whispered.

"You're always ready," I teased. "Tell me if I go too deep," I warned her, and slowly slipped inside. "I don't want to hurt you."

"I'll tell you if you do. I missed you so much," she said, reaching back. "Now stop playing with me and put it all in," she demanded.

I followed her command, and she shivered like a train was going past the house. I wasn't far behind. My sweet was dripping wet, throbbing around my cock. I stroked deep and slow nonstop, fighting the urge to let loose like a canon. "*How you doing, my love?*" I asked.

"Mmm hmm," she moaned.

"I'm about to--"

"Go ahead, I'll get you back up," she cut me off.

Her feet tucked below my thighs as she bounced and squeezed. I whimpered. When she rode me with such intense, orchestrated grips, I always shot quicker. Especially when her folds pressed against me in a back shot. "Yes!" she shrieked. "I feel your head swelling. Let it out, big boy."

When Nadia talked dirty to me, I was over. I stroked her harder, and she gasped softly under her breath. I lost control and plunged my way into orgasmic delight, gripping her waist and pulling her back next to my chest. My fingers travelled forward and held her belly. "Is everything alright in there?" I asked, kissing her shoulder. She turned around and nodded, then kissed my lips as our souls spoke to one another. I was complete.

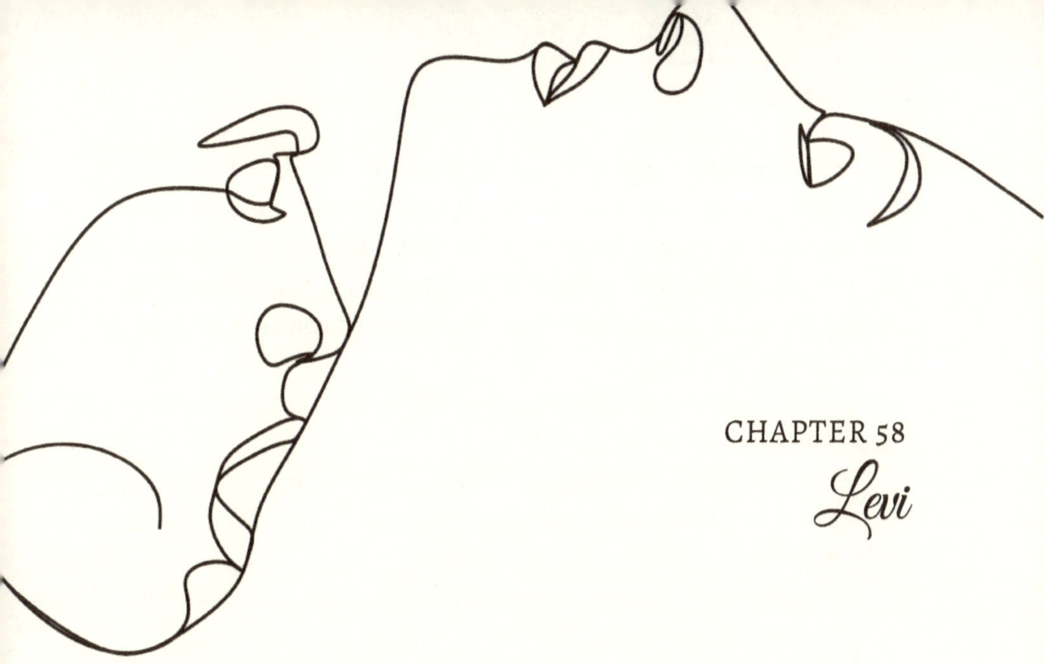

CHAPTER 58

Levi

The suite at the stadium was big enough for us to spread out and not be huddled under one another. I hadn't spoken to Taylor since our shameful display at the house Friday night, and my disdain for her put me in the familiar space of withdrawal when I learned about her affair. I buried the hurt and shame she brought upon me once. But after hearing about her shenanigans from early on, I accepted our marriage was an expensive sham.

I pretended to enjoy the game until Taylor's lying hazel eyes rested upon me. I had to get out of there before I further embarrassed myself. "We're winning by a landslide," I said. "I'm gonna step out and check out the shops. Maybe tailgate for a bit."

"I'll come with you. My cousins have a spot somewhere outside." Brian invited himself along.

The conversation with Brian was dry while we waited for the elevator. It arrived filled to capacity, forcing us to stand longer with a struggling conversation. "Are you sure it's cool I joined you?" Brian asked. "You seem like you need some time to yourself. Matter of fact, I'll go find my people's tent, and you can call me if you want to catch up."

"I was never going to the shops, B. I think I'll follow you and see what your fam has going on."

The elevator returned and took us down to the ground level. We sifted through the crowds to exit the gate, comfortable to speak freely with significant distance from the suite. "Let's find these fools so we can get you toasted and relaxed. Cheer up, man. You two will be alright. We've all had fights. That's marriage. It comes with being domesticated, I suppose."

"Easy for you to say. You're not the one in it." I huffed, uninterested in his opinion on the matter.

"True, but the past is the past. I admit I would be angry hearing about Khai and some other guy. But I'd also let it go. We have to. We're married."

"It appears only one of us is married in my house, B. Has Khai shared Taylor's little secret with you?"

Brian's face grimaced, and his shoulders tensed. He didn't have to answer verbally. I knew he knew. "I've never stepped out on my wife. And I could have several times. Even after we married. But the image of her being with someone else is recurrent in my head. I thought my being faithful would warrant the same in return. You know?"

"I've had my share of advances. Before and after Khai and I were married. When we were dating, I almost lost her, though. I was still playing around, and Khai grew suspicious and cut me off. We split for a while, then one night I saw her out with some cat. She was smiling a little too much with him, and I didn't like that shit. I had to tighten up and get her back," he confessed.

"How did you do it?"

"I went over and pulled up a chair to their table and told dude we had unfinished business."

"Say word."

"Word. I pulled out some cash and paid for their dinner and told him to leave. The rest is history."

"And how did you get past her you know...with ole boy?"

"Khai wasn't an easy lay, so in my mind I stopped it in time. Plus, I wasn't innocent, so I never asked and let it go."

"Do you ever hear from those other girls?"

"Yeah. One follows me online. Liking my pictures and shit. The other got married and invited me to the wedding. I wish you well, Ms. Thang, but I'm not coming to that shit." He cackled.

Brian gave me the laugh I needed to lighten up as we entered the wild and loud tailgating section. The aroma of mesquite, smoked food, tent-filled fans shouting at one another, and friendly camaraderie surrounded us.

Some folks wearing our team colors invited us over to join them for beers, and to taste their cook's special sauce. "Are y'all from the Queen City?" The cook's wife asked.

"Born and raised," Brian answered.

"Then help yourself to some barbecue. We have plenty," she offered.

"The beer is enough for me," I replied.

"I insist," the cook said. "My ribs are the best you'll ever try, and I look forward to you guys spreading the word about us back home. My sauce will be in stores soon."

We partook with their blessings and lost track of time, thanks to crowded conversations about our team's defense being the best in the league, the grill master's business plan, and wiping sauce from the sides of our mouths.

Khai called and summoned Brian back to the suite before we found his cousin's tent. "You go ahead without me. I'm going to hang out here for a little while longer," I told him.

I stayed in the tent and chatted with the chef long enough to taste the fresh slabs of ribs coming off of the grill. The tenderness and flavor had me hooked.

He gained a new customer, and I gained a new investment. After collecting his business card, I checked the status of the game. It was the end of the third quarter. I had overstayed my welcome with the grill master, and couldn't bring myself to return to the suite. I caught a taxi back to the house, packed my bags, and left Miami.

Taylor was livid I abandoned her. I could have handled my exit better, but for once I didn't think about her feelings. I thought about mine. And with the house to myself, I searched through her personal belongings. I went through coat pockets, purse zippers, and shoe boxes, and found nothing.

My father-in-law called to scold me, then I continued with my raid, checking Tyler's room for something to prove the feeling I had in my gut was right. After coming up empty handed, I gave up. Realizing I wasted the morning on a witch hunt, for Taylor's secrets were well kept.

I regrouped and grabbed a blanket from the chest and Tyler's favorite toy from his bed, then picked up my boy from my parent's house. We came back home after a half hour at the park, then I put him down for a nap. I watched him sleep trying to figure out how I was going to face his mother when her flight landed. Then it dawned on me. I didn't look under his bed.

I fumbled beneath the mattress while Tyler napped. He slept while I wiggled my forearm until my fingers felt a pointed edge. I assumed it was a loose spring and lifted the bed slightly to get a better view. The springs were all intact, and the pricking came from a sealed envelope addressed to Tyler.

I opened it, and read:

My dear boy,

It's your first birthday & I'm sorry I'm not there. Your mother and I have a lot of explaining to do when you get older, but I didn't want you to ever think I didn't want to be in your life. You mean the world to me. You come from a long line of broken households, and I didn't want this for you. When you are of age I will be waiting to do all the things I have imagined we would do together. Happy birthday. My first born son. I love you.

Your Dad

I seethed with rage. "Damn!" I shouted and woke the baby. I rubbed his back and put him back to sleep, then read the letter a second time in disbelief of the words. '*Who was this joker writing this letter to my boy?*' I wondered.

I looked at Tyler closely as he slept peacefully like the angel he is, and my mind drew another picture as a whirlwind of thoughts bombarded me. It broke my heart to think he wasn't mine, revealing the hidden violence in my bones as I punched a hole in the wall.

In the morning, I patched the hole and covered it with a photo waiting to be hung from the garage, then scheduled a paternity test.

As expected, Taylor arrived home ready to fight— yelling and cursing without any consideration of the baby. When she paused to catch her breath, I responded, "Tyler has already had a bath, and is sleeping. I'll be back in the morning for my things."

She followed me to the garage, slapping me, and kicking my car until I pulled out of the driveway. I looked at her one last time from my rearview, then grinned to myself when her shoe hit my window. I shook my head, then drove off, wishing my window was down so I could have taken her pump with me to piss her off further.

My night at a hotel near my office turned out to be a waste of money. Unable to sleep, I went to work earlier than normal, and watched the minutes turn on the clock. When it was time for the appointment, I scooped my boy from daycare and submitted to the paternity test— sick to my stomach.

We waited for Taylor to make it home in the foyer. Tyler was playing at my feet when she walked in ready to argue once again. She rolled her eyes at my luggage sitting at the door. "I see you don't plan on spending the night at home again," she said, blinking incessantly.

"Who is Tyler's father?" I asked.

"Come again?" She choked on her saliva.

"You've been busy, Taylor. Stop with the lies. Be a woman and tell me the truth for once. Who is he?"

"Where is this coming from?" She looked dumbfounded.

"You have been lying to me from the moment I met you. I saw the text on our honeymoon. You were seeing someone else while we were engaged."

"Levi."

"Do you even know who the father is? How many tricks have you been..."

She held up her hand. "Let me stop you right there. Don't sit over there and act all high and mighty with me. If you saw the text, why didn't you say anything?"

"Because I forgave you. I fooled myself to believe you were ending your affair, and taking our marriage seriously. How silly of me to think about the money we spent, and the embarrassment of calling it quits on the honeymoon. What were my friends going to think? What were my parents going to think, who warned me you were a little shifty and needed too much attention? I should have gotten an annulment when we made it home," I decreed.

"I wish you would have."

"So we agree, this is over. Now tell me. Who is his father? I know he isn't mine."

Her eyes turned pinkish in the corners with red dots forming like lasers. She held her lips tight and balled her fists. I braced myself to take more blows , determined not to leave until she answered me. "The test results say 0%," I said.

Her eyes dilated bigger than a coin. "I can't believe you had my baby tested behind my back."

"You don't have a leg to stand on when it comes to doing shit behind someone's back. Who is the father?!"

"It's Dylan!" she answered with a poisonous tongue and grin across her lips.

"Nadia's Dylan?" I confirmed in a high pitch tone.

"What do you mean 'Nadia's Dylan?'" Her eyes narrowed, lips pouted, and wiped the grin off of her face.

"Is he who you were texting on our honeymoon?"

"Yes."

A wicked laugh left my lips. I exhaled deeply and sucked my teeth. "You can have the house. If you can afford it. How many of our friends know?"

She huffed and folded her arms. "Have you ever had a thing for Nadia? I deserve to know after all these years."

"I wish I could hurt you right now and say yes, but the answer to your ridiculous question is no. You have always been jealous of her. And now you and her ex-boyfriend share a child. The boyfriend who treated her like shit, may I add. What a friend you are. Good luck to you." I chuckled on my way out.

"Get the hell out, Levi!"

She startled Tyler. I picked him up from the floor and kissed his cheeks. He laid his head on my shoulder, and I rubbed his back and whispered calmly in his ear.

"Give him to me!" Taylor continued to shout.

"I know he's not mine, but I'm not giving him to you until you calm down."

I pacified him in my arms while Taylor looked on with pure hatred for me in her eyes. He sucked on his finger and gripped tightly on my shirt. I sat with him and talked to him softly, holding back the tears in my eyes. "I don't want to leave him with you like this. Call your mother and see if he can spend the night with her until you get yourself settled."

She stomped out of the room, mumbling indistinctly. I sat with Tyler until my in-laws arrived, kissed Tyler goodbye, and carried my bags to my car. My father-in-law followed me outside. "What's going on here, son?" he inquired.

"I'm sure Taylor wants to give you her side of the story," I replied respectfully.

"But I'm asking you."

"We have called it."

"Son, we spent a lot of money on the wedding. How can you walk away from your family so easily?"

"Tyler is not my son," I announced stone faced.

"Say what?"

"You've been a great father to me, sir. But I have to get going."

We shook hands, and I drove away with shattered dreams. The tears I held back finally fell when the loneliness settled in, and the images of Taylor and Dylan agitated me through a sleepless night.

I agonized for weeks. The wife I adored stole my options, my dignity, and my son. Teaching me a valuable life lesson. Love can quickly turn into hate, and this was now my reality.

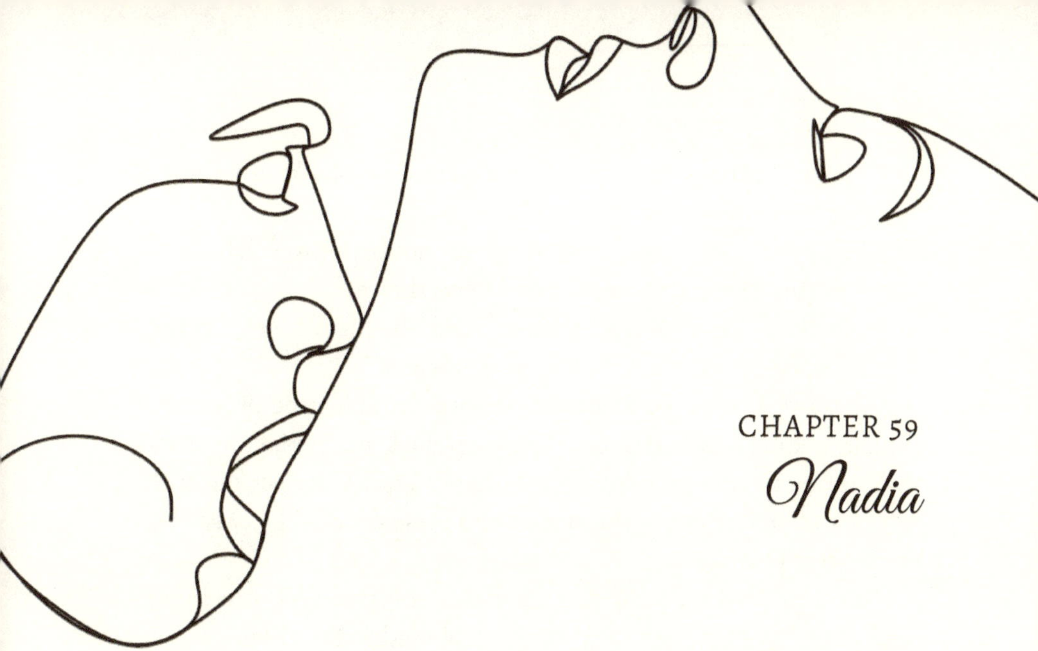

The holidays were difficult for some of us. Levi especially. Mash and I insisted he join us at Yohan and Olive's New Year's Eve Bash. It was the perfect way to thank him for fixing my Fleming Foul.

Olive did me a solid and introduced him to some of her friends. I didn't know who he ended up connecting with, but needless to say he was occupied for days after the party.

A few weeks later, we met the gang, minus Taylor, in Utah for the premiere showing of my short film Yohan brought to life. I was in the beginning of my last trimester, stretching out my sweaters and absorbing confidence from everyone who came to support.

An unlikely fivesome, Olive, Khai, Shannon, Isla and myself met in a bistro down from the hotel. It was the buffer space I needed to test Shannon's behavior around Olive. I led with, "Did you three drive Manny crazy on the plane?"

"He's flying in later on tonight." Shannon smirked at me.

I quickly grew nervous.

"Look at you. You can't hide your stomach anymore," she deflected.

"I know. I tried for as long as I could. You all met Olive in Paris, right?"

"Hello." Shannon leaned over and hugged Olive. "Yeah we met at one of those parties. How are you?"

"Happy to get a change of scenery, but not happy to still be in the cold. I'm long overdue for some sun." Olive shivered.

"I couldn't agree with you more," said Shannon. "We all should visit someplace tropical before the baby gets here."

Khai and I side-eyed Shannon. She was handling the presence of Yohan's leading lady better than I had expected, and testing my nerves with her sneaky motives. My eyes shifted towards Olive, sitting at the end of the table clueless she was in the presence of RT3. My chest burned from betrayal.

"Yohan reserved a room at a cigar club tonight. Will your significant other arrive in time to join them?" Olive asked Shannon.

"My husband should be arriving no later than seven o'clock," she replied.

"Great. He'll have plenty of time to settle in and join them. As for us divas, I booked an extra room and have a special night of pampering, amenities, and entertainment planned. You're all invited. I won't take no for an answer." She stared each of us in the eyes.

"We would love to," Shannon answered for us.

"Great. I'll see you all then. Ciao." Olive waved as she strutted out of the bistro.

"*Ciao.*" Shannon frowned and mocked her.

I braced myself for whatever was about to fly from Shannon's mouth. "What shall my excuse be for not attending that shit?" Shannon said.

"Oh, you're going," Khai replied. "We are keeping a close eye on you this weekend."

"Please." Shannon placed the back of her palm in front of her face. "You all know if I want to do something, I'm going to do it."

"How, with your husband in town?" I asked.

"Not to mention he's going to be smoking cigars with Yohan tonight."

"I've held up my end of the bargain. I was nice to your little friend. How did I do?"

I glared at Shannon and huffed. "You really make me uncomfortable," I said. Shannon stuck her tongue out at me and Isla chimed in.

"Taylor asked me to pass along her well wishes for you this weekend."

"I would have invited her, but Levi is here, and I think I have the right to be selfish this weekend. No drama," I said looking back at Shannon. "She said she would only come if Dylan was welcome. So, of course, I told her we would see her on the next one."

"I wish I knew what direction they were headed in. I definitely would have left him home this weekend if I was her. But hey. She continues to dig herself in a hole." Isla scrunched her lips.

"Especially when he refused to move in together," Khai added.

"Yes!!!" Isla's voice travelled past our table. "I confronted him, and to be honest, the brother is plain shady. He caused this woman to lose her friend, her husband, and her house. He wouldn't shack up to help with the baby full time, and wouldn't confirm if the rumors were true about him throwing and catching, so now he might be risking her health." Isla paused to catch her breath.

"What?!" We all gasped.

"I heard that rumor, but they say it about everybody these days." Shannon shrugged her shoulders.

With the conversation going from one extreme to the next, we wrapped up lunch and strolled through the exhibits, then stopped by a day party Mash was working.

They stayed at the party when I left to meet Yohan to prepare for our Q&A session, completely exhausted with no time to rest as I met up with the ladies in Olive's reserved suite.

Shirtless men opened the door, served trays of food and champagne, and danced in corners. "I may have misjudged Ms. Olive," Shannon whispered.

"Does this mean you're going to stop cheating with her man?" Isla asked.

Shannon ignored the question and grooved to the music in the background. "Look, our host is about to speak." She smirked.

"Welcome to The Olive Hour. Drink, eat, and enjoy that of your choosing this evening. On my soon to be husband's dime." She laughed.

More shirtless men walked from the back of the suite. She had male manicurists, masseuses, estheticians, and make-up artists divided into sections of the room. "I have to give it to your new best friend. She knows how to live this lifestyle," Shannon whispered in my ear. A certain sadness could be heard in her voice, and her eyes didn't shine with mischief as they had in the bistro.

Olive planned the perfect way to spend opening night at the festival, and surprised everyone in attendance with a designer clutch bag full of luxury samples and gift cards. The wait staff turned into exotic dancers once the pampering was complete, and when the fun was all over, she announced the get together was actually her bachelorette party. "Yohan and I are eloping in Vegas after the festival!"

I glimpsed at Shannon, wearing her poker face as I congratulated Olive. "Why didn't you tell me you two were doing the Vegas thing?" I asked.

"He sprung it on me as we boarded the plane. I put this shindig together today. Of course, with the help of his team and the concierge."

"I'm happy for you two. You have to come by and tell me all about it when you return."

"I will. I'll be spending all day tomorrow fitting for a dress, so I'll miss the showing. Can you forgive me?"

"You don't need my forgiveness. You're getting married." I squeezed her hand.

The girls and I retreated to Isla's room, the only private room amongst the group. Khai asked the burning question, "Are you okay, Shannon?"

"Why wouldn't I be? I'm married. He is about to be married. It is what it is," she answered without making any eye contact, and walked out of the room.

We didn't believe her spiel. She liked Yohan more than she led on, and was bothered by the way Olive flaunted him and their wealth in front of her. "Watch her for me, please?" I asked Khai and Isla. "I need to turn in."

I was asleep when Mash strolled in. He woke me, massaging my sore feet. "Today's the big day," he said, moving his hands upward on my legs.

"I'm ready to get it over with."

"Ready to get it over with?" He frowned. "This is the just the beginning."

"I'm worried about the backlash. Could be the pregnancy talking."

Seven o'clock arrived faster than I anticipated after a day filled with features, actor spotlights, and meet and greets. The lights dimmed in the audience, and my legs trembled forcefully. The row of chairs seated near me shook, bringing attention to my nervous face.

Yohan grabbed my knee. "I would have advised you to take a drink beforehand, but...the baby." He chuckled. "I'm removing my hand now before someone photographs it on your leg and turns this into a scandal. Then again, any publicity is good publicity," he joked, and lifted his fingers slowly. "You know I have two girlfriends in here watching me like a hawk."

I laughed at him making fun of his situation, and the vibration in my thighs slowly calmed. I pressed them together. "You mean your soon to be wife, and my friend you need to let go." I rose my brows at him, then glanced over at Shannon. "I told Shannon to end it with you."

Yohan sighed and settled in his seat. "I suspect she will after Olive's stunt with the bachelorette party. I love Olive, I do, but if I had known Shannon before, things might be different," he admitted.

"Oh God. Stop talking. I don't want to know anymore. Don't put me in the middle," I begged.

"You're such a square, Nadia." He laughed.

I made eye contact with Mash, clueless to what I was eluding to. His top lip puckered before he grinned on the side of his mouth. I shifted my eyes back towards the screen.

Hearing the audience laugh at the punch lines in my piece won me over, and the sound of clapping and cheering when the lights turned on settled my nerves.

"I knew I had a hit on my hands," said Yohan.

"I will forever be grateful you gave a newbie like me a shot." We shook hands.

"Now we go onstage and answer a few questions." He gestured the way. "Ladies first."

"Don't let me ramble," I said under my breath.

"If you're asked a question you aren't comfortable answering, do like we practiced. I'll save you."

Yohan saved me a few times during the Q&A until I was asked where I got the idea to write the short. As I stumbled in my response, the audience's stares petrified me. Shannon heckled, "Go ahead and tell them it's about me! I'm her best friend, y'all!" The audience laughed, and my speech settled.

"I wrote this out of fear I would never find my true self." I looked at Mash.

Yohan chimed in and lightened the mood. "Isn't her honesty refreshing? It's what attracted me to her work." The viewers applauded, and the session came to a close.

As I walked down the steps on the side of the stage, Mash presented me with roses and an endearing kiss. "I'm proud of you. You've arrived." He smiled. "One more thing. You have found yourself."

Yohan interrupted, "Nadia, have your entourage come to the suite for dinner. We'll head over to the after party from there."

Following orders, we met in the soon to be newlyweds' suite. Tables were shaped into two rectangles as hors d'oeuvres floated around the room to accommodate the mingling guests. Yohan tapped on his glass and toasted to our success. I blushed as clinking flutes offered us cheers, then stuffed my face on a four-course meal prepared by a world renowned chef.

Guests mingled to discuss the film after dinner was served. Mash stole my attention, lightly pinching my side. "What does this prick want?" he mumbled.

I turned to my left, greeted by Chili. "I arrived to the screening late, but I hear we got rave reviews," he said. "Congratulations."

"Yeah we did. Congratulations to you as well. You starred in it." I said through my teeth and a fake smile.

"Nice to see you both again." He placed his hand out in front of Mash. "How was your last tour? You are making some serious moves, man."

I stared Mash in the eyes until he countered with a handshake. "Yeah," Mash said, then barely embraced his hand. "Let's talk a walk."

Chili's eyes grew big. "Look, I actually came over to apologize to you both. I crossed the line and was hoping to leave all of that in the past and move forward."

"We accept," I answered.

Mash scowled at him. "My wife has apparently spoken for me. You take it easy."

"And congratulations on this, too." He pointed to my stomach.

"Thanks," Mash answered. "Glad you could make it out."

I hid my lips as Mash dismissed him, then skipped on the after party. Mash returned over in the night with bandages on his face, and bruises on his chest with the goofiest smile on his lips boasting about how he handled himself. "You should have seen the other guy," he said.

"I don't care about the other guy," I professed.

Seeing him riled up turned me on. I couldn't help myself. I initiated contact. "You feel like...you know...it's been a minute," I said.

"You know I'm worried about hurting you."

"I'll be fine. And I want it how you used to give it to me."

My God the frustration I felt having to settle for a gentle session. If I had gotten my way, I would have slept like the baby inside of me. Instead, I laid in bed rubbing on his scruff until he passed out, then traced the bruise on his chest, wondering if his temper would ever flame out.

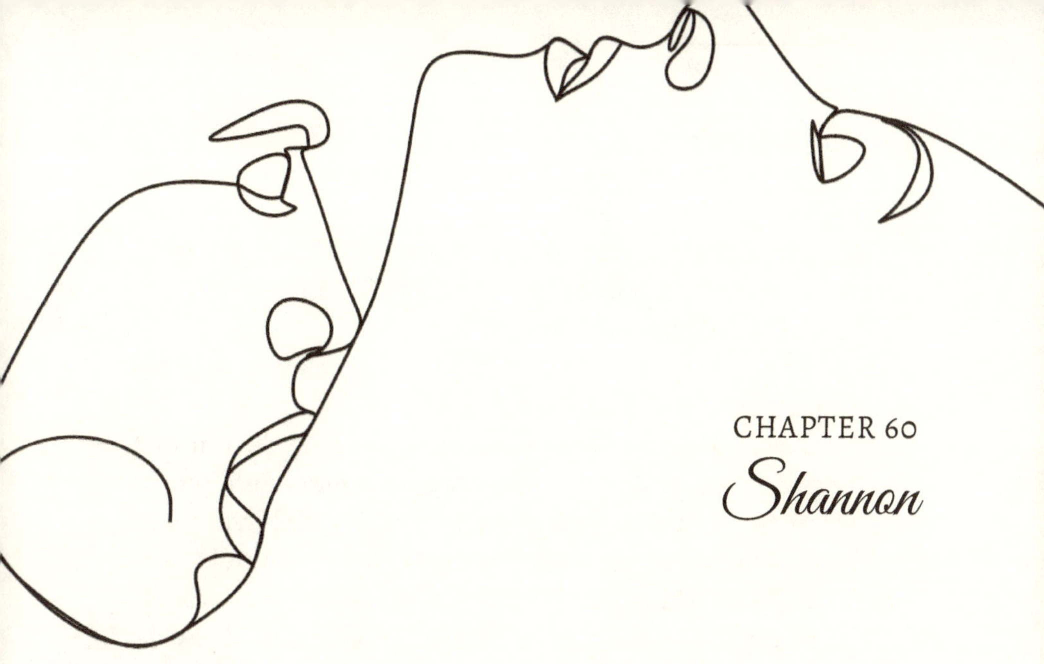

CHAPTER 60

Shannon

The after party was crowded, providing an easy exit for Yohan and I to get some one on one time. Something about our dynamic shifted, but before we could figure it out, Khai began texting me **California** like a maniac.

My pants were half-zipped and my buttons undone when I said goodbye to Yogi. It felt like the final goodbye— like we knew this was the last time we were ever going to be together, but neither of us would say the words out loud. We loved each other, and whatever unspoken bond we left behind in the room, I already missed.

I sadly kissed my lover and hurried back to the party, lashing out at Khai for interrupting my rendezvous. She warned me Olive was circling the room, and I apologized for barking at her for having my back. As we were making light of the situation, Khai grabbed my arm and pointed into the crowd, "One more thing. Lucas is here."

We grabbed the guys and gathered at the side of Mash's booth. When he finished his set, he beat us to the punch and told us he saw him in the crowd, too. We were so heavily engaged with one another, none of us noticed him standing behind us. Levi stood in front of all the girls, and Mash stepped forward, "Are you stalking me now? Or are you a fanboy?"

Lucas stepped in his face. "I told you I would get my revenge. Where is baby girl?" He grinned.

Mash formed a fist, and Manny intervened. "There are ladies present, cameras all around, and heavy security. Take this outside."

"Mash. Don't do it," said Khai and Levi.

He walked over to security and whispered something in their ear, then turned around and said to Lucas, "Let's go!"

We followed Mash and the two security guards to the rear exit. Khai begged Levi and Brian to talk some sense into Mash, but he wasn't listening. He had the look of the devil in his eye when he stared at Lucas, and Lucas had the eye of the tiger in his. "Nadia told us to babysit him," Khai whispered. "We can't let him do this. It's foolish."

Not a second was wasted. Mash took off his jacket and threw the first punch, hitting Lucas in the mouth. The condensation from his mouth formed a cloud, and all the guys sounded off, "Oooooh!"

"I told you, you hit like a bitch," said Lucas.

"This guy is mad disrespectful, Mash. Hit him again," Manny ordered.

Mash was way ahead of Manny's request. He landed a second punch to Lucas's chin, causing his head to fly backwards. "You can't say that one was weak. Hell, I felt it." Manny laughed out loud.

Lucas didn't insult Mash after feeling the heat from his fists and rushed him. They tussled, exchanging blow after blow as the frozen clouds from their mouths dripped of blood. Out of nowhere, Mash landed a right hook to Lucas's ear, forcing him into the circle surrounding them.

One of the security guards asked me, "What is this all about?"

Isla happily butted in and explained, "The black one is stalking the white one's wife."

"What a way to sum it up," said Khai.

"How would you describe it?" Isla asked.

"You could have said the taller one is stalking the smaller one's wife."

"I see your point. Give me a pass. It's cold as shit out here." She turned and smiled at the security guard.

"Get him off of you, Mash!" I shouted.

"You like this, don't you?" Khai scowled at me.

"Mmm hmm. Yes. I'm enjoying this very much. Something about a man showing his strength turns me on," I replied.

"*You here* with someone?" the other security guard asked.

"Yes, she is. But I'm not." Isla smiled.

The fight took a turn, and Lucas landed some stunners to Mash's lip and cheek. He then fell backwards into the circle. The guys threw him back towards Lucas who taunted him. "I don't hear your people talking shit now. Do I?" he bragged.

"Knock his ass out, Mash!" I shouted.

Mash started moving his feet and dodging Lucas's jabs. Lucas grew winded. "Fight me, prick, or are you ready to call uncle?" Mash teased.

Lucas jabbed Mash in the chest and stomach, landing a few in a row, then missing the next couple of swings. Mash blocked some of the punches, but was pushed against the wall as he moved. Lucas then pinned him against the bricks and delivered body blows to his side.

I got scared when Mash kneeled over, but then he stunned Lucas with an uppercut combination to the stomach and jaw. Lucas stumbled back. "I told Nadia I hate your punk ass." Mash walked towards him and swung, knocking him down on the snow-covered rocks.

Lucas began pummeling upwards, but never landed a direct hit. Mash dug deep and began striking him over and over, then choking him until the guys pulled him off of his tired body. He broke free from their grasp and followed Lucas crawling towards the wall. He grabbed the top of a trash can, and slammed it against Lucas's limp body. "Stay the fuck away from my family!" he roared.

"Okay, Mash," said Levi, holding him back.

"Pick his arse up and get him out of here!" Mash yelled to the guards.

We came inside from the cold, shivering our asses off, and huddled near the exit while the guys packed up Mash's set. "I'm going to say this, and I mean nothing shady by it. I'm turned on, too," said Isla.

"I know right." I slapped her hand.

"He's Nadia's husband and all, but if his fine ass fought over me like he did tonight, he would be in for the ride of his life. Don't tell her I said that." Isla swore us to secrecy.

"We won't. There's enough discord in our circle."

"Mr. Security Guard might get called up to my room tonight," Isla added.

"Don't do it!" said Khai. "Then again, have fun. Just be safe."

It was the quietest we had ever been. Mash gathered us all around. "No one mention this to Nadia," he said. "I'll tell her about tonight, after the baby is born."

"How are you going to explain those cuts on your face?" I asked.

"I have cuts on my face?" His voice rose as he pressed his fingers on his cheeks, searching for gashes.

"Everyone come to my room. You, too." Isla pointed to one of the security guards.

She put her nurse skills to use, and cleaned the cuts on Mash's face. When the last bandage was taped into place, he thanked us and took advantage of our sympathy. "By chance do you girls know why Nadia laughs at the mention of hummus?"

We glanced at each other and burst into laughter. Dying to know our secret, but concerned with déjà vu, Levi interjected, "If it's anything like the California story, don't tell him."

"Should we?" Isla asked.

"Can we?" Khai asked.

"Why not?" I said. "Hummus refers to you," I answered.

"Me?"

"It's our code word to describe non-*melanated* men."

"What the hell goes on when you girls get together?" Levi asked.

Mash stared at the carpet and finally laughed.

"Wow," he said. "I'm relieved it wasn't something bad. She had me going in circles with that one."

"Good grief. You women are animals," said Brian.

"And on that note, we are turning in. Ladies, remember— breakfast in the morning. Don't be late," Khai reminded us.

"And no one tell Nadia that wanker was here." Mash repeated.

The temperature during our walk down the snow shoveled sidewalk felt as cold as it did when we were watching the brawl in the back alley. The vibe was bittersweet knowing we were about to say goodbye to Nadia once again, but would soon link up in a few months to welcome her baby.

The barista drew our faces in our beverages, humoring us by drawing Khai's head extremely big in her latte. We laughed until we cried. "I should report him to corporate. My head doesn't look like this," she fumed, and turned to give him the evil eye. He winked his eye at her and blew her a kiss, then brought complimentary scones to the table.

"I had to get your attention somehow," he said.

Khai blushed and stopped complaining.

"I see a ring on your finger. You know where to find me if that doesn't work out. You ladies have a good day." He smiled and dropped a folded napkin with his number written on it.

"You didn't see that coming, did you?" I said.

"You didn't see last night coming," Khai shot back at me.

"What did she do?" Nadia asked.

"Nothing but talk, thanks to your snitch. And before you lose your cool, you'll be happy to know Yohan and I called it quits last night."

"Thank God!" Nadia testified. "I am relieved. Now can one of you tell me why my husband came to me bruised last night?"

"No, but we can tell you he knows what hummus means."

Nadia's face went blank, and her cheeks turned redder than when we were outside in the cold. "Who blabbed?"

"We all did."

"Well, that would explain why he was grinning from ear to ear when he got in. But none of you saw the commotion last night? Mash has a nick on his lip and bruises on his chest, but only wanted to talk about how bad the other guy looked."

Isla chuckled to herself. "I'm prying here. Did you get turned on seeing him like that?"

Nadia giggled. "How did we miss Isla has a fascination with boxers? Who knew?" she teased.

"And security guards," I told.

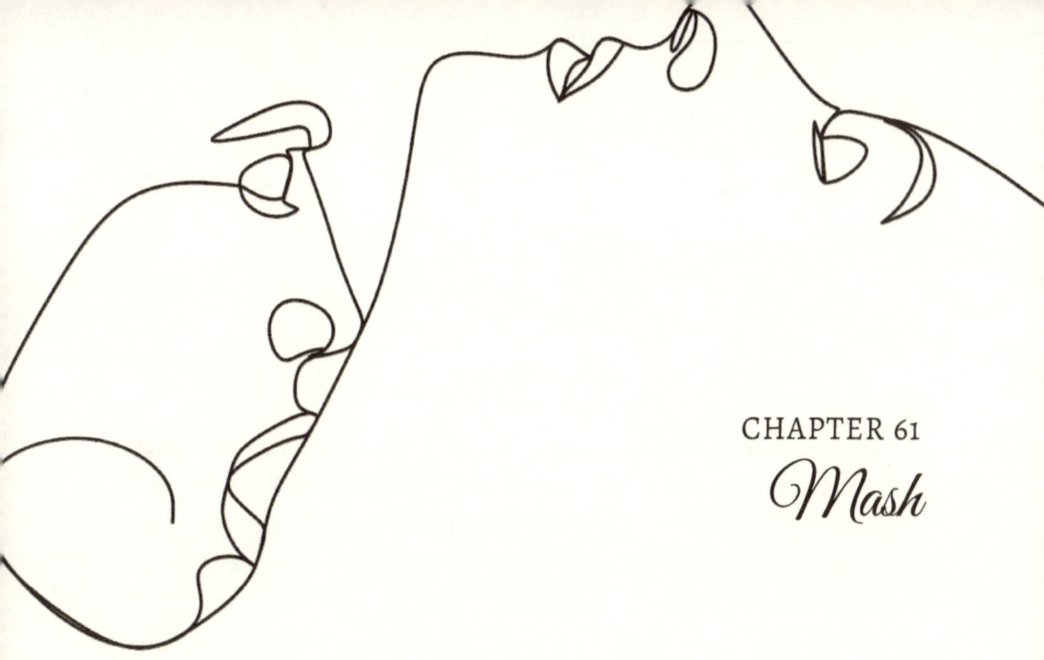

CHAPTER 61

Mash

The exhaustion from traveling and working on the road prepared me for when the baby was born. Levi warned me, "This is only the beginning of feeling exhausted all the time." I had no idea how it could get worse, but remembered to take heed.

The week of the due date fast approached, and I was surrounded by women. Mrs. Melton flew in from the states, and my mother from Italy. Our little family finally came together as one, and the love and energy was so infectious, it extended to my father.

It was the first time he and my mother were in a room together since I was a child. To my surprise, time had healed their wounds. They were civil to one another — uncontrived even -- and it was secretly what I wanted all of my life. "Your mother is still quite the head turner, son." Senior tried to rekindle their old flame.

"You're looking well, Senior," my mother replied.

"May I?" he asked.

"Sure," my mother responded, giving him her cheek to kiss.

"This boy finally made us old," said my father, *scruffing* my hair.

"Yes, he has. I've been waiting on this day for a long time. The suspense of whether it's a boy or a girl keeps me up at night. My son is finally giving me a bambino." My mother beamed and pinched my cheeks.

"How was New York?" I asked Senior.

"New York went smoothly. No need to ever go back," he answered.

"Good to hear." I shook his hand. "I'll let you two catch up. We should be eating soon." I excused myself.

For the first time since we wed, The Sharpers had a family dinner at an actual dining table. I sat at the head, and spoke of the changes I noticed in Nadia over the past few months. How she was less concerned about others or their opinions. How she had become more assertive and direct, calm, quiet and reserved. How she came into her own.

The veins in her temple moved so much, it was like watching her think from the outside. Then everyone laughed when I teased about how off balance she was the past month. She was ready to have the baby, and I was ready to meet the perfect reflection of us.

The excitement from the dinner helped get the ball rolling as a trickle of water shot down her leg before she made it to the loo. Mother Melton and I rode together to the hospital. My parents followed.

The closer the contractions, the stronger Nadia's grip cradled my hands. "Is there anything I can do?" I asked.

"Call my grandmother," she demanded.

Grams answered, "Is it time?"

"Yes, ma'am," I replied. "I hope to send you a picture shortly."

"How is my gal?"

"She's doing good."

"Put her on speaker!" Nadia yelled. "Grams, I'm never having sex again."

"Oh yeah. It's time alright." Grams laughed. "Stop lying to yourself. That boy is so good looking you'll be back in there with another one next year. It's going to be alright."

The nursing staff turned their backs to Nadia and laughed at Gram's humor, but the chuckles came to an end as the minutes turned to hours, waiting for the baby to make its grand entrance.

Watching Nadia in pain was agonizing. Mother Melton couldn't bear to see her like that, and took a break to check on my mother, while I stayed by her side, having the blood squeezed from my fingers.

Her breathing intensified when she let go of my hand. The screeching noise of her nails digging into the bed made my skin crawl. I stood and kissed her forehead. "Baby, you are doing great," I said for comfort.

"How would you know!" she yelled at me like the devil.

My eyebrows raised as her voice changed from the sweet melody that once serenaded me into a deep, salty baritone. The nurse buzzed for the doctor holding in her laughter and patted me on the back.

"I'm sorry," Nadia said, and reached for my hand. "I don't know why I'm being mean to you."

"Woman, you have held grudges against me longer than anyone I know. I can take it." I assured her.

"This is not the time to remind me of my flaws," she reprimanded me, out of breath with unhappiness spread across her face.

"What I'm saying is I'm not going anywhere."

"I want to bloody cry and scream right now," she said as a tear fell from the corner of her eye.

I wiped her tears as she wept, kissing her cheeks each time one fell, then smiled at the fact she used my slang to express herself. "Did I say something to amuse you?" she fussed.

"You said bloody."

"Did I?"

I nodded.

"Well, I'm bloody miserable right now!" she cried. "I'm scared."

"So am I, but did I let you drown?"

"No," she whimpered.

"Can't you swim like a fish now?"

"Yes!" She ugly cried and smiled simultaneously.

"She's crowning," the doctor announced.

"It's time, Sweets."

She pushed and pushed. Her sweaty palms gripped around my hands, and her neck rumpled and rucked from the strain. We were almost there but not quite enough. She rested her head back against the pillow, and I wiped her forehead with my palm, brushing the flyaway hairs from the side of her face. "How are we doing, lamb chop?" I asked.

She rolled her eyes at me. "How many more times do I have to push?" she asked.

"Give me a really good push this time, and it might be the last one," the doctor answered.

With everything Nadia had left in her, she pushed a few more times, and I witnessed my daughter slide into the hands of the doctor, covered in red and dark colored goop. I cut the cord and observed everything the staff did with my little bambino at the foot of the bed. The checking of her vitals and the cleaning of her eyes, nose, and mouth.

She cried as they wrapped her in a blanket and passed her to Nadia. "Look what we did," I whispered in Nadia's ear, then kissed her on her sweet lips, as she lied there half awake.

"Congratulations on your daughter," said the doctor. "You two have one beautiful kid."

"Is she beautiful?" Nadia asked near asleep.

"Like her mother," I said. "How are you feeling?"

"I just want to hold her for a minute then go to sleep." Her voice shook.

I snapped her picture then sent it to our parents and Grams. "She's so tiny. I don't see me anywhere in her little face. She looks like your mom— and you. Where am I, little girl?" Nadia teased her while circling her cheek with her finger.

"Do you want me to bring our parents in?"

She nodded.

I had my orders but found it hard to leave their side. "Why are you still standing there?" Nadia asked.

"I know it's just down the hall, but I can't move. I don't want to leave you two," I admitted.

"I love you. You know that? Now go get our parents. Please."

I directed everyone to the wash station, then led them to the room. Nadia appeared to be resting with our baby lying on her chest. Mother Melton went over to her daughter and kissed her cheek. Nadia leered, "Look what we made," she said, then signaled for me to pick up my baby girl.

I held her in my arms, ready to protect her from the world. Her little hand wrapped around my finger, then she opened her brandy colored eyes. The most beautiful baby in the world, and she was mine. I leaned down to smell the new life scent on her skin, and presented her to the people who came before us.

"Everyone. Meet Cassia Pilara Sharper."

Thank you for diving into my fictional worlds. To catch up with some of the characters from this series, read my novella, My Gift To You, https://books2read.com/mygifttoyou a Christmas romance where my ensemble casts from *'The Hummus Series'* & *'The On Track But Off Course Series'* collide to celebrate love during the holidays.

REVIEWS ENCOURAGE VORACIOUS INTEREST EVERY WHERE TO SUPPORT

ME, THE AUTHOR

I GREATLY APPRECIATE IT

ALWAYS THE BRIDESMAID
AN AFFAIR ABROAD
NEVER THE BRIDE
BUT THEN I MET HIM
T.K. RICHARDS

A TASTE OF THE FORBIDDEN
T.K. RICHARDS

BLEND
T.K. RICHARDS

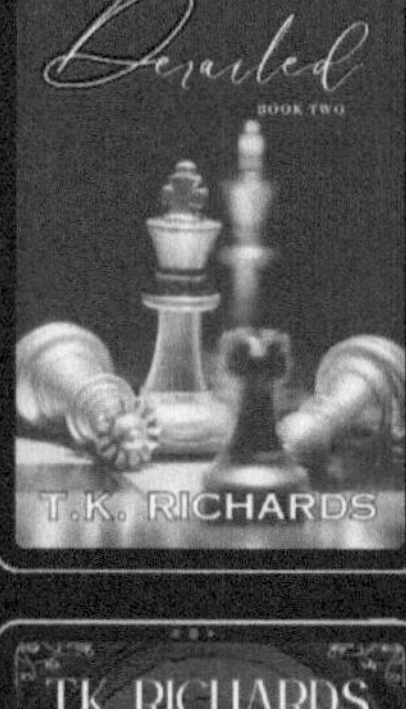
STRAIGHT Line
BOOK ONE
T.K. RICHARDS

Derailed
BOOK TWO
T.K. RICHARDS

THE Crossing
T.K. RICHARDS

LOVE IS A WICKED GAME.
JUKE
INTIMATE
EROTIC
ADDICTIVE
T.K. RICHARDS

TK RICHARDS
LOWCOUNTRY LEGENDS

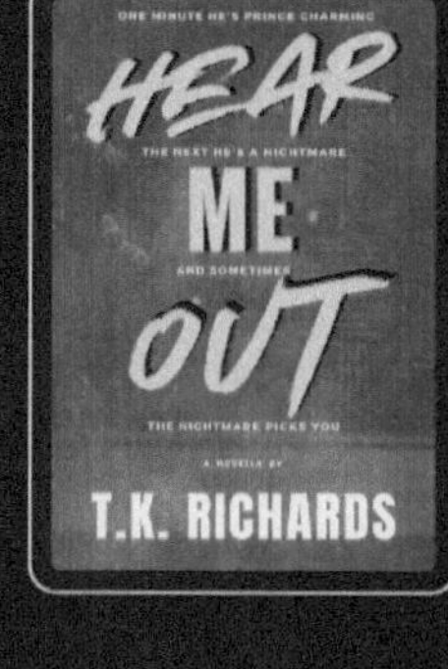
THE Vampiress
T.K. RICHARDS

ONE MINUTE HE'S PRINCE CHARMING
HEAR ME OUT
THE NEXT HE'S A NIGHTMARE
AND SOMETIMES
THE NIGHTMARE PICKS YOU
A NOVELLA BY
T.K. RICHARDS

Mikki & Mason
T.K. RICHARDS

EN ROUTE TO Emery
A NOVEL
T.K. RICHARDS

MY GIFT TO You
T.K. RICHARDS

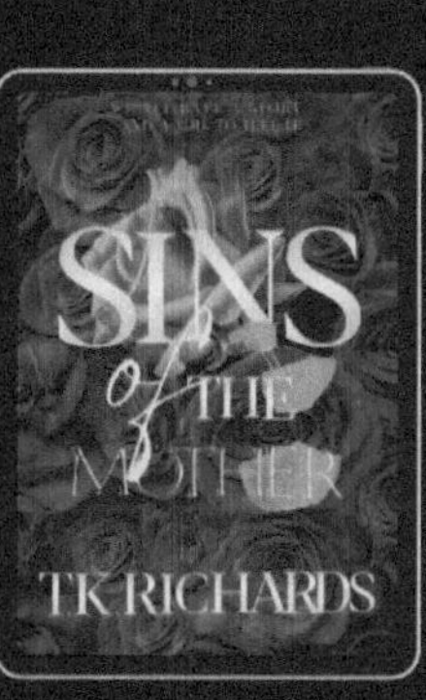
TIME CAN BE A GIFT & A CURSE
BUT IT'S NO MATCH FOR TRUE LOVE
CAN'T QUIT You
AN INSTALOVE NEW ADULT ROCKSTAR ROMANCE
T.K. RICHARDS

T.K. RICHARDS is a multi-genre author with popular novels and novellas in several genres of romance including Black, Interracial/Multicultural & Paranormal Romance, Speculative Fiction, Women's Fiction, and Domestic Thrillers.

A graduate of Limestone University, T.K. has honors in Expository Writing, and was also the Poet Laureate of her graduating class. When she is not writing, she is immersed in the world of tennis, and binge watching movies—mostly comedy as she loves to laugh.

For more information about **T.K. Richards**, visit her website at www.tkrichards.com and subscribe to her newsletter at: https://tkrichardsnewsletter.ck.page

Follow **T.K. RICHARDS** on the platforms listed below to interact with her personally:

instagram.com/t.k.richards

pinterest.com/TKWrites

tiktok.com/@tkrwrites

youtube.com/tkrichards

goodreads.com/T.k.richards

bookbub.com/authors/t-k-richards

amazon.com/author/Tkrichards

patreon.com/tkrichards

bsky.app/profile/tkrichards

Acknowledgments

Thank you to the readers on Kindle Vella for crowning The Vampiress in 2022 and 2023. Spreading the word about your love for this novel is greatly appreciated.

Special thank you to the following for your words of encouragement, support, and assistance in making the print version of The Vampiress exciting to produce, enticing to read, and visually aesthetic:

Racquel Henry
Kimani Lauren
Markeshia Kirksey
Ashley Coleman
Mia Lindler
Net Greene
Monica Manigault
Carolyn Taylor
Wakiza Hutchins
Jenn Lockwood Editing
Zack & Bria & Leon & Jagger & Lianna🤍

If I missed you, I still love you, and thank you for reading my work.